Now
It's
Time
to Say
Goodbye

ALSO BY DALE PECK

The Law of Enclosures

Martin and John

DALE PECK

Now It's Time to Say Goodbye

FARRAR, STRAUS AND GIROUX | NEW YORK

Farrar, Straus and Giroux
19 Union Square West, New York 10003

Distributed in Canada by Douglas & McIntyre Ltd.
Printed in the United States of America
Designed by Abby Kagan
First edition, 1998

LIBRARY OF CONGRESS CATALOGING-IN-PUBLICATION DATA

Peck, Dale.
Now it's time to say goodbye / Dale Peck.—1st ed.
p. cm.
ISBN 0-374-22271-1 (cloth : alk. paper)
I. Title.
PS3566.E245N68 1998
813'.54—dc21 97-26688

Grateful acknowledgment is made for permission to reprint the following: excerpts from "Bad, Bad Leroy Brown," with permission of Denjac Music Co. Copyright © 1972 Denjac Music Co./MCA Music Publishing (ASCAP). Administered by Denjac Music Co. Written by Jim Croce.

I wouldn't wish this book on anyone

except maybe Robbie Powell and Vaughan Jenkens

1

1.01

Justin

IF IT'S AFTER MIDNIGHT IT'S MY BIRTHDAY.

I once picked up a novel that started that way, but before I could read more than a few lines something distracted me. Though I remember the bookstore, which is closed now, and the distraction—he was about six foot three—I don't remember anything else about the novel, neither title nor author nor what came next, but even so, I've never forgotten that line. I don't know why. *If it's after midnight it's my birthday.* Evocative maybe, but also pretty meaningless. Still, it's stayed with me, popped into my head from time to time, and shortly after I left Galatea it came to me again. During my year there I was witness to one rape, several murders, and something that, context aside, I can only call a riot, but in twelve months not one single person celebrated a birthday. No, only the town observed its birthday; only the town, as Rosemary Krebs insisted all along, was important, and with that in mind I feel safe in saying that the story you are about to read is the story of a place, not a person. It is like a parade: though one marcher after another will step forward and claim to be the star, it is, in the end, the spectacle of stardom itself that lingers in the memory. And so I, first on, will now step aside, first off; but I leave this impression with you, a palimpsest that lingers behind the remainder of these words. If it's after midnight it's my birthday. In a way, I am striking a bargain with you: If you can make that one sentence mean something, then I promise to take care of everything else.

1.02

Melvin Cartwright

HE OPENED HIS EYES.

The porch light's glow pulsed through rain sluicing down his bedroom window. His eyes had their picka things to choose from—the mirror on the wall, the stack of read and reread detective novels in the corner, the photographs of his parents and sister—but they settled finally on the painting of Jesus he had made in Bible camp when he was eight years old. The rain-soaked light caused the Savior's heaven-gazing eyes to cry shadows of tears.

The phone rang again.

He knew before he answered what it would be. Not who. What. Wasn't no other reason for someone to call at such a ungodly hour.

He picked up the receiver, held it to his ear without speaking. A pause, and then a quiet voice came over the line.

"John Brown's body lies a-moldering in the grave."

Melvin bit back a sound, at once a laugh and a gasp. The laughter was for the silliness of the code, the gasp was a gasp of shock and acknowledgment. It couldn't be. But it had to be. It was.

He composed his voice as much as possible.

"His truth is marching on."

When the voice spoke again, it was in a more familiar tone, the exhortatory boom that could make a request for a glass of ice tea sound like a divine summons.

"Was down at Cora's Kitchen earlier this evening," the voice said.

"Have some-a that stew?" Melvin said.

"I did indeed."

"Had some myself," Melvin said. He paused for a moment, amazed at how easy this was, how natural it seemed, scripted.

Scripted is not a word he would have used.

Melvin cleared his throat. "Mighty good stew," he said.

"Indeed," the voice said again, and in a word ambrosial status had been conferred on beef, carrots, potatoes, pearl onions. A pause, and then: "DuWayne Hicks was down about the same time I was. Said he heard from Vera over to the new I.G.A. that Eddie Comedy's pulling up stakes."

"DuWayne shops at the new I.G.A.?" Melvin said. He was out of bed by then. He was at his bureau, pulling open a drawer. The long yellow spiral of the phone cord wagged behind him like a jump rope warming up, or maybe winding down.

"Well, that's another story," the voice chuckled, and, for a moment, things were almost normal. Then, in a voice deepened by seriousness: "Said he can't find work. Eddie Comedy said."

"Times *is* rough," Melvin assented. He had pants on by then, he had a shirt, he had the gun.

"That's true enough," the voice said. "Man has to go to extreme lengths to provide for his family." The voice broke the word *ex-treme* into pieces, held it out, emphasized extremity.

"That's true enough," Melvin repeated. The pistol's barrel tickled his balls, and he shifted it an inch or so to the right. *Ex-treme.*

"Yep, he had himself a round of goodbye drinks out to Sloppy Joe's. Told everyone this is it, see you later, be gone in the morning. Truck's packed and parked in the garage."

"Blazer, ain't it?" Melvin said. "Blue on bottom, silver on top?"

"Two-tone. I think they call that kind of paint job 'two-tone.' "

Melvin nodded silently. He allowed himself a look in the mirror: saw the close-cropped head of a black man, thirty-three years old going on some kind of zero. Reflected rain caused his image to cry the same fake tears as the painting of Jesus. Never liked the name Melvin. Momma called Malvernia: named after her. He suddenly wanted to ask her where she got her name, but she was dead now. Dead a whole year.

The voice filled his ear. "Well, I should be retiring."

A name he *did* like was Malcolm. Malcolm Cartwri—Carter. Malcolm Carter.

Ex-treme.

"Perhaps we'll be seeing you in church on Sunday?"

Melvin turned to the painting of the Son of God. Under a bright light you could see the faint shadows of numbers beneath the light brown hair, the pale pink flesh, the pure white of flowing robes—555, 666, 777—but in this light the face seemed almost real. As real as his, anyway, in the mirror, in the dark.

Tears coursed dryly down.

Melvin spoke slowly. "Tell the truth, sir, I been thinking-a pulling up stakes myself. Never mind a job. Man can't even find a wife in this town."

"Not at Cora's anyway," the voice said, and the two men shared a laugh again, and again, for a moment, things were almost normal.

"Been thinking bout heading west," Melvin was saying, and even as he said it he could almost believe he *had* been thinking about it. Never been westa the state line after all, and that was hardly more than a hundred miles away. A man had a right to see the world. A right, if not a duty.

"West, huh?" the voice said. " 'S a whole world out west." There was a pause. "I guess Eddie Comedy said he was heading east. Missouri, I guess he said."

Melvin nodded his head at no one. "East is nice," he said then, but the truth was he woulda preferred west. "Twenty-four heads east."

"Heads west too," the voice said, "but I guess Eddie Comedy said he's taking it east."

It was enough then, Melvin thought, it was almost too much. Anything else and he wouldn't be able to do it. Eddie Comedy had pulled a lotta shit in his life, but he'd never done nothing to Melvin—except for that, of course. And he hadn't really done that to Melvin.

Well, he thought, there wasn't no one to say he couldn't turn around when it was all over, turn around and head as far out west as he felt like it.

He looked in the mirror to check himself one last time, but as soon as he saw his face he realized he didn't know what he was checking for, and he shifted his gaze to the reflection of Jesus. He remembered then, for the first time in years, how Sawyer Johnson had deliberately ignored the numbers when he'd painted the same picture. His Jesus had brown skin and black hair, his robes were green and red and blue. Sawyer had used the pink only on the scarred palms of Jesus' hands, and he'd left the white out entirely. Reverend Abraham himself had pretended to scold Sawyer for the infraction, but twenty-five years later Sawyer's Jesus still hung in the Reverend's little office in the basement of the church.

Melvin wondered where Sawyer Johnson was now.

"I'm real sorry to hear you're leaving us too," the voice cut into Melvin's thoughts, and its veneer of sorrow was as thin as the paint on the cheeks of the Lord. "Maybe you'd like it if I sent Grady Oconnor round to help you pack up? In the morning, I mean. Not right now."

"No, not right now," Melvin said, and he thought, Grady Oconnor. He wouldn'ta thought Grady.

"Well then," the voice cut in again, as if reminding him that it wouldn't do no good to speculate, at least not now it wouldn't. "I guess that takes care-a just about everything."

There was a long pause then, and then Melvin heard the voice for the last time: "I wish you all the luck in this world, son" is what the voice said. "This world—and the next."

Melvin started to say thank you, but he realized the connection had already been broken. He imagined it: a brown thumb depressing a white button, a wizened hand with skin the color and texture of an old-fashioned grocery bag silently placing the handset in the cradle so as not to wake the sleeping members of the household. Melvin hung up his own phone just as quietly, even though there was no longer a household to avoid awakening. Momma died last year, Daddy killed in the Kenosha fire when Melvin was still a teenager. It occurred to him then: that was the reason he'd been picked this time. No one would ask where he'd gone away to, nor why. No one would miss him. No one expected him to say goodbye.

1.03

Justin

COLIN SAYS THAT EVERY ACTION IS PREDICATED ON two motivations. There is the reason that is spoken aloud, and then there's the reason that lies behind the words, the reason that, if unmasked, would reveal both words and action to be unnecessary, diversionary, a false move. This is the reason Colin came up with for packing everything we own and moving somewhere, anywhere, far away from the city: when the five hundredth person that we know dies from AIDS, Colin informed everyone, including me, then we will leave New York City and not return until the epidemic is over. He couldn't take it anymore, he said, he just couldn't stand it. Then, from his files—Colin files everything—he pulled his old phone books. "Andrew," he read aloud, and next to the number one I wrote "Andrew." "Barney," "Christopher," "David," "Edward," "Franklin," "Gregory," "Henry," "Isaac," all those good unabbreviated Christian names—well, not Isaac, I guess. By the time he finished reading there were more than two hundred names, and then I combed my memory for the names of boys and girls and almost-girls I'd worked with: "Jamal" and "Kareem" and "LaRhonda," and my list nearly equaled Colin's. And then we began searching. Colin had a single criterion—one thousand miles—so we started on the West Coast and in Europe. We traveled, eventually, to Johannesburg and Sydney, to Calcutta and São Paolo, we went all over the world. We ate up a year with our searching, and somewhere in that time I realized that my own desire to escape New York was as great as Colin's, even if my reasons were different. But even so, we ended up back in the city, knowing that not one of the places we'd looked at was a place we could run to. When we got home we found that the dying had continued unabated, and almost every morning the phone or the mail or the *Times* gave us the name of someone else, a john, a trick, a colleague, just someone met at a party or an artist whose work Colin had bought or an old dear friend, but by then sheer volume had reduced the dead to nothing more than names, and Colin's plan had reduced the names still further, until they were just numbers, and the numbers mounted higher and higher. We had fewer than ten to go when a dealer Colin knew told us about a painter he represented, a painter named Painter, Wade Painter, who lived in this crazy little town in Kansas. Kansas! Colin laughed aloud. Kansas! I echoed, but I didn't laugh. I remembered then one more number, one more name, and I added it to our list. "Martin," I wrote. The name seemed out of place, and I wondered if first I should have written the name "John." Well. Some people choose a place to be from and other people choose a place to go to; the very lucky do both and the very wretched do neither. Colin and I chose both, but even so, I don't think you will call us lucky men.

1.04

Welcome to Galatea
in Colorful Cadavera County
pop. 343
Incorporated Since 1976

1.05

Justin

FROM A DISTANCE THE ENORMOUS BLOCK OF CAST concrete that housed the painter named Painter looked like a cloud of solidified smoke. It seemed not to have been built but to have dropped from above, and as Colin and I approached it for the first time I could almost feel the ground vibrating from the impact. The flat edge of its roofline cut into a blue-gray sky like the blade of a knife and its walls were unrelieved by any detail or decoration save the occasional dark perforation of window or door, and the whole thing looked, I thought, like a single giant cinderblock, the beginning of some superstructure that would eventually house a race of giants, or the remnant of some colossal fortress. It would have stood out anywhere, but there, in that flat landscape of aluminum-sided asphalt-shingled farmhouses, every last one crowned by a dormer window and a deadened chimney, it was a monstrosity, the idea of *home* stripped down to its unbearable minimum: not safety but impermeability, not stability but stagnation.

"It's not exactly *Little House on the Prairie,* is it?"

"I think," I said then, but not to Colin, "I think I'm going to love this guy. Love him," I said, "or really, really hate him."

Before we could knock, the door sprang open. The boy who greeted us was not Wade Painter, I knew, because I had read Wade Painter's C.V. and I knew that he was forty-eight years old, and this boy was maybe eighteen. He was flushed and shiny and nearly trembling with excitement, and he was also black, which, I admit, surprised me a little, because Yonah had not mentioned a boyfriend and he had especially not mentioned a black boyfriend, and these were not the kinds of details Yonah Schimmel normally omitted, unless he omitted them purposely. "My name is Divine," the boy declaimed. "Welcome to Galatia!" He spoke as though he were welcoming us to Xanadu, and then, after the briefest glance in my direction, he gave Colin the longest once-over I've ever seen, and then he clucked his lips and shook his head and said, "My my *my.*"

Of hustlers—as of fools, witches, and wise men—it's been said that it takes one to know one, and after that one glance Divine avoided my eyes for the rest of the evening. He was a pretty boy, maybe even a beautiful boy, but the scar of vanity was etched into every one of his features. His copper-colored skin had been made slick and bright by too much time in a tanning booth, his bleached hair was intricately marceled and stiff and shining with gel. He wore tight clothes deliberately chosen to accentuate his long lean limbs, and when he spoke he put on this hangin-with-the-homies thang that just didn't work, and it took me only a moment to realize that Divine was some kind of actor, an actor who wasn't quite sure what role he was supposed to be playing, nigga, snap queen, small-town boy, so he tried to play them all.

The room he led us into was enormous and empty of furniture and even the naked eye could perceive that it was a perfect cube. Its floorboards were as dark as wet earth, but the walls and ceiling were as white and barren as a midnight fog. In the exact center of each wall was a doorway, and in one of these doors a woman now appeared, hesitantly: she put one hand on the door frame and stayed there, half in, half out of the room, as if awaiting permission to enter. I'd been surprised that the first person to greet us had been black, but I was positively suspicious that the second person was too, and it suddenly occurred to me that the three or four people I'd seen in town had also been black. Ah, Yonah, I thought, where *have* you sent us? and then I turned to greet this new person, who was introducing herself in a quiet voice.

"I'm Webbie," she was saying, and her tone of voice made me wonder how many times she'd already said it. "Webbie Greeving," she said now, raising her voice slightly, and then, slowly, she began to walk toward me with her palms outstretched, the way one approaches a strange, possibly vicious dog. The gesture startled me: it was the first time in a long time I'd thought of myself as dangerous.

When she was close enough I took one of her hands and shook it. "My name is Justin Time," I said, and I continued to shake her hand through the awkward moment that always follows this announcement. Webbie's hand was dry and light and I could hardly feel it in my own.

"Justin—"

"Time," I said, nodding, still shaking her hand.

Webbie's mouth hung open a moment, and then, with a start, she closed it and pulled her hand from mine. "I'm sor—I . . ." She shook her head slightly, smiled nervously. "Excuse me," she said, and then, in a calmed voice, she said, "Welcome to Galatia," and I noticed that in her mouth the word had three distinct syllables; in Divine's there had barely been two.

Webbie Greeving was around thirty, and you could see her body regarding the long slope of middle age: her hair, shoulder-length, relaxed, softly curled, was held off her face by a length of brown leather thong, and it was shot through with long gray threads and an occasional thin braid; but her face, round, bright, dark as walnut, was completely unlined. Even when she smiled—and she smiled now, uncertainly, quizzically, beneath my gaze—her face remained uncreased, as though her lips, which were paler and pinker than her skin, were expanding within a semisolid metal, like mercury.

One of her hands floated up to her face then. She used it to cover her mouth, but only for a moment; then she took her hand and placed it on her sternum, and even as I watched she unconsciously ran a fingertip along the bottom of one of her breasts, and it was this hand that suddenly endeared her to me. The gesture was many things, but it was undeniably, unconsciously sexual, and when she saw me looking at her hand Webbie pulled it from her breast as though it had burned her, but the hand went immediately, instinctively, back to her mouth, and I could see it tremble as Webbie tried to decide what to do with it. She put it finally, resolutely, in the pocket of the brown suede skirt she wore, and when she smiled at me again her mouth seemed somehow naked, without her hand to cover it.

"Thank you," I said then. "I, um, we, we're glad to be here."

Webbie blinked, just once, as though the effort of even pretending to believe me wasn't worth it; but she smiled as well, and I wondered how happy *she* was to be there. "Your travels must have exhausted you," she said, slipping into her own role as hostess. "May I offer you a drink? Ice tea, perhaps, or some wine?"

"I'll take some vino, woman," Divine said loudly, and I would have laughed if Webbie hadn't visibly cringed at the sound of Divine's voice.

Divine's arm, I saw then, was through Colin's, and he was leading him away. Webbie shrugged at me, and we followed them into another cube of a room. Four perfectly aligned Mission armchairs floated in an otherwise empty space; Colin had already sat down when we entered the room, and Divine, perched on that chair's flat wooden arm, was in the act of grabbing Colin's head with both his hands. This was hardly an unusual occurrence: my lover had a rather large head, and it was also completely bald, and people he hardly knew were forever putting their hands on it, touching it, rubbing it even. Still, I was impressed by Divine's boldness. He ran his fingertips over Colin's hairless skull without a hint of bashfulness, and then he began rubbing it hard, almost violently, like a fortuneteller warming up a crystal ball.

Webbie's eyes flitted from Colin's face to mine. We both smiled at her, but she still looked worried. *It's okay,* I mouthed; Colin merely closed his eyes. Webbie turned then, and grabbed at a bottle of red wine.

There wasn't a table in the room, so the bottle and five glasses were lined up against one wall on the floor.

She turned back to me. "I hope this will do," she said, holding a glass in one hand, pouring unsteadily with the other. "The wine club usually sends nice—" She smiled, shrugged. "It's a little difficult to actually, I mean, Vera's I.G.A., you can't just *shop* for—"

She just held out the glass then, and I reached for it with my numb right hand, but then stepped back. "Oh my God!" I said.

"What! What?"

"That's a *white* wine glass."

Webbie's eyes darted between my face and the glass, and when she finally realized I was joking she started to laugh, but then, before she'd quite begun, her face froze. She was looking past me, and, following her eyes, I turned, and there was Wade.

It seems important to mention that I didn't hear Wade enter the room. It seems, in fact, the most important thing I can tell you about Wade Painter—besides, I guess, besides the fact that he wasn't black. Wade Painter was the first person I ever met whose presence in the world seemed even more insubstantial than mine. It was as if it took more than one sense to locate him in space. Hearing alone wasn't enough: you had to see him too, and I immediately wanted to hold his hand, just to keep him from disappearing. But his hands were in his pockets, giving his body the shape of a lean egg, and he remained in the door, his face thin-lipped, close-mouthed, unsmiling. Wade *is* white, but after Webbie and Divine he just struck me as colorless: pensive, pale, gray maybe, not unkind, not uncaring exactly, but in some fundamental way resigned. There wasn't a drop of paint on him but he still smelled of it, a rich chemical loam of paint, turpentine, and some third element I didn't recognize but later learned was the soap he used, not on his brushes or his clothes, but on his skin, Lifebuoy, I found out, and I only remember it because, as a child, I always called it Lifeboy.

Everything seemed to have stopped when Wade entered the room, and everything started up again when, at last, he spoke. From lips the color and texture of two pumice stones issued a voice as dry as the pages of a history book. He said, as Divine and Webbie had said, "Welcome," but he didn't welcome us to Galatia. Instead, he welcomed us, as the sign printed by the Kansas Department of Transportation had, to Galatea. He shook my hand. He accepted a glass of wine from Webbie. Then, directing his attention to Divine, whose hands had been frozen on Colin's head since Wade had revealed his presence in the room, he said, "It is not a melon, Divine. You don't need to test it for ripeness before you take a bite." And then, turning abruptly, he walked from the room.

For a moment I wondered if he'd really been there or if I'd only dreamed him up. But even as I thought that, I felt a sudden ache in my hand, and I knew he had been there, because Wade Painter, whatever else he was, was not the kind of man you dream up, not the kind of man you imagine.

1.06

Lawman Brown

SHERIFF EUSTACE BROWN—PLEASE DON'T CALL HIM lawman, at least not to his face—occupied his cruiser, and his cruiser occupied the bare bluff. He'd turned off his headlights before heading up the hill but even so that darned shale cracked and popped so loud as he pulled onto the plateau that before he was stopped the three cars that was parked there had all started up their engines and was trying to pull away like hey, we was just getting ready to go anyway: Howard Goertzen's El Camino, Blaine Getterling's Chevelle, and a red '76 Monte Carlo he didn't recognize. Lawman Brown wrote down the Monte Carlo's plate number for future reference—nice cars, those seventy-sixes, last of the big Monte Carlos—and he added a mental note to let Rosemary Krebs know about Howard Goertzen's presence on the bluff. Howard Goertzen was, in the loosest of loose terms, Lucy Robinson's leading suitor, and anything that concerned Lucy Robinson concerned Rosemary Krebs, and anything that concerned Rosemary Krebs concerned Lawman Brown.

He didn't trouble himself with what Blaine Getterling got up to, although he had half a mind to stop him and ask if he had any idea where that boy Melvin Cartwright had got off to. Boy like that sneaks off in the middle of the night, you can guess he's up to no good.

He did wonder who owned that '76 MC. Wondered if maybe it was for sale.

The cruiser's cab smelled of clean car and fresh coffee, both courtesy of Nettie Ferguson, and when Lawman Brown was alone on the bluff he unbuckled his belt to ease the strain on his stomach and sighed as that ten pounds, oh, okay, twenty, as that twenty pounds he'd put on last Christmas eased free of its constrictions, and then he began to sip at his coffee through the nonspill lid of his QuikTrip mug. They called the lid nonspill because it was shaped like the top of a baby's cup: it had a raised nipple on one side, see, with just one single tiny pinprick of a hole in it, and in order to get any liquid from the cup you had to pull at the nipple, you had to put your lips right down around that nipple and *suck* that coffee into your mouth. Had to drive all the way down to the Big M just to get that cup, Lawman Brown did, though once he did get it he refilled it with the coffee Nettie Ferguson made at the station house, or he stopped in at Elaine Sumner's Sumnertime Café.

Thinking-a that made him think of Eddie Comedy, who'd been a regular at Elaine's café—no work, no wife, what else could he do? He was a good old boy, Eddie Comedy, willing to stand up for what he believed in, not like a lotta these kids nowadays, who didn't have nothing on their minds except getting their rocks off. Eddie Comedy always called a spade a spade—usually to his face—and Lawman Brown thought it was a shame that folks like Eddie Comedy had to go and leave town when folks like Melvin Cartwright would like as not show up in a day or two, smelling like cheap liquor and even cheaper women and telling everybody about it who didn't care to know.

After a few pulls from the nipple Lawman Brown took his gun from his holster and set it on his lap. The long line of the barrel pointed down the thigh of his loosened pants, and Lawman Brown was considering maybe getting out a rag and giving the barrel a few quick swipes when the cackle of Nettie Ferguson's voice came over the police radio, *Eustace, can you hear me? I know you can hear me, Eustace. Rosemary Krebs said have you found out anything about Wade Painter's visitors yet? Eustace? Eustace?* It was a downright disgrace, Lawman Brown thought, having to call Nettie Ferguson a police dispatcher when what she really was was a retired grade school teacher, and second grade at that, and rather than answer her he turned the radio off and he sucked at his cup of coffee and went ahead and pulled out his handkerchief and brought up the shine on his pistol. He wasn't in no hurry to head on over to Wade Painter's, that was for sure, it made him sick to his stomach just *thinking* about what those three characters might be getting up to in that house, which he tried not to do, to think about it, and instead he brought up the polish on his gun.

Surveillance is what he would say if Rosemary Krebs asked him how he'd spent his night. *Surveillance,* 1900–2000 hours. Wasn't nothing she could say to that.

Down below him Galatea was a small contained field of light on the rolling plain, its streets straight and sensible, gridlike you could say, just like any of those big cities back east. The grid was interrupted only by the sort of swirly plus sign where Route 24 crossed over Highway 9, and the whole map was as much a part of his unconscious as the lines of his hand inside his leather policeman's glove. He held his hand up then, his left hand, his right was busy with his coffee and he held his left hand up and squinted as he lined up his hand between his eye and the town until it seemed that Galatea rested on his palm.

Surveillance. 1900–2000. All clear.

He held on to the image for a moment, and then he curled his hand into a fist around an imaginary microphone and then, softly at first but growing louder and louder, he began to sing in a voice much deeper than his normal voice: "Well, he's bad, bad, Lawman Brown, baddest man in the whole damn town," and at the word *damn* he blushed a little, but he kept on singing.

1.07

Justin

WHERE AM I?"

Colin had waited to speak until we were seated around the circular table centered in Wade Painter's barren dining room, and I could tell from the look on his face that he'd been saving his question for just this moment. Colin has a thing about opening lines—a scene is made or unmade in its first sentence, he once said to me, which is fine as far as it goes, but Colin tends to forget that an opening line doesn't constitute the entirety of a scene: something has to come after. Something has to happen next.

Across the table from Colin, Webbie looked confused. "Excuse me?"

"You're in the dining room?" Wade said. "It's where we usually take our meals?"

Colin, realizing his line had flopped, tried to laugh it off. He took a drink of wine and said, "Forgive me." Colin never says I'm sorry; he always says forgive me; he always makes his mistake your responsibility. "My question was too vague," he said. "What I meant to do was ask about Gala—Gala—"

"Galatea," Wade said.

"*Galatia*," Divine said, putting so much spin on the word it sounded like *glacier*.

"Galatea," Wade said again, his tone uninsistent yet inexorable, like meltwater. "Perhaps we could answer your question better if we knew where your interest lay."

"In Gala—"

"—tea," Wade finished for him.

"He needs something to write about," I said then, but Colin spoke over me.

"I'm thinking," he said, "of moving here."

"He's blocked," I said. "He's been blocked for twenty years. He thinks he'll find something to write about here."

There was a brief silence, and then Wade said, "But surely Galatea offers nothing in the way of a subject for a writer such as yourself."

"I don't know *what* it offers," Colin said. "But really, moving here, if, indeed, we did move here, would have nothing to do with writing."

"Then . . . *why?*" Webbie said, her voice full of incredulity.

"New York," Colin said. He pursed his lips. "New York isn't exactly the place it used to be."

"What he means is, everyone we know is dead."

Divine dropped his fork then. It clattered to the floor, and after fixing me with an expression of absolute terror on his face, he disappeared beneath the table.

"And . . . Yonah?" Wade said. There was the slightest tremor in his voice, and I remembered hearing that a long, long time ago Yonah and Wade were said to have had something more than a professional relationship. "How is Yonah?"

"I think Yonah is doing well," Colin said carefully. "As well as can be expected." He shrugged. "We've been away so much this year."

I noticed then that my wine glass was empty and I reached for the bottle. It wobbled clumsily in my right hand and I had to concentrate so that I wouldn't spill the purple liquid on Wade's white tablecloth. "He can't be doing *that* bad," I said when I'd finished pouring. "He sent us *here*, didn't he?"

I was looking at Webbie as I spoke, and she brought one of her hands to her mouth. "I don't understand."

"Yonah can be a bit . . . intolerant," Wade said quietly.

"Yonah is a racist pig," I said, "and I bet he's laughing his ass off right now. What's left of it anyway."

"Justin," Colin said quietly.

"Yonah's a little *skinny* right now."

"Justin."

"Don't tell me to shut up, Colin," I said, and even as I spoke I remembered something Yonah had said when he sent us here, something whose meaning had escaped me at the time. "Jesus Christ," I said, "he called the place *Shvartzville*."

"I didn't tell you to shut up," Colin said when I'd finished. "I merely said your name."

"Yo!" Divine's voice came from under the table. He reappeared then, fork in hand, and looked at me. "How'd you get a name like that anyway? I mean, shit. Justin *Time*?"

"Well, *Divine*," I said, "that's really a question for Mr. *Nieman* to answer."

Divine turned to Colin. "So?"

Colin was silent for a moment, and then he shrugged and said, "It was just a bad joke. A bad joke that refused to go away."

"I'll say," Divine said, and turned back to me. "So what's your real—"

"Here," I said, "let me get you some more *vino*." I leaned across the table to fill his glass, and this time I did spill some wine, and Divine jumped back from the table to keep it from staining his pants. As I settled back into my seat Colin placed his empty glass down beside me and I filled it more carefully, and refused to meet his eyes.

"To return to your earlier question," Wade said to Colin.

If I'd still been holding the wine I would have spilled it again, because I'd almost forgotten Wade was in the room.

"My—"

"Galatea," Wade said, his voice so quiet I had to strain to hear it.

"*Galatia!*" Divine nearly yelled.

"Oh yes," Colin said. He paused, considered, picked sides. "Galatia."

"I was going to say," Wade said, "that Galatea has a rather *colorful* history"—he smiled briefly here, very briefly—"but I'm not really the person to tell it. Webbie is. She's practically the town historian."

"Well, my father, really—"

"Colorful?" Colin said, turning to Webbie.

Webbie looked uncertainly at him, and then she took a drink of wine and held her glass close to her chest. "Galatia," she said then, and nodded at Wade, "is really two towns."

"Two?" Colin said. "There hardly seem to be enough people here for one."

"There are three hundred forty-three—"

"According to that *sign*," Divine cut in, "which is *at least* two fucking years outta date." He looked at Colin. "I tell you what: this place is getting smaller by the *minute*. This place is turning into a goddamn *ghost town* right before your eyes."

Webbie waited until Divine finished, and then, in a voice that tried hard to remain smooth, she continued. "Of those three hundred forty-three," she said, "one hundred forty-seven live east of Highway 9 in a town they call Galatia, where they have lived for a century and a quarter. The other one hundred ninety-six," she said, and paused to sip at her wine, "the rest of the population live here in Galatea, where they have resided for just over twenty years."

"Hey, yo, Bopeep," Divine said then. "Can we just cut to the fucking chase? We all grown up here, no need to mince words. I mean shit, we gonna be dead and gone before you get to the point already."

Webbie took a long drink of wine, touched her hand to her mouth, then rested it on her chest. Divine didn't wait for her to swallow.

"So, like, this be the four-one-one," he said. "This be all you got to know. All you got to know is, everybody who lives in Galatia is *black*, like me and my mushroom-colored sister here. And everybody who lives in Ga-la-la-la is . . ." He paused, pursed his purpled lips, pointed at Wade. "Like him."

Wade dropped his eyes under our collective gaze, as if uncomfortable being the target of such direct scrutiny. Then, with the same bad sense of humor that had saddled me with this name, Colin brought a hand to his chest and said, "A *painter*?"

1.08

Webbie

THERE ARE TWO WINDOWS IN THE ARCHIVE. THE ARchive is the attic room in which my father stores the history of his town, and of those two windows, one faces south, toward Kenosha, and the other faces north, onto Matthew Street, onto the windmill and the willows and the steeple at the center of town—of Galatia, I mean, not Galatea—and, beyond that, onto the shining dome of the bald bluff, and it's there that I want to start, this time, rather than with Kenosha, where I usually start. We'll get to Kenosha soon enough.

Galatia is hemmed in on its northern border by a group of low hills collectively referred to as the bluffs, and it has long been a town joke that they are called the bluffs because they don't do a good job of even pretending to be hills. The name isn't capitalized and it doesn't appear on any map; indeed, it's rarely used even by Galatians, and only the tallest of the bluffs has its own name. It's called the bald bluff because it's hairless, by which I mean that it's grassless, its plateau a plate of white shale, brittle, easily chipped, and loud. Wagons passing over it in the last century must have produced a sound like Gatling gunfire, but only cars crunch over it now, and only at night, because the bald bluff has become Galatia's lovers' lane. But I prefer it during the day, especially in the morning. You can see it from anywhere in the valley that holds the town—a valley as shallow as the bluffs are short—and in the morning it seems not just to catch the light but to capture it, and release it in a magnified burst of liquid gold. In this drab landscape it is like a jewel, and I like to think that it was the sight of the bald bluff in the morning, and not just the presence of water, that caused the Five Families to stop here. But that's just historical fancy, as romantic as the notion that a pioneer would have dragged his wagon over the bluff to hear the shale crack under its wheels rather than pilot his way through the mud-swamped valley beneath it.

Galateans, with their propensity for name changing, call the tallest bluff *bare* rather than *bald*.

It is written, or so my father says, that the Five Families—the Greevings, the Deacons, the Johnsons, the Getterlings, and the Rochelles—stopped when they found mud. It was March 1859, sixteen months before the presidential election of 1860, but it was a cold and dry March, and where the Five Families had come across water during the course of their journey they had also come across white people. The mud lay at the absolute bottom of a small valley bounded by the bluffs to the north and unraveling in a series of dimples and bubbles in all other directions. At the point of the mud Reverend John Greeving dug a well, and by the time he had become known simply as Reverend Alpha he had built a windmill pump on the site, and for decades the drinking water of everyone who lived in town came from that well. In my father's Archive there is a photograph of sturdy women and restless children standing in line with metal pails and wooden buckets to collect the day's supply of water—it hangs on the wall, this picture, and I am sometimes able to glimpse it when my father enters or leaves the room. Another photograph is of all twenty-three black men, women, and children who founded Galatia. Seven men stand, seven wives sit on chairs hidden by their dresses, eight children sit on bare upturned soil. Through the stony expressions imposed on photographic subjects of the time there is still visible a certain amount of pride and fear and, above all, determination in their faces. One woman holds a baby, and the man behind her is the only man in the photograph wearing a hat. As in the famous mural of John Brown in the capitol building in Topeka—painted years after this picture was taken and restored, thirty-five years ago, by Galatea's very own Wade Painter—the hatted man holds a Bible in one hand, a rifle in the other, but he lets these weapons rest easily at his sides. He is Alpha Greeving—born John, but called, late in life, Reverend Alpha—my great-great-great-great-grandfather, and the man who built and first preached in the Southern Baptist Church of Galatia. Galatia, you see, differs in one fundamental respect from the few other all-black towns scattered across the North. Most of those settlements were founded in the wake of the Civil War by former slaves eager to forge some kind of new life, but Galatia—named after the biblical land of plenty—was founded in the heady days leading up to the war. It was settled, in fact, by a group of black people determined to bring Kansas into the union as a free state, and even today some Galatians, chief among them my father, are acutely conscious of the fact that not one member of the Five Families was a former slave; they weren't refugees or stragglers who'd wandered past the frontier's edge. They were, instead, pilgrims, and not surprisingly their descendants turned out to be puritans.

That black town, as some white people used to call Galatia, when they weren't just calling it Niggerville. Niggerville, by Bigger Hill.

Bigger Hill is Galatia's nearest neighbor, thirty miles south and west. Until 1974, there was Kenosha, which lay less than ten miles due south. Kenosha was once home to some five thousand white people, which in and of itself isn't significant: there are dozens of tiny and essentially all-white towns in Kansas, and Kenosha only merits a place in this story because it burned to the ground in 1974, and out of that fire Galatea was born.

I was fourteen years old at the time, so I have some memory of what occurred. It was July, I remember, harvest time, it hadn't rained in weeks; even the dew had a tenuous quality, and it was so hot that if there had been any sidewalks in Kenosha you could have fried an egg on them. If you're not from a farm town you might think this sounds ominous, but to a farmer it's the best possible weather for bringing in the wheat. Still, it's not without its dangers: the air around Kenosha's grain elevator was thick with incendiary chaff, and someone or something introduced fire into this atmosphere. Popular belief has it that Kenosha's most flagrant drunk, Gene Zwemmer, was the culprit, although how that legend got started is anybody's guess. At any rate, the immediate effect—an explosion whose fireball was sighted more than fifty miles away—leveled twelve of the elevator's fourteen hundred-foot towers and, as well, killed five people, Gene Zwemmer among them. Cottonwood trees more than five miles away were knocked to the ground, and despite the ever-blowing plains wind, what was left of the town was covered in a pall of smoke and ash for the next three days.

In fact, not much was left: the flash fire that spread from the elevator ate almost every building in town in less than an hour; two more people died. Everyone else escaped with their lives but almost nothing else, and by the time the fire brigade arrived it was all it could do to keep the blaze from burning across the prairie. The next day there was just smoke and the charred skeletons of buildings and, here and there, a few gutted brick structures, the bank, the school, the new grocery store, and I remember Galatia was abuzz with speculation as to what the survivors would do. The answer wasn't long in coming: less than two weeks later people—refugees really, homeless, penniless, and without any other prospects—began settling on lots carved out of the Krebs property west of Galatia. Big trucks arrived, houses went up, roads were graded. In the end, most of Kenosha's citizens moved away, but those who didn't have any other prospects accepted Rosemary Krebs' offer of cheap land and a fresh start, and as a daughter of Galatia I can imagine how seductive that must have sounded to a down-and-out field hand or counterman at the feed store: how many people can say they founded and named the town in which they live? For nineteen years they have held a picnic to remind them of their triumph. July 4th: Independence Day everywhere else, but here, in Galat*ea*, Founders' Day.

I suppose I could challenge the notion that a name makes any difference to the character of a place, or a person for that matter, but I know better. I know how suggestible human nature is. Perhaps a name doesn't alter the character of what it names, but it often has a profound effect on the people who use that name, and that is what matters in Galatia's case, and Galatea's, and my own as well. Though I've never been permitted to see my father's birth certificate—an "historical document" filed away for safety in the Archive—I have seen mine. My name is Webbie Greeving. My father gave me this name, and a history too. I suppose every father believes this to be his responsibility, but my father felt compelled to take it more seriously than most. My mother died as I was born; my father had wanted a boy. I list these entwined tragedies in the order I assign them, but I won't vouch that my father would rank them as I do. My father had intended my name to be W.E.B. Greeving: I was to be a teacher, a preacher, a prophet to the race, and not the mere historian I am—or, at any rate, that I was trained to be. Webbie isn't his idea of a compromise with reality, it's more of a joke; my middle name is Martina. But one letter appears before the word *Webbie* on my birth certificate—not an initial, you understand, but a single letter followed by a large space, as though my father had left himself room to reconsider—and this letter is, in legal terms, my first name. The letter is an A, but what if anything it was meant to stand for my father has never told me. A. Sometimes, when I feel optimistic, I think of it as a beginning that will never have to end, but usually I recognize it for what it is: nothing more than a story that was never told. A. My name is not Aaron, or Allah, or Arthur, or plain old Art. My name is Webbie, but I can't decide if that story is just a tiny, inextricable part of the story of my father's town, or if, as I hope, it can exist separately, and is merely waiting, like I am, to be pulled free. And I should tell you too that it galled me, it made me almost insane with fury, that someone like Colin Nieman could talk so cavalierly about moving here, when I was not even allowed to leave. You will note that I particularize my anger; I direct it only at Colin. Justin said very little while I told this story. He picked clumsily at Wade's bland food and spilled a lot of wine, but he still managed to communicate that he had no desire to be in Galatia, let alone to move there, and so, long before we became friends, we were aware of our commonality, and we became allies of a sort.

At the end of dinner five empty wine glasses wanted to be filled. Justin, drunk, filled his own first, and then, after a look around, he poured the remainder of the bottle into my glass. He touched his glass to mine, but he never said anything.

1.09

Justin

WELL, LOOK AT THAT," WADE SAID, BRAKING SUDdenly.

"What?" Divine said, poking his head forward from the back seat. "Lookit what? *What?*"

We were heading east on Route 24, the same road Colin and I had taken into town the day before; it was, it turned out, the only paved road that headed east from town.

Wade was giving us the grand tour.

"There appears to have been an accident," Wade said then, and as he spoke I noticed long trails of skid marks on the asphalt, a telephone pole with a shark bite of wood ripped from it. Shards of glass glittered among the dirty grass growing in the roadside ditch.

"Shit," Divine said now. "There don't *appear* to be no accident to me."

"Two," Wade said, easing the car onto the shoulder. "There were two cars involved."

"And how you know *that*, Magnum P. I.?"

Wade spoke as if to a child, although he didn't seem to be condescending. Well, I thought, Divine *was* a child. "Two sets of skid marks," he said. "Although . . ."

"Yes?" Colin prompted Wade.

"The skid marks run in the same direction," Wade said. "It *looks* like . . ." Again he let his voice trail off.

"Yo, Ellery *Queen*," Divine said, "let us in on what you done *detected* already."

"What it *looks* like," I said, my voice sharper than I'd intended. "It *looks* like one car ran another car off the road."

Wade looked over at me. He said, "It looks like one car ran the other into that telephone pole."

"She-*it*," Divine said then, but he sat back in his seat. "Sound like *some*body's been watching too many late movies. Thinking they done come across a *mys*tery or some shit."

Wade didn't answer immediately. He eased the car into motion, pulled onto the road. "I was just out here Wednesday," he said then. "There hadn't been an accident as of Wednesday."

"Yo, Wade man, whyn't you just call up Lawman Brown, get the *o*-ficial police report. Lay this matter to *rest* already."

Wade nodded his head, but he didn't say anything. Then, almost to himself, he murmured, "My father was killed in a car accident." He looked at me after he spoke, and because I had been looking at him, I met his eyes, and I nodded. "My mother died of natural causes," Wade said, "but my father died in a car accident."

I just nodded again and turned to the window. "My mother died of my father," I said. "I don't know what my father died of, or if he's even dead."

"*What?*" Colin said, throwing his face, his whole body forward. "*What* did you just say?"

I didn't answer him.

After a moment I heard Divine say, "Whyn't you sit back down, Mr. Colin Nieman? Relax, take in the sights. Trust me," he said, "we halfway between no place and nowhere, and we got a ways to go before we get home."

It was Sunday, I should tell you now. We'd been in Galatea, or Galatia, or wherever we were, for twenty-four hours. We'd slept on a square bed in the exact center of the floor of one of Wade's cubical rooms—there were nine in the house, I finally realized, laid out with the rigid symmetry of a tic-tac-toe grid. At the end of the evening Divine said goodbye to Webbie in a loud voice, pointing up the fact that she was leaving and he was not, but before Wade let her go he gave her a long tight hug, which I thought was sweet at first, until I saw the anxious drained look on Webbie's face; as soon as she was gone I grabbed my toothbrush, and I made a point of running into Wade just outside the bathroom door, and then I asked him point-blank what Webbie was doing here.

A look of something I want to call panic flashed across Wade's face. "I'm sorry?"

"It's obvious she doesn't want to be here."

"I invited her for din—"

"I mean in Galatia, Galatea, whatever you call this place. Why does she stay?"

Wade was silent for a long time before he answered. "She did leave once," he said eventually—and evasively, I thought. "She went to New York, actually. To Columbia. I believe she had only to write her dissertation in order to complete her Ph.D. in American history."

"And?"

"And her father had a stroke. He was bedridden for nearly a year, and his right side is still partially paralyzed. She's taken care of him ever since."

"When—"

"Eight years ago," Wade said, and then, with a long thick calloused finger, he touched my toothbrush. "When I was eleven," he said, "and I couldn't afford paintbrushes, I used to paint with my toothbrush. I brushed my teeth in the morning and then I painted with it all day, and in the evening I washed it out and brushed my teeth with it again. Eventually I got lead poisoning so bad that I had to be hospitalized, and when my parents discovered the paint-stained toothbrush they forbade me from painting ever again." Wade paused, and smiled his slight smile, and then, rather than continue his own story, or Webbie's, he asked me about mine.

"What happened?" he said, and he took hold of my right hand.

I looked down at the hand he was holding. By then even I didn't notice it very often, so slight were the remainders, the reminders of its injury, but once, long ago, it had been crushed so badly that it resembled a pulpy red ball, and for years afterward it had been twisted, stiffened, inflamed. Time and Colin's money had gone a long way toward repairing the damage, at least cosmetically; the only outward sign that remained was the fact that it was somewhat larger than my left hand—that, and a kind of clumsiness that seemed to take it over, especially when I was drunk. It would have taken a discerning eye, a painter's eye I want to say, to notice the difference; and it took another kind of seeing to notice that it still hurt me, especially on cold or rainy days. On other days I couldn't feel anything with it at all, but that night I felt the heat and sweat and clamp of Wade's hand clearly, pulling slightly, as though he were attempting to pull a past out of me that I had already decided would be better off erased, and for the first time in years I allowed another person to feel the weight of that story for just a moment, and then, with a reluctance that surprised me, I pulled my hand from his.

It surprised me when anyone noticed it, but it almost scared me when Wade did—vacant, absent I want to say *empty* Wade Painter. I wouldn't have thought there was anything left of him, in him, to be so perceptive, but before I could search for his own hidden story he sighed, and from the corner of my eye I saw his hand clenching and unclenching, and then he shrugged and he smiled and he said, "Good night, Justin Time," without a hint of awkwardness. "I will see you in the morning."

And in the morning our tour began. Wade showed us his studio first, a converted farmhouse that had once been his parents' home—dead, he said, when Colin asked him where they were now, dead and gone—and then, inside the dusty hull of an ancient green Galaxie 500, he drove us through the new, ugly part of town he called Galatea, and then the old, ugly part of town Divine called Galatia, and neither of them made any comment about the white wall of the grain elevator which divided the two halves of town, and on which only one name was written. The black letters began on one side of town and curved around into the other: GALATEA. That part of town had a bank, a church, a small restaurant, a hardware store, an I.G.A., a post office, a library, a school, and, according to Wade, ninety-seven houses, thirty-two of which were tin trailer homes scattered like dropped cigarettes in a trailer park called, in an amazing feat of nonimagination, Prairieview. In Galatia there were seventy-eight houses—no trailers—a steepled clapboard church that was, I have to admit, rather pretty, a general store, a café, and a narrow rectangular park that contained ten enormous willow trees and a single tall rusty windmill. One long S-curve of highway divided the town, and this highway split into two strands like a frayed rope, islanding the grain elevator in a river of smooth black asphalt; the skinnier length of Route 24 passed beneath the elevated walkway that connected the two wings of the elevator. Neither side of town had another paved road, but in compensation the dirt streets in Galatea were grandly named after presidents: Washington, East Adams, Jefferson, Monroe, West Adams; while the dirt streets in Galatia piously followed the books in the New Testament: Matthew, Mark, Luke, and John.

Both sides of town were full of empty houses. To be precise—to be as precise as Wade Painter unfailingly was in describing his town—there were sixteen in Galatea and thirteen in Galatia, and the sight of these ugly little dwellings cheered me a little because I knew that Colin could never lower himself to their standards. Colin had *closets* that were bigger than these houses.

"Make that fourteen," Wade said at one point, as we drove past yet another house with a FOR SALE sign in the front yard. This sign was freshly planted, the soil around the post still dark from recent turning.

Divine's head, spring-mounted it seemed, appeared from the back seat. "Yo, wasn't that Melvin Cartwright's place? I didn't know Melvin was gone."

Wade nodded as we drove past the house. "Last week," he said. "The same day as Eddie Comedy."

Divine sat back in his seat but his voice came floating forward. "They always take off in pairs," he said. "Man, that shit is fucked up. A couple more years, won't nobody be *left*."

Something funny happened when we returned to Wade's house: I climbed out of his car and I looked up at the imposing gray plane of his house and I had the distinct feeling that I was home. The feeling unnerved me so much that I grabbed Colin's wrist and looked at his watch, but it was a long moment before I could make out that less than an hour remained before we had to leave for the airport.

"Less than an hour to go," I said out loud, as much to place myself as to stress the point. I turned away from Wade's house, but the only other thing to look at was the distant horizon, a faint blur of land and sky so far away that I immediately turned back to Wade's house. The concrete looked cool and secure. It looked, well, it looked *concrete*, measured against all that emptiness, and I had to remind myself that it was just as empty inside as the sky it kept out.

"Yo, yo, Wade," Divine said then. "I got me some shit to do. I'ma head out now."

"Well, be careful," Wade said, quietly, seriously, and Divine flashed him a look before turning to Colin.

"Mr. Colin Nieman," he said, holding out his hand. "It has been my *distinct* pleasure to make your acquaintance, and I do hope we see you back here soon. Just remember," he said, "*the back door ain't never locked*," and I almost burst into laughter then, because Colin blushed so deeply he couldn't even answer Divine, who didn't bother to say goodbye to me before climbing into his car and speeding away.

"Well then," I heard Wade say when Divine was gone, "I suppose there's one more thing you should see."

I turned to him, but I was distracted yet again by the wide open prairie behind him. It was difficult to believe there was something we had yet to see: on that flat, barren landscape, how could you hide anything?

Wade stared at the wake of dust stirred up by Divine's retreat, and then, stirring himself, he said, "Shall we?" Colin nodded and climbed into the front seat of the car. I was about to get in back when I noticed Wade staring at me. He met my eyes for a moment and then he cleared his throat and said, "I think we can all fit in front."

This time we headed south on a narrow heavily cambered dirt road that quickly led us out of town, and I hummed the theme to *Gilligan's Island* under my breath until Colin elbowed me in the ribs, and then I stared silently at my feet. A moment later Colin slapped me on the knee.

"Hey! I didn't say—"

Colin cut me off. "Is that a *fire?*"

I looked up to see a huge black cloud clinging to the horizon. It was airy and low, and, though it did look like smoke, I sensed that it wasn't, because smoke rises and this cloud wafted just above the ground, like a hairdo held in place with not enough hairspray.

Wade's voice was calm. "That's Kenosha."

I didn't recognize the word until Colin said, "That town? The one Webbie told us about last night?"

Wade nodded. "On windy days the ash blows into the air and it looks like it's still burning." He paused, and then he added, "Just about every day is windy, around here."

He'd continued driving while we spoke—well, of course he had—and without warning he turned through a gap in a cedar break that had loomed up on our left. Before he turned I had thought that Kenosha was the one other thing Wade had thought we should see, but as soon as we entered the square cedar enclosure I knew that this was what Wade had in mind.

A house.

An enormous house, actually, a bona-fide mansion, built in the shape of a Swiss cross with four two-story arms and a steeply pitched roof. The house was as huge and simple and solid as a fact, and at the sight of it I felt suddenly weary, as if, once again, this land were stealing my imagination and leaving me helpless, unable to interact with the world around me, able only to describe it.

The walls of the house were built from huge limestone blocks of the palest yellow, the roof covered in some kind of black tile, and at its apex, a small cupola was just visible. The yard was flat and grassless and shiny in the setting sun, and I thought it was paved like a parking lot until I realized that the house was surrounded by a moat of obsidian flakes which caught the sunlight and produced an impression of oily depth. The setting sun came through another gap in the cedar hedge, this one perfectly aligned with one of the wings of the house—the west wing, I suppose it would be—so that a swath of light led straight to the house and snaked up the limestone wall in a bar as wide as a trellis. Where the light sank into the limestone it rendered the wall a wash of wet yellow, a transparent liquid yellow like clarified butter. The color reminded me first of aging paper but then I realized it was the same color I'd seen on some of Wade's paintings earlier in the day.

We sat silently for a moment, contemplating the spectacle. It was grand and grandiose, so obviously artificial that it seemed almost natural. It was in some ways the most beautiful house I had ever seen, but it was also the most oppressive—more oppressive than even Wade's house. It did not seem like the kind of place you could put a stamp on: it would put its stamp on you.

Colin cleared his throat. "Why—"

Wade answered him before he finished. "It's been empty for five years."

Colin said, "Is it—" and Wade cut him off again.

"Yes," he said, and he said it wistfully. "It's for sale." He paused then, and when he spoke again I detected something else in his voice, a challenge almost. "I'm not quite sure why I'm showing it to you," he said. "Rosemary Krebs will never let you have it."

I leaned forward then. If I was surprised at how quickly Wade had come to understand that Colin could never refuse such a dare, I was even more surprised that he had made it. But I was most surprised by the fact that Wade had surprised me, and I was beginning to realize that Wade wasn't quite as empty of emotion as he pretended, or wanted, to be. When he met my eyes, I saw in his a desire that was as naked as Divine's desire for Colin, and I sat back suddenly.

I looked at the house for a long time before I spoke. "Why don't *you* live here?"

From the corner of my eye I saw Wade turn back to the house; Colin hadn't looked away from it once.

"Because," Wade said finally, wistfulness and desire giving way, for the first time that weekend, to sadness. "Because," he said again, and I thought it was all he was going to say. But then he finished: "I've already built my house."

1.10

Webbie

THERE ARE NO BASEMENTS IN GALATIA. NOT ONE.

There are, each spring, a plenitude of flooded subterranean caverns in

Galatea, and any number of houses sitting at skewed angles on their cracked and sinking foundations, but in Galatia each and every house, no matter how tiny, is propped high and dry on wooden or limestone pillars sunk into solid concrete foundations and so rendered safe from a water table that rises right to the surface of the earth. It wasn't always that way. In fact, the Five Families lost their houses in a particularly wet spring just two years after they settled here, but when they built again, they built high, and no house is higher than Number 1 Matthew Street. Ten broad limestone steps lead to our front door, and when I was five years old and newly able to negotiate the steps unaided, I asked my father why we had twice as many steps as any of our neighbors. My father, that light and striding figure, replied, as he often did, without looking at me. Each of these ten steps, he said to the air, each of these steps brings us that much closer to God, and when he said that, I believed he spoke not to the air but to God Himself, and I thought that if I were as tall as my father then I too might see Him from the uppermost step.

But since my father's stroke each one of these steps has become his little piece of hell. His, and mine as well, for inside the house is Mother Mabel—my personal appellation for the chair lift which carries my father between the three floors of our house—but outside is Reverend Abraham's congregation, and the good Reverend considers it unmeet for the local representative of the Lord to be delivered to his constituency on a whining and slow-moving apparatus. And so, every Wednesday night and twice on Sunday, once in the morning and again in the evening, there is my father's command, *Lend me your arm, daughter*, a summons delivered in a booming voice so that all who have gathered to greet the Reverend as he leaves his house for the Lord's can hear this amicable exchange between father and daughter, reverend and parishioner, master and servant.

Halfway to Heaven, he said when I was five. Look out the Archive window and you just might see God looking back in. But of course the Archive was reserved for my father, and if any divine visions ever appeared he never allowed me more than a glimpse. Lend me your arm, daughter, he declared now, three times each week, and I would have left the arm with him if I could have, but he required the body attached to it as much as he required the arm itself.

The Sunday of Colin and Justin's visit was no different, except I had a hangover, and my father's stentorian bellow against my eardrum was even more painful than usual.

"Lend me your arm, daughter," he cried out. He hooked his walking stick over his weakened right wrist and gripped me with his left hand. His fingers bit into my arm as we prepared to make our way down the steps, and his grip was so tight that I imagined that the hand holding my arm was not that of an invalid but of a jailer—as if it were not I who escorted my father, but he who escorted me.

At the bottom of the steps three old women waited to see my father to church. For as long as I could remember my father had referred to these three women as his Church Ladies and, in fact, their given names were Faith, Hope, and Charity. You might think such a woeful conglomeration of names was bestowed by a single too-pious mother, but in fact Faith Jackson, Hope Rochelle, and Charity Getterling, though contemporaries, are unrelated, the surviving members of the Five Families of my father's generation.

"Morning, Reverend Abraham," the Church Ladies called out in unison, as they have called out numberless times before. They stood below us, three old but sturdy black women dressed in shiny polyester dresses dotted with toast crumbs and smelling of equal parts soap and perfume and bacon.

My father hung his not inconsiderable bulk from my arm, threatening to pull it from its socket, and then, slowly, we began our descent.

"The Lord has given us another beautiful day," his voice, the one aspect of his person—besides his weight—that remained undiminished by infirmity or age, hollered into my ear, and the Church Ladies called out their assent.

"Sure is a beautiful day, Reverend," Charity Getterling sang forth.

"As beautiful as the Lord makes them, Reverend," Hope Rochelle assented.

"Not a cloud in sight, Reverend," Faith Jackson affirmed. "Nothing in the sky but the birds."

My father didn't answer. His left leg swayed from one step to the next like a Slinky; when his right leg followed it his entire body was supported by mine.

Then, in a tone not as radiant, as reverent, as she normally used, Charity Getterling spoke. "Might be one little cloud in the sky today, Reverend."

"Not so much in the sky," Hope Rochelle clarified, "as on the horizon."

"Moving away, you could say," Faith Jackson appended, "leaving the sky clear as it was before."

My father stopped with a lurch, nearly knocking us both to the ground, and, although I would have thought it impossible, he managed to tighten his grasp on my arm.

"Tell me the news, ladies."

"Melvin Cartwright," Charity Getterling said.

"Gone away," Hope Rochelle explained.

"But so did Eddie Comedy," Faith Jackson added, and forced a smile into her wrinkled visage.

My father's hand seemed to spasm on my arm. His fingernails pushed through skin and flesh right to the nerve, and it was all I could do not to cry out.

"Melvin Cartwright was a good boy, and Galatia will miss him," he said after the briefest of pauses.

"Oh, yes, Rev—"

"But not," my father sternly cut off Charity Getterling, "not as much as he will come to miss Galatia."

At that the ladies fell conspicuously silent, the silence of mourners who have gathered to remember a pious brethren only to discover that their lost congregant was a practitioner of some secret vice.

My father, looking down on his chastened ladies, seemed to take pity on them. "We shall remember Melvin Cartwright as he was, and pray the world does not treat him too harshly. Perhaps," he said, as, with another lurch, he started us off again, "perhaps one day he will remember the simplicity and piety of the place which first cradled him, and he will return to us."

"Oh, he *will* remember, Reverend," Charity Getterling said.

"And *we'll* remember, Reverend," Hope Rochelle echoed.

"Remember and remember and remember," Faith Jackson repeated as grit crunched beneath my and my father's feet.

There was silence then, on the part of actor and audience alike, while we finished our journey. The Church Ladies watched us tensely, and I knew that if my father toppled forward they would have thrown their bodies under his to protect him from steps whose edges time had done nothing to soften. By then my hand had gone cold, almost numb, and my shoulder burned with each jolting step.

At last my father's bad foot touched the sidewalk, and then, with one last lurch, his good foot was beside it. I panted, wet with sweat and dizzy with exertion, as, with a buzz, the Church Ladies burst into speech.

"Why, Sister Webbie, I do believe you grow more and more like our lost Emily with each passing day," Charity Getterling said.

"She was a beautiful woman, God rest her soul," Hope Rochelle answered for me, and Faith Jackson, as she always did, finished up.

"Well, anybody can see that you sure are an asset to your father."

"We have Sister Emily to thank for that," my father said now, his voice—a gift from God, the Church Ladies have called it—level, untrembling. "As the years go by, a little more of Webbie fades away and a little more of her mother emerges."

He delivered his speech without looking at me; instead, he lifted his walking stick from his right arm and placed its tip firmly against the earth, and then, as jauntily as his crippled frame would allow, he took a step toward the park. The Ladies clustered around him immediately, ready to offer support if it became necessary, and together they set off for the church, leaving me, for the next hour at least, free. My father had long since given up insisting that I accompany him to church, because the sight of my yawning face was even more damning than my absence.

Now there would be one more absent face in church: Melvin Cartwright's. Once, when I was sixteen or seventeen, I had let Melvin Cartwright kiss me. I had kept my lips sealed until he'd reached under my ribs and tickled me, and the moment my mouth opened to laugh he'd shoved his tongue deep inside. Curiosity more than anything else impelled me to let it remain for a moment or two before I pushed him away; now I pushed the thought of him away as well. But my body, more nostalgic than my mind, let go less easily: my hand, I noticed, was on my rib cage, just beneath my breast, just above where Melvin Cartwright had touched me. But when I looked down and saw my hand and tried to remember Melvin's touch, or anyone else's, all I felt was Wade's parting embrace from the night before.

I shivered in the hot sun, shivered it all away and turned back to my father and his retinue of Church Ladies. They seemed hardly to have moved, and I was struck then by the contrast between the speed of thought and the slowness of lived life: my father and the Church Ladies walked so slowly that a puffball overtook them and disappeared in a shaft of sunshine. They walked toward their congregation, diminished by one more, dwindling with a progress as slow but steady as their own, and the earth they trod on, bound tightly in scrub grass, refused to take the impress of their feet. Only the gouge left by my father's cane appeared at regular intervals, each dimple as tiny as an egg cup, as innocuous and as useless, and yet in each of those perfectly formed dimples I could see the history of Galatia, also tiny, also innocuous, also, I suppose, useless, but it was beautiful too—almost perfect, given the country that produced it, and I was suddenly filled with a great tenderness for my hometown. I suppose it was Colin and Justin's presence that produced this wave of nostalgia, of love almost, for a place that I normally considered a prison rather than a home, or maybe it was Melvin's absence.

My shoulder burned from its recent load and my head throbbed from that last glass of wine and there was nothing I could call my own, not even these aches, but for a brief moment it was all outweighed by the sight of those four frail figures taking slow, measured steps on their way to the house of the Lord, and I kept watch on them, until they were safely inside.

1.11

Justin

THE DRIVE TO THE AIRPORT TOOK THREE HOURS. IT'S an exaggeration to call the gray strip on which we traveled a highway: it was a road. It embodied roadness. You felt the distance you'd covered, the miles yet to come; you had a sense of being suspended as well, between places, between decisions. Though I'd known from the moment our plane dropped below cloud level yesterday that this place was all wrong for us, I'd kept my tongue in check all weekend, and even now I let the road signs speak for me: Russell, Waldo, Paradise, Natorna, Codell, Plainville.

Plainville. What could I say to that?

It wasn't until we reached the airport that the twentieth-century sight of jets lumbering into the air shook me from my stupor, and I was able to think again, to make judgments, to reach conclusions, and I realized then that all of Kansas, and not just that narrow interminable road leading to and from Galatea, had given me the feeling of being between places, of being in a state of suspended animation. Difference is relative. The difference between a sand dune and the Atlantic Ocean is elemental, but five summers in Colin's house in the Pines hadn't taught me this; it took instead the blurring sameness of a weekend in Kansas, where prairie grass gives way to wheat gives way to parched earth, to point it out to me. Kansas was a state of broad vistas, but my eyes had been compelled to the ground the entire time I was there, as if there was something fascinating in the granularity of the soil, or something terrifying in the never-ending sameness, the distance one would have to travel before reaching the horizon.

Now the car shook slightly as another jet heaved itself off the ground, its wings seeming to flutter and flap behind a veil of exhaust.

Colin shook himself slightly as well, and then he slipped a twenty dollar bill between the closed sun visor and the roof. You might think he was merely leaving an extravagant tip for the person who would clean our rental car, but in fact his gesture was directed at me. The twenty was the equivalent of an opening line. It was Colin's way of starting a new scene.

With a drawn-out sigh, he turned to me. He looked at me for a long time but I refused to acknowledge him, and stared instead at jets taking off, or landing, or at empty sky. The airport in Wichita, Kansas is not a busy airport, so mostly I looked at empty sky.

At length Colin cleared his throat. He said, slowly, carefully, "Just-in-time?" using a voice that only I was privileged to hear, his weak voice, the voice of his childhood, a voice that can only speak in questions. He said, "Your father killed your mother?"

I pretended to be angry, but in fact I was surprised: after all this time what he still wanted was my story, and then, when I thought that, I *was* angry, and I said, "Fuck off, Colin."

There was another long moment of silence, at the end of which Colin reached into his wallet, extracted a twenty, and, with fingers that shook slightly, and without seeming to notice the tip he'd already put there, he slipped it into the space above his sun visor. When he'd finished he sighed again, and I realized he hadn't forgotten about the first twenty: he was merely acting. He was starting the scene over.

He spoke this time in his grown-up voice, the voice that could only make assertions. He said, "That house was beautiful."

"We're going to miss our plane," I said, but even as I reached to open the door Colin pressed the button that locked all the car's doors. I suppose I could have unlocked them—an identical button was on my side of the car—but I didn't. I just sat there. I waited. But this time Colin outwaited me, and when I could no longer take the silence I said, "That town would *kill* me."

There was a third pause, but at the end of this break Colin didn't add another twenty to the first two. Instead, he unlocked the doors, and opened his, but before he stepped out of the car he said, "They took Yonah to the hospital this morning." He stood up then, and when he spoke again it seemed he addressed not just me but Kansas itself, and this airport, and the world it reached out to with its thousands of airborne tentacles, and what he said was "Two. Just two."

1.12

Divine

ONCE UPON A TIME THERE WAS A LITTLE OLD SHACK about a half mile from the Big M Truck Stop. Nothing special bout that shack: it'd been built outta cheap-ass plywood years before I entered this world, and by the time I saw it its roof was sagging like the back of a thirty-year-old plow mare. Inside it was all dusty and shit, or mold, somebody once told me that shit was mold, but I mean, whatever, it don't really matter. I only bring it up cause I guess you could say it was on account of that shack that some of us finally figured out things had well and truly gone to shit in Galatia. I mean, we all knew things was fucked up before, but afterwards, well, afterwards we realized there wasn't no going back.

Used to be I visited that shack on a regular basis. The Big M, see, the Big M's on I-70 where it intersects U.S. 288. That's a real place—you can look it up on a map—and there's like a whole *cluster* of diesel fuel stations built around a parking lot that makes a football field look like a city back yard. What I'm saying is, there was plentya places to park, but I always stashed my car in that shack cause it wouldn'ta done no good for nobody to see it down to the Big M two, three times a week—and you'd be surprised at how many cheap-ass farmers drive a half hour outta they way just to save a dime a gallon on gas and bone up on some-a that stale lemon meringue pie they serve in the restaurant. But I didn't go there for gas or dinner. You ask Wade, Webbie, they'd say I went there to turn tricks, but they don't know shit. Why I went there was to look for Ratboy.

That time, the time I'm talking about, that time when I got there

there was already a car there, a truck actually, parked inside the shack. I could see it without even opening the door cause the walls was so fulla holes and shit, some beat-up Chevy pickup it looked like, but I couldn't tell if there was anyone in it or not cause it was too dark, and I didn't go inside to find out. I don't believe in ghosts or no shit like that, but the last thing a nigger needs is to get caught in a white man's barn—and one good piece of advice my daddy give me was he said if it don't have a black man's name on it, then it belongs to the white man. Now, normally I suppose I woulda gone on back to Wade's, but that wasn't a normal day. Nothing *like* normal. That day Colin Nieman had been in Galatia, and even then, hours after he'd left, just thinking about him was enough to send a little shiver up and down my spine, and I needed something to get him off my mind, and so, truck or no truck, I pulled my car to the leeside of the shack, locked it up, and made my way to the parking lot.

I tell you what. It never took long at the Big M. If I'd still been smoking I wouldn'ta had time to smoke me even one cigarette before this guy rolled down his window and asked me—this was a new one, even for me—if I wanted some potato chips.

Which he called *tater chips*.

He had a truck that smelled like cigarette smoke and cheap coffee spiked with even cheaper whiskey, and all that shit was like wrapped up in three hundred miles of Kansas dust and sweat, and so was he for that matter, and so he became just another trucker. He was a gypsy type, you know what I'm saying, probably just some half-breed Mexican, and his face was rough and stubbly and his fingernails were dirty and tasted like salt-and-vinegar potato chips, tater chips, what*ever*, by the looka things they was the only shit he ever ate. His English was a damn sight worse than a wetback's, but we didn't talk much. I knew he wouldn't undress, just like ease open his fly—man, they always sigh when they do that, I mean *always*, and I just wanna say to them, Buy some bigger *clothes*, motherfucker, buy you some clothes that *fit*, and sure enough this guy pulled down his zipper, but he opened up his flannel shirt too and I was all like, lucky me. I'd just worn a T and some baggy jeans and baseball cap, you know, I'm keeping it real, you know what I'm saying, I'm keeping *up* with what's *down*, and like Harry Houdini I slipped outta my clothes with the greatest of ease, and then this guy like *falls* on me and starts rubbing his shit all over me like he was some steel wool pad or some shit trying to scrub me clean, and like his underarms smelled like milk gone bad a *long* time ago. He was all like, "I vant to fock your bott," like someone outta some dumb-ass Count Chocula movie, and I found my jeans and fished around in the pocket and come up with a rubber and lube, for the mess, you know what I'm saying, the mess more than anything else, you don't have to worry too much around here but I do *not* like to douche every goddamn time, it dries me out, yeah, *somebody* out there knows what I'm saying, and so I gave him the merch and then I just rolled over and sighed. It's the sigh that really gets them going, when you combine it with the sight of naked ass—especially if that ass is as fine as mine. That sigh's like, I'm leaking, baby, you better find that hole and plug it *up*.

So listen, boys and girls, cause Divine is gonna give you the lowdown on doing it way up. My advice is simple: don't try this at home—although it'd be a damn sight easier at home, as opposed to the cab of a semi. I tell you what, it takes practice, not to mention a flexible spine, to take a dick that's shorter than the stomach it sticks out of and give your man any real satisfaction, let alone get something for your own self. I mean, most of these fat-ass Mexicans or gypsy types or whatever the hell he was just kinda grab your waist and close they eyes and start poking around with they little dicks at any old place on your butt cheeks and carrying on the whole time like they was Jeff Stryker or something, like woo-hoo! they giving it to you *now*, motherfucker! Yawn. But Divine has had years to practice, and it turned out Vlad the Impaler wasn't no stranger to the back door either, and all in all we had ourselves a fine time. And let me tell you one more thing: Webbie'd never believe it, but if there's fucking going on, like as not it's me fucking their sorry asses. These good old boys want the one thing their tired-ass wives can't give them—and about the only thing they liable to give me is a case of V.D. But don't you worry about Divine, I know how to look after myself. This may be the nineties and shit, but time moves a little slower in the middle-a fucking nowhere, so you don't got to watch your ass like you do in someplace like New York City. I mean, Webbie with like twenty fucking years of college said she couldn't even *guess* why Colin Nieman would want to look at Galatia, let alone think about moving here, but I could give her five reasons right off the top of my head. A-I-D-S was the first four, and the fifth was: it ain't round here.

So. There's them that pretend they don't know what's going on while they do it, and there's them that can't shut up with the gay shit in between mouthfuls of me. Some of them pretend I'm the woman, and some of them pretend they the woman, and every once in a while they wanna hold me like a baby when it's all over, which I have to admit I'm a sucker for that shit. Most of them give me something, like twenty bucks if I'm lucky, more likely a case of beer or a pack of cigarettes or something, which I always take even though I do *not* smoke no more. One guy even gave me a case of motor oil, said it was all he had. I take what they offer cause it makes it easier on them, especially the white ones: you can *take* sex, but you can't really *pay* for that shit, but everybody in America knows you can pay for a person, and that kinda keeps everything simple, you know what I'm saying? It's like, you're you and I'm me and here's twenty bucks to keep it that way. What Vlad did was give me my lube back, and then, like, he gave me the goddamn shit-covered scumbag too, handed it over with this like smile like it was a chocolate rose or some shit like that, and I was like what*ever* and sorta took the thing between two of my fingers, and then for like dessert or some shit Vlad was like sticking four of his dirty fingers in my mouth and I sucked on them, but all I tasted was me, and I pushed him off.

"Hey," I said, dropping the condom behind the semi's little mattress. "You ever come across somebody calls himself Ratboy?"

"Ratty?"

"Rat*boy*."

Vlad shook his head, and his jowls flapped around on either side of his mouth like one-a Howard Goertzen's daddy's hogs. Now that it was all over I could see he was some *skanky* shit, that was for *damn* sure. "Nuh-uh."

"How about Lamoine?"

"La-whuh?"

"La*moine*," I said, like Jesus Christ, don't no one speak fucking *English* no more? "Short, white, kinda funny-looking face, buck teeth."

He scratched his belly this time, which was even uglier than shaking his head. "Nope."

Well, I just jumped out of the cab then, naked as the day I was born. I mean, fuck that shit, he wasn't no good to me. I got dressed underneath his rig. Even before I was finished I heard the creaking and moaning start up above me, and I felt a touch of professional pride at the thought of him bringing himself off a second time, cause I knew what he was thinking about was what he'd just done with me. And then I was all like laughing and shit, thinking about the used rubber his wife was gonna find when she cleaned out his truck for him. I was like, explain that shit to the bitch, motherfucker.

Now. Let's talk some *real* spooky shit. Spooky is a starless night on the prairie, a mile walk through a night blacker than Webbie's pussy, clouds pressing down on you like a sweat-soaked sheet. Before I was even halfway back to the shack the lightning started, and I tell you what: them flashes lit a fire under my black ass, you know what I'm saying. But not even the nigger who took second place in the state cross-country championships—I had a twisted ankle or I'da won—can beat a Kansas thunderstorm, and before I was even halfway to the shack I was soaked through. Then, I don't know, then all the sudden I had this like flash of me and Ratboy on top of the grain elevator. We used to meet up there sometimes, get drunk, make out, just shoot the shit, but the time I'm remembering we hadn't really done nothing cause somebody or other'd busted up Ratboy's face and his lips was too swelled up to even kiss. But then like the rain started, like ice cold freezing rain, and I wanted to go but Ratboy just sat there and so I sat there too. I always did what he did, when I had the guts. And then eventually Ratboy was like, "Kiss me," and I was like, "But your lips," but then I saw through the dark that the swelling had gone down. The rain, you know what I'm saying, that goddamned ice cold freezing fucking rain musta done it, and I kissed him and even though neither of us said it I knew we was both thinking the same thing: that something, the rain or something, would always come along and fix things, and I'm here today to tell you that we was wrong—wrong that day on top of the elevator, and wrong again that night outside the Big M when I dragged my soaking wet ass into that old shack and damn near busted my knee on the grille of Eddie Comedy's pickup truck, which I didn't notice at first, cause what I noticed first was the smell.

You read about that shit in books and shit, and, like, you see people in movies, they walk into a room and crinkle up they noses like, god*damn*, that's some nasty shit, but let me tell you: not all dead things smell the same. What I mean is, there's something inside a human being that can tell the difference between a dead dog or cat or cow, which I've all smelled, and a dead person, which I hadn't never smelled before, and I was like shit, man, I do not *need* this in my life right now.

At first I was like, maybe I should just say fuck it, not even turn around and see what up, just open that shack door back up and get in my car and haul ass back to Galatia, but then I got to thinking about fingerprints and shit, and like who mighta seen me down to the Big M, and so, real slow like, like if I turned around fast it'd be worse, I turned around. I didn't see no body at first, just that truck, and right off I recognized it was Eddie Comedy's truck. Galatia's not such a small town you know what kinda car everybody drives, but I'd been in the back of Eddie Comedy's truck once or twice, you know what I'm saying, and besides, Eddie Comedy was kinda on my mind, what with him having just taken off and shit. Eddie Comedy's truck with its extra-fancy two-tone paint job looked like it'd been wrapped nose first around a telephone pole. I mean, the grille had a dent in it bigger than my body, and I was all like, damn, motherfucker, you musta been going fast.

I swear to God, I was thinking all that shit, I mean, like, for a moment I didn't think about that telephone pole out on Route 24 east of town, and I didn't even think of looking behind the wheel. It was like Eddie Comedy was somebody I knew, not somebody who could be rotting away in a shack in the middle of a field.

But you know, there's only so long you can look at a dented grille and so finally I looked up, and the first thing I saw was that there wasn't no windshield left in Eddie Comedy's truck. No glass at all.

The second thing I saw was Eddie Comedy.

A body don't change that much in three, four days, a week, whatever. At least not in that light it don't. Eddie Comedy's face was kinda . . . kinda swelled up I guess you'd say, like his cheeks was stuffed with food or some shit. It was all swelled up but it was kinda saggy too, like it'd been swelled up bigger than it was swelled up when I saw it, and well, the right side of his face was kinda messy, with some kinda dark gunk caked in his hair and making it stick straight out from the side of his head. Other than that he looked pretty much like Eddie Comedy. I mean, Eddie Comedy wasn't exactly known for his expert grooming or anything like that, he'd always been pretty much of a slob. His mouth was open and his eyes was closed, and if I'd heard snoring I coulda believed he was just sleeping off a bender.

And then I noticed the hole. It was on the left side of his head, right by his eye, just a single dark spot. I guess I woulda thought there'd be blood or something but there wasn't no blood around this hole, just a sort of black crusty cap that wasn't quite the same thing as a scab. It was about the same size as if someone with a long fingernail had taken their pinky and gouged out a little piece of Eddie Comedy's skin, and then I looked over at the right side of Eddie Comedy's face, at the bloody hair sticking straight out from the side of his head, and then I looked over at the passenger seat of Eddie Comedy's truck and it took me a moment to recognize what I saw there cause it was kind of covered with, well, with goo and shit, and even as I beat it on outta there to my car I was like, *Aw shit*, and I was like *shit* as I started up my car and *shit* as I floored it and then I was like *shit-shit-shit!* as I tore around the corner and felt the whole fucking car shake as it scraped along the side of the shack, ripping off my goddamn sideview mirror in the same way that a bullet had ripped off Eddie Comedy's ear and threw it on the seat across from his head.

And I tell you what: I read the books, I seen the movies. I knew what I shoulda done is gone back and found my sideview mirror and not left it behind for nobody to find. But the fact of the matter was I'd just looked at Eddie Comedy and he'd looked back at me and he only had a single ear fastened to his head. I had two ears on mine, two cute little ears that my momma used to tape to my head at night to make sure they'd stay nice and flat, and I had every intention of holding on to both of them. I put that gas pedal on the floor and I didn't even *think* about slowing down until I was in Wade's driveway, and then when I did get there I stepped outta my car and I looked at the naked spot where the mirror shoulda been. I put my finger on the little piece of metal still stuck to my car. A half hour after the fact it was still hot, like ripping it off had taken a lot of effort. It wasn't really hot enough to burn but even so I jerked my finger back and stuck it in my mouth, and I had a little flash as I sucked on my own skin that leaving that mirror behind was a big mistake. It was Lawman Brown I had on my mind when I thought that, but as it turned out it was the mailman who brought that mirror back into my life, though not for a hell of a long time—not till I'd almost forgotten about it really—and not in a way that I'd've ever expected.

1.13

Justin

IN THE BEGINNING HE WAS EVERYWHERE. BEHIND ME, beside me, in front of me. He opened every door for me, locked me up safe and sound every night. He splayed me, played me. I've never done so little to receive so much. His love was hungry, greedy. He ate me, yet after each meal I came away full. His love was needy, but it was me he needed, and only me. When I got scared I felt like a sacrificial lamb, slit, spitted, turning on a stick; but usually I felt like something gilded, an icon, an altar even. Colin was the one who was split, worshipper and worshipped. His two halves communicated through me. He wasn't just everywhere: he was *inside* me. He was omnipotent, but I—I was illuminated.

Colin was attempting to buy the limestone house. I was waiting to see if Colin would be successful. By then I was skilled at waiting for Colin; waiting had, since the beginning of our relationship, characterized the way we dealt with each other, although the term *waiting* was not one which either of us used. *Exploring our options* was how Colin put it most often; *being bored* was my particular favorite. Colin was exploring our options re: the limestone house, he was making a few telephone calls re: Rosemary Krebs, he was seeing if there was a story re: Galatea; and I was being bored while he did these things. I was filing my nails while he worked his fingers to the bone. I was spending the money he gave me so selflessly. I was retreating into memory while he planned our future life. All of these last phrases are Colin's, are options he explored and abandoned, one by one, and he abandoned them all because, in the end, they came down to the same thing: I was waiting, and Colin was waiting, for what would happen next.

So. Love is a flower. Love is a long-lashed multitude of white honeysuckle, a soft abundance of heart-shaped leaves, a blanket of evening perfume. Love is a clinging vine, a creeping tendril, a covering thing, inching its way up the bars of a trellis or along the brick face of a building. A worming inside, a warming, a weeping outside, a light touch that refuses to release itself, that doesn't know how. A shifting, a shimmering, a concealing and then a changing, a changeling, dangling over the abyss, one leg up, one step down, stasis, not stasis, revolution, return finally, to the covering, the creeping, the clinging. So. To everything that grows spring comes, to everything comes winter. But here's the rub: love is a flower, but it's not a perennial. Once it dies, it's dead.

A week after we returned from Kansas, Yonah died. Colin called Wade to tell him. When he hung up the phone I asked Colin what Wade had said, and Colin said, He said, I'm not surprised. And then Colin added—he had to add—Only one left. Only one to go.

I cut him the first time. My wristband was spiked—I was still doing the punk thing—and I sucker-punched him when he tried to walk away from a fight. He still has the scar, a little lightning bolt at the base of his occipital bone. I have a scar too, under my eye: he cut me with the diamond on the ring his father had given him; he had backhanded me. I cut myself the third time. I waited until he was asleep and I sliced my wrist, my right wrist of course, the wrist that led to my bum right hand, and then I dripped and slithered my way to where he lay sleeping on our bed, and I let my blood fall into his open mouth until he awoke, choking. He sputtered first, spewing blood, and then he screamed, and then he sat as if paralyzed, his body and mine covered in a fine red mist. "Just don't swallow," I said. "You practice good oral hygiene, don't you?" I followed him when he got up and staggered to the bathroom. "Walk like a man," I taunted, "it's not like I *shot* you or anything." Colin pulled open cabinets, drawers, spilled objects onto the floor. "What're you looking for? Mouthwash? Rubbing alcohol? Want me to get some *bleach*?" In the end he gargled with hydrogen peroxide because it was all he could find. When he stepped out of the shower he was more red than when he went in, but, even so, he was shivering, and he knew what the stakes were: for me, and, as long as he kept me, for him.

We seem to have just missed the beginning of something, Colin said to me, just one day after Yonah's death. Some trucker discovered a smashed-up truck last night, Colin said, apparently the same vehicle that ran into that telephone pole Wade showed us, only the truck was stashed in a shack about thirty miles from the telephone pole. Paint chips, Colin said in answer to my unasked question, that's how they knew it was the same truck. And, he continued, after a pause, there was a corpse in the truck. Another pause, and then: The mystery is, the man didn't die in the accident. Someone blew his brains out. Another pause, a quieter voice: Guy had a funny name, what was it, Carmody, no, not Carmody, Comedy, yeah, that's it, Comedy. Funny name, huh? This time Colin refused to speak again, and so, at length, I said, I think I have a temperature, to which Colin said, Oh, fuck you, Justin. You want to live in the past, fine, wallow in it for all I care. Fuck *you*!

Zach was Colin's friend. He made one vow: to outlast his cat. This is the story Colin told me: when Zach tested positive he went home and his cat jumped into his lap. He thought, Jesus, this cat's going to outlive me. He said, Everybody buys a cat knowing that one day it'll die and they'll be sad for a while and then they'll get a new cat or a new dog or whatever, a parakeet or a lizard or something. And here was Zach, and he had this eight-year-old cat with a life expectancy greater than his. So he vowed that the cat would go to its grave first. Well, for five years everything was fine. And then he started to get sick. And then he got sicker. And then he got *real* sick. By then the cat was old. She'd slowed down, but she was in good health. Zach stopped feeding her, but between his home-care worker and his friends there was someone there nearly every day. He tried to kill her once, but she was more spry than he was, and she managed to hide on top of a bookshelf. A few years passed this way. No one was quite sure how Zach held on, or what he was holding on to. But he called last night. He said, One year for a cat is equal to five years for a human. He said, AIDS is like that, except one year for a P.W.A. is like ten years for a human, or twenty, or thirty. And then he said, The bitch is *dead*. And he was too, when we got there this morning.

These people are all *nuts*, Colin reported. The woman who used to own the limestone house left it *in her will* that no member of, who is it, the *Krebs* family could ever buy the house or the land, but when I asked the agent *why* all he could tell me is that Rosemary, I guess that must be Rosemary Krebs, Rosemary and Bea, he said, were not the best of friends. And so this Krebs woman, Rosemary, who apparently owns more or less everything else in, what's it called, Cada*vera* County, Rosemary Krebs *did* manage to get the executorship of Bea's estate transferred to the largest real-estate brokerage in St. *Louis* of all places, I mean, we're talking about the firm that sold the plot the goddamn Gateway *Arch* was built on being handed what amounts to a nickel-and-dime deal *five hundred miles* away. Not exactly high priority, if you see what I mean. And then on top of it all she's applied to every government agency under the sun to landmark the place so it *can't* be sold. Seems there's a fucking burial mound on the property somewhere, nothing more than a hole in the ground the size of a walk-in closet which had like *one* skeleton in it, this skeleton and some primitive pottery balls or something, whatever they were they weren't even *glazed*, and no one has the slightest fucking *clue* where the skeleton is now. Oh, and *since you ask*, Mr. Curiosity, Colin said, no, there hasn't been any movement on the Eddie Comedy front. Lawman Brown hasn't got a clue, is how Wade put it. Now Colin paused. He asked after you. Lawman Brown? I said. No, Colin said, Wade did. And what did you tell Wade? I said. I told him that you were fine, Colin said. I said your condition was unchanged.

You turn your back on them, but that's what lets them enter you. You know what I mean, don't you, boys—and a lot of the girls out there, I bet you understand too. You roll over, you turn your face from them, your eyes, your mouth, your nose, your ears even, your ears point forward and when you roll onto your stomach they join all those other cranial senses in *rejecting the man who's about to fuck you*, and don't think he doesn't know this. Oh, he'll pretend, he'll say, It's an expression of your trust when we do it this way blahdy-blahdy-blah, he'll say that after you've turned, after a moment of silence while he contemplates the facelessness of the nape of your neck, your nippleless back, maybe he'll already be sliding a finger between the cheeks of your ass, feeling, probing, he'll say, I could do anything to you, but you trust me don't you? and there'll be that little questioning lilt at the end of his speech, the request, please, affirm me. So you sigh, you lower your head, raise your ass a little, widen the distance between your legs: *that* mouth doesn't speak, and against its silence he too is silent, all business, his unanswered question hanging in the air for as long as he can keep it up. Sometimes he'll bring your head close to his head: in order to do this he's got to pull you to him, by the hair, if you've got any, or an ear, or your neck, he'll pull your head back until one of your cheeks is up against one of his and then he'll try to catch a glimpse of where you're looking before he kisses you, that neck-twisting maneuver that looks like a praying mantis eating her mate. More often than not his tongue will settle for your ear, a garbled squelching taking the place of language between you, and far far away another blind eye will feel around for something it *knows is there* but can't see or touch. The first time Colin finished fucking me—the first time, in fact, we had sex, nearly two full years after we'd met because he wanted to wait until I was legal—he walked from the bed to the bathroom to fetch a towel and I watched him go, Colin, I memorized the shape of his back and buttocks, Colin, his hams and calves and the backward swing of his arms, Colin, the cap of his skull, Colin Colin Colin, I watched him because I wanted to know just what would be hiding under his clothes when, finally, he left me.

But he surprised me. He outwaited me, as, sometimes, he is able to do.

It was the evening of Zach's memorial service.

Colin said, "I closed on the house this morning." He said, "It's ours."

"It's *yours*. Own it in good health."

"Justin—"

Suddenly my patience was at an end.

"Enough, Colin, it's enough already. Listen to me, Colin. There's only one way you're going to leave AIDS behind, and that's if you leave *me* behind."

"Justin—"

I grabbed him then, I used my unfeeling hand and I pulled him close. I would have liked to reason with him, but it never worked that way with us: the gaudy script we followed required shouts first, then silence, then tears, and so I hissed in his ear, "I consider it my task in life to tear down every wall you build, whether it's with words or distance or money. As long as I am with you, you will never forget what you're running from."

"Justin—"

"That is *not* my name."

This time Colin grabbed me, with both hands, practically lifting me from the ground by my shirtfront. "Then what *is* your name?"

This time I let my silence answer, and it said nothing. Nothing is my name.

1.14

Wade

DIVINE WAS SLEEPING.

He slept naked, of course, on that and every other night he spent with me. He slept naked every time I saw him sleeping except for the first time, outside the steps of the new library. He slept naked in my bedroom with the heat turned up high in the wintertime or the air conditioning turned off in the summertime so that he could lie atop the sheets because, even asleep, Divine organized his life around the principle that *someone* was watching him. If this is what some people mean by the term *vanity* then it was a conditioned vanity, for Divine had always been on display, a beautiful baby who became a pretty little boy who had become, by the time I knew him, a ravishing teenager. When company came over, he told me once, his parents didn't say, Whyn't you get Reverend Abraham a iced tea. They said, Whyn't you sing "Swing Low" for the Reverend. They said, Whyn't you dance like Michael Jackson. Divine starred first in his living room and then on the high school stage, and the track team, and the Big M Truck Stop, and my bedroom: he slept naked and he slept atop the sheets and he slept on his belly with his back arched and his ass pushed ever so slightly into the air. His face nestled between two plumped white mounds of pillow and only his penis was hidden, beneath his body, and his hands as well, beneath the pillow, and when I asked him why he always hid his hands and his penis he frowned and he said, "God don't like to look down on the idle and unemployed," and he pulled the pillow over his head.

It was morning. The night before Colin Nieman had called me to say that he had managed to outmaneuver the obstacles Rosemary Krebs had erected, that he had purchased the limestone house, that he would be moving into it a few days hence.

I put a hand on Divine's shoulder. His copper skin was smooth and soft and warm and just slightly damp, like a pipe with hot water coursing through it, and I let my hand rest on him for just a moment, and, as lightly as I could, I shook.

"Off duty," Divine rasped, so quickly that I realized he had already been awake. "Go way."

"I need to draw you," I said. "While the light's still good."

"It's the sun, not a piece-a meat. It don't go bad."

"It's a beautiful morning. You won't even have to get dressed. Just come out to the studio with me. You can even go back to sleep when we get there."

"Why can't I go back to sleep here?"

"You know. I need to draw you in your room."

"*My* room? Can't hardly call it my room when you keep it locked against me."

"Divine—"

"Aw, c'mon, Wade, let me off the hook for once in your goddamn life. I didn't hardly get no sleep last night."

"And whose fault is that?"

Divine's eyes were still closed, but the effort of keeping them shut showed up in his wrinkled brow and pursed lips. "Offhand, I'd say it was yours. Less that was someone else fucking me last night."

"Colin's coming back. He's coming on Saturday. He's coming for good."

Divine's eyes sprang open. "They coming back? They actually *moving* here?"

"Not them. Just Colin. Just . . . Justin's staying behind."

A slow smile crept across Divine's face and it didn't stop until it had split his cheeks from ear to ear. "Well, I'll be goddamned."

"Get up. Let's go."

"Getting up and going," Divine said, and he sat up, stood up, jumped up and down, and then stretched his arms up to the ceiling and dug his toes down into the floorboards. He held the pose just long enough to say, "Sure you don't want to fuck me? Might be your last chance."

I turned away from him and started for the studio. I turned away from him not just because I wasn't sure that I didn't want to fuck him, and not just because I knew that it might be my last chance, but because Colin Nieman had said that Justin Time would not be coming to Galatea. After a moment I heard Divine start after me, the pads of his feet slapping out a rapid staccato on the floor as he skipped past me, still naked, opened the door, and danced out into a drizzly fall morning.

"Shit!" he screamed, stopping, turning, staring at me. "You said it was *warm*, you . . . shit!" He just jumped up and down then, all the muscles of his body laid out in corded lines beneath skin studded with goose pimples and droplets of water, the slick gravel popping beneath his bouncing feet, but before I could answer him the morning air was rent by the short sharp blast of a siren.

Divine stopped bouncing and turned toward the yard. His mouth fell open but no sound emerged.

Later Divine told me it had started for him nearly two weeks earlier, when he came across Eddie Comedy's body in that shack by the Big M, but it didn't start for me until that morning, when I looked through the rain and mist and saw a pair of wipers swishing slowly back and forth across the opaque windshield of Lawman Brown's police cruiser. It sat, framed by the emptied shell of my parents' house, in the middle of my back yard. There were no tracks in the silvered wet grass, so I knew he must've driven it there some time in the wee hours and then waited for us to make our appearance. That he knew to wait outside the back door meant something too, but I didn't think about that until later.

What sunlight there was bounced off the windshield and rendered the interior of the cruiser invisible, but as we watched, the door opened slowly and the bare balding head of Lawman Brown appeared, followed a moment later by his hand carrying his hat, which he squared atop his head before he stood and began walking toward us, one hand resting on the butt of his gun, the other on the bulk of his stomach.

Divine stood on the gravel path, naked, shivering slightly. His skin was so highly buffed that the rain sat on it as it would on a freshly waxed car, in perfectly round, individual drops, and, briefly, I wished that I had my charcoal and paper with me, because I wanted to draw him then and there, with the rainwater studding his body, but then I realized I would not be able to draw in the rain.

When Lawman Brown was close enough to hear me without my having to raise my voice, I spoke.

"Morning, Lawman."

He took a few more steps before he answered.

"My name," he said, "is Eustace, and my title is Sheriff, and I'd appreciate it, Wade, if you'd afford me the respect that title deserves."

"Morning, Sheriff Brown," Divine said then, and the wheedling tone in his voice made me look at him. He was still shivering, but not, I realized, with the cold. He was terrified.

"Morning, Reggie."

When Divine didn't say anything I knew something was really wrong, because Divine allowed *no one* to address him by the name his parents had given him.

"Little cold for sunbathing, ain't it, Reggie? Kinda cloudy too. Aw, what am I saying, your people don't . . ." The broad brim of Lawman Brown's hat craned dramatically left and right. "Don't see no heated swimming pool, so I can't imagine you're gonna go skinny-dipping." He paused again. "So what's up, Reggie? Where's your clothes?"

Divine nodded his twitching head at me. "He, he was gonna draw me."

"*Draw* you?"

"Perhaps we could arrive at the point, Eustace. We all have work to do."

" 'S'is how Reggie here dresses for work?" He nodded his hatted head once at Divine, then again at me, and then he turned back to Divine and said, "You wasn't maybe . . . working out to the Big M a couple-a three weeks ago, was you?"

"I don't never go to the Big M," Divine said. "Why would I go to the Big M?"

"I think it was a Sunday night," Lawman Brown said, and then he named a date.

"Eustace," I said. "Divine was here that night. We had company that night, that's why I remember. Webbie Greeving, and two men from out of town."

For the first time since coming outside, Divine lowered his hands to cover his genitals. The runneling rainwater flowed down his body to just that spot and leaked out between his fingers, and I had the distinct impression that the spilled liquid was something precious, and I was watching it being lost forever.

"Webbie was here on Saturday, not Sunday," Lawman Brown said now, "and your visitors was gone by 14:30 Sunday afternoon. What time I'm talking about is oh-one hundred hours, Monday morning to be precise. Big M Truck Stop, northwest parking lot. Sure you wasn't—"

"You found the mirror!" Divine bleated out. "I was just getting some food and gas, Lawman, some, Wade, he needed something from the paint store in Bigger Hill and I, aw shit, aw goddamn, that goddamn mirror!"

"Reggie, I'd appreciate it if you refrained from taking the Lord's name in vain. And my title is not Lawman, it is *Sheriff* Brown, and I'd appreciate it if you'd—"

"Eustace, what the hell is this about?"

"And I would appreciate it, Wade, if you would refrain from interfering in official police business, which I will remind you is an actionable violation of the law. Now, Reggie," Lawman Brown said, shaking his reddening face quickly and flinging accumulated water from the brim of his hat, "what's this dad-gummed mirror you keep talking about?"

Divine looked confused. "You didn't find it? I thought, you knew I was there, I mean, my sideview mirror, I—"

"Enougha your prattling on, Reggie." Lawman Brown stopped then. He drew himself up to his full height, cleared his throat, and, in his best approximation of officiousness, declared, "Reginald Packman, I am here to take you into police custody for questioning in conjunction with the murder of Eddie Comedy. You are not, I repeat *not* under arrest, but there are some questions I want to ask you. You have five minutes to get yourself inside and cover your nakedness, and then we going down to the station house. I mean we're."

Divine stared at Lawman Brown briefly and then he turned his panic-stricken face to me. It was a wide-open face, at once begging for a savior, but also, and just as powerfully, inviting betrayal.

"Wade?"

"Get dressed," I said. I would have liked to have told him that I would take care of it, but I didn't know how to take care of it. I didn't know what needed taken care of. There are people who can make that sort of blind promise, but I have never been one of them. I felt myself shrinking, retreating from the scene at hand.

"Wade?" Divine said again. The word floated past me as though I were not there.

"Get dressed," Lawman Brown said. "You got four and a half minutes left."

Then Lawman Brown and I were alone together. We didn't speak. We didn't even look at each other. The sun was still low in the sky behind him, and I looked at the thick gray expanse of cloud it tinged yellow and orange and dusky ocher, and Lawman Brown looked somewhere else. One minute passed, two minutes, three minutes, four. Five.

Lawman Brown cleared his throat. I wasn't sure if it was a prelude to conversation of if he was merely phlegmy. He spat, and then returned to silence.

Five more minutes went by.

Lawman Brown cleared his throat again. "Uh, Wade?"

I turned from the rising sun to look at him. An afterimage painted his face a hepatitic yellow.

"You wanna see what's keeping him?"

Once, when we were in high school together, I had painted a smiley face on the seat of Lawman Brown's desk at school. The boy Eustace, plump and pimply, had sat on it unknowingly, and for the rest of the day he had walked around with not one but two dopey grins, one fore and one aft. Though he could never prove I'd done it, he had been wary of me ever since, and without Divine's cowed presence his bluster dissipated and he was just another tubby policeman with a doughnut problem.

"Uh, Wade?"

"Be my guest, Eustace. You are the sheriff, after all."

I left him then, and went to my studio. He found me, fifteen minutes later, in Divine's room. He was sweaty and out of breath and his hat sat at a skewed angle on his head.

"He's gone!" he panted. "He done run off!"

"You sound surprised."

"Listen here, Wade. That boy was seen by half a dozen folks messing around that shack where Eddie Comedy was found. Now I ain't saying he had nothing to do with it but all the same maybe he knows something he don't know he knows. He—"

His voice broke off as his eyes, which had been wandering the walls of the room, finally made out what was on them.

"Is that . . . Divine?"

Once upon a time the room we stood in had been my bedroom. For years I had painted its tiny white walls with imagined vistas of escape and revenge, of freedom from my parents and Galatea and all of Kansas. Thirty years later it had become a monument to Divine. It was virtually covered by drawings of him: drawings on the ceiling and the floor as well as on all four walls, drawings on the back of the door and drawings on the window. Day after day I had posed Divine in the middle of that room, naked, and then drawn whichever part of him wasn't hidden by the sun's glare. I had drawn his hands, I had drawn a single finger. I'd drawn his body without his face, his face without his body, I'd drawn all of him. One time I drew his shadow only, and left his body itself out of the picture. Now, four days before Colin Nieman was due to return to Galatea, there were more than two hundred drawings in the room; there was space for just one more, and it was that picture I had meant to draw when I'd awakened Divine in the morning, that space I had meant to fill.

It occurs to me only now that my drawings of Divine sound ominously like the list that Colin and Justin had compiled. I offer this bit of information as illustrative, but I am not sure what it illustrates, about me, or about Divine, or about Colin and Justin. You might expect me to be bothered by that but I am not. There are those persons—Colin Nieman was one of them, as was, for that matter, Divine—who believe in the meaning of things, and the importance of meaning, and there are others, people like me, people like Justin, who do not see an intrinsic meaning in things but instead see only the meaning that people bring to them. There is a third type of person—Rosemary Krebs was such a person, as was, I think, the person who had orchestrated the murder of Eddie Comedy—who is less interested in the source of meaning, of information, than in the ways that information is or can be put to use. Webbie Greeving was a member of this third class, although she would not like to admit it.

"Uh, Wade?"

In my hands there was a sheet of blank white paper. Before I answered Lawman Brown I tacked it to the empty space on the wall. I looked at the rain through the thin slices of window that showed around my drawings of Divine, and, still addressing the window, I said, "Where did the animals flee during the flood?"

"Uh, Wade?"

"The rain came down, the waters came up, you remember the old song, don't you, Eustace? Where did all the animals go?"

"They climbed on board the ark and—"

"Whose ark?"

"Noah's—"

Lawman Brown's voice broke off as he finally understood what I was talking about. The room was quiet save for the light patter of rain outside. I listened to the drizzle, tried to feel what it felt like and see what it looked like as it left the clouds, as it fell through the sky and struck the soil and mixed with the water already there, and at some point a thin breeze slipped through the window and rustled the drawings of Divine, and this new sound roused me to speak.

I said, "I think you know where to find what you're looking for, Eustace," but when I turned my head to look at him I saw that he had already gone.

1.15

Justin

FIVE HUNDRED PEOPLE HAD DIED, AND IN RESPONSE Colin had bought a limestone mansion that was less than one hundred miles away from the exact center of the country—which is to say, about as far away from the epicenters of the AIDS epidemic as you could get without leaving the country. He was going out there, he said, he was going to Kansas whether I went with him or not.

Five hundred and one, if you count someone called Eddie Comedy, whom I did not but Colin did. I didn't count Eddie Comedy not because he hadn't died of AIDS but because he didn't have anything to do with my going or staying, and Colin counted him because he did. Have something do with Colin's desire to go, I mean: Eddie Comedy, Colin said, was going to write Colin's new novel for him, and when I suggested to Colin that that was going to be a little difficult given that Eddie Comedy was dead, Colin had said that he was *using a metaphor*, and I was attempting to remember the expression Colin had worn when he said this, *using a metaphor*, I was attempting to remember what it was about Colin's expression that had frightened me so much that I had been forced to leave the house immediately.

I was remembering Colin's blank gray eyes and the particular lightlessness of his skin and the thin horizontal line of his upper lip as he said the words *using a metaphor* as I made my way north on Seventh Avenue. I was walking on the east side of the street, between Twelfth and Thirteenth; I had, without planning it, walked to St. Vincent's, but on this particular occasion I had not walked into St. Vincent's because everyone was already dead, and so I walked past the chapel entrance on Twelfth and past the emergency room entrance on Seventh and past the main entrance on Thirteenth, and as I crossed Thirteenth I decided that I would get on the subway at Fourteenth if I hadn't figured out what it was about Colin's expression as he said *using a metaphor* that had upset me, and I would ride the subway as far north as it would go. It occurred to me too, as I crossed Thirteenth Street, that north was the one direction that Colin had never considered. South, yes; east and west, fine; north, not an option.

It was a warm fall day but my skin suddenly goose-pimpled as I imagined Toronto, Anchorage, Vladivostok, and I realized then that what had so upset me about Colin's expression when he had said he was *using a metaphor* was that there hadn't been one, an expression, I mean. Colin's face had been grim and determined as he said that he was going to move to Kansas with or without me and his face had been full of a guilty excitement as he said that Eddie Comedy was going to write his new novel for him but when he said that he was *using a metaphor* his face had suddenly frozen into a blank mask, and all at once I understood that Colin was going to go to Kansas, not so that he could write a novel about Eddie Comedy and whatever it was that had killed him, and not, for that matter, so that he could get away from the AIDS epidemic. Colin was going to go to Kansas so that he could get away from me. The metaphor Colin was using was Eddie Comedy's death, and the thing it stood for, the thing elided, was me.

I decided that I would get on the subway anyway. It would take me only to the Bronx and then it would turn around again. There was, in other words, no real point in getting on the subway unless I decided to get off it and seek some other means of escape, but I had no intention of getting off it, at least not until it came back here.

Then, up ahead, I noticed a fat white man enter the subway station at the southeast corner of Fourteenth and Seventh, and, without quite realizing I was doing it, I waited for him to resurface, because that corner of the street is only an exit from the station. But he didn't come back up, and as I got closer to the intersection I saw several more people go down the same stairs, and none of them came back up either. I looked at the other three entrances: I saw crowds of people rushing into the subway station as though it were a vacuum sucking them in, all kinds of people, fat and thin, young and old, black and white, male and female, healthy and sick, they all walked right up to those descending staircases and disappeared, one after another after another, and not one of them came back up. I'm not just saying that the people I saw go down didn't come back up, I'm saying that no one came up—*no one*—and I knew that if I went down those stairs then I too would not come back up.

What was it Divine had said? They always go in pairs.

When I got home I threw the papers that were on Colin's desk to the floor and I made him fuck me right there, right where he wrote, or, I should say, where he didn't write his second novel, and just before he came I pushed him off me and I stood over him and I said, You will never leave me. I may leave you one day, but you will never, ever leave me. He sprawled in his chair: beautiful perfect stunned Colin, his penis still hard and still covered with little flecks of my shit and my blood and his black condom, and you would think that his face would reveal *something* about how all this affected him, but no. It remained as expressionless as when he'd said he was *using a metaphor*, and I was suddenly afraid that he would make a liar of me. I have to go pack, I said then. If we're leaving this weekend, I said, I'd better go pack.

1.16

Divine

I TELL YOU WHAT: I DIDN'T KNOW ANYBODY IN GALAtea even heard about Noah's ark, let alone knew where it was. I guess you can't even count on black folks keeping their own secrets anymore—and don't give me no shit about Old Lady Beatrice. Bitch was so wasted by the time she showed up here it was all she could do to climb the stairs of the house she bought off Donald Deacon, so don't be telling me she went off for no ten-mile walks in the fields. Folks said the only reason Donald Deacon had to sell out to a white couple was to pay off the debt his brother run up building a boat the size of Texas in the middle of a goddamn Kansas cow pasture. Folks said if it hadn'ta been Bea and Hank it woulda been Rosemary Krebs, and all things considered most people think he did the right thing by taking a chance on a unknown commodity.

Me, I bet it was Webbie. Told the story, I mean, about Noah Deacon and the ark he spent his whole life and life savings building. There's just some people that have to tell stories, and Webbie Greeving was one of em. Webbie told Wade, and Wade, well, Wade told Lawman Brown, that motherfucker, and landed my ass in jail. Though I have to say Lawman Brown didn't seem like no stranger to the ark when he found me there. Fact was, it looked like the ark had seen a fair bit of action since the last time I'd been there, rubbers and beer cans and shit all over the place, and like cans of food even, and the ashes of fires they'd been cooked in. Well, it wasn't nothing I hadn't done myself, except for the food. Not the smartest idea in the world, building a fire inside a great big dry wooden box, but I suppose it beats eating the shit cold.

Questions. He said I was just there for questions. Nigger's heard *that* line before. And like what the fuck did I know about Eddie Comedy besides the fact that his dick hair was as dark and kinky as mine, and the thing that stuck out of it was a little bit on the little side? That, and the fact that the hole the bullet made coming out his head was a hell of a lot bigger than the one it made going in. You gotta lock my ass up to ask me that?

But he did, and then he left me there. Fucking iron cage in a goddamn motherfucking basement, and I tell you what: fluorescent is *not* optimum lighting conditions for my complexion. Not even a goddamn window to let me know whether the sun was up or down, just some skinny-ass bed with a smelly mattress thinner than the blanket on top of it and one of those toilets with no seat, and nothing to eat neither. I mean, fuck, not even a goddamn phone call.

"You ain't under arrest" is what Lawman Brown said. "If you ain't under arrest you ain't entitled to a phone call. Besides," he said, and I could tell he said it just to be nasty, "who you gonna call? *Ghostbusters?*"

" 'Who I gonna call?' You best watch it, Lawman Brown, you spend so much time hanging round black folks you starting to sound like one."

Well, that got him, but afterwards I wished I hadn't said it cause all it did was make him mad, and then he left me alone down there. Nothing to do but sit and stew and try to hold it all in, cause I tell you what, there was no *way* my pretty little ass was gonna set down on some goddamn piss-covered commode. I wouldn'ta guessed Rosemary Krebs' new jailhouse saw so much action, but if that commode was any judge there'd been a goddamn parade of prisoners in and outta there, eacha them with a aim about as good as a blind grandma shooting crows at midnight. I mean, shit, how hard is it to hit the fucking *bowl*?

When I heard the key rattling in the lock down at the end of the hall—the cells had bars in front but cinderblock walls at the sides, so you could only see what was in front of you, which was a cement wall about three feet away—I figured it was just Lawman Brown come back to bother me with some more-a his dumb-ass questions. But even before I could see anything my mouth was all like watering and shit cause I could smell the rich thick smell of fresh-cooked ham.

"That you, Cora Johnson, or am I hallucinating?"

She lumbered into view then. Thirty-seven I guess she was, a year or two older than Webbie, but she coulda passed for fifty. My momma always said that's what worrying did to you: put lines in your face and gray in your hair long before you was due, but I guess Cora had reasons to fret, what with being a single mom trying to raise a son who was always in and outta the hospital on accounta his asthma, and running a café on her own—although I guess there was Rosa. I always forgot about Rosa, even though it'd been four years.

Cora was holding a picnic basket big enough to feed a family of five, and she looked at me for a minute before she set it down on the floor and stood up. She seemed kinda stiff, not like her back was hurting, I mean, but like formal and shit, but I suppose talking to somebody who's on the inside of a cage'll do that.

"Baby boy," she finally said, "what mess you done got yourself in now?"

"I ain't done nothing, Cora. Nothing at all."

"Lawman Brown"—Cora swallowed—"Sheriff Brown just thought you needed a change-a scenery, that what you telling me?"

I looked at Cora for a minute, and she dropped her eyes to the floor, but before she did they kinda flashed to her left, and I realized he was down there, at the end of the hall, and then, as loud as I could, I said, "Since when does Lawman Brown need a good excuse to lock up a black man?"

"Don't play that game with me, Reginald Packman. Man ain't no frienda mine"—Cora swallowed again, but went on in a normal tone of voice—"he ain't no frienda mine, but I ain't never known him to hassle black folks. Without a reason." She smiled when she said that, just a little smile on the right side of her face, but I smiled back at her.

"My *name*," I said then, "is Divine."

Cora frowned then, but then she smiled again. "Yeah it is," she said, and she laughed, some weird-sounding shit, I gotta tell you, echoing around an empty cement basement. "Divine," she said. "I forget. *Divine*."

"Is what's in that basket for me? Or were you maybe on the way to some orphanage I don't know about?"

"You practically an orphan," Cora said. "Aw, I'm sorry, Reg—Divine. I shouldn'ta said that." I didn't answer her, and after a minute Cora said loudly, "Well, technically I'm supposed to tease you a little, try and get you to answer some questions before I open up the basket, but . . ." She shrugged, pulled up a metal folding chair, dropped down into it the way people who stand on their feet twelve hours a day tend to do. She flipped the basket open and after rummaging around a minute pulled out a slab of pink, pink ham, one side marbled brown and white with a nice thick crust. "Lawman Brown said no forks and knives, sorry. No plates even. 'Can't have the prisoner doing harm to hisself.' "

"You just hand that shit over, Cora Johnson. I don't need no fork and knives to eat shit right now."

"Watch your language, boy," Cora said. She'd started to hand the ham over, but she held it just outta reach.

I smiled. "I'm sorry, Miss Johnson, ma'am. Please may I have that ham now, please?"

She smiled back, and handed it to me. "It's still Mrs. actually, if you wanna get technical about it."

I didn't answer her cause my mouth was already fulla ham. It was still warm, and I ate it down in three or four bites. Cora had another thick slice ready for me when I'd finished, and then one more, and when I'd finished the third slice she handed me a napkin and I wiped off my greasy fingers and mouth. She was looking at me kinda funny when I finished, so I said, "What up, Cora? There food on my face?"

"Huh? Oh, no, no, you clean." She fished in the basket, came out with a baked potato. "I just cut it and put some butter on it upstairs, so watch out, it's still hot." I was trying to suck the meat outta the skin without being a complete pig when Cora kinda cleared her throat and said, "He, um, Lawman Brown, he wanted me to ask you about those two men."

"What two men?" I said between bites.

"Those two that was at Wade's. New York City, I think he said they was from."

"Colin and Jason. Justin, I mean. Justin."

"That their names? He didn't say. He just said to ask you."

"Why? He think they killed Eddie Comedy too. Or is he still stuck on me?"

"Aw, baby boy, nobody thinks you had nothing to do with Eddie Comedy."

"Easy for you to say, you on the free side-a these bars."

Cora grabbed for some more food then. Cornbread. Buttery, and still hot.

"So, uh, what you know about them men?"

"Probably not much more than you. Rich. White. *Mighty* white. The older one, Colin, he's a writer."

"Are they?"

"What? *Gay?*"

"Like you and Wade?"

I laughed out loud, and before I thought about it I said, "No, Cora, they ain't nothing like me and Wade," but then as soon as I said it I realized it wasn't really true. "But they *are* gay, if that's what you asking."

Cora handed me a slice of cherry pie.

"So how's Sawyer?"

Used to be Cora said which one if you asked her that question, but now she just said, "Oh, he's fine. Breathing easy."

"And Rosa?"

Cora looked at me for a minute before she answered, and when she did it was in a quiet voice. "She's fine, I'll tell her you asked."

She just sat there then, outta food and outta questions—or outta questions she was willing to put into words, and I was just about to ask her what she knew about Colin and Justin, like maybe Lawman Brown had told her something, but I was cut off by the rattle of keys in the lock. Cora's head jerked around, then she stuck her hand in the basket, grabbed some napkins, shoved them at me through the bars.

"You clean yourself up with these," she said in a loud voice. "I'll be back with breakfast in the morning, need be." She was dusting off her skirts as though she'd been the one spilling crumbs all over herself. "You be good, this mess'll be over before you know it," she said, and hurried off outta sight.

"Bye, Cora," I called after her, and then I said something I don't say too often. "Thanks."

I heard the door close down at the end of the hall, but there wasn't no key rattle. I waited, but there wasn't no rattle.

"Might as well come on out, Lawman Brown. I know you there. I ain't gonna say nothing incriminating to the walls anyway."

He waited a moment, like he was still fooling me, and then he just started humming that goddamn song, what's it called, "Leroy Brown." When he was in front of the cell he broke off his song and looked me up and down like he'd never seen me before. "My *name*—"

"—is Eustace, and your title is sheriff. I know the drill, Lawman, save it for someone who cares. How long you gonna keep me in here without no charges?"

"Law says I can hold you seventy-two hours." Lawman Brown patted his stomach. "Without no charges. Three days."

"Three days!"

"Course, you could see daylight a lot quicker if you'd just come clean."

"Come clean about *what*? I done told your cracker ass I don't know shit."

"What was you doing out to the Big M then?"

"I told you. I was looking for somebody."

"Looking for somebody, huh? Like maybe Eddie Comedy?"

"I done *found* Eddie Comedy a long time ago. I was looking for somebody *new*."

Lawman Brown looked like he was gonna say something, and then he just looked like he was gonna spit.

"You people make me sick, you know that. Sick."

"I thought before you said it was us who was sick. Now it's you? I can't keep up with you, Lawman, you always changing your story."

"You know what I mean! You—" Man's tongue got all tangled up then, and after a minute he managed to close his mouth. His hand went straight to his gun then—I never saw a man who loved touching his gun more than Lawman Brown did—and he kinda rocked back and forth on his heels. "So tell me, *Reggie*," he finally said, "who was you looking for, if you wasn't looking for Eddie Comedy?"

"I was looking for—"

"And don't gimme none of this 'Ratboy' story. I've had enougha that."

"I was looking for . . . Lamoine. Lamoine Wiebe."

"Lamoine Wiebe. The same Lamoine Wiebe who run off two years ago?"

"*You* say he run off. I think one-a them truckers took him."

"And what? You think if maybe you ask around they gonna tell you? Yeah, I took that boy, cut him up and scattered his body from here to Mt. Rushmore." He laughed. "Try a little harder, Reggie."

"Well, it sure as hell beats what you doing. Which is nothing."

"Listen, some sixteen-year-old juvenile delinquent runs off that's his own business. I talked to Carol, as far as he's concerned good riddance. And as far as I'm concerned good riddance. Galatea's better off without his kind."

"He eighteen now. His birthday was in August."

"Yeah it was. If he was alive to see it." Lawman Brown stepped right up to the bars. "If some pervert didn't get him by now, then the AIDS will. Or did, for all you know."

"You think your cracker ass is safe, motherfucker, but you just wait. It gets dark out every night, motherfucker, it gets dark every fucking night."

Lawman Brown leaned right into the bars then. His stomach bulged between them, and a few inches under that was his gun.

"I ain't scareda the dark, Reggie."

"Yeah, well, you better be scareda what moves round in it."

"You're talking a lot now, Reggie, but you ain't saying much. Why don't you tell me something I want to hear. Something I can *use*."

"What you could use is a good fuck. Maybe lighten you up a bit."

"I've had just about enougha talk like that, Reggie."

"Pardon me, *Sheriff* Brown. I ain't so used to filling my mouth with *words*."

Lawman Brown's eyes went wide then. He made that spitting face again, but he didn't spit.

The whole time I'd been talking to Lawman Brown I'd been holding the napkin Cora'd pressed into my hand when she left, and now I let go of it. It was so quiet in there you could hear it hit the floor, right in between two of Lawman Brown's loud gaspy kindsa breaths.

"Oh, dearie me," I said, real quiet, "I seem to have dropped my napkin." And I got down on my knees to pick it up.

Now there was just Lawman Brown's breathing, a getting quicker in-and-out through his nose. There's a certain kind of breathing a man gets when he's in that position, you know how to listen for it and it'll tell you more than words ever could. When you hear that breathing you know that not even shame and grossed-outedness is gonna turn him back. And Lawman Brown was a single man, a regular in church on Sunday. He'd been waiting for this for a long time.

I put my hands on the cold steel bars. My left hand was six inches from the butt of Lawman Brown's pistol, but I used my right hand instead. I wanted to make sure he was nice and distracted before I—

"Uh, Eustace?"

We both jumped. I fell backwards and hit my head on the commode, and Lawman Brown kicked over the chair Cora'd been sitting on. It clang-a-langed off the cement walls for what seemed like hours before it was finally quiet.

"I just came in to see if Reggie needed something to eat."

The voice was Nettie Ferguson's, I realized then. Bless her heart, I wouldn't've guessed she cared.

Lawman Brown busied himself setting the chair up and shit, which he seemed to find some kind of majorly challenging task. "The prisoner's been *fed*, Nettie." He kept his body turned away from her, to hide what I could still see.

"You left your keys in the door, Eustace," Nettie said, and I heard her rattle them. She rattled them again, but she didn't come down the hall.

The incriminating evidence, you know what I'm saying, had faded away by then, and Lawman Brown turned to Nettie Ferguson. "I'll thank you kindly, Nettie, not to mess with matters of law enforcement. Your secretarial duties should be more than enough to occupy your attention."

"Where does chicken-fried steak fit in, cause that's what I got."

"Just gimme the keys, Nettie. There's no reason to keep this boy here any longer."

He straightened himself—his back, I mean, though his pants coulda used some fixing up too—as Nettie Ferguson hobbled her way to the cell. When she got there she squinted at me down on the floor over the top of her cat's-eye glasses. She couldn'ta looked any more like a second-grade teacher if she'd tried.

"My goodness, Reggie, you've certainly grown."

I tried to laugh at her joke but it didn't really work. "Afternoon, Mrs. Ferguson."

"It's nighttime, Reggie. It's nearly eleven." She looked at me a minute longer, and then she said, "What're you doing on the floor, Reggie?"

"I, uh, I just dropped my napkin." I grabbed it and waved it at her, but she'd already turned away from me and was giving the keys to Lawman Brown, and I turned and threw the napkin in the commode.

When I turned around again Lawman Brown was putting a key into the lock on my door. He stared real hard at the keyhole. He didn't look at me at all.

"Can I go home now?" I said in my sweetest voice.

Lawman Brown looked at me through the bars before he turned the key, and then, when he did turn it, it made the exact same sound as when he'd locked me up in the morning. "Hmpf," he said. "That's the one thing you ain't got. You may have a lotta things, Reggie Packman, but you ain't got no family and you ain't got no friends and you ain't got no *home*."

1.17

Justin

ALMOST EVERYTHING WE OWNED HAD BEEN PACKED. The few things that remained and had once seemed central to our lives were revealed as odds and ends now, incidental, and, by and large, disposable. "Do you want this?" I said. I held an eight-stemmed candelabrum, Danish, 1920s, its slim iron arms coated by a dusty patina of rust. It was small, and held only small candles, and once Colin had read me small books by its light: Shakespeare's *Sonnets*, Gardner's *Grendel*, More's *Utopia*. "No," he said, and I set it aside. "Do you want this?" Colin said. He held the large spherical aquarium which for three years had held my Japanese goldfish. A power failure, a cold snap, and a vacation had conspired against them: we came home to find them suspended in a block of ice. "No," I said, and Colin set it aside. "Do you want this?" I said. I held ten sheets of paper on which were written five hundred and one names—someone called Nolan had been scratched out and replaced by someone called Oren; Nolan had not actually died. "No," Colin said after a long pause, and I set the names aside. Sometime later I heard the clink of metal striking glass, and I looked up to see Colin squeezing the candelabrum inside the aquarium. He had found candles somewhere, and he lit them, and then he set the name-filled pages inside the aquarium and placed the slotted metal lid on top of it. The paper blazed brightly for a moment but quickly turned black and broke into tiny pieces. For a long time they skittered nervously through the heated air trapped within the aquarium, and occasionally one would reignite in a tiny short-lived burst of flame. But then, when the candles finally went out, the flakes settled on the floor of the aquarium and they lay there in a film of cold, dry, silent ash. It seemed to me that everything that needed to be said was there, in that ash, but it wasn't enough for Colin. I heard his throat clear, I heard his breath catch. I was surprised to see tears on his face, and when he spoke I realized that sometimes it *is* necessary, no matter how futile the effort seems, sometimes you have to say it out loud. He was looking at the ash when he spoke, and what he said was "Goodbye."

2

2.01

Justin

ON THE SECOND OF THE SIX DAYS WE SPENT UNPACKING—on the second, I mean, and not on the first; it took me two days to stumble across it—I opened a door I thought I had opened many times before and found something which was not ours but which had, I assumed, belonged to the people who had lived in the limestone house before we had, an old white couple who had showed up, we were always told, like us, "from somewhere else," and bought the place from the black family which had owned it since Galatia's founding. I wasn't sure what I found. I wasn't sure, I mean, if it was a rock or if it was some kind of unglazed pottery. It felt more like a pumice stone than bisque, and it looked like pumice too: it was gray, spherical, a little smaller than a baseball, and when I touched it ashy grains flaked off beneath my fingers. Still, it seemed too . . . well, too *round* to be natural, and when I lifted it—it sat on the floor in the middle of an otherwise empty room—it rattled quietly, although I found no trace of a seam, no sign that it had ever opened to allow something to be sealed inside it. The object, whatever it was, was immediately precious to me: it was mysterious and even though it was plain it was also pregnant with possibility, and it was, as well, one of the few things in the house which didn't have Colin's name on it, and so I slipped it in my pocket. I claimed it, in other words, and I hid it. I claimed it from Colin and I hid it from Colin, and later on I wrapped it in a piece of chamois to smother its rattle, but I left it in my pocket and

I wore the same pants for the next four days, until I found a better place to keep it safe.

We finished unpacking early in the evening of our sixth day in the house, and afterward we ate our first meal in the dining room. One of the room's windows was aligned with a gap in the cedar enclosure, and through it I could see six of the Pleiades. I wasn't sure if the ragged edges of the untrimmed hedge were obscuring the seventh; vaguely, I remembered something about a missing Pleiade, but I couldn't remember if that was just the myth or if it also pertained to the constellation. Colin would have known but I didn't ask him; instead, after dinner, I went outside to see if I could make out the seventh star. I crunched my way across those awful rocks, sharp and slippery beneath my shoes, while the thing in my pocket bounced lightly against my thigh. After four days I still thought of it as that, as a thing; I hadn't come up with a name for it, perhaps because I sensed that it already had one and that, in due course of time, I would find it out. I left the cedar enclosure behind, headed into the fields. A cold breeze carried the faint scent of wood smoke. I climbed a small rise—even *hill* seems too ambitious a term for that little swell—but as soon as I descended its other side the bright light of the limestone house disappeared and all I could see was dim prairie, as featureless as fog and unrolling endlessly in all directions, and my mind was filled with a vision of Catherine lost in the moors. I know, I know: you're thinking, he knows the constellations, he doesn't need landmarks. But I didn't know the constellations as ancient mariners did; to me, they were nothing more than celestial decoration. Though I might lose myself in stargazing for a moment or two, they could never help me *find* anything. What I mean is, they could never help me find myself, and I turned and ran back inside.

And inside, there was Colin. Or, rather, his voice, drifting down from somewhere above me. "Justin," it called, "Justin, come here." I went from the first floor to the second; he wasn't there. "Justin," I heard, "Justin, come see what I've found." I went from the second floor to the attic; he wasn't there. "Justin, Justin, Justin," I heard, and as I contemplated the stairs to the cupola I wondered how it was that Colin's voice, Colin's normal speaking voice, had carried from up there to the distant rooms of the first floor. But that isn't the sort of fact one can stare out, and so, turning slightly—the stairway to the cupola was even narrower than my shoulders—I climbed up, the skin of my arms prickling against that illusory dampness one feels in very, very cold stone. The room at the top of the stairs was filled with dust and the light of a single low-wattage bulb and Colin, and when I pushed open the door he smiled at me and said, as he always said, "Just-in-time," and I turned from him and his smile and his name. Narrow slitted windows were set into each of the room's eight walls, which were covered by a hand-painted fresco of hundreds of birds, badly cracked, faded, but still, even in this light, wild and weirdly colorful, but for the moment I ignored the birds and went instead to a window. I looked for the Pleiades. I was above the top of the cedar hedge, and the constellation shone clearly in the naked sky, and I counted. Six stars. An occasional twinkling blip suggested the possibility of a seventh, but none of them stood up to a direct gaze. In the end I had to concede that there were only six stars in the Pleiades, and when I had reached that conclusion I let my eyes drop, briefly, to the land beneath them, and it was only as I contemplated the prairie's vastness from the safety of the cupola that I realized that it wasn't the house beneath me which frightened me. It was the land it was built on. It was the prairie. The limestone house was large, but not large enough to get lost in. The prairie was.

"Justin?"

Colin tried to keep his voice level but I could hear his impatience. Colin doesn't like it when someone else's reverie lasts longer than his own. Mine, at any rate, ended when he spoke, and I turned to him.

The dust and the light playing on the dust and the birds all around him made it seem as though Colin, naked, bristly, beautiful Colin, were floating in space. I was impressed by the sight but I was also put off by it, because I knew he had planned it that way: Colin is always finding the appropriate frame for himself, for his beauty. But the prairie managed to upstage him. Through a window behind him I saw a flickering, too large and too close to the ground to be another star.

"Justin?"

I pushed past Colin without answering him. A moment later he spoke again, and I recognized his words as the ones he had uttered when we had seen the gray pall of Kenosha on the horizon.

"Is that a *fire*?"

It was a fire. The night and the bland terrain made it hard to get any perspective, so it was impossible to tell if it was large or small, close or far, but it was definitely a fire burning somewhere between the house and the horizon, visible through a gap in the cedar enclosure.

After one look at the distant flames Colin ran from the room behind me, but I remained at the window a moment longer, caught by something I couldn't quite name. And then I realized: the fire was perfectly framed in the window and in the gap in the hedge. Whatever was burning out there, it had once been important to someone who had lived in this house. And I couldn't help but feel that whatever was burning out there was meant to be seen by us.

I turned from the window then, I headed toward the door. Before I reached it I saw an old skeleton key sticking from its keyhole. Like the thing in my pocket, I didn't remember seeing it before, and thinking that, I reached for what was in my pocket. I reached for the key as well. I unwrapped the chamois and rattled the thing that I had unwrapped and then I put it down in the center of the room. It just sat there. It was tiny on the floor, still nameless, still unknown, but even as I watched, it became a sort of egg, a single egg surrounded by the room's thousand birds. I shut the light off then, and both birds and egg disappeared; I closed the door and locked it and dropped the key in my pocket, and I said, out loud but to no one in particular, "From now on, this is *my* room." And then I went, with Colin—and with everyone else in town—to discover Noah's ark.

2.02

Webbie

THERE WERE SOME PEOPLE WHO THOUGHT IT WAS still a secret, but it was not a secret. By *people* I mean, specifically, black people, and by *secret* I mean something which they believed was known only to them, and even by those limited definitions it had never really been a secret. My father had told me that when I was very young, and when I asked him why it wasn't a secret he had laughed mirthlessly and said, Who do they think he bought the wood *from*?

Seventy years old, that wood was, and half hollow from decades of gnawing termites and mice, the only living creatures it ever housed. Dry as dust as well, thanks to the barn. It probably took a single match.

Even if there *had* been a black lumber company from which Noah Deacon could have purchased his lumber, one did not build a barn in the middle of a Kansas cow pasture without someone taking note, particularly when that barn was a hundred twenty feet long and fifty feet high at the top of its steeply pitched roof. Noah Deacon built a huge hollow shell: only enough wood went into the barn to hold it up, but even so, that was an enormous amount of wood for these parts, at that time. People disagree about the year in which Noah began his "side venture," as they called it, either 1925 or 1924 or possibly even 1923, but no matter when he began it, when it was finished it was the second-tallest landmark, natural or artificial, in all of Cadavera County. Only the bald bluff was taller. From the top of the one you could see the top of the other, but only if you knew where to look, and if you knew what you were looking for. There were more than a few people who knew where to look but very few who knew what they were looking for, which is perhaps what Galatians meant when they called the barn, and the boat that hid inside it, a secret, but in that case it was just as much a secret from them as it was from white people. It grew straight up from the soil and sat there as plain as the hand in front of your face—but, as my father used to say, even your own hand is invisible when your eyes are closed.

On the night it burned I went to the top of the bald bluff. Everyone else in town, Galatians and Galateans alike, most of them for the first and all of them for the last time, made their way across Colin Nieman's property to see the creation that had been a part of local lore all their lives. But I went to the bluff. Like most people, I had not known where to look before, but now I had a clue, a waving flag really, a beacon, and I watched that sign flicker in the distance, a bright but contained ball of fire some ten or fifteen miles away. An oblong shadow laid itself down on the prairie between me and the fire, and though it appealed to me to imagine that the shadow was the dense knot of people who had gathered to watch the fire, it was probably nothing more than what it appeared to be: a shadow, laying itself down on the prairie.

The barn—its size and its location—was strangeness enough, but even after it was finished wood kept coming in, and that was what set people talking. Truckloads of wood, truckloads of thick dark beams as long as the new telephone poles that were just beginning to be seen down Bigger Hill way, but these beams were squared off, like oversized floor joists, and many of them appeared to be warped, according to those who caught glimpses of the trucks before they turned off the highway. The trucks hauled their loads of mysterious timber out to Noah Deacon's hollow barn, and when they pulled back onto the highway their flatbeds were empty and jangling, and they rattled back to wherever it was they had come from. The men Noah Deacon had hired to help him build the barn had been let go by then, and whomever he hired to help him build the boat he erected inside that barn remains completely unknown.

What is known is that a little over sixty years earlier the annual springtime flooding was more severe that year than it had been the year before, so severe, in fact, that the south fork of the Solomon River jumped its banks and wiped out the two-year-old village of Galatia—and, incidentally, revealed the entrance to the Cave of the Bellystones. Noah Deacon, one year younger than the village he lived in, claimed to remember that flood clearly, and at some point he also began to claim that another flood was coming, a bigger flood, a flood to rival the Great Deluge of Genesis. Reverend Alpha's successor, the second Reverend Greeving, Reverend Able, had remonstrated with him: the Lord had promised never again to destroy the world by water. Did Noah not remember the covenant of the rainbow at the flood's end? But Noah Deacon had been granted a vision, and he would be true to it. If people chose to ignore him, well, the first Noah's warnings had gone unheeded in his time, and, undeterred, he set to work. He was indulged if not actually aided in his task by his family because, in the first place, they had the money to indulge him, and, in the second, because they owed that money to him. No matter how much time and money Noah Deacon wasted on his side venture, he labored equally hard on his main venture, the crops and the cattle, and under his husbandry the Deacon holdings grew larger and larger. Their luck seemed almost magical: their wheat yielded twice as many bushels per acre as did their neighbors', they got their cattle to market a day before the market glutted and prices plummeted. No matter how much money flowed into Noah's side venture—people called it that because calling it Noah's ark was hard to do with a straight face—there always seemed to be more than enough extra cash to go around.

More to the point, even as Noah busied himself inside his barn his brother Donald was busy back at the limestone house, adding the two wings that gave it the cross shape it has today. Noah Deacon bought a thousand gallons of pine pitch to ensure that his vessel would be watertight, while Donald Deacon lined the cold stone walls of his mansion with mahogany and teak and fruitwood panels; Noah Deacon built tier upon tier of stalls for the animals he would save, while Donald Deacon built large opulent rooms and threw fancy dress parties for everyone in town, and at Donald Deacon's parties no one commented on Noah or on his ark because of the general belief that such a project, which might be seen as a white man's eccentricity, would be considered proof of a black man's insanity, and if word got out to the white people who ran the rest of the state then old Noah Deacon would be carted off to the madhouse and the key to the Deacon family's prosperity—and, as well, to Galatia's prosperity—would be gone.

I must confess that it was a strategy I never understood: how the silence of black people, among black people, and about black people, was meant to keep secrets from white people. Who did they think he bought the wood from—and the nails, and the pine pitch, and the dozens and dozens of paired stuffed animals? But that is not or at any rate was not the point: the point was that Noah Deacon built his ark and Donald Deacon built his mansion, and Galatia chose to keep its eyes fixed on the visible monument, the structure which spoke more highly of African-American industriousness and prosperity, and their bubble didn't burst until Noah Deacon finally died at the advanced age of one hundred and nine, at which point the second and third mortgages came to light, the massive debt, the fragility of the entire enterprise. Later it was said that nearly all this debt had been accumulated by Donald Deacon and by his son, Donald Junior. That, in fact, Noah's ark, however expensive it might have been, had been finished before the Depression was over, and all that Noah had done for the last forty years of his life was tinker a little, acquire a rare trophy, a dodo bird or a passenger pigeon. It was, in fact, the architectural excesses of Donald Deacon the first that had sunk the family deeper and deeper into debt, and it was Donald Deacon the third who inherited this mess upon the death of his great-uncle. He made one last-ditch effort to save the farm: he drilled for oil, and found none. The Deacon family's luck seemed to have died with Noah, and a few years after his death Donald found himself faced with one choice: sell, or have everything taken by Rosemary Krebs' bank. He sold, and then he left. Or perhaps I should say, he sold, and then he fled.

But long before then his uncle's ark had receded into legend. There were reasons, I suppose, not the least of which was the fact that nearly everyone who had been alive when Noah Deacon began building the ark had died long before he did; those people who were still alive had been children at the ark's inception, and most of them behaved as if those old stories were just that: stories, that they or their parents had made up to amuse themselves. And then, too, there were other things to worry about. There were, for one thing, the new owners of the Deacon spread, Beatrice and Henry. For another, Rosemary Krebs. In the light of that, one old man's eccentricity seemed not important at all.

Myra Robinson once told Wade, who told me, that she didn't think Beatrice had any idea about the ark's location, or even its existence. I wonder. Perhaps, like me, she merely avoided looking for it. Rosemary Krebs, I later learned, also avoided the ark. On the day it burned she stayed home; she sent Phyneas on ahead, and Lawman Brown, and trusted to their reports.

For his part, Noah Deacon stopped talking of the ark and the coming flood long before he died. Indeed, he stopped talking of almost everything. I remember him, just barely, sitting in church each Sunday, his mouth resolutely closed through each hymn, his only greeting a doffed hat and his only farewell that hat being replaced on his head. Just one time did I hear him speak. It was dark, a glowering afternoon in late spring, the sky thick with clouds and the air filled with dust and leaves harried along by the wind. I was hurrying home from church with my head bowed against the dust when I walked straight into Noah Deacon's legs, as thin as fenceposts but just as sturdy, and before I could say excuse me he cupped my jaw with one of his dry old hands and he looked, first, deep in my eyes, and then he looked up at the sky, and then he looked back down at me and he said, with great solemnity, "You best get on home, little Webbie. Look like a blow coming up. Look like it might rain."

The fire burned for three hours after it was discovered. It was a clear night, and it was possible to make out the plume of smoke that rose into the air by the stars it hid behind it. The next day, Alice Gunderson, calling on my father, told me thank God there wasn't no wind last night or it coulda been a lot worse. As it was, Quincy Cross and George Oconnor hauled a couple of tractors out there, and they were kept busy plowing under as much dry grass as they could. Occasionally, Alma Kiehler told me, a little ball of fire would detach itself from the main blaze and float out into the fields—just like a strawberry plant sending out a feeler, Alma Kiehler told me—but the air was so still that men armed with fire extinguishers and bags of lime and sand were able to squelch each of these offspring before they grew into anything substantial. No, Victor Bradfield told me when I ran into him at the I.G.A. a few days later, there wasn't nothing much to do except watch. First time, he said, first time he could remember everyone in town coming together like that, and, though it was usually my place to make such comments, Vera Gatlinger beat me to it. "What about Eric Johnson?" Vera Gatlinger asked Victor, but Victor just stared into his grocery cart for a few minutes and then he turned to me and he said, "I don't recall seeing you out there, Miss Webbie?" I couldn't find the words I needed to explain that no, I had not gone out there, I had not wanted to discover yet another of the symbols of my past just as it was being destroyed, and so all I said was "You didn't see me at Eric Johnson's lynching either."

2.03

Justin

YOU MUST BE MR. NIEMAN,'' ROSEMARY KREBS SAID AS she opened the door of her large white pillared house. She spoke in a breathless Southern falsetto, the kind that always seems to me to convey a sense of distaste, and after Colin had passed by her incredibly tiny body, most of whose height was contained in a sort of yellowish beehive, she said to me, "And you must be his son."

I fought back a laugh. "If Colin were my father he'd be breaking two laws in this state, and not just one."

I waited then, as Rosemary Krebs looked back and forth between us and tried to stare out a filial connection. I stared back in wonder. She wasn't even five feet tall. She couldn't have weighed more than eighty pounds. Her fingers seemed almost as small as pretzel sticks.

At last she spoke. "Please excuse me," she said. "Reginald led me to believe that you were related."

"Reginald?" Colin said.

"Related?" I said.

Rosemary Krebs ran her hands down the immaculate apron that covered her white silk blouse and gray wool skirt. When she spoke she addressed herself to Colin. "Reginald Packman," she said. "Wade's young friend. He told me you had moved here with your boy."

2.04

Divine

DWARF WHITE BITCH. FUCK HER. LIKE I EVEN GOT *TIME* to have dinner at her house. And fuck Wade too. He wanna strap Webbie on like a beard—like anybody could believe he was fucking *her*—that's his problem, you know what I'm saying. I got better things to do with my time.

Wade's always ragging on me about how I'm gonna catch some shit one-a these days, and I tell you what. Sometimes I wish I *would* catch something, just so I could pass it on to him. Pious-ass motherfucker. I mean can you even *imagine* Wade Painter scratching at a case of crabs? I know I can't.

It took T. V. Daniels a pack of cigarettes to come outta Sloppy Joe's. I know I said I don't smoke no more but sometimes you have to make allowances. The parking lot was motherfucking *cold*, you know what I'm saying, and the burn in my lungs felt kinda good. But of course that burning doesn't really warm you up, and I was shivering and just about ready to pack my shit up and go when T.V. come waddling round the side of the pool hall. His shit was all like bulging outta that mailman's uniform, which the reason he was still wearing it, most folks said, was because the U.S.P.S. was the only company that made clothes big enough to fit him.

I tell you what: that man gained five pounds every fucking day he was *alive*.

I swirled the worst of the cigarette taste outta my mouth with my tongue and spit—about the *only* thing T. V. Daniels won't put in his mouth is a cigarette, you know what I'm saying—and then I called out, "Hey, T.V."

He jumped so hard he nearly fell over, which woulda been a sight. The Chee-tos in the little bag he was eating from flew all over the place. "You scared me," he said, looking down on the ground like maybe he was considering picking up his Chee-tos.

Like maybe he could bend over.

Well, I just put one foot up against my car, set my shit up and made sure he took a good look. "Aw shucks," I said then. "I bet you say that to all the guys."

2.05

Justin

A SKINNY OLD MAN BOUNCED INTO THE FOYER, FIVE strands of hair combed over his bald pate like an unscored musical measure. "Well, hello-o," he said, announcing in four syllables that he was, unmistakably, a fool. He led with his hands like a partnerless dancer. "I'm Mayor Krebs," he said, pumping Colin's arm, then mine. "Phyneas is the name, but most folks just call me Mayor. Easier to say, I guess. You folks registered voters?"

I blinked my eyes, then realized we were meant to answer him. "In New York," I said. "Colin is, I'm not."

"How bout that excitement the other night?" the Mayor was saying. "That was something, huh?"

Colin cleared his throat. "I thought it was rather beautiful."

"Well, I suppose things burn down all the time in the big city." The Mayor continued smiling and nodding his head up and down, and then he turned back to me and said, "That's quite a shiner, young man."

I looked at Colin, then back at the Mayor. "Moving accident. I walked into a—"

"Oh ho ho," the Mayor was chuckling to himself. "The big city. The *big* city," he said a little louder. "Big city politics," he said, and the first word sounded like *beg* in his mouth: *beg city politics*. "Well, we'll take care-a you, don't you worry. Galatea may be a small town but she's got a lot to offer in the waya politics."

"Phyneas," Rosemary Krebs said then, her intonation as slow and careful as an animal trainer's. "Perhaps you would close the front door, while I show our guests into the parlor."

A Victorian suite of brocaded gold-tasseled furniture huddled together in the parlor, as if afraid of the red and green gilt fabric that crept up the walls. A love seat whose dark varnished wood was only slightly less crenolated than Botticelli's clamshell held the Galatean version of a young lady: she sat bolt upright, and though the effort to appear polished was written on her face, her manner was that of a majorette rather than a debutante. A matching armchair held a matching woman, who was obviously her mother. Both women had hair that was dark and tightly permed, faces that were too tanned—though it seemed time had done it to the elder and a machine to the younger—and their small chests were almost defiantly displayed in the low-cut fronts of their dresses.

Again I failed in repressing a chuckle—not at the women, but at the reasoning which had led Rosemary Krebs to invite them to her house that night.

"Myra Robinson," Rosemary Krebs said, "and her daughter, Lucille. Myra, Lucy, may I present Colin Nieman and Justin—"

"Time," I finished for her.

"Justin Time," Rosemary Krebs repeated in a level voice. Lucy," she said, still addressing me, "is Winter Homecoming Queen."

"I'm sorry," I said, but my words were drowned out by the rustle of Lucy's purple satin prom dress as she sprang to her feet.

"Pleased to meet you!" she said, her white gloved hand shooting out from her side.

"Lucy," Rosemary Krebs said quietly. "You are shaking his hand, not returning a volleyball serve."

At Rosemary Krebs' words, Lucy withered and her outstretched arm drooped a little, but before it could fall to her side Colin stepped forward and caught it in one of his hands and kissed it. "*Enchanté*," he said.

Lucy's face turned a red that clashed hideously with her dress, and she yanked her hand from Colin's and turned, in desperation almost, to me. She seemed caught by my right eye for a moment, and I wondered if she was staring at the new bruise or at the old scar. Her words, when she spoke, were clearly rehearsed. "Mrs. Krebs informs me that you hail from New York City. Is that where you are originally from?"

"Originally?"

She foundered slightly. "I mean, is that where you were born and all?"

I felt Colin watching me intently, but I spoke only to Lucy. "No," I said. "Were you?"

It seemed that her eyes glazed over then. "Was I what?"

"Born." I paused. "Here."

Clever Lucy: after a moment she clapped her hands together delightedly and said, "Oh, you're teasing me!" She looked at Rosemary Krebs, who seemed satisfied with her answer, and then she sat herself down without another word. Her back bowed for a moment but then she caught herself, and her spine straightened like a snapped bowstring.

Colin extended his hand to Myra then, who, rather than shaking it, used it to haul herself to her feet. She was, judging from Colin's strained expression, not quite as slim as her daughter, and even from across the room I could smell Binaca and, underneath that, the whiskey that laced her breath.

"Pleased to meetcha," she drawled, or slurred—slurred—and then, without bothering with me, she sank back to her chair. When she stood up a small bulging purse had swung wildly from her shoulder, and when she sat down it bounced off the chair arm with a heavy sounding clunk. Myra stilled the purse against her stomach and patted it contentedly.

"Well, I do believe we've all been introduced," Rosemary Krebs said, a touch of relief in her voice. "Would anybody like a drink before dinner?"

"Oh, I'll just have whatever Ms. Robinson is having," I said. "That would be Ms. Robinson the elder."

Rosemary Krebs smiled weakly and said, "Phyneas?"

"No, nope, not me, I'm fine, thank you, dear," the Mayor said, and then, when his wife continued to stare at him, he slapped his forehead and said, "Oh yeah, sure, right, what am I thinking, silly me." He turned to the Robinsons. "Myra, Lucy, Cokes for y'all?"

Myra just waved a hand, but Lucy said brightly, "Yes, thanks!"

Colin said, a bit unsurely, "I'd like a gin and tonic, please."

There was a brief silence, and then Rosemary Krebs said, "This is a dry house, Mr. Nieman."

It certainly was.

"Of course," Colin said, and again I noticed Myra patting her purse, a not-so-private smile on her face. Colin cleared his throat. "Just a seltzer then."

"A what?" the Mayor said.

"Water," Colin sighed. "I'll just have water."

Years later, it seemed, Webbie and Wade finally arrived. By then I had pulled every hair out of my head, one by one, until I was as bald as Colin, and Myra had more or less moved into the bathroom. Though I'd tried, I'd never managed to nip out at the same time she had, and the most I could do was inhale the intoxicating aroma of liquor and breath freshener she left in the bathroom in her wake.

Instead of shaking Webbie's hand, I grabbed her arm and mouthed the word *Help!* But she looked as out of sorts as I felt, and she only smiled weakly, and patted my arm.

Suddenly Wade's voice scratched into life. I had already learned that if Wade Painter spoke without first being spoken to, then it was likely that what he was saying was important.

"Rosemary," is what Wade said. "What has that incompetent lard-ass you call a sheriff managed to discover about Eddie Comedy's little accident?"

I realized then that Wade, like Myra Robinson, had not come to dinner unfortified.

Rosemary Krebs allowed a long silence to follow Wade's outburst, and then, in a voice that ruled out any sort of reply, she said, "Nothing. Absolutely nothing."

2.06

Divine

WHEN T.V. SCOWLED AT ME HIS FACE LOOKED LIKE A peeled potato or some shit like that, a potato that was all pocked and puckered from where you've had to dig out the bad spots. It was enough to make me lose my appetite, you know what I'm saying, but nobody ever said life was easy.

"So," I said, "you make it out to the fire the other night?"

"No."

"Course not, why should you." I smiled at him. "Quite a sight, I heard."

"You didn't make it out neither?"

"I got better things to do than watch some old barn burn down. Besides, I been out there lotsa times."

I guess what T.V. did then was squint, though what it looked like was his eyes was receding into his head.

"So is it true? Was it true? Was there really a boat out there, a, a, an *ark*?"

"Ark, boat, barn, whatever. Never looked like mucha anything to me."

T.V. looked into his empty Chee-tos bag for a long time, like maybe a Chee-to would turn up if he looked hard enough, and then he sighed and threw the bag on the ground.

"I heard some kids from down to Bigger Hill was messing around out there, that's what I heard. Started a fire to keep warm and got all burned up."

"Messing around?"

"Hey, what you want anyway?" T.V. said then. "I got to get home."

" 'What I want'?" I said. "I don't want shit. I already got everything I want."

"Why're you bothering me then?"

"Am I bothering you? I just thought I was saying hi-lo to a old acquaintance I hadn't seen for some time."

"You saw me last week."

"They started a fire to keep warm, huh? I guess they wasn't messing around too much if they needed a *fire* to keep warm."

"Aw, don't start on that stuff with me. I don't want to know about that stuff."

"What stuff is that, T.V.?"

I noticed then that T.V. was all like sweating and shit. I mean, like, think about that shit: forty degrees, tops, a stiff breeze outta the northwest, and here was T.V. sweating so hard he had to try to wipe his face on his coat sleeve. Which he couldn't do very well, cause like when he tried to raise his arm and lower his head at the same time this big old wad of *something* just sorta showed up between his shoulder and his neck.

I had to look down so I didn't stare. "Well, I guess no one won't be messing around out there no more."

"Look here, I got to get home. You got something you need to say to me or are you just out to bother me?"

"Seems like a far piece to go just to mess around. I mean, all the way from Bigger Hill."

"That's just what I heard," T.V. said. "I don't know if it's true or—"

"So, T.V., how's work?"

T.V. tried to look suspicious, but since it involved scowling and squinting and such, it didn't really work. Man's face was so fat he couldn't really make expressions, if you know what I'm saying.

"Those new fellas, they get a lotta mail. Mail out a lotta stuff too."

"I bet they do," I said. "Mr. Colin Nieman, he's a important writer. One-a the things writers do is write letters."

When T.V. squinted his eyes looked like a snowman's eyes that've been pushed too far into his head. I mean, *shit*.

"Just a hunch," I said, "bout dinner, I mean," and then all nonchalant like I unbuttoned my coat. "So, T.V., you seeing anybody?"

"Huh?"

"You know, T.V., you about that age when boys start taking a interest in girls. Shaving in the morning, putting on some-a the old man's cologne. You know, T.V. Messing around. Keeping warm." I shivered a little. "Sure is cold tonight."

T.V. just glared at me, which glaring he could do because it didn't really involve movement of the face. He was thirty if he was a day, and shit, I guess I'd have to admit that comment about his old man was in pretty poor taste seeing as how the guy'd only bought the farm like a year or so before his momma, so I laughed a little and shrugged and I got all like contrite and shit. "Just wondering," I said. "You know, if you was seeing anybody."

T.V.'s voice was all like hoarse and shit when he answered me, a bit hungry even. "I ain't seeing nobody."

"Well, don't you worry. You got a real nice personality and I'm sure you'll meet somebody soon." I shivered again. "Brrr!"

T.V. suddenly leaned back onto the hood of his car, which that shit like to flip over. I mean I swear to Christ one-a the back wheels actually rose up off the ground. "Look here, what you want?" T.V. said, all like desperate and shit now. "It's late, I'm tired, I got to work in the morning."

"I done told you, T.V., I don't want nothing. I just come here to see if I could offer you anything. You know, old friend to old friend."

"You come here just to see me?"

"Express for you, T.V."

"Well, I don't need nothing."

He tried to make his voice all like noncommittal and shit, but he wasn't fooling no one. He was all like staring at his feet and shit. Or something, I guess, I don't suppose he could see his feet. Maybe he was looking for his Chee-tos bag.

I kinda lifted myself up off my car like I was just stretching a little, you know what I'm saying, and then all casual like I walked towards him. I walked real slow and shit, like I was just strolling, like I was just taking in the sights in that three or four feet between me and T.V.'s stomach, like I might stop anytime. There was this like bulging action going on beneath T.V.'s stomach that looked like a tent that'd blown over in the middle of the night, and don't get me wrong, I'm not talking about just another roll of fat. By the time I got right up next to T.V. he was practically hyperventilating, and when I put my hand on his shoulder I think he woulda jumped except I don't think he was like *able* to.

Then I was all like squeezing his shoulder and shit. "Yo, T.V.," I said. "Everybody needs something." I squeezed again, just cause I liked the way his shoulder like give and give and give, kinda like Play-Doh. "You sure I can't help you out?"

T.V. was all like refusing to look up at me. "I ain't your friend."

"Aw, T.V., I'm hurt."

"I hate you."

"Well, of course you do. But don't you need something from me too? Ain't you a little cold? I know I sure am."

"I hate niggers in general."

And they hate you too, is what I didn't say. When they can be bothered to notice you. But I didn't say nothing. I didn't have to.

T.V. didn't say nothing neither, just tried one more time to wipe that sweat outta his eyes. I almost felt sorry for him then, I have to tell you, if I'da had a handkerchief I think I woulda wiped the sweat outta his eyes and left it at that. Yeah, yeah, it's a nice thought, but . . . But I didn't, so I couldn't. Instead I moved the front of my left thigh so it was just barely touching the inside-a T.V.'s right knee. I was trying to maneuver so I could get my right leg up against his left one but hey, he was just too wide for me to touch botha them.

"Don't think of it as help, T.V. Think of it like delivering the mail. That's just something you do for folks. It's your job. Me, this is what I do for folks."

I tell you what: for a big fat man, T.V. could sure move fast when he wanted to. I didn't even see it coming, it was just like all the sudden T.V. mashed my head down. I'da preferred to use my hand, you know what I'm saying, but both of them was otherwise engaged in holding his stomach out the way—like if I didn't hold it up it was gonna fall down and smother me or some shit—and as it was the whole thing was over in less than a minute.

What can I say? For a fat man he sure shot a thin load.

Afterwards T.V. was feeling around below his stomach, trying to find his dick so he could stuff it back in his pants, and I was all like reaching into my pocket and pulling out my most recent letter to Ratboy.

"Hey, T.V., can I give you—"

"What is it *now*?" T.V. wailed, so loud that I have to admit I was kinda startled. I looked around but there wasn't no one coming outta Sloppy Joe's. T.V.'s hands was scrambling blind down there, and I wondered if maybe I should help him find it, but I decided the best thing to do was just wait.

When he'd finally managed to fix himself up, I said, "It's just a letter, T.V."

"Letters go in the mailbox."

"I know, I know, I don't mean to make you work overtime or nothing. I just thought, since we was both right here and all . . ."

He seemed to have a change of heart then, and like I just said, sometimes he could be quick. He snatched that letter outta my hand like it was a ham sandwich. He looked at the address for a minute, and then he looked at it for a minute more, and then he looked at me.

I just looked back at him.

"Don't you worry, Divine. I'll make sure it gets where it's going to."

The return address said Divine.

He tried to put the letter in his pants pocket but he couldn't find it, so he ended up just shoving it under his belt. I thought I should say something, but I just shrugged and said, "I knew I could count on you, T.V."

T.V. kinda smiled. Even that was hard for him. It turned out he had his own hankie, it was in his breast pocket, and he pulled it out and used it to wipe the sweat outta his eyes. "Sure you can count on me, Divine. After all," he said, "what're friends for?"

2.07

Justin

ROSEMARY KREBS STOOD BESIDE HER CHAIR IN THE dining room. The finials atop the chair's back, carved in the shape of acorns, were nearly as tall as she was, and when she sat down it looked for a moment as though the two posts had stabbed through her shoulders.

"Well," she said, "are we all here?"

"Now we are," Myra said, rushing into the room. Her nose and cleavage—and purple dress—were freshly powdered, her lips wet and shiny. She sat down without looking at anyone.

From the corner of my eye I saw Lucy grimace. As my "date," Lucy had been seated to my left, and I was seated to the Mayor's left; as my "dad," Colin was seated across from me on the Mayor's right, with Myra on his right. Webbie sat beside Myra, though I could hardly see her through an enormous candelabrum placed in the middle of the table, and Wade was seated across from her. The candelabrum generated an enormous amount of heat, and the violet flicker bulbs in the chandelier which presided over the room played havoc with Rosemary Krebs' honeyed hairdo.

Colin cleared his throat. "I, um, I hate to rub salt into an open wound."

"Beg pardon?" the Mayor said.

"Mr. Nieman?" Rosemary Krebs looked at her hands, as if searching for a laceration.

Colin manufactured a rueful smile. "What I mean is," he said, "that I, like Wade, am rather curious about the story of Eddie Comedy."

The Mayor's face lit up for a moment, and then just as suddenly it darkened, and he nodded his head so solemnly that I thought he might actually say something of substance. But he merely continued to nod for a while longer, until, shaking his head as if to clear it, he said, "You wanna help yourself to some-a that chicken there, Justin, maybe get it started?"

"Sheriff Brown has led me to believe," Rosemary Krebs began, and then she stopped. "Sheriff Brown has led my husband and myself to believe that he is investigating every possible . . ." Her voice trailed off as, with great delicacy, she placed three wedges of beet on her plate and passed the bowl on to Wade.

"I believe the word you want is *lead*, Rosemary," the Mayor said, tonging two pieces of fried chicken onto his own plate. "Although maybe you should ask Mr. Nieman about that, seeing as he's the writer and all."

"I think *lead* is the right—"

"Perhaps you could wait to have seconds, Phyneas, until all our guests have been served."

The Mayor grinned sheepishly, and put one of the pieces of chicken back into the serving dish.

"Every possible lead," Rosemary Krebs said then, smiling at Colin as he served himself a chicken leg. "As you might imagine, this sort of incident isn't all that common in Galatea, but nevertheless, Sheriff Brown is an experienced law enforcement officer, and the Mayor and I have every faith in his capability to bring this matter to a swift and speedy conclusion."

"Swift *and* speedy?" Wade said loudly. "My goodness, Rosemary, that is confidence." He paused long enough to receive the bowl of mashed potatoes from her, and with gestures made flamboyant by alcohol managed to splatter two huge dollops onto his plate before handing it on to Lucy. "Far be it from me to call your faith misplaced, Rosemary, but Eustace Brown couldn't find his own . . . *hand* if it wasn't attached to his body."

"Green beans?" Rosemary Krebs offered the bowl to Wade, but before either of them could say anything the Mayor chuckled loudly.

"I hate to take sides against my own wife, Wade, but I gotta admit I don't know what the hay Rosemary sees in that man."

"Oh, I suspect I can answer that one for you, Mr. Mayor. Eustace Brown is a man of limited imagination, and like most men of his type he *is* rather proficient at one thing: taking orders."

" 'Mr. Mayor,' huh?" The Mayor held the bowl of green beans in his hands. "I never heard that one before. 'Mr. Mayor.' "

"Phyneas," Rosemary Krebs said. "I'm sure Mr. Nieman would like some vegetables."

"Oh, of course, of course," the Mayor said, dutifully passing on the green beans.

"He called up Dad," Webbie said then.

"Eddie Comedy?" the Mayor said.

Webbie put a hand over her mouth. "No, no. Lawman Brown. He was asking if he knew where Melvin Cartwright was."

"Perhaps, Miss Greeving, since Sheriff Brown spoke to the Reverend, we should leave the matter between the two of them."

Webbie reached for her napkin then, dabbed at her lips for food she'd not yet tasted. "Well," she said, quietly but persistently, "Dad was discussing it with the Church Ladies right afterwards, so I guess it can't be that much of a secret now."

At that, Myra Robinson laughed loudly; after a glance at Rosemary Krebs, Lucy tittered uncertainly.

"The Church Ladies?" Colin said. "Melvin Cartwright?"

"Melvin Cartwright," the Mayor drawled, his voice full of officiousness and chicken, "was a black boy about Webbie's age, a well-mannered black boy if you ask me, who just happened to move off right about the same time Eddie Comedy did. Lawman Brown seems to've taken the notion that the two actions are somehow related, which strikes me as . . ."

"I believe the word you are searching for is *ludicrous*, Phyneas."

"Well, I was thinking *silly*, actually, but thank you, Rosemary, I think *ludicrous* does fit the bill."

There was a long silence then, broken only by the thin clink of silver striking china and the occasional snap of a chicken bone. The Krebses' dining room was large, but its space was eaten up with dark furniture whose chunky carved surfaces were obscured by a fog of lace. White webbing covered everything, windows, table, sideboards, and circular doilies lurked beneath every piece of ornamental crystal, silver, or china. The whole thing felt eerily like a scene out of Ibsen: all that was needed was the gunshot in the next room.

Suddenly Wade set his fork and knife down with a clang.

"But don't you *think*," he said, and it was unclear to whom his *you* referred, "don't you think it an odd coincidence that the Eddie Comedy–Melvin Cartwright situation should so closely parallel the situation between my father and Gary Gables?"

"Wade," Webbie said then, in perhaps the sharpest tone of voice I'd ever heard her use. "Gary talked about moving for months before your father's death." She gulped at her water immediately after speaking, wiped her mouth with the back of her hand.

"I thought your father died in a car accident," Colin said.

"He died in a car, yes. I don't know about the accident part."

"I don't understand."

"Of course you don't," Wade said sharply. "You're not from around here, why should you."

"Wade," Webbie said again, her voice pleading this time. "Please—"

Wade spoke over her. "My father's car," he said. "Nine years ago, my father's car, like Eddie Comedy's car, crashed into a telephone pole on, as it happens, Route 24, approximately two miles east of town. He went through the windshield. He died, though, not of his injuries, which might in any case have proved fatal, nor of a gunshot wound, but of exposure. He lay, exposed, by the side of the road, for nearly twenty-four hours. But what concerned me—what, I should say, concerned my mother, because I was not here at the time—what concerned my mother was the fact that in addition to the damage caused by the telephone pole there was also a dent on the side of my father's car, and flecks of turquoise paint there, which suggested that my father's car had collided with another car, presumably before it collided with the telephone pole."

"Wade," Webbie said one more time. "It was blue. Blue. There are lots of blue . . . things."

"You think this Gary . . ."

"Gables," Webbie said.

"You think Gary Gables—"

"I had the paint analyzed, Webbie. It was a General Motors–issued, DuPont-manufactured pigment called, specifically, 'Cherokee turquoise,' and used on Buicks, Pontiacs, and Cadillacs from 1978 until 1984. Gary Gables drove a 1982 Pontiac Le Sabre."

"Le Sabre is a Buick," Webbie nearly whispered, "and the Cherokee didn't work with turquoise." She folded both hands over her mouth and left them there.

"You think Gary Gables ran your father off the road!" Colin was fighting to keep a smile off his face, but it was possible to see words, paragraphs, whole chapters unrolling in his eyes. He said, "But why did it take twenty-four hours for the accident to be discovered?"

"East of town," Wade said.

"You mean, east of Galatia."

"What I mean is," Wade said, glancing briefly at Rosemary Krebs, "east of *town*. What I mean is that my father was a vile man. Not just a child abuser, not just a wife beater, but an almost rapaciously cruel racist. My *father* once attempted to prevent Abraham Greeving from voting in the mayoral election, and when someone challenged him on this he said, out loud, in public, my *father* allowed as how he knew niggers couldn't be *owned* no more, but that didn't mean, as far as he knew, that they could *vote*."

"But he voted though," the Mayor said. "Reverend Greeving. I saw him drop the ballot in the box myself." The Mayor chuckled quietly. "Still lost though."

"And you still won, Mr. Mayor. Yes, we all know."

"You think," Colin said, "you think *people* deliberately ignored the accident."

"It was Howard found him. Howard found your daddy."

It was Lucy who'd spoken, and, at her words, Wade turned on her sharply. "Yes, Lucy, Howard found my father, but where, oh where is yours?"

Lucy gasped and clapped a hand to her mouth.

The room was silent after Wade spoke, and into this silence Colin breathed a single word.

"Fascinating."

Across the table from Lucy, Myra dropped her head. One hand stroked her purse longingly, while the other covered her mouth. Still, it seemed as though she might have been laughing under her breath.

"What happened to your father was a tragedy, Wade." Rosemary Krebs had adopted a soothing, political tone, the kind of tone that incites me to almost murderous rage. "I'm sure I speak for the Mayor when I say that we are all deeply affected by the loss."

"Twenty-four hours," Wade said. "The wreck had broken both my father's legs, his pelvis, and his right arm. His left shoulder was also dislocated, two of his ribs had cracked and punctured his liver, and there were twenty-three separate pieces of glass lodged in his face, including one piece as large as a quarter that had pierced his right eye, and despite these injuries my father still managed to drag himself exactly thirteen feet from where he'd landed. He made it to the bottom of the ditch beside the road, but he couldn't make it back up, and he lay there for twenty-four hours before Howard, thank you very much, Miss Robinson, before Howard Goertzen decided to stop and see if anything was *wrong*."

Beside me, Lucy spoke to her lap. "Howard said he saw the car in the morning. He said he saw it in the morning but he didn't think nothing about it till nighttime, when it was still there." She looked up suddenly, not at Colin but at me. "Howard's *white*."

"Oh, Wade," Webbie said then. "Gary had been talking of leaving town for months before your father's death. *Months*."

"Yes," Wade said. "He talked about it for months and months and months, but he never seemed to leave. Not until the day my father had his accident." He stopped then. He looked around the room slowly, as if defying anyone to speak, but no one took up his challenge. Finally, his eyes met mine over the top of Lucy's head, and he stared at me with such open longing that, after a moment, I had to drop my eyes. "Well, my goodness," I heard him say then. "All this, and nobody's even mentioned Eric Johnson yet."

I looked up just in time to see Rosemary Krebs stand up.

She smiled as she spoke. "Would anybody like dessert?"

I noticed then that there was no food on her plate, and though I tried, I couldn't remember her ever putting anything into her mouth.

2.08

Divine

THE THING ABOUT SEX IS THAT IT'S OVER TOO DAMN fast. I mean, if killing time is what you want to do then turn on the TV or some shit like that, you know what I'm saying, cause like fucking don't take up more than an hour or two and that's counting foreplay *and* afterglow, and sucking off a fat mailman in the parking lot of a pool hall takes about ten minutes, counting conversation and clean up. What I mean is, me and T. V. Daniels was through with our business and it wasn't even nine o'clock. What I mean is, everybody I knew was still at dinner at Rosemary Krebs'—everybody except my parents, who last I heard was somewhere down in Florida, and me, who was all alone in my car. I don't mean I was lonely or nothing. I was just bored and shit.

So I decided to go out to Noah's ark.

But Noah had built his barn and his boat both outta wood and nothing but wood—he didn't even use nails cause like supposedly they didn't have no nails in the Bible, which if that shit is true then what was it they stuck through Jesus' hands and feet when they put him on the cross? And then too, he, Noah, he went and filled the whole thing up with straw. *Straw*, like he was gonna feed it to all those stuffed animals he stuck in there. Now, I freely admit that I am not exactly given to common sense, but even I could tell it was just a plain *miracle* that shit didn't burn down a long time ago.

Nigger was crazy, there ain't no way round that. Say whatever else you want to about him—good farmer and family man and shipbuilder—Noah Deacon was fucking *whacked*.

Me, I think T.V. was talking out his asshole when he said some kids from down to Bigger Hill had started the fire, but I do know of more than a few folks from Galatia who'd used the ark at one time or another. Although I have to say it wasn't the kinda place you hurried back to. Any old barn that filled up with straw is just as likely to be filled up with rats and mice, and any place filled up with rats and mice is gonna have its fair share of snakes, up to and including rattlers. The one time I ever messed around there, it was, um, I think it was Lyle Goertzen. No, it couldn'ta been Lyle, Lyle was white and I never woulda brought a white man out to Noah's ark. It was Bruce Cardinal, I think, our second go-round if I remember right, but I don't remember much except the smell of vegetable rot and the sound of things rustling through that straw, which is a shame, cause Bruce had himself one hell of a nice dick, mmmm-hmmm, I remember *that* well enough, and I remember that he seemed to've acquired a fair bit of experience with it between our first and second get-togethers. But still and all, a good fuck's not worth risking snake bite, and what really creeped me out was all those stuffed animals and shit, we're talking regular barnyard animals, horses and cows and pigs and chickens, although Noah had got himself a couple-a buffalo and a paira Texas longhorns—well, all of em was in pairs, of course, I mean, it was Noah's ark, right?—and all of them was rotting from the inside out. I mean, it was enough to make you lose your lunch, let alone your hard-on, and after that one visit with Bruce, I guess I was thirteen or fourteen, I never bothered going back there until last week, when I was trying to get away from Lawman Brown.

I swear, I can*not* guess how Wade knew to tell him where I was going. Sometimes that man does astonish me.

I was so caught up in thinking about all this that I almost missed it completely. The ark, I mean, or what was left of it, which was basically ashes. I couldn'ta been going more than five miles an hour, there wasn't no road that led out there and it was totally goddamn dark too, and you can't imagine what a coyote den can do to your alignment even at like twenty miles per. I was sorta looking at the horizon, like I guess I expected to see the ark in the distance, you know what I'm saying, but of course it wasn't there no more, and then like all the sudden it was like I'd driven into a cloud or some shit. It was the ash, of course, blowed up by my engine, but that shit totally freaked me out. I stomped on the brake but even before I'd totally stopped I was like, Chill, Divine, it's just some ash. Which was still blowing up from under the car and shit, you know what I'm saying, what with my headlights and all it kinda reminded me of those scenes in alien movies where the spaceship lands. The whole feeling was kinda creepy and shit, but it was definitely cool too.

After a little while I shut the car off but I left the headlights on. It took a minute for the ash to settle down and shit, but after it did I was all like ho*ly* shit. I mean, I tell you what: as far as my headlights was shining the land was totally smooth and powdery white. It was like, I don't know, like being in the middle-a the desert or some shit like that, like being on the moon even. It was really beautiful is what it was, but it was kinda sad too, because all that ash wouldn'ta been there if the ark hadn't burned up, but it was like the fact that the ark *had* burned up was part of what made the ash so beautiful. I mean, knowing what made it and all, the reason why it was there. It was like the ark got a lot more interesting after it wasn't there no more. Well, I guess I know all about that shit, Mom and Dad, Ratboy, hell, even Eddie Comedy, they was all gone now, and they seemed to matter a lot more since they went away.

Every once in a while a little breeze would pick up the ash and move it. It was pretty much a quiet night and the breeze was quiet too, I mean it didn't make no noise, but one minute the air would be clear and dark and the next it would fill up with ash and the way my headlights hit the ash made the air seem all sparkly and shit, and I guess I got kinda caught up in that or something cause when I first noticed myself noticing him I could also tell that he'd been there for a while and I just hadn't registered it—Colin Nieman, standing at the far enda my headlights' reach. I could tell it was Colin Nieman just by the size-a him—wasn't no man in Galatia or Galatea as big as Colin Nieman, and then plus too there was his clothes, well, specifically his coat, this great big black trenchcoat-type thing which you'd also never see on the back of a red-blooded Galatean man, and of course there was that head, that great big bald head, as round and white as a cue ball.

As soon as I saw him I jumped outta my car. "Colin!" I yelled out. "Colin, it's me! It's Reggie!" Well, I guess that was how much he surprised me, if he made me use that old name.

I tell you what: that ash was deep. It was like running through snow. And I coulda sworn it was still warm too. It was pretty goddamn cold out, but I swear my feet felt warm, sinking into soft dry stuff.

Out there in the distance Colin pulled one-a his hands outta his pocket. I thought he was waving at me but he was just putting a hat on, some kinda stocking cap is what it looked like, a white stocking cap which once it was on his head I couldn't see where the cap ended and his skin began. But I guess I didn't think too much about that. I mean, it was fucking freezing. But then I got a little bit closer and he pulled the hat down over his head and at first I thought it was a ski mask but after another couple of steps I could tell it wasn't no ski mask, it was just a sack, a white sack with a couple-a holes cut out for the eyes, and then, you know—hey, I ain't the stupidest nigga in the world—then I got the idea that maybe it wasn't Colin Nieman. Some things went through my head then. I was still running toward him, toward what I thought'd been Colin Nieman but which I was now pretty sure wasn't Colin Nieman, toward, I guess, toward my idea of Colin Nieman, and that idea just reeled me in like a fish. And what I thought about first was Ratboy, about the time he'd come in from the Big M with cigarette burns all over his body, and then what I thought about was Eddie Comedy with his brains and his ear splattered all over the seat of his truck, and I thought about Justin Time. I'd seen Justin a couple-a days ago at Wade's and, well, he'd had a black eye, Justin did, and, you know, what he said was that he walked into a door while he was moving stuff in. And then I thought about Colin Nieman again, which by that time I was practically right in front of him, and I stopped running.

I still don't know if it was Colin Nieman out there that night or not. I mean, I've had a hell of a long time to think it over, all the facts are in, you know, but the jury's still out. The one thing I do know, in case you're wondering, is that Rosemary Krebs' dinner was over by nine, nine-thirty, and I figure it was about ten by then. I mean, I'd like to just say it wasn't Colin—and I'm pretty sure it wasn't—but still, if I said that I'd be fudging things a little. Not that I'm all that stuck on the truth usually, but this one time I want to get the facts straight.

Whoever it was he just stood there the whole time I ran up to him. He pulled the sack down over his face but then he put his hands back in his pockets and he just stood there. What with the black jacket and pants and boots he was wearing, he practically faded away into the night, I mean the ash or something was stinging my eyes, making them tear up a little, things got kinda blurry and for a minute all I saw was the white blob of his head floating in the sky, which it took me a moment to realize what it reminded me of but what it reminded me of was a bellystone, and then my vision cleared, and I took one more step toward him, and I stopped. I noticed one last thing: that there was something, writing I thought, but it mighta just been a design, stitched into the sack with dark shiny threads. I was pretty sure it was writing. He just stood there after I stopped. I'd like to tell you that he stood there looking at me but it was too dark for me to see his eyes.

"Colin?"

I don't know how long it took me to say this, but when I did he kinda jumped a little, like he'd forgotten I was there.

"Is that you, Colin?"

He didn't answer me, didn't say nothing or shake his head, or nod it for that matter. He just stood there, but I thought his left hand was kinda fiddling round in his pocket. It was hard to tell in the dark.

"It's, um, it's Divine. Is that you, Colin?"

He came to me then, and what can I say, Colin or no Colin, I could tell just from the way he picked his feet up and put them down that he didn't mean me no good. But I couldn't move. Part of it was like the ash was quicksand or some shit, but part of it was the fire that'd made that ash. It was like I wanted to disappear too, like Noah's ark, like Noah himself. It was like whether or not the man coming toward me was Colin Nieman or the bogeyman or the devil I knew that sooner or later he would fade away in his black coat and black pants and black boots, he'd leave a little after-image of his bellystone sack-covered head but then that'd disappear too and then I'd be even more alone.

I tried to say his name one more time but when I opened my mouth nothing came out. It was like those dreams, you know, when you try to talk but you can't. It was just like that.

His right hand came outta his pocket then. His right hand came outta his pocket and right off I noticed it was carrying something, metal maybe, or glass, something shiny and silver and hard-looking is what I noticed at first, and all at once something clicked and I realized what it was was my sideview mirror that'd broke off that night when I found Eddie Comedy down by the Big M, and that was about all I had time to think about cause in one like smooth move that hand was up in the air and then *bam!* it came down on my head, and it was lights-out for Divine.

2.09

Justin

AFTER IT WAS OVER I WASN'T QUITE SURE WHAT HAD happened. What had been said and what had been implied. It all seemed to make sense during dinner, but as soon as the meal was over Wade left, and Webbie left with him, and in their wake they left behind nothing more than a vague enervated unease. It had seemed fairly clear that Wade was accusing the man called Gary Gables of his father's accident, and it had seemed clear, if somewhat less clear, that he was implicating the town of Galatia in his father's death, and perhaps he had also been implicating Galatea. It was hard to tell what he meant by the word *town*. And then there was the matter of Eddie Comedy, as well as Melvin Cartwright. And Howard Goertzen, whoever he was, and Eric Johnson. And Lawman Brown. And Reverend Greeving, and the Church Ladies: who in the *hell* were the Church Ladies? I wanted to go home and try to sort out all the names and stories that had come up during dinner, the pieces of stories, but Colin accepted Rosemary Krebs' offer of coffee, "in the parlor," she said, "where the atmosphere will be more relaxed."

On the way to the parlor Myra Robinson announced that she had to nip to the powder room, and I dropped behind everyone and followed her down the hall, and then I waited for her outside the bathroom.

She was zipping her little purse shut as she opened the door, and I served up my widest, most desperate smile.

"Please," I said, "I would *kill* for a nip of whatever it is you have in your purse."

Myra hesitated a moment, then motioned me into the bathroom. Her flask was cheap and tinny, and so was her whiskey.

"I hope I'm not making a terrible impression," Myra said. "I'm really *not* a drunk, not really. But I couldn't see any other way of making it through an evening with Her Royal Highness."

"Please," I said, and took a third long pull. "You don't have to explain anything to me."

Myra smiled and said, "Of course, I couldn't possibly let you date my daughter, knowing that you're a drinking man."

"I don't think that will be a problem."

Myra looked puzzled for a moment, and then she took the flask from me and raised it to her lips. She drank from it, screwed the lid on tight, dropped it in her purse. "Well, goddamn," she said, and tossed her hair. "Well, I *was* wondering. Does this mean I got all dolled up for nothing?"

The word *wondering* came out *wundrin*.

"Actually," I said, "I take it back."

"You—?" Myra smoothed the top of her breasts, the front of her dress.

"No, no, no," I said. "Not that. We're both queer as the night is long. No," I said, "I take back what I said about explaining. I *do* want you to explain some things to me. Some holes in Wade's story."

"Holes?"

"Gaps, elisions, evasions, whatever. I had the feeling I was getting the abridged version."

"Huh?"

"There was something he wasn't saying, wasn't there?"

"Oh!" Myra said. Her eyes widened, and she turned away from me. "Oh. I suppose there was a lot of things Wade wasn't saying, but I'm hardly the person to ask about that." She looked intently in the mirror and then, unconsciously it seemed, she patted her hair. "We, um, we oughta be getting back."

"Myra." I put my hand on her shoulder, and she nearly jumped. When she looked at me, I saw that she was not merely being evasive. She was terrified.

"Yes?"

"For the record," I said, and I smiled, "I think you look fabulous."

"Fabulous!" Myra mimicked me, and then a laugh that smelled slightly bitter from alcohol passed her lips and she said, "Aw, you wouldn't want to date Lucy anyway. When all's said and done she's just a stuck-up little prig who wishes her mother was more like Rosemary Krebs. Rosemary *Crabs*," she said, and made little pincer movements with her fingers, and then she reached into her purse and pulled out a tiny atomizer.

"You certainly came well armed."

"You ain't seen the half of it. Now open wide, and pray this ain't my Mace." Before I could decide whether she was joking I felt the tingle of breath freshener on my tongue. She paused when she had finished, still facing me. She was looking at my eye. "I, um, it's not really my place to ask, but did he—"

"The bruise?" I said. "No, I walked into a door." She looked at me funny and I said, "No, really. There are a lot of doors in that house."

"I know exactly how many doors are in that house. I cleaned it for twenty years."

"You—"

"I didn't mean the bruise," she said. "I meant the scar."

"The scar," I said, surprised that she had seen it, and I touched it with my hand, the hand that I had been surprised that Wade had seen, and I wondered if all my secrets were so transparent. "No, that wasn't Colin. Colin tried to fix that." I smiled at her. "You cleaned our house."

"Twenty years, but I'm all retired now. Bea left me a little something in her will. Enough to get by on anyway, although sometimes I give Elaine Sumner a hand at her café."

"Another story," I said.

Myra smirked. "Now, don't follow too close on my heels or it'll look suspicious. My *heels*," she repeated, looking down veiny legs at a pair of three-inch wooden-soled Candies. "My aching ankles. Oh well," she said, "fabulous!"

When, a few minutes later, I returned to the parlor, Lucy was explaining to Colin how she'd been a finalist in the Miss Kansas contest. Poor

Lucy. She sat precariously close to the edge of her chair, and in the stiffness of her spine all I could see were future back problems.

"The Miss Candy-Ass Contest, I think you mean," Myra said as I walked into the room, and Lucy fixed her with a scowl that would've ruined her Poise score.

"Mo*ther*!" she said, but she recovered quickly. "Well, let's not talk about that anyhow," she said, and she attempted to smooth her feathers with a gesture that wrinkled her dress. "Or you may just see a side of me you wouldn't like too much. Ha ha," she added, as though the idea of an unlikable side of her would've never occurred to us.

I noticed then that Phyneas Krebs had dozed off at one end of the couch. Rosemary Krebs sat silently beside her husband. She was staring fixedly at Colin, and then she turned slightly and met my eyes.

"I trust that you and Mr. Nieman have had a pleasant evening."

"Oh," I said, "of course, of course. Pleasant company, pleasant evening, that's what I always say."

"That's good," she said, "because I'd like to ask you for a repeat performance."

"Repeat?" I said. "Performance?"

"The Mayor and I are throwing a little mixer," Rosemary Krebs said. She didn't look at her quietly snoring husband. "I think you young people call them 'dances' nowadays."

Lucy Robinson laughed loudly.

"What's the occasion?" Colin asked.

Rosemary Krebs did something then. It took me a moment to realize that what she was doing was laughing.

"Does one need an 'occasion' to celebrate?" She laughed a little more, an odd noise: it sounded like she was having trouble breathing. "The Mayor and I host the Founders' Day Picnic each summer, but this fall has just been so . . . troubled. It seemed like everybody could use a chance to unwind." She smiled. "So. It's this very weekend, in fact. I know it's short notice, but I'd like to extend a personal invitation to the four of you."

"We'd be delighted, of course," Colin said immediately, and I turned to him suddenly, but he was facing Lucy. He seemed about to ask her something, but Rosemary Krebs spoke first.

"Please," she said, "if you will allow me to broach a somewhat . . . sensitive topic?"

Colin turned back to her. "Of course," he said, always a master of these kinds of questions of etiquette. "Please, speak freely."

"Our friend," Rosemary Krebs said, "Wade Painter."

"Our friend," I said.

"As it happens," Rosemary Krebs continued in a quieter voice, "Lawman Brown was never able to locate Gary Gables. But, other than the odd coincidence of timing, there was nothing to indicate that Gary Gables or anyone else in Galatia had anything to do with Odell's death. It is simply a sad fact of life that more people leave this part of the world than come to it."

"Odell?" Colin said.

"Galatia?" I said.

"Forgive me. Odell was Wade's father's Christian name." Rosemary Krebs allowed herself a discreet, delicate swallow, and when she resumed speaking she was practically whispering. "I hate to speak so . . . frankly, but I should tell you that Odell was known to . . . There was a question of alcohol in the incident. In fact, the county coroner went so far as to suggest that had Odell not been as intoxicated as he was, he never would have been able to crawl into the ditch. He *said*"—she paused, smoothed her skirt with her tiny hands—"he said that Odell was so drunk he probably didn't even realize he'd been in a wreck."

"But what about the paint?" I said, and barely managed to stifle the burp that followed hard on my words.

Rosemary Krebs turned to me. "Mr. Time."

Lucy giggled, and I jerked back from the name. No one had ever called me "Mr. Time" before, and I didn't like the way it sounded.

"I'm sorry," I said, "it's just that—"

"No, no, don't be sorry. Your concern is completely understandable." She paused a moment. "But, nevertheless, ungrounded. Eustace was able to ascertain that, at the time, nine years ago, at that time there were forty-six different automobiles in the town of Galatea, all of which had been painted 'Cherokee turquoise.' "

"Eustace?" Colin said.

"Lawman Brown," Myra reminded him. She laughed, but it was a nervous laugh. "He come sneaking around everyone's house in the middle of the night, scraped a little piece of paint off their cars until finally Vern Gatlinger's Doberman took a good-sized chunk outta his rear end, and then he just asked people for their auto records." She laughed again. "That man."

"Galatea's a GM town," Lucy said then.

I turned to her. "As opposed to . . . ?"

She looked at me with a confused expression on her face. "Well, Ford, of course. Or Chrysler, I guess, but nobody around here really drives a Chrysler."

"At any rate," Rosemary Krebs said, "I thought I should attempt to elucidate Wade's . . . misgivings."

"Well, yes, thank you," Colin said, and he turned back to Lucy. "I believe, young lady, that we were talking about *you*."

"Oh!" Lucy said, looking up suddenly, the color returning to her cheeks in a sudden blush. Her back straightened with an almost audible snap. She turned to Rosemary Krebs nervously, took a deep breath, and smiled, first at Colin, and then, more determinedly, at me. "I had to choose this year between being a drum major and a cheerleader, and so actually"—*ackshully*—"I already added a new cheer."

She looked around sheepishly, and when no one spoke she smiled hesitantly and stood up. She closed her eyes and her lips moved as she mouthed the words to herself, and then her eyes opened and her hands began to push imaginary pom-poms through the air—the rustle of her dress mimicked the sound quite well—and she began to chant:

Galatea, Galatea,
you're the best!
Galatea, Galatea,
beat the rest!
Galatea, Galatea,
charge ahead!
Galatea, Galatea,
knock 'em dead!

She finished, flushed, with a whoop and a little jump, and then she looked around at each of us for approval. When no one said anything immediately her shoulders drooped slightly and she said, "Well, I guess it does work better when there are five of us." In a slightly pleading tone, she added, "It's for football. At the end I do the splits." She was practically whispering as she finished. "I'm the only girl who can."

2.10

Divine

I REMEMBER IT WAS WARM. I REMEMBER IT WAS REALLY warm and then all the sudden it was cold, it was *really* cold, it was ice-fucking-cold and it was completely dark. It was pitch-black. It was so totally dark that I couldn't see nothing no matter how hard I tried, and I remember that my eyes hurt with how hard I was staring into the darkness trying to see something, anything, and then I opened my eyes and it was still dark. Still dark, but not pitch-black, not dark like it'd been before. Up above me I could make out long wispy clouds and on the other side of the clouds the stars, a million million stars that seemed like just barely over my head, like maybe if I lifted up my arm I could grab a handful of them. But I didn't. I didn't lift up my arm. I knew better. I knew that even if the stars was within reach that the motherfuckers would move away from me if I tried to grab them and so I just lay there and let them fill up my eyes for a while. Then there was the ash. It was just a smell at first, a dryness, a burning, a rotting all rolled up in one, and then it was a taste too, those same things, dry-burn-rot, all gummed up in my mouth, and even as I was working up the strength to spit it out a breeze come up and all the sudden the air was filled with glittering ash, it was like those clouds that was up above me had come down and swallowed me, or maybe I'd floated up into them, and it felt like that for a minute, for just one sweet minute it felt like I was up in the air with the angels and the wind all around me and the stars too, the stars was floating above me and beside me and below me and I thought, *Oh, Jesus Christ, Jesus H. Christ. I'm dead.*

2.11

Justin

COLIN WORKED ALL NIGHT. HE TYPED LIKE A HACK REporter, with just two fingers. He struck the keys of his anachronistic manual typewriter—a Remington, just like the rifle—with a sound like . . . well, with a sound like old typewriters make. It was the sound Colin lived for. He said it made him high, that sound, and when he was on a roll he typed for hours, gobs of black ink filling up page after page of creamy white typing paper that Colin had mailed from a stationer's in Paris, each ream individually packaged in its own monogrammed cotton sack. Sometimes Colin filled entire pages of this paper with gibberish until inspiration struck again, but that night his typing had a realness to it, a measured staccato of characters and spacing and carriage returns, and I knew that he was actually working, writing, transforming or at any rate transcribing tonight's dinner conversation into yet another attempt at his second novel. I wondered how close he would get, this time, if he would type all night only to burn everything he had written in the morning, or if he would get carried away and write for a few weeks or months or years until a scattered stack of pages sat on one edge of his huge mahogany desk like a single heavy cloud settling down on the plain. I wondered which would be finished first, the story Colin was telling or the story that Webbie had begun the first day we were here and that Wade had added to tonight, the story that Galatea was telling. If it sounds like I'm making a race out of it, it's because I knew that it *was* a race, and Colin knew it as well: as soon as he was finished with his novel he would be finished with Galatea, and even though I hoped he would finish soon I hoped, too, that Galatea would beat him. In spite of myself, I had become hooked. I wanted to know the rest of the story. And I was able to want that only because I thought Galatea's story was over, just as I thought our story, mine and Colin's, was also over, that it was merely a matter of filling in the pieces. If I had known what the town had in store for us then I would have gotten out of bed and destroyed Colin's manuscript for him, shredded every last sheet of paper in the house and thrown his typewriter down a flight of stairs. And why not? I had done it before, and it saved us then, for a while anyway, it had saved us. It had saved us for this.

2.12

Webbie

YOU OWN IT."

"I do?"

"Didn't anyone bother to tell you? It's on your property."

"Ah." Justin looked up at me. "Colin owns it."

He turned back to the halves of my father's bellystone that he held in his hands. The petrified burr of an ancient seed pod rolled around in the dimple of the half in his left hand.

"I found one in our, in the limestone house."

"You did? I didn't know Beatrice had a bellystone."

"A what?"

"They're called bellystones. Well, some people call them prairie pearls, but most people call them bellystones."

"Some people?"

I shrugged. "White people."

Justin laughed. "But what are they?"

"No one knows. It's uncertain whether they're natural or artificial. There's absolutely no record of them before their discovery. None of the local Native American tribes has any information about them. Nor"—I smiled wryly—"does the white man."

A corona of long invasive gouges ringed both halves of the bellystone in Justin's hand, and he ran a finger over them—a finger which, I noticed, seemed slightly crooked. "Ugh," he said. "What did . . . your father—"

"My father."

"What'd he use to open it up?"

"A screwdriver," I said. "And a hammer."

Justin winced, as though the blows had been directed against his own body, and something in the gesture caused me to look at his bruised right eye. For the first time I noticed the faint shadow of a scar ringing it. Only pieces of the scar were visible, tiny red-pink ticks notching the pink-white of his skin, but it seemed as though the scar might once have completely encircled his eye. It was hard to tell because of the faded bruise on the side of his head, but even so I wondered what might inflict such a scar. The jagged end of a bottle maybe, an unshod horse's hoof, a belt buckle secured with a belt around an attacker's hand? Then I wondered *who* might inflict a scar like that.

Justin didn't seem to have noticed my examination. "You're saying they all came from a what, a mine or something, on our property?"

"It's called a cave. The Cave of the Bellystones."

All at once his face lit up. "I want to see it. Take me there."

"It's not really a cave," I said. "It's just a hole, really, a pit dug into the ground, with a pile of stones on top."

"They're so beautiful."

"No, they're not. They're mysterious, and that's not the same thing." I nudged it with my finger. "I mean, look at it. It's just a gray lump. The only thing interesting about it is where it came from, how it got here."

"Where *did* it come from?"

I shrugged, pointlessly, since Justin's eyes seemed fastened to the bellystone. "Some people think they might have been formed in the gullet of one of the aquatic mammals who lived here millions of years ago, when the Plains were an inland ocean. Others think that a lost tribe of Indians possessed a seamless potting technique, although innovations in ceramics are more associated with the tribes of the Southwest. Most people go for the whale theory."

"Now I really want to see this cave. Come on, let's go."

"Your stone. Bea's stone. Is it whole?"

"Yeah."

"Wade has a whole one too. All the rest of them, I guess there were about a hundred in all, all of the ones I've ever seen have been opened. Supposedly Noah Deacon found a lump of gold inside the first one he ever opened, and after that everyone . . ." I shook my head. "I really can't go. Someone needs to be here to help my father up the steps."

"You mean your father wants *you* here to help him up the steps."

"Same difference."

"No, it's not. You said that when you're not around he just comes in through the back door and takes the chair lift."

"I call it Mother Mabel. The chair lift, I mean."

"But of course. Mother Mabel, and Faith and Hope and Bestiality." He rolled his eyes. "You people in this town have the funniest names."

"You should talk," I said. "*Justin Time.*"

"Excuse me? A William Edward Burkhardt Du Bois Martina Greeving?"

I laughed. For the first time in my life my name felt like a little bit of a blessing, rather than a curse, a shared joke rather than a joke at my expense. "Really, it just says Webbie on my birth certificate. And don't blame me. I didn't pick it out."

"Maybe you should pick out a new one. Although *I* think Webbie's a lovely name."

I shook my head. "I'm a firm believer that people can't just change their names."

"Sure they can. Look at Divine."

I rolled my eyes.

"Well, come on. You don't think my parents actually *named* me Justin Time, do you?"

I almost gasped. I suppose it had occurred to me, but I'd rejected it out of hand. I shook my head then, as if to rattle this new piece of information into its appropriate slot, and my rattling shook more words out of me. "I'm beginning to think I tell you too much."

Justin still held the split scarred bellystone in his hands, and he gestured with it now. "I wouldn't worry about that. Everyone does."

"What, are you some kind of father confessor?"

"Well, no one's ever accused me of being the daddy type, but you'd be surprised at some of the things people tell me."

All at once he turned away from me in a manner that was becoming familiar. He looked back at the bellystone, and then he tried to fit the two halves together. Even as he nudged the pieces together I could feel him retreating into a distance that wasn't contained by a Sunday afternoon in my father's living room. He held the seamed bellystone in his hands absolutely still, as though it were filled with water, and I could see his eyes filling with the prehistoric moment when it was formed. Behind Justin's eyes the bellystone's seam disappeared, water swirled into the house, the walls of my father's living room became the stomach of some great whale and the bellystone rolled around in it, slowly gaining mass as sticky stuff from the stomach's lining coated it layer by layer, year by year. Time passed. The whale died, settled to the bottom of the ocean floor, the water retreated from the corpse. Flesh rotted, withered, dried, blew away like dust, left behind a skeleton and then not even that. Just more dust, and the bellystone, which, even more slowly than he had closed it, Justin now opened.

"Most people," he said then, neither looking at nor speaking to me, "most people are driven by a need to confess." He looked up at me, his eyes, his entire face blank, as though it were waiting to have an impression stamped on it. "But some of us, unfortunately, solicit confessions. Some people tell secrets, and others are told them. And most people, if you look hard enough, will have left some kind of record. And right now," he said, suddenly smiling away his blankness. "Right now I want to know the secret of the Cave of the Bellystones."

In the end I acquiesced, and I drove us to his house. Justin had me park outside of the cedar enclosure, and we skirted it on our way to the fields.

"Those stones," he said, and shivered.

"I know exactly what you mean. When I was a kid I read this terrifying account of the La Brea tar pits, about how they consumed thousands and thousands of dinosaurs over the eons, and ever since then I've never been able to walk on that moat without expecting to be swallowed up, just like those dinosaurs."

Justin laughed a little and nodded his head, but it was a distant laugh. His face wandered the horizon until a circling hawk caught his eye; a moment later they were distracted by the silver flash of the withered leaves of a cottonwood stand moving in the cold wind.

I watched him look around, aware that the landscape wasn't really holding him in. Amazing, I thought, all that space, and still his mind needs to go beyond it, go somewhere else. I wanted to ask him where, but I didn't know how, so instead I asked about Colin.

I asked him how Colin's writing was going.

"His writing."

The wistfulness that had been in Justin's voice was gone now; his tone had hardened, and even though he shoved his hands in his pockets I could still see that they were balled in fists inside his jacket.

"Something he said at dinner the other night. When we were talking about Wade's father, and Gary."

"And what did Colin say?"

"Careful," I said, as Justin nearly stepped into a tangle of barbed wire. The wire spiraled off of a series of withered fenceposts that had fallen to the ground. "I think . . . yes. We just have to follow this fence," I said, "or what's left of it. It should take us all the way there." I paused. "He said, 'Fascinating.' "

"Fascinating, huh?" Justin snorted. It was an odd, dangerous sound. It made me realize for the first time the degree of animosity between him and Colin. "Fascinating." With quick steps, he began walking the fence's wavering line across the prairie, and I hurried to keep up with him. "What *I* find fascinating about Colin's writing is why no one's ever spotted the fundamental difference between *Beauty* and *The Beast*."

I tried for levity. "Ouch. I just have to wince every time I hear those titles." Justin didn't answer me, so I said, "But what *is* the fundamental difference between *Beauty* and *The Beast*?"

"You've read them?"

"Yup. Did my homework."

"What's *Beauty*'s first line?"

I smiled, and in a deep voice I intoned, " 'My name is Colin Nieman.' "

"And?"

"And? Oh, right. 'My name is Colin Nieman, and I swear that this is the truth.' "

"Perfect," Justin said. "And the first line of *The Beast*?"

"Um . . ."

" 'Because the beast has no name,' " Justin recited, " 'he is always on the run.' "

" 'He moves through the darkness,' " I finished, " 'because he cannot stand the sun.' " I laughed. "It's a little overblown, don't you think. I mean, the rhyme and all?" I waited, but Justin said nothing. I sensed that it was analysis he wanted, not judgment, and I thought for a moment and then I said, "One of them starts with a name, the other with namelessness."

"It's not *just* namelessness," Justin said then, "it's an assertion that something can't be named."

"I think you might be reading into the line a bit," I said, but Justin seemed weirdly intent on what he was saying, and he waved my protest away.

"Look at the book again, you'll see I'm right."

"Fine," I said, "but that still doesn't tell me what you mean."

Justin sighed, a small sound that, like my words, seemed to disappear on the prairie. He trudged resolutely on, and I fell behind and waited for him to sort out his thoughts.

I turned around and saw that the Deacon house was almost invisible now, its cupola just crowning a small rise in the land. In the other direction, in front of us, a low gray cloud of ash indicated the position of Kenosha.

"What *is* a name?" Justin said then, but before I could answer, he said, "A name is a declaration. It says, I believe in the power of words to describe the world."

I didn't answer him. I was thinking: *prairie, cupola, ash, wind, fence.* These were the words that were in my head, these were the words I used to describe the world. They seemed to be doing their job just fine.

"Don't you see?" Justin went on, holding his hands in front of him, empty now, but still carrying the ghost of the bellystone. "A name and what it names are the simplest one-to-one correspondence between words and real things. *This*," he said, and he made his hands look like scales, "equals *this*. This *means* this." I just waited, and after a minute Justin went on. "There is faith in *Beauty*, faith that words, that its words, have meaning and are useful. That faith is not present in *The Beast*."

The fence curved down into a dip in the land then, and the sound of our footsteps changed as we worked harder to keep from slipping on dry loose soil. Kenosha's ashes disappeared; I knew that the cupola would be invisible behind us. Curve, change, slip, disappear, invisible. Isn't that what was happening, what we were doing?

"So what happened?" I said out loud. "What made Colin lose his faith?"

Justin looked at me, and I knew from his expression that he wasn't telling me the whole story, and that he wouldn't. Justin Time, Webbie Greeving, Colin Nieman. Galatia, Kenosha, Galatea. "Nothing" was all Justin said. "Nothing happened—to Colin."

There was an answer in his words to a question that had yet to be asked, but there was also something in his voice that silenced me, and we didn't talk for a few minutes. I had thought we were still a ways from the Cave when we topped a hill and there, suddenly, it was.

"Oh my God," I said.

"What? What's the matter?"

"What do you mean, what's the matter? Look at it."

"I don't know what I'm looking at. Is something wrong?"

"Is something *wrong*? Jesus Christ, they've built a fence around it. A cap. A, a, a goddamn witch's hat."

"Wait a minute. You mean this building isn't the entrance?"

The entrance to the Cave of the Bellystones had originally been a conical pile of stones, not bellystones, just regular stones, although they'd been cut roughly into spheres. They were primarily yellow limestone; some white shale and gray flint had been worked in, and here and there a piece of granite embedded with glassine sparkled among the softer, duller rock. The pile had been nearly twenty feet high, maybe half that in width, and it was split by a single slit that led to its hollow core. Inside that core had been a notched pole that dropped down into the cave. But now the cone of stones was covered with rough planks. The planks resembled a tepee more than they did a witch's hat, and I wondered, through my anger, if that's what the cone had been meant to represent. I'd always opted for a slightly more Freudian interpretation, mound, slit, hole in the ground, but sometimes a pile of stones is just a pile of stones.

"Webbie?"

My hands were in fists, and I made myself uncurl them before I spoke. I breathed in and out deeply. I tried to relax. "Oh, Justin," I practically cried, "they've ruined it."

He didn't have to ask who. Spray-painted stencils read "DANGER—NO TRESPASSING—BY ORDER OF THE POLICE DEPARTMENT OF GALATEA."

The planks were faded and worn. I realized they must have been erected while I was away at school. They could've been up for a decade, longer even. I suddenly remembered: I was thirty-four years old. Cora Johnson was thirty-seven. She had an eight-year-old son with asthma, she had stretch marks at the sides of her breasts from the time they'd been full with milk. You could see the stretch marks in the summer, when she cooked in sleeveless blouses.

Justin had gone up to the door and was rattling it, lightly at first, then roughly. A large padlock whined against the metal clasp it held closed. I watched him look around for something to break the lock with. Only pebbles were visible, a few scattered prickly-pear cacti. Not even grass grew on the sand-swept floor of the valley that contained the cave. The only thing it held was wind, which blew into it and seemed to get trapped, whirled around in futility, then dissipated in defeat, leaving behind a swirling track as though a giant snake had rolled across the sand.

Justin gave up, turned to me. There was a bemused smile on his face. "I almost feel, I don't know, affronted. I mean, I *own* this."

I tried to laugh it off with him. "Oh well," I said. "I'm sure she did it legally. Public menace, lost cattle, children, whatever."

Justin shrugged. "Whatever," he said. "It doesn't matter." He looked at me for a moment, turned back to the flat boards. He put his palms against them. "So tell me," he said, pushing here, there, "what's inside? What am I missing?"

"Now?" I said. "Not too much. A dry smell, a ceiling shorter than you are, rectangular niches cut into bare earth walls. Maybe a snake or two, or a pack of kangaroo rats."

"But not both."

"No, probably not both."

He turned back to me. "What keeps the ceiling from collapsing?"

"Grass roots. Just like sod houses."

Justin looked around. "There's no grass growing here."

"Not anymore."

Suddenly Justin started walking toward me. "So," he said, "what else was there? Before they emptied it and sealed it up."

"Blankets," I said distantly. "There used to be blankets there, and kids used to shimmy down the pole and fuck on them. It was absolutely dark. Totally. It was even more private than masturbating."

He was still walking toward me.

I found myself blushing, and I was embarrassed by my embarrassment. Justin was walking toward me. It seemed like he should have reached me already, but he was hardly any closer.

"And you, Webbie? Did you fuck here?"

"Did I fuck here? I've never even fucked in Galatia, in Kansas even. I think if I fucked in the same state that my father was in I'd just . . . explode."

"Maybe you used another name."

"Another name?" I said, thinking, at first, that he meant a pseudonym, a stand-in for Webbie. "You mean, for fucking?"

Justin didn't answer me. All of the sudden he was right in front of me, and he stood there without speaking, and his silence seemed to draw the words out of me.

"We didn't call it anything. There was nothing to call it."

Justin still didn't answer me. He had gone from being impossibly far away to being much too close to me.

"Oh my God," I said. "*You* wrote it, didn't you? Colin's second book. *The Beast*. You wrote it."

He stared at me for a moment, and I realized two things: that he had meant for me to discover his secret, but that he hadn't wanted me to say it out loud. He turned away from me then, and began walking toward his house.

"Justin?"

He didn't say anything. I'd like to say that his silence was answer enough, but I wanted something more concrete, and I said, "Justin, answer me."

He just kept walking.

"I took you here, Justin. I showed you the Cave, I gave it to you. Now you have to give something to me."

He stopped this time; he turned. "It's always mercenary, isn't it?"

"Excuse me?"

He screamed then. He screamed, but the land was so big it didn't really matter. "People always want to *buy* things! No one ever gives them away, no one ever accepts gifts. They always want *money*."

"Justin, I—"

"Yes, I wrote the fucking thing. I wrote it, and yes, it's a little overblown. I was sixteen, and he stole it from me. I would've given it to him,

I would've given him *anything*, but no, he had to take the one thing that belonged to me and make it his. And now he's going to take Galatia from you, he's going to take Eddie Comedy and Odell Painter and Melvin Cartwright and Gary whatever-his-fucking-last-name-was, and he's going to find out who this Eric Johnson is that everyone refuses to talk about, and he's going to take him too, and Divine and Wade and you. Okay? He'll take all of you, okay? Are you satisfied? *Okay?*"

He turned to go again, but I stopped him one more time. "And your eye," I said. "Did he do that too?"

He put a finger on it, first on the remains of his scar, which were invisible in the bright afternoon light, and then on the soft purple bruise beside it. He smiled at me, a smile that was not without mirth. "Yes," he said, tapping the bruise hard enough to make me wince. "But I hit him first."

This time when he turned I let him go. I watched him begin the long walk back to his house. Which was really Colin's house, which had been Old Lady Bea's house, which had been the Deacon spread for over a century and unowned by millions of Native Americans for millennia before that. But none of that history really mattered, I realized: only the present counted, only the here and now. Millions of dead Indians, a family of niggers, one old white bitch: all of them had been supplanted by a bald white faggot and his bruised and scarred houseboy, and they would be gone too, one day. I turned then, and looked back at the capped entrance to the Cave of the Bellystones. Maybe it was less of a tepee, more of a Quonset hut. But that didn't matter either, nor did it matter what had once happened on the other side of that door, whether the door itself was locked or unlocked. For the time being it was a door, and it was closed, but I knew that if I needed to, one day, I would open it.

2.13

Justin

STEEL RIBS HELD UP THE FLACCID TIN SKIN OF THE gymnasium, puddles of light splashed on the floor. Red and black lines offered the blueprint of a basketball game, but the only takers were Galatean couples, heterosexual Galatean couples, white heterosexual Galatean couples—all those adjectives, and we haven't even gotten into fashion yet. Men, following their bellies, led wives or girlfriends; a trail of perfume lagged behind the women. On the stage four potbellied and balding white men played a cover of "Caribbean Queen," and the dim dull thump of music stalked the gym and its occupants. Beside me, Lucy sighed. It was a sigh of contentment.

"Isn't it pretty?"

She meant, I suppose, the metallic streamers that drooped in uneven arches from the ceiling, the multicolored balloons that hung from longer and shorter strings and listed in warm air currents that unfortunately weren't present on the gym floor, which was chilly and smelled faintly of the locker room. Lucy herself *was* pretty, dressed in a purple minidress and white tights and pumps that matched her dress. Her eyes, lost in mascara and shadow that went with her dress and pumps, were at least an inch higher than mine, and her thick hair, piled high in a French twist, added another half foot to her height. Her nails, I noticed, had been painted a light robin's-egg blue which didn't really go with her dress, and when Lucy saw me staring at them she put her hands behind her back.

"It was the best I could do." She tried to laugh, a horsy kind of laugh, like Chrissy on *Three's Company*. "How many girls do *you* know who buy their nail polish in the housepaint section of the hardware store?"

"I don't think you want to know the answer to that question."

Down on the floor, Lucy's tapping foot occasionally matched the rhythm of the music, but usually she missed the beat by a wide mark. She saw me staring at her foot and laughed. "Things'll pick up soon," she said.

"Pick up?" I said. "As in levity, or levitation?"

She looked at me with a puzzled expression on her face, and then, as I was learning about her, she laughed her confusion away. "Oh, you!" she said, and smacked me with her purse.

"Ouch!" I said. "What've you got, a brick in there?"

"Just girl things," Lucy said. "Nothing you'd understand."

"You'd be surprised," I said, and again Lucy just stared at me. "Oh you!" she said again, but this time I dodged her purse.

"Hey kids," Myra's voice came from behind us, "shouldn't you be dancing or something?" Myra's question seemed slightly surreal, given the band, and what they were playing, and how they were playing it.

"Mo*ther*!" Lucy said, and her purse flew, but Myra seemed to know to avoid it.

Colin's hand snaked across the small of my back then. "Hey," I said to him, meaning hi, but he put his hands in his pockets before I could catch one of them with my own.

"Well, if you kids don't get on out there, me and Mr. Nieman are gonna have to show you up."

"Mom, don't you dare! You'll embarrass me to death!"

"Well, that seems as good a reason as any. Mr. Nieman?"

"Please," Colin said, "whenever I engage in the task of embarrassing someone's daughter—especially the beautiful daughter of a beautiful woman—I insist that she call me Colin."

Myra giggled. "Oh you!" she said, and Colin took her hand, but before they went off he turned back to me.

"Do you remember where you put my black wool coat?"

"It should be in the bedroom closet."

"That's funny. I looked there, but I couldn't find it. Oh well." He shrugged, and he gave Myra a tug, and they danced away from us just as the band launched into something that was meant to be, I think, "Brown Sugar."

"Oh God," Lucy said. "I hope no one sees her."

I indicated the otherwise empty gym floor, the perimeter of Galatean couples. "It's a little hard to miss them, don't you think?"

"Oh no!" Lucy said then. "There's Brenda and Lee Anne and Shelly. Dance with me, quick."

I stepped back before she could catch my arm. If push came to shove, I wasn't so sure I could beat her in a wrestling match. "I don't dance, sorry."

Lucy looked at me as if I'd said I breathed water. "I'm sure you're fine. Come on."

"I'm sorry," I said, "I lost my leg in a boating accident, and it just hasn't been the same since."

"What? Which one—oh!" Lucy forced a little laugh. Her purse arm trembled a little but remained by her side. "This is no time for jokes. Come on now, let's go." She caught my arm this time, but I managed, with difficulty, to stand firm.

"Don't get me wrong," I said, trying to pull free, "but this kind of sitcom intrigue really isn't my style. And I *don't* dance."

Lucy stopped pulling, but she kept hold of my arm. "I don't get it."

"Look, there's something I should tell you." I heard myself say that, and I was forced to laugh at myself: who was purveying the sitcom mentality now? Lucy's hand tightened on my arm, as if this were just a ploy of mine to distract her, but before I could speak again a shrill female voice cut me off.

"Lucy! Is that your *mom* out there with that *bald* guy?"

"Oh God," Lucy breathed, "oh God oh God oh God. They'll *never* let me live this down." She visibly shrank as the three girls moved in on us; three boyfriends, who seemed to recognize that tonight the gym wasn't their turf, hung back, though I felt their eyes noting me inside the circle of girls.

"Hey Bren, hey Lee, hey Shell," Lucy said with forced brightness. "Hey guys," she called to their boyfriends. She took a deep breath, smoothed the front of her dress. "This is Justin."

"Hey," I said, and then I straightened a little and said, "Hi." Straightening didn't help: the girls were still taller than I was. I'd been surprised by the general largeness of the Midwest farmers' daughters, but I suppose emphasizing gigantism wouldn't have worked in that Beach Boys song.

Lee Anne smirked at Lucy. "Where's *Howard?*"

"Oh, puh-*lease*," Lucy said, her lips curling off her teeth in disgust. "This is *Justin*," she said firmly. "He just moved here. From New York City."

"Huh," Brenda said. I suspected the girls knew that much about me already. Now they examined me sharply; their eyes traveled up and down my body, as if, if they looked closely enough, they could discover some alien feature, a third ear, fingers without nails, cuffed trousers.

Eventually Lee Anne bit her lip and the tips of her teeth came away fuchsia. "He's cute?" she offered hesitantly.

"Well, he's a lot cuter than *Howard*," Shelly said.

"Not to mention *younger*," Brenda said.

"Not to mention *thinner*," Lucy said, and, at that, the girls broke into hysterics.

"You guys are *too* mean," Lee Anne said, and then, in the same breath, "Hey, Lu, who's that bald *geek* your mom's dancing with?"

Lucy blushed. "That's Mr. Nieman. He's from New York too. They, um, they bought the limestone house."

"Huh," Shelly said. "Is he your daddy or something?"

"Not anymore."

A confused look went around the circle of girls, and then Lucy came out with an "Oh you!" The circle of girls blocked my escape route, and I caught her purse full in the stomach.

"He's a writer," Lucy said while I was recovering. "Mr. Nieman, I mean. You're not a writer, are you?"

"Not anymore," I said again, but this apparently didn't merit a purse swing.

"He's really famous, if you've heard of him," Lucy said. "Mr. Nieman, I mean."

"Hey Lu," Brenda said quickly, "Shelly's driving down to the Big M on Monday night." She leaned forward, whispered conspiratorially, "We're gonna go see that shack where they found Eddie Comedy."

"Yuck! That is totally gross!"

"Oh, Lu, get over yourself," Shelly said. "You know what my mom said? My mom said Melvin Cartwright did it. That's why no one can't find him anywhere. She said"—Shelly paused significantly—"she said it was *revenge*."

Lucy's face fell on the last word. I thought, in fact, that she might be going to faint.

"Revenge?" Lee Anne said. "For what?"

"Duh," Brenda said. "For Eric Johnson."

"That's enough," Lucy said. "I don't want to hear no more."

"Lu—"

"I said *enough*! Besides," Lucy said, catching her breath, "Mondays is cheerleader practice, so I couldn't make it anyway." Her hands went to her head then. They were trembling slightly, but they steadied as they touched her frosted hair as though adjusting a homecoming tiara.

I found myself reaching up then. I slipped a finger into Lucy's hairdo. I wasn't sure if I meant to be tender or cruel, but I ran my finger along a lock of Lucy's hair, and when I finished, a single long black strand hung down her forehead, its pointed end just touching the side of her nose. Lucy stood unnaturally still while I touched her, and when I was done she almost crossed her eyes to stare at the hair. She looked as though a snake had crawled out of her hairdo.

"There now."

"What now?"

"It's much sexier that way," I said, and Lucy's breath came out in a long slow exhalation that swished the curl back and forth. "Exactly," I said, "you keep doing that and you're bound to land yourself a real man." And then, without waiting for her to smack me with her purse, I pushed my way through the girls. In New York I could have disappeared into the crowd, but here I had to settle for distance, and I walked as far from them as I could.

2.14

Webbie

WHEN I GOT TO THE GYM I SECRETED MYSELF IN A corner. I was able to spot Justin almost immediately. He, too, stood by himself, swaying slightly in a jacket that was too thin for the cold outside. When I saw him I was struck anew by his fragility. He was too skinny, I thought, much too skinny. I wanted to take him to Cora's, she'd put some meat on his bones. Even from a distance I could make out a pimple on his chin that seemed dangerously large and red, and all at once I realized I had come to the dance to see him because I knew that not only did he not belong here, he could not survive here. He would be gone soon, and then I would be alone again, shuttled between my father and his Church Ladies, and Wade and Divine.

I hesitated a moment, unsure as to what I should do, but Justin turned his head and saw me. He smiled and trotted over to me, clutching an empty plastic cup. When he kissed my cheek my nose filled with alcohol-laden breath.

He held up his cup. "The lady may keep a booze-free house, but at least she's smart enough to serve it at parties."

"You should probably thank the Mayor for that. He's the politician." I paused, smiled. "So, um, how are you doing?"

"I'm 'doing' a date."

"I saw Colin—"

"Not Colin," Justin said, and then he sort of jerked his head.

"Huh?"

Justin jerked his head again. "You'll understand if I don't turn around, but . . ." He jerked his head one more time.

"Oh!" I said, and I scanned the crowd. "You know, I don't think I've ever seen anyone do that in real life. That look-where-my-head-is-jerking thing. It's something you see onstage, or in mov—*oh*!"

My eyes suddenly met Lucy Robinson's, and as soon as they did she ducked behind Shelly Stadler.

"You're here with Lucy Robinson?"

"We're the talk of the town. Thank you, Rosemary Krebs."

I saw Colin and Myra on the dance floor then. "But surely she figured it out? I mean, she's prone to delusions of grandeur, but she's not dumb."

"I suspect she figured everything out just fine," Justin said. "I suspect," he went on, "that this is all for Lucy's benefit, although I'm not sure *how*."

"You poor thing," I said. I tapped his empty cup. "Can I get you a drink or something?"

"A drink," Justin said, "would be divine," and then he rolled his eyes. "Let's hope *he* doesn't show up."

"Speaking of Divine . . ."

"Hmmm?"

"I was talking to Wade the other day. He said Divine's been acting a little weird lately."

Justin was playing with his empty cup, rolling it between his palms, and he said absently, "Weird?"

"Well, he had a big bruise on his head for one thing," I said, and, after hesitating a moment, I touched the faint greenish tinge on the side of Justin's face. "And he refused to get out of bed for like three days or something. Wade said he's been writing letters again."

"Divine's been writing letters?" Justin put an arm on my shoulder, and began steering me toward the bar.

"For three days."

"I think I'm missing something. Besides a drink, I mean."

We were at the bar by then, and I ordered a whiskey from Dave Helman, who was playing bartender for the evening.

"Look," I said when Justin had his drink. "Divine has this thing he does." I paused when Justin rolled his eyes. "I mean, besides that. He's been writing letters for years to somebody he calls Ratboy. He calls them his insurance."

"Ratboy? Insurance? I'm really lost now."

"I can't help you with the Ratboy part. But the insurance part is, as far as I can tell, blackmail."

"Blackmail."

"Well, what Divine's doing falls somewhere between what Joe McCarthy did, and that lady on *Romper Room* who used to look in her magic mirror and read out the names of all her friends." Justin only looked at me blankly, so I continued. "Divine says he's written down the name of every man in Galatia he's slept with. Not just the names, but all those little details, birthmarks and tattoos and, and—"

"Penis size?"

"Thank you. He said he's written all this down and mailed it off to this Ratboy person for safekeeping. He says that as long as those letters are safe then no one will bother with him."

Justin sipped at his whiskey. "Well, I have to admit that I'm rather amazed at the amount of *fagginess* he gets away with in a town like this. It's kind of awe-inspiring." Justin smiled. "Letters. What a charming anachronism. He doesn't really think it'll work, does he?"

I was just about to answer when a voice called my name.

"Why, if it isn't Webbie Greeving. I never thought I'd see you at one-a these things."

I turned then, and saw Cora Johnson striding up to us. She seemed even taller than I remembered, and a little heavier, but her skin was that same beautiful deep reddish brown that she'd always been so proud of. Sawyer's plump body trailed behind her, wheezing slightly, and clutching at the asthma inhaler that dangled around his neck.

I could feel the stiffness in my face. "Cora!" I called out, too brightly.

We hugged then, Cora crushing my head to her chest, and I tried to say hello to Sawyer, but he hid behind his mama and only peeked out shyly.

"Cora," I said, "allow me to introduce you to my good friend Justin . . . Justin Time." My eyes met his, and he smiled a little and shrugged his shoulders. "Justin, this is my oldest friend in the world, Cora Lewis—I mean, Cora Johnson, and that little munchkin hiding behind her skirts is her son, Sawyer."

"I'd watch who you was calling old, girl," Cora said to me, taking Justin's hand and shaking it warmly. "Cause wherever I am, you can't be too far behind. Sawyer, come on out and shake the man's hand. He don't bite."

Sawyer came out only long enough to put a pudgy palm in Justin's thin one, and I noticed again that its fingers, Justin's fingers I mean, were all slightly crooked. I looked at the scar around his eye again, at the bruise.

"Justin just moved here," I said. "That's his, um, friend dancing with Myra Robinson. Colin Nieman."

"I suppose I coulda guessed that even if I didn't already know it," Cora said. "Ain't so many new faces in Galatia that you gotta wonder who's who." Cora looked down at Justin with a mischievous smile on her face. "Your friend sure is bald," she said.

"Speaking of new faces," I said, and laughed nervously, "how's Rosa? Is she here?"

"Rosa's doing fine," Cora said, and then she reached out and shook Justin's hand again, and I realized then that she was as nervous as I was. "She stayed in this evening. Got to get up early, you know, and she's not mucha one for crowds."

"No, I guess not," I said.

There was a long moment of silence then, and I could see that Justin was a bit confused on how to proceed. Well, I was a bit confused too.

"You hear the latest?" Cora said then.

"The latest . . . ?"

"Apparently that shack, the one where they found Eddie Comedy? Apparently it burned down."

"What?" I said. "When?"

Cora looked at her watch. "Bout two hours ago. Sheriff Peterson down to Bigger Hill called the station house, Nettie Ferguson got the call."

"Well, I can't believe I didn't hear it sooner then," I said, and Cora and I laughed a little. Justin's eyes flitted back and forth between us but he said nothing. "Well," I said. "Well. First Noah's ark, now this. Did Sheriff Peterson have any idea who was responsible?"

"Nobody seems to know nothing bout nothing." She shook her head. "Strange days is upon us, Rosa says, and I'm inclined to agree. Strange days indeed." There was a lull, and then Cora said, "Well, don't let me keep you two. You looked like you was deep in conversation."

"Oh." I waved a hand.

"I'll see you soon," Cora said. Her hand on mine startled me, and it was all I could do not to pull back.

"Soon. I'll come by the café someday, if the Reverend ever lets me out of his sight."

"I seem to recall you was pretty good at giving the Reverend the slip whenever you wanted to." I searched for a recriminating element in her words, but I couldn't find one. "C'mon, Sawyer," Cora said then, and taking his hand, she led him away.

When she was safely out of earshot Justin said, "I sense another story there."

I laughed a little, and waved my hand again.

"I leave it up to you," Justin said.

"Oh, Justin," I said, and when I looked down at him he looked at me with such a stricken expression on his face that I brought my hands to my cheeks and found they were wet with tears. "Isn't it awful," I said, "I mean just *awful*, how people grow apart?"

Justin didn't answer me immediately, but stared behind me. I turned, and saw Colin twirling Myra in a slightly wobbling pirouette on the dance floor, and as he dipped her backwards nearly all the way to the floor her yelp rent the air of the gym.

He turned back to me. "I think I know what you mean."

My eyes found Cora's retreating back. "It was stupid for me to come here," I said. "I don't even *like* dancing." I turned back to Justin. "Forgive me for leaving you in the lurch," I said, "but I think I'm going to go home."

Justin nodded his head. "Get me a refill first?"

I laughed, took his glass from him. "I haven't had a hangover in a while, but I seem to recall that chocolate milk works well." We laughed together for a moment, and if I had known that those bubbly giggles were the last sounds I would ever hear from him I would have thought up joke after joke to keep him laughing forever. But all I did was dab at my eyes, and I said, "Later. The story, I mean. I'll get you that drink now."

2.15

Justin

MY HEAD WAS SPINNING, AND NOT JUST FROM ALCOhol. It was filled with so many names, so many little pieces of stories—Webbie Greeving and Cora Johnson, Divine and Ratboy, Lucy Robinson and Eric Johnson—and these names swirled in with those already there, and, despite all my efforts at resistance, I felt myself being drawn into Galatea's sucking spiral.

Webbie Greeving and Cora Johnson.

Divine and Ratboy.

Lucy Robinson and Eric Johnson.

And suddenly, in my drunken half-sleep, I understood what I was being told. Webbie and Cora, Divine and Ratboy, Lucy and Eric. They had all been lovers. I knew whom Webbie had visited the Cave of the Bellystones with, I knew who had broken Divine's heart and left him to chase after the likes of Wade and Colin, I knew why Lucy Robinson looked at a loosened strand of her own hair as though it were a snake growing from her head. It's what every prostitute learns sooner or later:

that most people have only one secret, and that secret is whom they truly love.

I allowed myself to say his name out loud.

I said, "Martin."

2.16

Webbie

THE LIGHT WAS ON IN MY FATHER'S ARCHIVE WHEN I got home, but the room, as always, was silent. He'd been up there a lot in the past several weeks, and more than once I'd picked up the phone only to hear him on it. My father loathed telephones, and more than once had threatened to have the line taken out of our house, so the fact that he was using it at all hours of the day and night was as sure a sign as any of his agitation.

It had occurred to me once that my father might use the Archive to masturbate, but sustaining that idea also meant sustaining an image of my father's erection, and that just wouldn't do, wouldn't do at all.

In my room I slipped out of my clothes, slipped into my nightgown and into bed. There was a faint scent of perfume on my blouse, Cora's perfume I knew, and I thought then of her wrists and her throat and her skull just behind her ears, her "pulse points" as she'd taught me to call them years ago, when she taught me the proper way to put on perfume.

The blind was down and the curtains drawn and there were no streetlights in Galatia: my room was pitch-black. If I stared at the ceiling, I could almost smell dry earth in my nostrils, the faint tang of old sex.

Everyone in town had gone there. It was a place you had to visit at least once, the way a New Yorker makes a token pilgrimage to the Empire State Building or a Parisian takes a trip to the Eiffel Tower. I put off going for years and years. The unknowable past of the place frightened me: by the time I was a teenager my father had taught me the lessons of the historian too well, and I didn't like the thought of something that invited questions but offered no answers. When I finally went there I was eleven, and I only went at the insistence of my best friend, Coretta Beech Tree Lewis.

Cora was three years older than me, already tall and beautiful, with full hips and breasts and a red tint to her skin that spoke of her Native American ancestry. Umber, she called it sometimes, that tint, burgundy, sepia, sienna. I'm not just black, I'm Siennese. Her grandpa on her daddy's side had been half Cherokee—her middle name had supposedly been her great-grandmother's—and she was the most beautiful girl in town, hands down. She had huge almond-shaped eyes that were even blacker than mine, and no man, not even my father, could deny her when she turned those eyes on them. With a glance or a stare or a wink she could turn a man on and off like a faucet, and if that didn't get her what she wanted then she had only to open her mouth and sing. My father liked to call her our own Mahalia, but Cora, who smoked cigarettes, drank beer, and was taking me to the Cave of the Bellystones to show me where she'd lost her virginity to Sawyer Johnson, Cora called herself a siren. "Woe to the man who hears my voice," she used to say to me behind my father's back. Woe, woe, woe! I adored her.

"Girl, you think it's just there to bleed?"

Cora was teaching me about my pussy. Kenosha was a cloud on the horizon, a tangible scent. Behind us, smoke curled from three different chimneys in Old Lady Bea's house. It was the middle of summer vacation.

"You think, what, it's just a one-way street? In and out, honey, in *and* out."

A blush made me as red as Cora. I could feel it all the way down to the palms of my hands. Before I could answer Cora started laughing at me.

"You think I'm just trying to be dirty. But you'll find out one day. Sex isn't just dirty—it's funny. It's a laugh and a half. First time you see some boy scrunching up his face when he's finishing, I bet you'll wanna laugh your head off. I told Sawyer he look like he drunk up a glass of lemonade when he thought he was getting milk. A hot toddy instead of ice-cold beer, a Harvey Wallbanger instead of a Shirley Temple."

"And what he say?"

"He said all that talking about drink made him thirsty again."

The way Cora said *thirsty* made me blush again, and my blush sent Cora into another fit of laughter. Her hand flailed, fell on my shoulder, the palm damp from the day's heat. That palm had curled itself around Sawyer's buttocks, his penis, its fingers had traced the space between his thin lips and dark gums. I tried to act casual, but I shrugged her hand off as quickly as I could.

"Okay, girl," Cora said, "I'll stop teasing you, but first you gotta say it."

"Say what?"

"Pussy."

"Is that supposed to liberate me or something? Maybe I should just burn my bra in the park."

"You wearing a bra now? That's so cute."

I blushed; Cora laughed. She said, "I just want you to say it so you'll know the right shape to make your lips when you give a blowjob."

I'd never heard the term before, but it didn't matter. I clapped my hand over my mouth and Cora laughed in delight.

"Come on, girl, say it now. Pussy."

I sighed through my nose, a long wheeze of air.

"That's a useful skill too," Cora said. "Now say the word."

"Pussycat," I said. I giggled.

"Uh uh, no cats involved. This ain't the Jazz Age. Pussy."

"Pussy," I said. Silently, I mouthed "cat."

"Louder."

"Pussy!" I yelled. This is what an empty field and a strong wind are for: to swallow up, to blow away embarrassing words. "Pussy!" I yelled, and imagined the word fleeing from me. "Pussy!"

"Cock!" Cora yelled.

"Cock!"

"Shaft!"

"Shaft!"

"Tool!"

"Tool!"

"Prong!"

"Huh?" I said. "Like the video game?"

"No, that's Pong. Prong. Prong!"

"Oh, enough already," I said. There was silence for a moment, wind, grass moving, the hum of taut barbed wire. Then I said, "How come there are so many words for a man's, um, you know—"

"Webbie!"

"Okay, okay, for a man's *dick*, but there's just the one word for women."

"Well, there's two answers to that," Cora said. "On the one hand, you could just say it's a man's world and leave it at that."

"Uh-huh."

"And on the other hand you could say cunt, box, snatch, fish, twat—"

"Okay, okay! I get it already."

"And that's just the hole. We ain't even got around to the clit part yet."

"*Okay.*"

The fence curved down into a dip in the land then. Our feet slipped on dry loose soil. Kenosha's ashes disappeared, but the smell intensified. Cock, shaft, tool, prong, dick. I giggled. Cunt, box, snatch, fish, twat. I didn't want sex as much as I wanted a magic marker and a bathroom wall. I wanted to be *bad*, not to *be* bad.

"Hey, Cora?"

"Hey what?"

"Have you seen it?"

"Webbie!"

"No, no, not Sawyer's, um, Sawyer's dick." I took a breath. "You seen Marsha's baby?"

We'd reached the bottom of the hollow by then. It was soggy down there, and we stepped from one clump of grass to the next to avoid sinking into the mud.

"Yeah," Cora said, stepping carefully. "I seen it. Him. I seen him."

"So's it true?"

Cora started back uphill before she answered, and when she did speak it was only to say, " 'S'what true?"

But I knew why she equivocated. I had a hard time saying it myself. "Is it . . . is it . . . ?"

"White?"

"Yes!" I nearly yelled, startled by the word itself. "Is it . . . white?"

"Whiter than a white man," Cora said. "With pink eyes, hair like a rusty steel wool pad, and hungry all the time."

"Yeah?" We were nearly to the top of the hill. "And it don't have a daddy either?"

Cora laughed a little. "Girl, you are the most innocent creature I ever met. Just because Marsha don't have no husband don't mean her baby don't have a daddy. He a albino, not Jesus Christ. And would you stop calling him an it. He a boy. His name is Eric. Eric Johnson. And if I marry Sawyer Johnson one day then he gonna be my nephew."

2.17

Justin

MYRA SHOOK ME AWAKE WITH ONE HAND. WITH HER other she held two drinks, her fingers stuck in the cups, her fingertips invisible beneath dark liquid.

"My heroine," I said, rubbing my eyes.

"Don't get your hopes up. It's just Coke. I think you've had enougha the hard stuff for one evening." She hiccuped then, and giggled. "So've I, for that matter." She sipped at her Coke and then she said, "So, Lucy scare you away?"

I shrugged. "Aw, you know."

"I expect I do," Myra said, and sipped her drink.

"Don't worry, I'll make sure she gets home okay."

Myra smiled appreciatively, but she only said, "Don't take too much trouble on her account. Lucy's a pain in my ass, but she can take care-a herself."

I noticed Colin among the dancers then, dancing alone. A lone figure on the other side of the gym might have been Wade, or it might not have. "So," I said eventually, "having a good time?"

Myra shimmied a little. "You know," she said, "it's fun to dance with other people every once in a while, instead of, you know, at home by yourself."

I nodded. "Tell me to butt out if I'm butting in, but, um, where *is* Mr. Robinson?"

"Mr. Robinson?"

"Your husband? Lucy's father?"

Myra stared at me blankly for a moment and then she said, "Lucy's father." The smile on her face was sad and whimsical, and then it hardened for a moment into anger, and then it disappeared, and she said simply, "He left." Something in her tone kept me from pushing further, but after a moment Myra said, "I don't suppose anyone has let you in on the dark moment of Galatea's shining history? The flip side to all this business?" She jerked her thumb at the dancers and the stage beyond them.

" 'Dark moment'?"

"*Dark* is the wrong word," Myra said. "That's what's funny about this town. Everything you say is loaded. Anyway," she said, "you know how Galatea was founded?"

I nodded. "Webbie told me," I said. "Galatia, then Galatea."

"That's it," Myra said. " '*I* before *e*, except after *c*.' That's it in a nutshell." She said, "Well, things've been quiet for a long time. I mean, most black folks don't like white folks, in general, I mean, as a general principle, and most white folks don't like black folks either, but generally they stay out of each other's hair. Like tonight, for example." She indicated the crowd: it was no longer all white, but I could see fewer than a dozen black men and women among the hundred-odd Galateans. "Oh hell," Myra said, "this could get all elaborate but let's just cut to the chase. Ten years ago, my husband helped a gang of, of, of *fuckers* to lynch a thirteen-year-old black boy. They strung him up by his thumbs overnight, and then the next morning a few men, my husband among them, went back and finished the job."

For a moment I could only stare at her in stunned silence. Finally I managed to say, "By his thumbs?"

Myra sighed. "He was a thief. Anywhere else, he'd just be called a shoplifter and get a slap on the wrist, but in Galatea a thief is a thief, and—"

"An eye for an eye—"

"A tooth for a tooth, and a thumb for a can of peaches. And"—Myra gulped, sighed, took a long drink—"and my daughter, Lucy."

"Lucy?" It came back to me then, my dream. "Oh my God," I said. "Lucy."

"Lucy said he put his hands inside her panties."

After a month of silence and equivocation, it was too much too fast. I had to backtrack. " 'A can of peaches'?"

"Peaches, candy bars, sandwich meat, whatever." Myra shrugged her shoulders. "Some people said he never stole nothing but food. I don't know. He never stole nothing from me."

Again I waited, still attempting to process this information, and then I said, " 'Finished the job'?"

"Stan said they used sticks to knock him outta the tree, like he was a pin, a pin, a pin—"

"A piñata."

"They buried the pieces of him. Stan said *the pieces*. Somewhere, who knows where." Myra waved a hand. "And then, you know, there was afterwards. Afterwards Stan had time to think about what he'd done."

"And he left."

"He left."

Myra didn't speak again. I said, "You're leaving something out." It was what I had said about Wade the other night, at Rosemary Krebs' house, and Myra answered me the same way she had then.

"I expect I'm leaving a lotta things out. I expect a lotta things were left out when Stan told the story to me. Still and all, the long and short of it is that my husband and a bunch of other men in town covered up a murder by calling it frontier justice, but my husband at least had the character to feel guilty about it, so he took off."

"Do you, do you know where?"

Myra seemed not to have heard. "Okay," she said. "Here's one thing I left out. The boy was white."

"The boy?"

"His name was Eric Johnson. And he was white. He was, how do you say it, an albino. He was as ugly as anybody I've ever looked on, living or dead."

"Oh," I said, and then, because I couldn't think of anything else to say, I said it again. "Oh."

"You see what I mean," Myra said, "about everything being loaded around here."

"I think I'm beginning to. I think so, yes." I returned to my earlier question. "You have no idea where your husband went?"

"Don't know. Don't want to know. I'm ashamed to admit I ever married a man who could do such a thing."

We seemed to be finished then. The only thing I could say was "Wow," and then neither of us said anything for a long time, and then Lucy showed up.

"Mo*ther*," said the girl who had been killed for. She seemed not to notice the strained look we gave her. "Isn't one date at a time enough for you?" She turned to me. "And I hope you weren't planning on abandoning me all night. Lee Anne and Brenda and Shelly are already going to have a *field day* with my mom and Mr. Nieman."

I looked at Myra one last time, but she seemed to find the logo at the bottom of her plastic cup more interesting than her daughter. "I'm sorry," I finally said to Lucy. "I'll drive you home."

Myra looked up suddenly. "No, you won't," she said. "You all can catch a ride home with me and Mr. Nieman."

Lucy tossed her head, and the strand of hair I had freed earlier splayed across her face. "Are you trying to com*plete*ly embarrass me? I am seventeen years old. I cannot be seen catching a ride home with my *mom*."

"Well, you can walk then," Myra said. "And I don't want you riding home with none-a those boys neither. They ain't in no better shape than Justy here."

Lucy rolled her eyes. "Like I *would*."

"Myra," I said. "Mrs. Robinson?"

She turned to me. "Yes."

"It's Justin," I said. "Just-in."

She smiled. "Got it," she said, and she turned back to Lucy. "Whatever you do, I want you home by one." She kissed her quickly, before Lucy could step away, and then she skipped back onto the dance floor. It is perhaps melodramatic of me to point out that in the months to come that kiss would be all Myra Robinson had to remember her daughter by, but I point it out anyway, because Myra herself never seemed to remember it.

2.18

Webbie

WE HADN'T BROUGHT A FLASHLIGHT. IMMEDIATELY INside the pile of stones it was dark and we didn't have any kind of light. The path turned, the sun disappeared behind us, and I felt Cora's hand wrap around mine.

"Here," she said, "grab this."

She curled my fingers around something hard, round, dry, and, in spite of myself, I giggled.

"Don't get stupid on me, girl. I don't want you falling and breaking your leg."

I sobered quickly. "What do I do?"

"There's notches. If you take off those silly shoes you wear, you can feel them with your feet. It's just like a ladder, only a little more slippery."

"I don't know about this, Cora."

"That's probably for the best. Now go."

I used my toes to take off my shoes. My right one fell on the ground, but my left one fell into nothing. A second later I heard a dull thump. Not a second: two seconds.

I said, "Two seconds. Cora, that's twenty feet."

"It ain't no twenty feet, girl, it's more like ten, and besides, what's the difference? Don't fall and you won't get hurt."

I stopped protesting then, realizing that if I kept it up I'd succeed in psyching myself out. And I really wanted to see what was down there. Well, not see. Feel, hear, experience. I thought of Jimi Hendrix, and his zit-spotted face. My father told me he had used drugs, that's why he'd had acne even as a grown-up. That's why he was dead. I tried to imagine Marsha Johnson's baby's face too. Eric Johnson. Some people said his father was a white man, but my father told me Eric had been born out of wedlock, and that's why he looked the way he did.

"Webbie?"

I grabbed the pole with both hands. I stepped out, felt around with my right foot until I found the pole, a notch to rest it against. The bump was smooth, fit into the arch of my foot. My left foot went out, and then I was hanging off the pole.

"Here goes nothing."

"Here *you* go," Cora said. Her hand found my head, a finger landed right on the thin line of bare skin between the two plaits of my braids.

I slipped down, her hand slipped away. I went slowly. It wasn't hard at all. My feet went down first, then my hands. Feet, hands, feet, hands. I'd done this on the monkey bars at recess, on a rope hanging from the ceiling of the gym. I was skinny, agile. I was wearing shorts. I could do this.

The pole vibrated as Cora swung onto it above me. I heard the sounds of her descent. Something ripped.

"Shit!" she said.

"Don't you dare!" I giggled.

"Now who's being sick?" Cora asked. "I snagged my dress."

"Well, *I* didn't make you wear it."

"*Girl,*" Cora said, and then she was silent. There was a second quick rip, and then the sound of her continued descent.

Finally, ground. I didn't trust it at first, tamped around with my feet while still clinging to the pole, but it seemed solid enough, nothing slithered and hissed away, no bones cracked. I stepped away from the pole, immediately tripped over something soft, and I screamed as I fell on my ass. The smell of ash and sweat filled my nostrils, an odor so rank that I screamed again.

"What!" Cora yelled. "What's wrong, Webbie?" I heard her scrambling down the pole. Scrambling toward me. For just a moment I exulted in a feeling of helplessness and rescue. "Webbie, girl," Cora called, "where you at?"

I hadn't realized how dark it was until Cora spoke, and I realized she was on the ground with me. I could see nothing, absolutely nothing. In a small voice I said, "I don't know."

And Cora was there. She stepped toward me, her foot landed half on my ankle, I screamed one more time and she fell down beside me. She put a hand on my stomach and squeezed, as if making sure I wasn't a wraith.

"Girl—" she began, but the sound ended in a spurt of laughter. I laughed too, and then we lay there for a long time, just laughing, breathing heavily, laughing and breathing.

Finally, I spoke. "What's that smell?"

"One thing at a time, girl, one thing at a time. First off, you okay?"

"Well, you stepped on my ankle, but I think it's okay. It's, I'm fine."

"Okay," Cora said, her voice still serious and thoughtful. "That smell," she sniffed, "is ashes. And *that* smell," she said, sniffing again, "is sex. You tripped over a blanket and landed your ass right in somebody's campfire."

"Oh, gross. You mean I'm covered in ashes? My daddy's gonna kill me."

"You ain't the one wearing the white dress. Shit," she said, "ripped *and* stained. Ain't that a sight. Oh well," she said, "you just leave Reverend Abraham to me."

"Cora—" I began, but her voice cut me off.

"My sins have been washed clean in the blood of the Lord.

Now I clothe myself in the beauty of His Word."

Her voice filled the cave, bounced back and forth off the walls, more blues bar than church choir, though I didn't know that then. I waited until the silence had managed to reassert itself, then said, "I don't know that song."

Cora giggled. "I just made it up. The Reverend won't recognize it either, but he'll be too embarrassed to admit it."

I giggled too at the thought of my father, fooled. I laughed aloud, my head thrown back, my mouth wide, tasting ash on my tongue. My father, the fool. My elbows, propping me up, were embedded in something soft, ash, I supposed, though it felt slimy. Cora's hand was hot and heavy on my stomach, and my right ankle was crossed by Cora's left. I wiggled mine.

"That you, girl, or some Indian ghost come to take revenge?"

"I'm not doing nothing," I said innocently.

"In that case—" The sand shifted beside me. Before I realized what was happening, the hand that had been on my stomach slapped down on my ankle. I screamed again, fear and delight, as she yanked my ankle and rolled me over and away from her.

"Cora!"

Cora giggled. I heard her scrambling across the cave. The echoes made the sound impossible to trace.

"Cora, where are you?"

More giggling. The sound seemed to hang physically in the air, like a layer of smoke. I stood up slowly, to hear it better, but before I could straighten fully my head hit something soft but unyielding. Cold dry soil filtered down the back of my shirt. Yet again, I screamed.

"Cora!"

Nothing now. Nothing at all. I couldn't even hear her breathing, though my own gasps rent the air.

"Cora, please, I'm scared."

Still, silence. Silence and nothing. Quickly then, or I knew I'd start crying, I began to move. I knew the cave was small, hardly bigger than my father's living room, smaller than the dais at church. I had been told this. The bellystones were gone, the skeleton bundled up and carted off somewhere. The worst thing I was likely to trip over was a beer can half filled with stale beer and soggy cigarette butts. I knew this.

I stepped slowly. It wasn't really walking, it was stepping, one trembling foot after the other, head held low to avoid the roof, step, and step, and step. I tried trailing a hand above my head, but that knocked grit into my hair and on the back of my neck, so I held them in front of me, like a blind woman would—I *was* blind—and I stepped forward.

Step, and step, and step. Cora refused to make a sound. I could hear her thinking, though. Come this way, she was thinking, I want to be found.

I didn't call out to her. I didn't say anything. That wasn't what she wanted. She wanted me to find her. I was finding her. My hands hit a wall, or, rather, my right hand hit a wall but my left continued forward another foot or so. I moved it around, found the margins of the space. It was the size of a bread box. I knew what it was. It was empty now, but I knew it had once contained a bellystone.

I made my way along the wall until I found a corner. The cave was rectangular. Four walls, and I stood at the intersection of two of them. I walked the length of the second one. My foot tripped over something hard, metallic, round; it crunched and sloshed as I stepped on it: a beer can, half full and stuffed with soggy cigarettes.

I reached a second corner. I turned, walked down the third wall. My hands passed over the empty space of niches. Some were small, the size of toasters, others as big as ovens. I didn't have to check to know that they were all empty. I knew they were empty. It saddened me a little, not the fact that they were empty, but the fact that I couldn't even pretend one of them might still contain a bellystone.

A third corner, a fourth wall. I turned. It was only a few steps before I felt something where I knew nothing should be, nothing that was part of the cave.

"Cora?"

She didn't say anything, but her stomach moved in and out under my hands. The sound of her breathing came to my ears. She put her own hands forward, and used them to cup the undersides of my breasts, but she didn't say anything.

"Cora," I said again. It wasn't a question this time. It hadn't really been a question the first time, I realized, it had been a request, though I didn't know what I'd been asking for.

Cora did. "Girl," she said, and it was all she said, but it was all she needed to say. Her voice was thick and hoarse and there was nothing else she needed to say, and what I thought was, poor Sawyer.

My hands were still on her stomach. I'd felt the one word form there, *girl*, the tremblings, vibrations as they bubbled up and out of her.

"Is this where you did it, Cora? Is this where you fucked?"

Suddenly her hands leaped from my breasts to my wrists. She clasped them tightly, but all she said was "Girl!"

"Did you fuck here, Cora? Is this where you fucked?" I didn't need to ask. I already knew, as much as I knew the size and shape of the Cave of the Bellystones, as much as I knew that there was no such thing as buried treasure and that the hands that had held my breasts and now held my wrists had once held Sawyer Johnson's cock, his dick, his tool, his prong, rod, prod, shaft, his, his, his johnson.

Poor Sawyer, I thought again. Poor Sawyer, poor Marsha, poor Eric, poor everyone who would feel this awful, awful desire.

I flipped my hands around, and then I was holding Cora's wrists. I twisted the skin in my hands, twisted back and forth. In school we called this an Indian burn because it made your skin turn red, but Cora's skin was already red.

"Ow! Webbie—"

"You got to tell me, Cora, tell me and I'll let go."

She was bigger than me, older and stronger, but she only pulled weakly at my wrists. "Webbie, please," she said again.

"Tell me, Cora," I said. I said, "I found you, and now you got to tell me."

"Yes!" she said then. "Yes, okay, yes."

She pulled away then, she had answered me, we were even and she could pretend to be in charge again. The sound of our breathing filled the room. When she pulled her hands away from me, I knew that's how it would always be for me. I would not do things. I would know things. I would find them out.

"Let's go," Cora said then.

"I got to find my shoe."

We felt around the floor. Cora gave up after a few minutes, said that we'd never find it, but I knew how big the room was, I knew everything that was in it. I patted my way across the floor, slowly, carefully, I knew now that I could find anything if I only looked carefully enough. My shoe tried to hide—it was half filled with sand, buried under a blanket—but I found it, emptied it. I couldn't wear it as I climbed up the pole and the pockets of my shorts weren't deep enough to hold it, so I tucked it into my waistband. The rubber of the sole was cold against my stomach, but in the time it took to climb the pole—"Over here, Cora," I said, "this way"—it warmed, became hot even, even hotter than me. My other shoe waited at the top of the pole, and I slipped them on, one hot, one cold. It felt odd for a moment, but on the walk home they both returned to normal, a little scuffed maybe, but otherwise just the same.

2.19

Justin

LISTEN: THE NIGHT WAS COLD AND THE SKY WAS CLEAR and the frosted ground broke under our feet like ice. Listen: the roads were straight and narrow, as you would expect the roads in Galatea to be, and they moved us inevitably toward our destination. Listen: my name is Justin Time, and now it's time to say goodbye.

"You're drunk," Lucy said.

"Yes, I am," I said tersely.

"You're not old enough to drink."

"Yes," I said, "I am."

"I don't know why you talk to me like that. I'm not, like, as, as . . ."

"Naive," I said.

"As naive as you think I am."

I tried to take the edge out of my voice, but I said, "Yes, you are."

"Well, so what? Is that so bad?"

"Only you would know the answer to that question."

"It's terrible!" Lucy said then. "I want to *know* things, I want to *do* things. I wanna have some *fun*."

"Do you think that knowledge and action are necessarily fun?"

"Huh?"

"Well, say, what if you go out looking for *knowledge* and you meet a man and he's very sweet to you, he kisses you on the neck and buys you perfume and clothes and jewelry, and then he asks you to live with him forever."

"Great!"

"And then he pulls out a knife and rapes you and carves X's into your nipples, not deep enough to scar, just deep enough to bleed."

Lucy was still smiling when I finished speaking, but then her face, a moment behind my words, clouded, and a long thin plume of breath escaped from her mouth. "You're sick. You are, like, totally sick."

"And you've learned something."

"That is *not* what I want to know. I want the first half of the story, not the second."

"I know what you want. You want to inherit a fortune without anyone having to die. You want to build a castle without ever lifting a brick. You want to have children without ever giving birth."

"I take it back. You're not sick. You're just really, really mean."

"And you're a fast learner."

Lucy sighed again. "Look, why're you being so mean to me? I mean, I thought we were on a date and all. It's okay if you're not, like, into me, but—"

"Lucy, I'm a fag."

Lucy's shoulders bunched up then, but she tried to pass it off as a shrug. She affected nonchalance, which is to say, in her case, that she pretended to be bored.

"I know."

"Colin is my lover."

"I *know*," she said again, and then, after a moment, her eyes went wide. "Did he? The knife?"

"Do you think I'd still be with him if he had?"

"Oh, right," she said. She looked almost disappointed. "But it really happened? I mean, someone. . . ."

I nodded.

She looked away from me then. "Something bad happened to me once," she said, so quietly that her words almost disappeared into the sound of our footsteps. I looked up suddenly, surprised to discover that we were out of town now. Frozen fields unfolded on either side of us; Lucy's house was a mile ahead, the limestone house a mile beyond that.

"Your mother told me," I said.

"Told you?"

"About Eric Johnson."

"She *told* you about Eric Johnson?"

"She told me you lied."

"Why, you little faggot!"

Her purse caught me square in the face, and I nearly fell over. I stumbled backward, both hands over my face. "You bitch!" I yelled through my fingers, and when I took them away I saw Lucy facing me, arms akimbo, tiny breasts heaving inside her coat, breath steaming and iridescent in the night light. She was sobbing.

"Oh shit," I said. "I'm sorry. I didn't mean to sound like I was blaming you for . . . I know you didn't mean for it to happen." Actually, I didn't know that, but I wanted to give her the benefit of the doubt.

She just stared at me for a moment, and then she wiped her eyes with the back of her hand. She withdrew a tissue from her purse and blew her nose. She turned then, and started walking again, and I followed. We didn't speak for several minutes. The porch light on Lucy and Myra's house came into view. The branches of a leafless mulberry tree beside the road creaked and clacked, and occasional gusts of wind slithered through the grass in the ditches and fields. And there were our footsteps, and the ground like breaking glass, and the sound echoing back and forth between the trees. I lagged a pace behind Lucy, watching her long white-stockinged legs wobble each time the heel of her shoe stabbed the dirt of the road, and only when I caught up to her did she begin speaking.

"I don't know *what* I expected to happen," she said. Her voice was slightly uneven, snuffly. "I mean, I was seven and all, I didn't really realize what he'd done—I mean, what he could have done. I just knew that it felt bad, and I wanted him to stop."

I wanted to ask her questions, the kinds of questions I could ask someone in New York, but I felt, suddenly and clearly and for the first time, the awful weight of the silence that seemed yoked over everyone in Galatea. Still, I fought against it. I said, "You're saying it really happened."

Lucy didn't answer me immediately. When she did speak, her words came slowly, deliberately. "He was the ugliest thing you ever saw. You ask anyone, they'll tell you. Even my mom once said he had a face like a plate of mashed potatoes left out overnight. And I was just staring at him that day, I couldn't get over how ugly he was, these big cracked puss-oozing lips and beady bloodshot eyes, and that hair, I mean, it was just like those black girls that bleach their hair orange, only even uglier, and frizzy too. And his skin. You ask anyone, they'll tell you, Eric Johnson—oh!"

Lucy pitched forward as if thrown. She fell, tumbled, sprawled across the ground. I turned, saw a human shape that seemed twice as big as mine, and then I caught a fist in my face. I don't remember falling, I just remember a steel-toed boot catching me in the ribs, and in the silence I heard them crack beneath my coat and my skin. I lost my breath then, but not consciousness, and I saw the same boot kick Lucy. The boot kicked her in the chest, it kicked her in the stomach, it kicked her in the crotch—and I focused on the boot because I recognized it. The boot belonged to Colin. Like me, Lucy was unable to speak or even breathe for a moment, and the only sound was Colin's boot striking her body, and she pitched about with each kick, and the man's great black coat flapped about like the wings of a hobbled angel. The coat was a bat's wings, a dragon's, the coat was the shimmering trail of a jet plane rending the sky. The coat was Colin's, and all the sudden my breath returned in a long sob of pain like a newborn's first cry, and the man turned at the sound. I saw Lucy convulsing, and I saw, for the first time, his head: his head was covered by a white sack with two holes punched out for the eyes. His hands—gloved in Colin's gloves, in tan lambskin as soft as a fresh-shaved cheek—his hands dropped on me like crane buckets, one on my throat, one on my testicles, he palmed me with them and he squeezed, suffocating me, crushing my balls. I tried to writhe away and I tried to strike him but my body was useless to me. My body has always been useless against Colin's. In what seemed like seconds purple spots began to glow in the night sky. I was virtually unconscious when he lifted me, and then I was above his head like a trophy. The pain in my balls was unholy: it seemed older, somehow, than my body itself, and I couldn't remember what breathing was like. For a moment all I saw were twigs patterned across the sky like torn lace, and the stars beyond them, and then I felt my body slip in the man's awkward grasp, and I saw a long thin gold crescent where the black of the land met the black of the sky. Rather than attempt to recover me he threw me away, and I almost didn't realize I was airborne because I was so busy breathing, and then the frozen ground knocked me out.

When I opened my eyes my mouth was stuffed with something and my limbs wouldn't move and our attacker lay over Lucy's body. All his weight seemed to rest on his right hand, which cupped Lucy's throat as he'd cupped mine, and his thumb was shoved in her open mouth. Her coat was open, her dress simply gone, and the shredded mess of her tights looked somehow worse than her torn skin. He was raping her already, and though something dark and shiny—blood, I suppose, Lucy's blood—covered his penis, it was still the only part of him that was visible, and it was white, and even through everything else I still recognized that Galatea had changed me, because, before coming here, I would not have noticed what color his penis had been, unless it had *not* been white.

With his left hand he was repeatedly smacking Lucy's face. He was smacking her just hard enough to keep her awake. I must have made a sound then, because he turned his covered face to me for a long moment, but he didn't stop raping her, and he was still looking at me when his body twitched and shuddered with his silent orgasm, and then he fell on top of her, and he knocked his sack-covered head into hers again and again, a horrible thumping noise like two blocks of wood striking each other, proving that this was no scarecrow with a head filled with straw. He sat up and he smashed her body against the ground. He stopped suddenly, and in the silence I heard my own gagged sobs. He dismounted Lucy's body slowly—her body didn't move, it just didn't move—and he scooped his flat hands under her and slung her over his right shoulder. He walked unsteadily toward me then, Colin's boots and Colin's pants, and when he got to me he just stood above me for a moment, Colin's shirt and Colin's coat, and he swayed slightly, Colin's gloves, Colin's necktie, he swayed like the branches above his head, Colin Colin Colin, and I knew I was being told to remember this moment. He fumbled in his pocket then, he pulled out something. He pulled out a mirror, the side-view mirror of a car door. He maneuvered it until something in my eyes must have let him know that I could see my face, the face that he wanted me to look on for the last time, the face that I was looking at when he fell on me. The weight of his body and Lucy's body slammed his knee into my groin, and it seemed I vomited and began choking at the same time as he smashed the mirror into the place where Colin had smashed his fist so recently, and then I lost consciousness again. And what made it all worse was that no one uttered a single word during the entire attack, not him, not Lucy, not me. Lucy and I had tried to speak and failed, but our attacker hadn't even bothered to try, not word nor sigh nor prayer. Not even a grunt.

2.20

Webbie

I WAS ALWAYS AWARE OF THE FRAGILITY OF THINGS AS a child, of the process of decay. This is unusual; such knowledge is, I think, an adult preoccupation, not a juvenile one. Children, dimly cognizant of their own weakness against an inhospitable world, turn to their parents for support and protection. Gradually they lose this feeling as they mature, become stronger; they learn that the things they live with, whether china teacups or limestone fenceposts, are as subject to the erosion of time as they are.

But I was different. I always knew I was strong—*superior* is the word my father used when he wanted to chastise me; *pride* was the favored epithet among the Church Ladies, as in "Pride goeth before a fall." But my sense of pride, or superiority, or strength, was relative, rooted less in myself than in an acute awareness of the fragility of the things that made up our household. I remember the life cycles of dish towels, from starchy newness to stained but sturdy drying implements to hole-filled dust cloths to eventual end in the fireplace (the buildup of lemon Pledge made them excellent firestarters: one match and *whoosh!*), as though the entire process, which must have taken years, had happened in a sped-up film. I can see the new set of china we got when I was eight moving in with the remainder of our old set. The old china, almost every piece chipped or cracked, had an ornately drawn blue teapot in the center of every plate, saucer, or bowl (reminiscent of Wedgwood but marked Franklin Mint); the new china was simpler—my father had let me pick it out—and it had just three bands of gold circumscribing the ridge. A bit plain, if you ask me, Hope Rochelle had sniffed, but I persisted in setting the table with it anyway, so that all the place settings matched. Meals were never just my father and me in those last heedless years before Rosemary Krebs arrived; there were always the Church Ladies, and sometimes members of their extended families, or other members of the congregation; it wasn't until my father's stroke, and my return from Columbia, that we began eating alone. But the new china, like the old china, became old. The gold rims faded and flecked off, edges chipped, things dropped and broke into pieces. Soon enough—too soon, in my conflated memory—there were the few remaining pieces of the new china and the fewer remaining pieces of old china, and then it was time to buy china once again.

I was eleven; I remember because it was just a few weeks after I'd visited the Cave of the Bellystones with Cora Lewis. I remember cleaning out the cupboards to make room for the newest set of china, and at the back of one cabinet, a dark dry corner where we kept gunnysacks of potatoes and onions, I found a dust-encrusted plate which, when washed, yielded an unfamiliar pattern. A ring of roses, red once, but faded now to a pale pink, circled the plate, linked by a green vine that had once been continuous but that was now broken into pieces by faded patches. I looked at the plate: it sat in a sink of steaming water and shimmered slightly through the haze of mist and liquid. I took the plate out and set it with the others in the strainer—the new old china, the old old china, and this, the old old *old* china: my mother's china—and then I took the plate out of the strainer and I held it in my hands for a long moment, I stared at it, I memorized it, the way it was and the way I imagined it might have been once, brightly colored, flamboyant even, offering up spicy meals of jerked chicken and shrimp jambalaya, and then I let it drop on the floor. I picked up the pieces and I used a hammer on them, and when the plate had been reduced to a gravelly pulp I got out the rolling pin and I ground it down into a powder, a fine powder, nearly as fine as talc. The kind of powder that stuck to my fingers when I handled my father's bellystone.

I was crying by the time I had finished. I was eleven and I had just lost my best friend—things were never the same between Cora and me after our trip to the Cave—and now it seemed I had lost my mother for the second time. Full of remorse, I swept the dust up; I put it in a little plastic bag. For a long time I thought about making something with that powder. I would mix it with water, form a paste, I would work it up into a clayey dough and shape it into . . . what? An ashtray? A cup? Another plate? In the end I could never decide, and I left the dust in the bag. It's in a drawer somewhere. It is waiting, as I am waiting, and now Lucy Robinson is waiting, to be discovered, to be made whole again, made into something new.

3

3.01

Colin

HOW TO BEGIN? WHERE? THUCYDIDES BEGINS HIS ACcount of the Peloponnesian War by placing it meticulously in time, dating the harvest, the season, the reigns of certain kings and the lengths of certain treaties, and at the time I read his history I was struck by the contrast between his efforts and the simple line at the top of the page that had been added by the book's publishers fifteen hundred years later: "Outbreak of War, 431." Perhaps I should start there: On November 11, 1994, one hundred thirty-five years after the founding of Galatia, eighteen years after the incorporation of Galatea, seventeen years after her birth, ten years after the boy Eric Johnson was lynched, nine years after the death of Odell Painter and the disappearance of Gary Gables, eight years after Reverend Abraham Greeving's paralyzing stroke and the return of his daughter Webbie to Galatia, six years after the return of Wade Painter, eight years after the birth of Cora Johnson's son, four years after the arrival of Rosa Stone, two years after the death of Old Lady Beatrice, two months after the death of Eddie Comedy and the disappearance of Melvin Cartwright, one month after the arrival of Justin and myself in this town, and fourteen years into the AIDS epidemic, the girl, Lucy Robinson, was kidnapped by an unknown man who attempted further to implicate me in the kidnapping. It is in my nature to believe that the true boundaries of stories are births and deaths, but for once I will ignore my nature and say that this story, like Thucydides', begins with a declaration of aggressions. I do not know where it will end.

3.02

Lawman Brown

HE STAYED UP LATE AND DID THE MATH.

Originally he had planned on being a presence at Rosemary Krebs' mixer, but she vetoed that proposition right off the bat. She said she thought people was less likely to relax and unwind with what she called "a guard on duty," which Lawman Brown didn't quite like the sound of that, but hey, after the past few months he could use the night off.

It never was his best subject in school, math, but this was pretty simple math. It went something like this:

Five minus three equals two.

In school there'd been a harder kind of math which they called story problems. What made story problems harder was that they mixed up the numbers with a bunch of words so that what you had to do, first of all, was go through and pick out the numbers from the words, and then you had to go back through and figure out how the numbers went together so that you could make simple math out of them. According to that way of thinking the math went something like this:

Five men walk into the fields one night. All five of the men are wearing hoods over their faces and all five of them are carrying torches. All five are wearing shoes, for that matter, but, see, that's how they try to confuse you in story problems: they throw in extra details that don't really matter, not just the shoes, but the torches and the hoods and some rifles too, which in the end doesn't affect the main fact, which is that there are five men.

There was a sixth person there that night, not a man, a boy, but he doesn't figure into this equation. So you are left with five. This sixth person was also wearing a hood, but unlike the other hoods his hood didn't have no holes in it, zero, although the hoods that the men were wearing all had holes in them, in four cases two holes, in one case three holes, and through this extra hole, by Lawman Brown's reckoning it was the eleventh hole, through it came the one voice that was heard that night, and what that voice kept saying was "This is for Lucy, boys, remember that. This is for my daughter."

He wasn't supposed to say that, Stan Robinson, he was supposed to play along with the idea that none of the five men knew who any of the others were. But Stan went on and on about his daughter, his Lucy, and even if you hadn'ta recognized his voice or his tall skinny body inside that ghost costume sheet he was wearing, Lucy only had the one daddy, and there you were. And he didn't make much of a secret about it, afterwards. In fact, he let everyone in town know what'd happened that night, in the fields, with the torches and the hoods and the rifles and the rope, which was why everyone knew about it.

See, it gets hard to find the simple math when the problem is put in terms of a story. The story tends to take over. But Lawman Brown had had ten years to whittle away the story, all the different stories, and he had the numbers down cold.

The first number was definitely five.

What he didn't have down cold was the names that went with those numbers. Or, at any rate, all the names. What he had was Stan Robinson. Stan Robinson had let everyone and their mother know that he was number one. And then, well, number two pretty much had to be Odell Painter. And number three was more or less a shoo-in too: Eddie Comedy was number three.

Minus three.

That was what he had, so far, but what that meant was that there were two names, two numbers he didn't have.

Five minus three equals two.

He wrote it down. He had written it down before but he wrote it down again, he put it in a nice neat column. He wrote:

Stan Robinson
Odell Painter
Eddie Comedy
____
____

The two blanks were for the names he didn't have, and he stared at them, at the blanks, for a while, as if they might magically fill themselves in, and then when that didn't work he did something he'd never done before, which what he did was he wrote down the name Melvin Cartwright beside the name Eddie Comedy. And then above that he wrote the name Gary Gables beside the name Odell Painter. And then all the sudden he had a flash and he wrote down one more name, and two more blanks, and then what he had was this:

Stan Robinson–Sawyer Johnson
Odell Painter–Gary Gables

Eddie Comedy–Melvin Cartwright

___________–___________

___________–___________

The God's honest truth was that it was enough to drive you crazy, to look down at that list and suddenly realize what'd been going on by dribs and drabs and creeps and crawls and general subterfuge, right under his nose but so slow that even he, the man charged with preventing this sort of thing from happening, hadn't ever quite realized it was happening.

But who woulda guessed Sawyer Johnson? He was the kind of boy you could almost like, Sawyer Johnson, a real hard worker, a regular churchgoer, a family man—well, almost. He was the kind of boy you could almost feel sorry for, if you happened to know, as Lawman Brown happened to know, if you happened to have access to certain documents that only Lawman Brown and maybe Reverend Greeving had access to, documents which told you what his own wife had gone and done. Which didn't have anything to do with the problem at hand. But still.

The phone rang then, distracting him. It was always something, distracting him.

3.03

Cora

NIGHTTIME: TEATIME THEN BEDTIME, EVERY DAY NOW for four years. Sometimes she takes me straight to sleep. It's like that, like when she takes my hand she leading me somewhere, and where that is is sleep, and, you know, it's a long day's work between Sawyer and the café and we neither of us is as young as we used to be: sometimes sleep is all it takes to make us happy. But just as often we take the long road there, not like me and Sawyer used to, but not as different from it as I'da thought. But either way it's never a worry in the world, not at night, not in bed. Not with Rosa.

But on the night it happened—this'd be the night before everyone found out about it, the night we could all still claim innocence—Rosa stayed down in the café and made me wait up hours for her. I heard her down there, polishing up what was already shiny, smelled a pot of twenty-four-hour broth going on to simmer, and then finally I heard the click and rattle of the venetian blinds when she pulled them down, which Rosa don't ever pull down the blinds unless she really bothered by something. Looking back, I almost want to say she knew something was up, but that night I figured it was I'd come home from Rosemary Krebs' little dance thing smelling like cigarette smoke and liquor. The smoke was on my clothes—it was from other people's cigarettes—but the liquor was on my breath, and, you know, Rosa's a bit like Rosemary Krebs in that she don't hold with drinking, and I figured she maybe just needed a little time to cool off.

By the time she come up the oils in her tea had separated out from the water and floated on top in soft circles. I'd fell asleep but I woke up when she came into the room. Rosa. She musta been really upset cause what she did then was she put a nightgown on over her dress and then she let the dress fall out from under it, the dress and then her panties and her bra, but she kept on the little bootie socks she wears insteada slippers and when I asked her why, she just said her feet was cold.

In bed she turned out the light and put one cold hand in my warm one and she gave me a squeeze, which I took as some sorta invitation.

"Rosa," I said, "Rosa, honey, I'm sorry about going out tonight, but you did say it was okay with you."

"Oh no," Rosa said.

"Yes, you did, you said—"

Rosa squeezed my hand then, a nicer way of saying shut up than saying shut up.

"It's not that. It's not the dance. It's just."

"Just what, honey? What's wrong?"

Rosa's hand was all warmed up by then. I used the nail on my pointer finger to tickle her palm. She laughed a little but I could tell she was doing it just for me.

"Don't mind me, Cora. You know how I get sometimes."

"Well, I do know. It don't make me feel no better knowing, but I do know."

"Oh, Cora. My Cora. I'll be okay. I'm just a little outta sorts is all."

She squeezed my hand again, a long tight squeeze, but this time I didn't shut up. I didn't say nothing right off, but I did eventually, and what I said was "You know, maybe I could help you feel better, maybe I could feel a little better myself, if I just knew where you come from. What it was happened to you that made you come here."

"Girl, you been asking me that for years. For four years. Whyn't you say what you mean?" In the dark her voice sounded almost normal. You'd have to know her like I do to know something was missing—and you'd have to know her better than I do to know what to call the part that was missing.

"Where you come from?" is all I said again.

"What you mean is, where'm I going?"

"You going somewhere?"

"I ain't going nowhere."

"Then where you come from?"

"*Nowhere.*" She sighed now. She rolled onto her side, facing me.

"Nowhere," I said after her. "Then you ain't going back where you come from?"

"No," Rosa said, "I ain't going back there."

That was enough, that night. Anyway that was all she give me. I didn't never want to lose Rosa the way I lost Sawyer, but if I did lose her I didn't want it to be to the past. Go forward, away from me. That's what Rosa said when she blew the seeds off a dandelion puffball. She said it was something she learned to say when she was a little girl. But you see what I mean. Go forward, away from me.

3.04

Colin

HE WOULD NOT SIT IN A CHAIR. HE SAT ON THE FLOOR. He leaned against the wall. There was the wall, the one he leaned against, and there were three others, and there was the ceiling and the floor, and there was Justin. I saw him through a window set within one wall. I saw his arms, folded over his stomach. I saw his leg, tucked under his body, and his head, lolling against the wall. There was his closed mouth, and there were his open eyes, and there was blood all over him. Illuminating the entire scene was a single bare lightbulb, a hot glowing tear dangling from a frayed black wire which seemed to trail behind it like a streak of mascara. Directly beneath the bulb, Justin's foot tapped the floor. The foot cast a tiny shadow when it lifted up, but the shadow dwindled away to nothing each time the foot struck the floor. If it made any noise, I couldn't hear it.

He was big and burly, the man whom everyone called Lawman Brown. He was nearly as tall as I was and twice as big around, and his right hand never strayed from his holstered pistol for more than a few seconds; the other hand tended to sit on his belly. He sighed occasionally, heavily and sourly, as he padded around the station house; he moved papers, opened drawers, hummed a song under his breath, but he didn't say anything.

The song was "Leroy Brown."

I had not wanted to speak first. I had wanted Lawman Brown to set the tone of the scene; I'd wanted him to tell me what was going on, but the sight of Justin's battered body coupled with Lawman Brown's unending drone finally drove me to speak.

"Excuse me?" I said. "Sheriff Brown? I think Justin should be taken to a hospital."

Lawman Brown looked up from a tabletop. He squinted at me, as though trying to remember who I was and why I stood in his office. After a moment his eyes dropped back to the table and he resumed sifting the scattered pages there. "He can go to the hospital in a minute," he said. He picked up a note card, squinted at it, tossed it back on the desk. He drew himself up to his full height then, and regarded me with a thin accusatory stare. "He needs to answer me some questions first, and then we'll see about the hospital."

"Oh, Jesus Christ—"

"Mr. Nieman. Mr. Nieman, I would be most appreciative if you refrained from taking the Lord's name in vain in this station house."

"Will you *look* at him? He's shaking, he could be having convulsions. He's covered in blood."

"What I see," Lawman Brown said, not looking at Justin, "what I see is a shivering boy with what looks like some scrapes and bruises." He shrugged. "You'd be surprised at how much blood a body can spare, Mr. Nieman. But I tell you, Mr. Nieman. I tell you what. What I do not see is a seventeen-year-old girl who was last seen with your . . . *friend* here."

"Is *that* what this is all about? If I have to call my lawyer that badge'll be off your chest so *goddamn* fast—"

"*Mis*ter Nieman. Mr. Nieman. I asked you once about taking the

Lord's name. Please don't make me ask again. Now," he said, "you may very well be calling your lawyer later on this morning, but if I were you I'd let him get a good night's sleep, as I think you'll be wanting him at the peak of his abilities. And as for this badge." He took his hand off the butt of his gun to finger it for a moment, and then he returned his hand to his gun. "The only man who can take this badge off my chest is Judge Jackson Jameson Culpepper the Third, and J.J. ain't due back here until the Monday after Thanksgiving, when pheasant season opens. So if I were you."

For the first time I sensed something more than mere spite in his tone. "What are you getting at?"

Lawman Brown paused for a moment, and then he walked to a gray metal cabinet, unlocked and opened it, and pulled out a dark pile of cloth. He unfurled it, and then he said, "Mr. Nieman, do you recognize this article of clothing?"

"Of course I do. It's my coat." It was, in fact, the coat I had been unable to locate when I left for the dance, and I saw now that it was filthy, covered with dark wet smears.

"You sure about that?"

"Of course I'm sure."

"You can provide proof?"

"Well, I don't have the receipt on me, if that's what you mean, but I can assure you it's a twenty-five-hundred-dollar greatcoat purchased from Giorgio Armani in Beverly Hills. I sincerely doubt that anyone else in Galatia has a similar item of clothing."

Lawman Brown nodded, as if to indicate that he, too, doubted that another such item of clothing existed in Galatia, and then he said, "Mr. Nieman, this coat was found approximately ten feet away from your young friend in there."

"He must have borrowed it."

"He was wearing his own coat."

"Perhaps for Lucy."

"Miss Robinson was also seen leaving the party wearing a coat. Not this one." I started to say something, but he cut me off. "Mr. Nieman, I don't wanta act hasty or nothing. What I mean is, I don't wanta have to place you under arrest just yet, because I would *hate* to have to start filling out the paperwork at this time of night. But I would appreciate it if you would just sit tight and shut your mouth until I finish questioning young Justin in there."

"Why, you piece of small town shit."

"Mr. Nieman. Mr. Nieman, I'm real glad you said that. Now I no longer have to pretend I like you. So let me tell you. If that boy in there provides me with *any* reason to believe you had something to do with the disappearance of little Lucy Robinson, I'm gonna make you wish you'd never even heard the name of Galatea. *And may I remind you,*" he went on, and for the first time his voice betrayed a hint of nervousness, "sodomy is illegal in the state of Kansas."

He turned then, and placed my coat back in his cabinet, and locked it, and then he left the room I was in, for the one which held Justin.

Within minutes I heard shouts from the interrogation room. Lawman Brown's voice, not Justin's. There was no sound from Justin.

I went to the room's window, but Lawman Brown had drawn a blind on the inside of the glass. The shouting had stopped though, and I left the window to look for a phone. I found the line eventually: it led into the locked metal cabinet. Bastard, I thought. I suddenly wished that I'd joined the cellular phone craze, but even as I thought that my mind spun the thread out a little farther and I realized that even if I had bought a cellular phone I'd have left it at home when I went to the dance. In that tiny room, with Justin locked away from me, it seemed a huge defeat of my imagination, and I slumped into a chair. My head fell into my hands and I almost started crying; only the thought of Lawman Brown's imminent return kept me from giving in. For once in my life I could imagine no alternative, no escape route: every little story I conjured up led directly to the room I was in, and to Justin's battered body in the one next to it. I'm not sure if it's a measure of my delusion or of my despair, but the one action which could have averted this night—not moving to Galatia—never occurred to me at all.

Time dragged by. Minutes, hours, I couldn't tell. Eventually, in desperation, I pulled my journal from my pocket. I had meant to write an entry on the day—it seemed worthwhile, recording this day's events—but when I opened the book my eyes were caught by these words:

Most people have seven holes in their head.

It was something Divine had said a few nights ago, over dinner at Wade's house. He had said, "Most people have seven holes in their head, but Eddie Comedy had eight," and then he said, "Oops," and he said, "I mean, nine," and he collapsed in a fit of laughter. He had been very drunk that night, and I had been very drunk too, but I had remembered the line because it seemed like a good opening line for a scene, and I had scratched it down in my journal upon my return home. Now, looking at the line again, I suddenly found myself writing:

I only have six.

I had seven holes in my head, just like anyone else: I had two eyes, two ears, two nostrils, and a mouth. What I mean is, when I wrote *I only have six* I was not writing about me. I did not know anyone who only had six holes in their head; I wasn't even sure how one could be reduced to such a state, barring genetic abnormality, but nevertheless, I wrote *I only have six*. And then I wrote:

There are other ways I could introduce myself.

By then "I" was not even remotely me anymore: "I" was not Colin Nieman, and "I" was not stuck in a police station at two in the morning in the middle of Kansas, with the bloodied form of my lover locked in an interrogation room ten feet away. "I" was somewhere else. I wasn't sure where "I" was, yet, but I had only to decide. And then I was off:

> *Most people have seven holes in their head. I only have six. There are other ways I could introduce myself. I could offer my age, height, weight, eye color, I could describe where I was born or what I do for a living or I could just tell you my name, but, given the fact that none of these characteristics is in fact immutable or even particularly relevant, at least not to this story, perhaps all I should write is that instead of the usual seven holes that are in a human head, I possess only six, and, though it is not, as I have already stated, particularly relevant to our story, I will offer the little narrative which explains how this came to be. To be brief: a bad coke habit destroyed my septum, and, for all intents and purposes, I have only one nostril—*

A clunk shook me from my reverie. Lawman Brown was coming out of the interrogation room. He pulled the door firmly closed, gave the doorknob a little shake to demonstrate—to me, I suppose, as much as to himself—that the door was locked. I capped my pen as soon as I noticed him, folded my notebook closed. The ink was still wet and would probably smear, but I thought it best to close the notebook. As it turned out, I could have left it open.

Lawman Brown had locked the door, and now he stared at the notebook in my lap.

"Well, that's a fancy little book you got there, Mr. Nieman."

I shrugged.

"Nice pen too." Lawman Brown smiled briefly; I wasn't sure why. "I ain't never seen a book like that before, Mr. Nieman. What is it you do with a book like that?"

"It's a notebook. I use it to keep notes." I started to put it inside my jacket pocket, but Lawman Brown held up his hand.

"No, no, no, Mr. Nieman, don't put it away just yet. Such a fancy notebook, I'd like to look at it a while longer."

He began walking toward me then. One hand was on his pistol, as always, the other extended toward me.

"Maybe you'd even let me hold it. That's real leather, ain't it?"

I nodded.

"Well, I bet it's some soft leather. Could I? Hold it?"

"I don't suppose I have a choice."

"Everybody has choices, Mr. Nieman. Right now your little friend in there is choosing not to say anything unless I allow you in the room with him. Right now I'm trying to choose between letting you in there or letting him maybe think about his choice awhile, until, say, until the sun comes up and everybody can have a cup of coffee and not worry about being able to get back to sleep. And right now you're trying to choose between letting me see that fancy little notebook in your hand or taking a nap downstairs."

I held the notebook out to him.

Lawman Brown took it without comment. He didn't waste any time examining the leather: he flipped directly to the last entry. He squinted as he read, patted his pockets for, I assumed, reading glasses, didn't find them, and continued reading. It took him several minutes to read what I had written—I gave him the benefit of the doubt, and assumed that the ink had smeared—and while he read he glanced up at me often. At last he snapped the book closed.

"Well."

"Yes?"

"Well," Lawman Brown said again. "That is certainly something interesting to be writing. Given the hour and the circumstances."

I shrugged. It was the first thing he had said all night which I could not dispute, and I didn't see any point in making something up.

Lawman Brown peered at me again, and I realized with a start that he was looking at my nose, and when I swiped at it nervously he raised his eyebrows and nodded his head. Without bothering to ask, he took the notebook to the metal cabinet and locked it inside, and then he turned back to me.

"Well, I *never*," he said, and then he had to unlock the cabinet again, so that he could use the phone to call Nettie Ferguson.

Forty-five minutes later, Nettie Ferguson waddled into the station house, old and plump and arthritic. Silver cat's-eye glasses dangled from her neck on a waist-length chain and a bag large enough to contain a well-fed toddler hung off one rounded shoulder, and when I saw her I was washed with relief, because Lawman Brown had been humming "Leroy Brown" under his breath for more than thirty minutes, and I was beginning to believe that I might actually commit a crime after all.

"This better be good, Eustace, or I'm gonna give you heck come Monday morning." She noticed me then, and introduced herself. "Nettie Ferguson," she said, "pleased to meet you." She dumped her bag on a table and began to rummage through it. "Usually he lets everyone get a decent night's sleep, me, him, and whoever, and he takes care-a business in the morning. I believe I am quoting you, Eustace, when I say that no question was ever answered on a empty stomach or half a night's sleep." She turned then, holding in her hands an old-fashioned tape recorder spray-painted with the incongruous slogan *Danger—No Trespassing—by order of the Police Dept. of Galatea*. "Well," she said, "let's get this over with. Sooner he starts talking, sooner he stops, and we can all get back to bed. Why, Eustace Brown, what is the matter with you? I don't believe I've seen you look so anguished since that time your Silver got humped in the schoolyard when you was still at Kenosha High."

Lawman Brown had stood silently through Nettie Ferguson's speech, and now he cleared his throat nervously and said, "Nettie, I think you oughta brace yourself. This ain't the typical case of drunk driving or rowdiness out to Sloppy Joe's."

Nettie Ferguson turned to me and winked. "I seen it all in my day, Mr.—"

"Nieman," I said.

"*Oh*," she said, feigning surprise. "*You're* Mr. Nieman. I been wanting to meet you since I heard you was moving into the limestone house. Now, don't you run on outta here without you let me ask you a few questions first."

"Nettie," Lawman Brown said. "It's getting mighty late."

"Mighty early in my book. But whatever."

Again Lawman Brown hesitated, and then he spun on his heel with a loud rubbery squeak and led us to the room. His key slipped neatly into the lock, the doorknob turned without a sound. "Well," he said, entering the room, "Mr., um, Mr. Time, we're all here now."

In the presence of Justin's bruised and bloody body, even Lawman Brown seemed cowed, and it took all my strength not to go to him: I knew Lawman Brown would just make him suffer more if I did. Justin's face didn't register that he'd heard Lawman Brown. He stared straight ahead, at the two stumpy legs protruding from the floral print of Nettie Ferguson's dress. At the sight of Justin, Nettie's breath caught in her throat with a choking sound, and after a long pause she lowered herself cautiously, heavily, into a chair, and she stared fixedly at Justin's body.

"Nettie," Lawman Brown said, "you can start that thing up anytime now."

Nettie held her glasses to her eyes with one shaking finger—I think they shook even when she wasn't nervous—and then, after a bit of study, she used one swollen finger to start the tape recorder.

Lawman Brown said, "Any time you feel ready, Mr., um, Justin. You just begin at the beginning and tell it straight through, just like it happened."

Justin raised his eyes then. He raised them as he'd raised them five years ago, when we first met, and it seemed to me that he was remembering that moment, just as I was. He looked at Lawman Brown as he'd looked at me, blankly, unknowingly, and then he shifted his vacant gaze to me, and then he settled on Nettie. He smiled, just slightly, and Nettie squirmed slightly in her chair; if she'd been a Catholic I'm sure she would have crossed herself, but as a Baptist she had to be content with several deep breaths.

The tape recorder whined as it turned, like a dog worrying the boundaries of a chicken coop, and then Justin began speaking. His eyes hadn't changed, but his smile had opened and words tumbled out of him like marbles from an upended jar.

"Listen listen listen, for I will only say this once and then I will never speak again. He had the biggest hands I have ever seen, and the biggest body, and he wore your clothes. He made no sound. He moved inside our sound and then he stole our sounds from us. Our footsteps were his footsteps, our cries were his cries, but all our cries were silent. He came from behind us, but it was as if he came from inside us. It was as if *we* had made *him*."

At Justin's words, so obviously *composed*, no matter how distraught his tone or desperate his appearance, I found myself on my feet. "God damn you, Justin," I screamed. "Don't do this!" But Lawman Brown pushed me back into my chair, and Justin went on as though I didn't exist.

"He hit Lucy. He hit me. He kicked me. He kicked Lucy. He lifted me up. He gave me the sky. He threw me. He threw me away. He went on Lucy. He was *on* Lucy. He covered Lucy, and he covered himself. He covered us all. Black gloves, black boots, his pants were black, and the sack that covered his face was gray, but his dick-his dick-his dick was white."

There was a muffled sound from Nettie Ferguson, but Justin did not stop speaking.

"He finished with Lucy, finished her, ruined her, ended her, he lifted her to the sky and he showed her to me and he showed himself to me and he showed me to me, he showed us all ourselves and then he fell on me, he did and Lucy did, Lucy who was in his arms and I who was on the ground and then *I* was gone, and when I opened my eyes he was gone, and Lucy was gone, and I was gone again, and gone forever."

He turned to me. His eyes fixed on my eyes and went wide with something, with surprise, I think, or terror, or a memory of love.

Lawman Brown's eyes darted back and forth between us. "What is it, Justin, what're you trying to say? Are you trying to say Mr. Nieman? What, Justin, *what*?"

Justin did not take his eyes from mine, but the expression, whatever it had been, faded from his eyes, and then there was nothing there that I could make out. In his final act of communication he shook his head from side to side.

"He smelled like ashes," he said, and then I never heard him speak again.

3.05

Divine

I TELL YOU WHAT. THE FIRST TIME THAT MAN FUCKED me I knew all the reasons why. He didn't make one wrong move, just lay me down on the cold tile floor in his office like I was a sack of feathers he was about to take a nap on, and then what was the really fucking and I do mean *fucking* amazing part was that when he slid into me it was all different. It was . . . what? It was like he was pulling on a glove or something. Not one part of me from my head right down to my toes felt any further away from him than my asshole, pardon my French, but it was like *all* of him was going inside me and I was like just this skin he was stretching out and slipping on over his own—like I was still the sack but now he was the feathers, I guess, to get back to what I was saying before, and like together we made this *one* new thing. When it was all over he said, I hope you don't live to regret this, which I admit kinda flipped me out, and I figured the best thing I could do then was just leave. Which I wish to hell I had.

3.06

Cora

WHEN I WOKE UP THAT MORNING I NOTICED FIRST OFF that it was wintertime. Fact was Christmas was just over a month away, but the weather'd been slow in changing that year. There'd been hot spells in October, kids running around in shorts and no shoes, and Maven Getterling was still selling me squash, acorn, spaghetti, and butternut, come November. But that morning when I woke up I smelled Rosa's coffee downstairs and the first thing I thought was one blanket wasn't enough no more. There was frost on the windowpanes, and the clickety-clack of frozen branches against the north wall of the bedroom had that hard sound they get after the sap freezes under the bark, and for the first time that year I had the particular winter sensation of not wanting to get outta bed. Sleep's something I never quite reconciled myself to—the sand dripping out the hourglass of your life while you just lay there, deaf, dumb, and blind to it all—so you know that if Cora Johnson rolls back over when the alarm goes off then it must be mighty cold out indeed.

Sometime later I opened my eyes and Rosa's hip was warm against my arm. It was still dark, but the darkness was shot through with gray, just like Rosa's hair.

"Coffee," she said.

"Coffee," I said, and took the cup she offered me. It was strong, nearly as pale as she was with the condensed milk she stirred in. "Mmmm-

mmmm," I said, "thank you, ma'am." A few sips later I noticed the look on her face. "Rosa," I said, "you look like you run over the neighbor's dog. What's wrong, honey?"

"Grady Oconnor been by. Said he run into Nettie Ferguson coming home from the station."

"What?" I looked at the clock. "At five in the morning?"

"That white girl," Rosa went right on, "the one you told me about once, the one who—"

"Lucy. Lucy Robinson."

Rosa nodded again. "She gone missing. They think those men in the limestone house, they think they . . ." She took a deep breath. "They got the older one under what she called house arrest, which she said ain't the same thing as actual arrest. She said he can't leave town until everything's . . . sorted. The little one's in the hospital down to Bigger Hill."

The wind dropped off at just that moment, the branches stopped scratching at the wall. In the silence I could hear Sawyer's snoring in the next room. Sawyer's got asthma and the adenoids, and so when he snores it sounds mighty peculiar, but still, it's a kind of a comfort to me, that sound, cause it means he's still breathing.

For a moment I tried to fight it. "Missing. What's missing? She probably just went off with her girlfriends, or maybe her and Howard finally—"

"It ain't like that," Rosa said. "He, whoever it was, he . . ." She just shook her head, kind of sagged a little. "Grady said they out there, they, um, they scraping the road for samples."

Sawyer snored, the branches clacked against the window. Downstairs in the café a buzzer went off, breakfast muffins, corn and bran. Just a normal winter day.

"Samples?"

"Forensic evidence." It was like Rosa had to step away from herself just to say the words. "Blood," she said. "Semen. Tissue."

"Tissue?" At first I thought she was offering me a Kleenex, but she wasn't, she wasn't at all.

"Little pieces of her skin," Rosa said. "They scraping little pieces of Lucy Robinson up off the road."

3.07

Colin

BESIDES MY COAT, THE ROAD WHERE JUSTIN HAD BEEN found and Lucy had disappeared yielded up a synecdochist's treasure: boot prints, here and there, large and heavy enough to have left their stamp in frozen earth, fiber samples, frayed white filaments from Lucy's stockings, torn purple swatches of her dress, coarse black threads from my coat, and hair samples as well, long brittle black strands that were clearly Lucy's, shorter softer brown strands that were Justin's. Lawman Brown seemed to find the lack of any third type of hair significant, and when I asked why he found this significant he looked at my head and he said, "Well, Mr. Nieman, it looks to me like you don't got no hair." There were ashes, so many that it seemed they had been scattered on the ground deliberately, and there were Lucy's shoes, still buckled. There was blood, hard brown shiny beads scattered across the road as though they had spilled from a snapped necklace, and there were other beads as well, other drops of frozen liquid, but they weren't brown. They weren't blood. Semen separates as it freezes; the heavier sperm settles to the ground in a thin white layer, the prostatic fluid sits atop it like a dollop of milky glaze. Lawman Brown used the blade of a pocketknife to scrape the three semen samples he found into three different evidence bags, and when I asked him why he separated the samples, Lawman Brown looked at me as though I had insulted him, and then, brusquely, he said, "Just in case." It took me a moment to figure out what he meant, *just in case*, but then I realized he meant *just in case* more than one man had attacked Lucy Robinson. He scraped the semen samples into separate evidence bags *just in case* Justin and I had done it together.

3.08

Divine

FOR THE RECORD: I DECLARE MY INNOCENCE IN THIS

matter. I didn't plan what happened, it just happened. I went over there to see if there was anything I could do for them, for *both* of them. Okay, okay, so I don't really buy that shit either, but the truth is I don't got a good reason for why I went over there. I mean, it certainly wasn't to get *fucked* or nothing. I *mean*. But Colin opened the door and his face was just so wild, so crazy, so hurt, I couldn't help myself, I gasped, and then Colin was grabbing me and pulling me into the house and pushing me ahead of him into his office. Tell the truth I was scared at first, I mean no one can work a phone like Nettie Ferguson and by noontime wasn't nobody in town didn't know about the question of his coat, and plus too and I mean of course there was what had happened out to Noah's ark, which I didn't know *what* had happened, exactly, but something like two weeks later I still had a lump on my head the size of a golf ball, which thank *God* my hair covered it up okay. But all the same I'd been wanting to get my hands on that man for so long, and, well, when he put his hands on me there was just this feeling in them, in the way they held me: saying no was *not* an option.

Like I was really gonna say no.

Oh okay, I admit it. Part of me wanted it to happen right there, right then, I mean so soon after. I'm not proud of that or nothing, but there you go. What I mean is, part of me went so far as to imagine I was Lucy Robinson and the tile floor beneath my head—expensive tiles, I couldn't help noticing, I heard tell that Old Lady Bea bought her those tiles off the floor of some castle in Europe—and there was a part of me imagined those tiles was a frozen road and it was pretty easy to close my eyes and imagine Colin's head stuffed inside some kinda sack, or something, Alma Kiehler who I got the story from, Alma was kinda vague about the sack part. Alma got the story from Cora Johnson who got it from Rosa Stone who got it from Grady Oconnor who along with DuWayne Hicks had been the very first people to get it from Nettie Ferguson, so you can see how things might get a little fucked-up in the telling. I mean, Alma even went so far as to say he whoever it was was wearing a Klan hood, which when I asked her why in the world would somebody put on a Klan hood to rape a *white* girl she didn't have no good answer for me, she just kinda shrugged and allowed as how she *thought* that was what Cora had said but maybe . . . This is what I told Alma: I told Alma that I expected they'd find out that the sack had been white and small and close-fitting, with just two little holes cut out for eyes, and not no big pointy-topped Klan shit.

I didn't mention the writing part since I didn't know what the writing said, or even if it was really writing.

Alma asked me how I knew what I knew and I just told her I know what I know, and left it at that.

Anyway.

I usually prefer to take care-a business on my stomach, you know what I'm saying. But Colin put me on my back, legs up in the air, and it was pretty clear that the reason didn't have nothing to do with comfort or fit or anything like that. He wanted me to watch him. He wanted me to watch him fuck me, and I did, and he stared right back at me and I swear to Christ he didn't blink once. He didn't have no lights on in the office where we did it, and even though it was broad daylight that house had a way of making its own shadows, and in the half dark everything was kind of creepy, halfway there I guess, halfway between being what they was and being something else, and just like part of me could imagine we was out on that frozen road another part of me could just as easy imagine that we was upstairs, you know what I'm saying, up in Colin's bed, silk sheets, soft pillows, big thick blankets and all that shit. And then like I said afterwards Colin said, I hope you don't live to regret this, and then I *was* scared, and kinda thrilled too, and if it hadn'ta been November I'da hightailed it outta there without no clothes on and run stark naked through town like those old time brides who used to hang the blood-stained sheet out their bedroom window the day after their wedding night. But I stayed right where I was, call it afterglow or some shit like, and a minute later Colin said, I'm going to the hospital to see Justin, which I hadn't even thought about *that*. Colin didn't ask me if I was staying or going, didn't ask me if I needed nothing, he just stood up and turned around and walked away from me, and I lay there and watched the fine shape of his ass until it was outta the room. I heard him go up the stairs, heard him come back down, heard the front door open and close. His car spit chunks of that obsidian against the side of the house when he tore outta there, and then that was it. Silence. Late-afternoon winter sunlight. A cold draft on my skin, a tightness on my stomach from where the cum, my cum, was drying. *His* cum was inside-a me.

It was the humming that got me up. It was one-a those quiet noises that seem to grow louder and louder and louder in your eardrums till you can't think about nothing else, like a ticking clock or water dripping out the faucet in the middle-a the night. I got up, looked around, and I mean, I tell you *what*. What a room that was. What a *fucking* room. It was about the same size as my parents' house, that room, and all it had in it was this like enormous desk at one end, mahogany I guess it was, with a black and white marble top, and this leather couch at the other end, which when I saw that shit I was like, why didn't you fuck me there, asshole, insteada bruising my delicate body on that cold-ass tile floor. Which my body, I noticed when I checked it out, my entire body was covered in little pieces of gold. Tiny little flecks all over me, and when I looked at the floor I saw that the whole thing was covered in gold, it was like confetti, you know what I'm saying, and at first I thought, what kinda crazy fool sprinkles gold dust on his floor, but then I got the idea to look up and I saw that, like, the ceiling in Colin's office was crisscrossed with thick dark wood beams and it was the beams that was flaking off all that gold, I guess they'd been gold-leafed by Old Lady Bea at some point but by the time I first saw them half that shit musta been on the floor, which by the looks of things Colin never bothered to sweep up. Like I said, what a fucking room.

I noticed the humming again, and right away I saw the source of it: an old electric typewriter on Colin's desk. I suppose there's nothing too weird about that, except right next to the electric typewriter was an even older manual typewriter, and both typewriters had sheets of paper sticking outta them, and then next to the manual typewriter was a notebook, and the notebook was open, and there was even a pen laying on top of it.

Well, what would you do?

What was in the electric typewriter was this:

> *Later on I wore a small padlock hanging from the hole in my nose. I don't know if the coke would have destroyed my septum on its own, but someone offered to do it for me. He was a big tall bald man; he said, I'll give you a thousand bucks if you let me have your padlock, and I was reaching for the key before he could get his wallet out. No, he said, no key. He put his hand on the lock, let what was left of my septum hold the weight.*

Well, I read that and I was like, oh *shit*! I'd never read Colin's other two books cause Webbie made them sound pretty goddamn boring, but this shit was okay. But then I looked at what was in the manual typewriter, and what was in the manual typewriter was this:

> *It happened in an alley. I had ducked into the alley to urinate, and I hadn't even finished when he grabbed me from behind. He threw me against the wall I had just wet, then pulled me just as roughly off the wall, and even as I turned to look at my assailant he pulled a hood over my head and it was only when I felt cloth enveloping the skin of my*

face that I panicked, and I made the mistake of standing up fully and slammed the crown of my head into the stone ceiling of the alley.

And then, well, then I looked at the notebook:

Justin—hospital, bring Bactrim
Gas
Lawman Brown
Wade
Ira and Wyn—how much is gram/coke?
Setting? Here? Mississippi? Morocco?
Motive?
Gun
Harrod's—more paper
IGA—lightbulbs, bleach
Dinner at "Big M"? Roast beef?

There was a little check next to Lawman Brown's name, and another one next to the name Ira, and another next to the coke thing, and there was a check next to the word *gun* too, and I was kinda wondering what I was looking at, like, was it a shopping list or a To Do list or was it like some sorta notes for whatever it was that Colin was writing, or some kinda combination of all three—and if it was a combination then where did what was real end and what was made up start? Like where, specifically, did the word *gun* go? And I was still trying to figure that shit out when I looked next to the notebook and I saw a little bag with what looked like typing paper sticking out of it, and I mean it wasn't just a little bag, it was—and I mean I just *knew* this, as sure as you know the sound your momma's footsteps make outside your bedroom—I knew that what I was looking at was the same kinda sack that'd been over whoever's face it'd been out there to Noah's ark, the same sack that'd covered whoever it was who held down Lucy Robinson on that deserted road which was probably a fuck of a lot colder than the tile floor in Colin's office. I mean, it was a plain white sack with a little cinch string along the bottom that you could use to tighten it around your neck, and there was stitching across the top of it too, thick dark silk threads which spelled out SUPERIOR BOND in such fancy letters that it was hard to read them in the bright light of afternoon, let alone in the middle of a field at night.

Next to the sack was a pair of scissors, and that was all I saw cause when I saw that shit I was outta there, and I mean O-U-T out, gone, goodbye, I mean get me the *fuck* away from that shit cause I do *not* want to know *no more.*

3.09

Cora

THE SUN WENT DOWN THE NIGHT AFTER LUCY ROBINSON disappeared. The sun goes down every night but you know what I'm saying. That night darkness seemed like a little bit of a blessing, a little bit of a curse too. The streets in Galatia is never what you'd call busy, but that night they was positively deserted. Talk about a ghost town: Galatia didn't even seem that alive. It was out-and-out dead.

Rosa closed the blinds again. She closed them slow, real slow, one by one, and then she made her way to the door. She looked through the glass for a long time, and then, reluctant, she flipped over the closed sign. She turned the bolt in the door last, a tiny careful movement that always ended with the heavy bolt clunking into place. She always tended to close up slow, with long looks outside as if she wished for just one more customer. At least that's what I used to think, till one day I asked her about it and she told me she hated the sound of a locked door. Said she was never sure which side of it she oughta be standing on. But that night, well, that night inside definitely seemed like the best place to be. It was kind of eerie, kind of, it was downright awful, me having Lucy Robinson to thank for another night of Rosa.

Sawyer was sitting at a table, breathless from the effort of pushing his toy cars across its surface. As Rosa come over to me she reached out a hand and ran it over his head, and as she pulled it away one of his cars left the table and traveled over her arm. Sawyer's lips flashed with spittle as he made the sound of the car's engine, and I gave Rosa a cup of coffee. That's how our day went: she made me the first one in the morning and I made her the last one at night.

"What's wrong?" she said to me, just like I said it to her that morning. "You look like you got ideas in your head."

"Oh, ideas." I shook my head, and heard a memory of the beads Sawyer used to put there.

Rosa took my hand, held it a moment, then put it back on the counter. "Tell me."

"I just been thinking."

"What you been thinking?"

"I been thinking that people ain't gonna be able to keep pretending that he had anything to do with what's happened much longer. I mean, there ain't no evidence. There ain't no proof. A *coat* ain't proof."

"Brish, brish," Sawyer said. I looked over and saw that there'd been a crash at the table. "Whoo, whoo, whoo," Sawyer said, pushing an ambulance to the rescue.

"There was the . . . other stuff." Rosa blushed a little.

The ambulance nudged the wrecked cars. They rolled over. "Putt, putt," Sawyer sputtered, and then "Vroom" as they took off again, repaired, unscratched, unscarred.

"Yeah," I said. "There's that. But I don't put too much truck in that I mean."

"What you mean?"

"I mean, I heard it that he was with Myra Robinson till midnight, and the way everybody's got it figured what happened happened right around that time. And so like then it could only go two ways. Either he was with Myra, or Myra's lying to protect the man accused of doing, of doing *that* to her daughter. And you know I tell you. Last time—the *last* time this happened I didn't have my Sawyer, I could kinda believe folks when they said that maybe Myra, and Stan, Stan too, maybe the two of them was making something up to protect their daughter. But now I know that you can't, you just *can't* do that to flesh of your flesh, blood of your—girl, why you looking at me like that?"

Rosa had a funny-sad expression on her face, and I couldn't tell which half was covering for the other half.

"Girl. Cora. Cora, honey, I know you think everybody cares about they children like you care for Sawyer. But."

"But."

Rosa didn't finish the thought, and I didn't either. I guess I knew well enough what she was saying.

After a minute Rosa squeezed my hand again. She stirred her coffee but didn't drink from it. "What you think gonna happen?" she said. "If you right, I mean. About Colin Nieman."

"That his name? Nieman?"

"Nieman. Means No-man. In German."

I didn't bother to ask Rosa how she knew that.

"Well, come on, Rosa, you know as good as I do. White folks don't like to blame their own, even if they, if they gay. It's just a mattera time before they come looking around this side-a town."

I suppose it must seem funny to you, me saying something like that to Rosa. I mean, she being white and all. And it's not like I ever forgot she was white, no matter how she talked. But all she said was I know, I know, like the ways of white folks was as strange to her as they was to me.

"They ain't no more Eric Johnson to blame," I said. "Ain't some poor boy who nobody's gonna defend. And I'm scared. This time it's gonna be all of them against all of us. This time it's gonna be like, like a, like—"

"Like war," Rosa said.

Well. *Like hell* is what I was thinking of, but *like war* pretty much fit the bill too.

"Brish, brish," Sawyer said, as the cars, one in each hand, crashed into each other all over again. "Whoo, whoo, whoo" went the ambulance, speeding, once again, to the rescue.

Rosa jumped a little at the noise. "Well. Well, well. It's been a mighty full day. I think I'll turn in."

"Whyn't you take Sawyer on up with you. I'll just finish down here."

"Cora?"

Rosa took my hand again.

"No, no, baby, I'm fine. I—" I sighed. "I just need a little time to sort things through."

Rosa nodded. She smiled. She let go my hand, but slow.

"Sawyer, honey."

They went.

A restaurant's a great place to think when it's closed. You know, all those empty chairs, those bare tables: they need people at them. If they ain't around your mind fills them in. And you know, I had choices. There was more than one person I might wanta think about. But one boy pushed all those others outta his way, in death just as he had in life.

That boy, Eric Johnson, was Sawyer's nephew. He was ugly, smelled bad, and seemed to know how to do one thing only: eat. I never seen anyone who could put away more food than that boy could, except of course T. V. Daniels, but that's a whole nother story, a great big novel even. Oh, they said he was a thief, Eric, and I suppose he was, but to the best of my knowledge he never stole nothing but food. Certainly he hung round here a lot, where there was always a lotta food. The restaurant wasn't open then—I didn't open till after Sawyer gone, and Sawyer didn't go till after Eric did—but I always liked to cook, and many's the time I turned round to catch that ghost running out my kitchen with a pie or a pan of brownies. Once he made off with a whole plate of fried chicken, me and Sawyer's supper and lunch the next day too, and I woulda wrung his neck the next time I seen him if it wasn't bigger round than my hands. Oh, he was big all right, but he was quiet too: that boy learned from a early age that he was a whole lot better off if people didn't see him coming or going, and damn if history didn't prove him right. Every once in a while you'd hear about some peculiar bit of strangeness he got up to, like the time DuWayne Getterling caught him in a open grave—DuWayne's Aunt Baby was due to end up there a couple-a hours later—but I just asked DuWayne, Was he eating something? and sure enough, he was eating a bowl of macaroni and cheese he took from the wake table. Well, I said, you wanta hide on the open plain, a hole in the ground's about as good as you gonna get.

Sometimes I'd catch him before he could get away, and then he'd stand there with his hands full of whatever. One time, I remember, one time it was a bowla candied apples that was supposed to go into a pie.

"Uncle Sawyer said I could have some," he said, not scared, but testing me. He was squinting, but I knew that was cause his pink eyes couldn't take the sun. Whatever. I don't really like to describe him cause it just ain't fair to the boy. He didn't make hisself that ugly.

Now, Sawyer was ten miles away in the middle of a field, and Eric and I both knew he hadn't said no such a thing. But all I said was "This ain't Uncle Sawyer's kitchen, is it?"

"He said I could have whatever I wanted."

"Ain't nobody can have whatever they want, boy. But if you want some-a them apples all you got to do is ask. But I bet they'd taste a sight better after I bake them up in a pie."

"I don't want your apples," he said, and spilled the bowl all over the counter and run out the door. But the minute I turned my back he was in again, stealing something else. And I'll say this for him: he always brought the dish back. I don't know if it was a attempt at good manners, or if he just knew there wouldn't be no more food if I didn't have something to cook it in. But he always brought the dish back.

Anyway, I guess what I'm driving at is, he was weird, but it never struck me as nothing out of the ordinary, at least not given the circumstances. I mean, life had never been easy for him in Galatia, but by then Rosemary Krebs and her crew had made it clear they not only intended to stay where they'd settled but take over the entire town, and it seemed that everybody on both sides of Highway 9 needed somebody to take out their aggressions on. Poor Eric: he was like a bowling pin waiting to be knocked down. And, you know, Reverend Abraham wouldn't want to admit it but menfolk messing around with females that're smaller than they is ain't exactly unheard of, even in a sleepy town like Galatia—and that sort of thing always brought up the question of who Eric's father was, but Marsha, Sawyer's sister, Eric's mother Marsha was too busy drinking to tell anybody that. So Eric had two strikes against him from the start, but he wasn't dumb: he knew what he could and couldn't get away with. He spent so much time round here cause he knew me and Sawyer was softhearted, too wrapped up in each other to worry that much about a missing can of green beans or a hand-sized gouge out of a pan of cornbread.

I'm trying to add it all up, see, just like I did then, and just like I did then I get the same answer: it's not that Eric Johnson *couldn't* do something like bothering with Lucy Robinson's privates, but I think he wouldn't. Eric Johnson may have had white skin, but he was a nigger as far as white folks is concerned, and every nigger knows which way the wind blows when you're hanging from the lynching tree. It blows back and forth, back and forth, and once it starts it don't never stop.

3.10

Colin

BEFORE I DID ANYTHING ELSE WITH DIVINE, THERE WAS something I had to be sure of. He waited a few days before coming over again, and when he did come he didn't call, just knocked at the door and stood there silently when I opened it, a sheepish grin on his face, his eyes aimed at my midsection.

"I want to read you something."

Divine looked up at that, and at first I thought I saw fear in his eyes, but a moment later it passed. He looked at the book in my hands for a moment, and then he cleared his throat and said, "Read away."

"My name is Colin Nieman, and I swear that this is the truth. Once upon a time—"

"Wait a minute," Divine cut me off. "You reading that, or are you telling me?"

I just looked at him.

"Oh," he said, "this is *your* book, ain't it?"

"This is my book," I said. "This is *Beauty*."

Divine didn't say anything to that, and after a moment I looked down at the page again, even though I could have recited the words on it from memory.

"My name is Colin Nieman, and I swear that this is the truth. Once upon a time I had hair on top of my head. My mother called me a true blond: my hair was the color of white gold, and she encouraged me to wear it long, longer than any boy I knew, longer even than most of the girls. I believe she encouraged the growth on top of my head as a distraction from the rest of me, for I was the ugliest child you have ever seen, fat, cross-eyed, buck-toothed, pigeon-toed, possessed of a posture and clumsiness rivaled only by certain invertebrates. Adolescence added all its usual woes to this unfortunate situation, and during those years my hair was my one consolation. It was long and never really thick, and I usually wore it parted in the middle and plaited into a single shining braid that hung down the center of my back. Sometimes, though, I wore it free, and on those occasions the wind would swirl it about my head. The strands flashed across my faulty eyes, and if I stood very still and let my vision blur then I could convince myself that I, like Jesus, was haloed in light.

"When I was twelve years old my parents separated; my father won custody of me, and the first thing he did was send me to a military school, and it was there that I made a series of discoveries which I contemplated on the long walks, and then runs, I took every morning. Morning's deserted hours were the only time I would exercise, for I couldn't bear to see people stare at my ponderous body wiggling and jiggling and huffing and puffing along its tortured path. One of the first things I discovered was that if I pulled on my penis it became hard, and that if I continued pulling then I could achieve a certain pleasurable effect which I don't think I need to describe. Then I discovered that if I beat up other boys they would leave me alone, and if I beat them up more than once they would do things for me. Finally I discovered that if I made other boys pull on my penis—and suck it, and take it up their asses—that, in the first place, it was more pleasurable than pulling on it myself, and, in the second, that the boys were even more willing to do things for me than when I beat them up. At the time I considered this state of affairs convenient but not necessarily useful, because I had nothing, really, for the boys to do. I only asked them to do what they were already doing: pulling on my penis, and sucking it, and taking it up their asses.

"All of these discoveries occurred during the same period that dark hair began slowly appearing on my arms and legs and chest and groin, and the blond hair on my head began to disappear, and by the time I was old enough to choose between college and a war I was completely bald and I had what amounted to a harem of boys who would do whatever I told them to. In my last week of boarding school each of these boys approached me in turn and asked to know where I was going, so that they could follow, and my reply to each of them was the same: why do you want to go with me? Because you are beautiful, each of them said, each in his own way and in so many words, but I believed none of them. I had lost my only beautiful feature—my hair—or, at any rate, I had lost the only feature I esteemed, and I sent them all away. I went neither to college nor to war, but instead, and, on my father's money, to London.

"But I never forgot what the boys had told me—what they had all told me—and this is what I realized. Have you ever wondered what happened to the ugly duckling who one day realized he was a beautiful swan? This: he was condemned to a life of swimming around a smelly pond pelted by stale bread crumbs thrown by gaggles of dirty children whose one desire seemed to be to wring the breath from his neck with clutching fingers. But the peculiar way I discovered my beauty also let me in on beauty's true secret. For most people, beauty is a source of weakness, an enslavement inside one's own skin to an adulation that is really hatred. But beauty *can* be a source of power: it is powerful in those who hate the very thing in themselves that other people consider beautiful. When, years later, I entered the gay world, I learned to think of this relationship in different terms: those who are imprisoned within their beauty are called bottoms, and those who use it to ensnare others are called tops, and those who don't possess beauty are, fortunately or unfortunately, called nothing at all."

When I snapped the book closed Divine jumped up. I looked at him, saw that he was shivering, but before I would let him come inside I had to know.

"Did you understand that?"

Divine's eyes flashed left and right, as if the right answer might be written on the walls of the limestone house.

"Could I maybe come—"

"Did you understand that?"

"You had blond hair?" Divine blurted out.

"I had blond hair."

He tried to laugh, but it didn't really work. "You was fat?"

"I was fat. I ate all the time."

"And you wore glasses?"

"I wear contacts now."

"I didn't real—"

"Did you understand *any* of that?"

Divine gulped. "Not a word."

I grabbed him then, by his shirtfront, and pulled him inside. With each word I'd read to him my desire for him had increased, and I started to push him down on the rug in the foyer. But Divine stopped me. He used one hand to take the copy of *Beauty* out of my hand, and he used the other to touch my erection through my pants. As he was kissing me I heard the sound of my book striking the floor somewhere behind him, and when he was finished kissing me, I said, "The floor's nice and all, but could we maybe use the *couch* this time?"

3.11

Divine

Dear Ratboy,

Well I ain't heard from you in awhile but I know how you always got things up in the air and are busy keeping busy so I'm just gonna assume things is going OK with you. Everythings okay here too, you know G. nothing ever changes here ever or maybe I should say the more things change the more they stay the same. You know, theres been a little of this and a little of that but nothing worth writing home about—ha ha.

Well I bet I can guess what your thinking, your thinking who was it this time. Well I tell you what this time it wasn't no hog shit smelling cracker like Howard Goertzen, no it wasn't, nor no cute but dumb nigga like that Melvin Cartwright—who speaking of which did I mention in my last letter to you that its starting to look more and more like it was him who put that ~~bulet~~ bullit threw old Eddie Comedy's head and then took off for parts unknown? OK so maybe there has been a little bit of excitment around here but you know niether of them 2 was so exciting that you miss them when they're gone, but thats neither here nor there, I was telling you about who it was this time. Well. You remember that man I told you about, that new one who just moved to town? Colin Nieman? (I think last time I wrote Neeman or something like that but N-I-E-M-A-N is how its really spelled) Well. I can't hardly write just thinking about it, my hand starts to shake and the pen like to fall out my hand and I tell you what even my butt starts to sweat, I guess all I can say is he was the best one since you Ratboy, the first one who knew what it was he wanted and how to get it and I hope you don't get no dumb ideas like maybe I'll go and forget you or nothing like that cause the truth is he was so good he was almost as good as you he was oh I don't even no how to describe it except to maybe just say that he was so good that it only makes me miss you more and more and more. You know you will always be #1 in my book and I hope you will please write or inish-e-ate (I don't know how you spell that word) contact sometime soon.

Your main squeeze,
Divine (a.k.a. Reggie, in case you forgot)

3.12

Cora

NOW SOME SECRETS, KNOWN AND UNKNOWN:

Nine years ago, when I was twenty-eight, I left the man I been married to for ten years because he would not give me a child. That man was Sawyer Johnson, and for ten years I made his breakfast, packed his lunch, had his dinner ready for him when he come in from the fields. I washed his dishes, washed his clothes, washed his body even, when he was too tired to do it hisself. And don't think I did this outta some notion of wifely duty. I did it cause I loved him. If I hadn'ta loved him I wouldn'ta married him, but I wouldn'ta married him if I hadn'ta thought one day he'd give me children. But we was young, he said, let's get a little older first, and we was poor, let's get a little richer, and we was having too much fun. And that man did give me pleasure: every night, sometimes in the morning too. And not just pleasure. He give me comfort too. He rubbed my hands when they hurt, and my feet, and my neck and shoulders, and every spring he picked the first flower he saw blooming and gave it to me. Sometimes he sat me up between his legs all through the dark hours of the night, his willy laying up against my backside, hard sometimes, sometimes soft, and he braided my entire head of hair for me, finishing up with a row of seven cobalt beads so their glass roundness cooled my cheek every time I turned my head. But I tell you that not once—not one time—did that man plant his seed where it could do any good, and the day after our tenth anniversary, after he kept me up all night long making futile love, I packed me a bag and took the money that until that morning I didn't realize I'd been saving for just this reason, and I caught the Greyhound bus to Kansas City. For seven days I put up in a motel room that had more different kinds of bugs in it than there are people in Galatia, until it was my time, and then I spent the next seven nights with seven different men. I met them in the blues bars, and I tell you what, it was hard some nights, giving up that music for a man who probably wouldn't even last till the first verse come back around. But I did what I had to do, and I come home, and when I got back here Sawyer didn't ask me nothing. But a few months later, when things started to get obvious, he tucked his pretty but useless tail between his legs, and nobody in Galatia seen hide nor hair of him since. He said one thing before he left. He said, I never did you no wrong. And let the record show: Sawyer Johnson never did me no wrong, and I give my son his name to prove it, and I wish to God he was his boy. I don't know if it was the name or if it was my eye in Kansas City, but Sawyer looks enough like my husband did that it answers any questions people might have. Not that they ask questions: nobody asks questions like that in Galatia. They just look at the three pictures over the counter: the first Sawyer, smiling with that mouth that been places, and me, staring with them eyes that maybe seen more than a polite woman should, and the second Sawyer, still too young to be blamed for our mistakes, and then they pick up that fifty cents they was gonna leave me, and they hide a dollar bill under their coffee cup instead.

After Sawyer, Rosa. They say some people can't live with other people, and other people can't live without them. I know which kind I am.

How Rosa know to come here I'll never find out, unless one day she decide to change her mind and tell me. She showed up one night towards the end of winter, four years ago plus I guess it was. She had a single suitcase in her hand and no more dust on her than you'd get walking to here from the I.G.A. No car in sight, and I hope you don't think there's a train that stops in this town. Am I too late for dinner? she asked me, like she come in every night.

Like I been expecting her.

I did what anybody'd do. I asked her what's her name, and what she told me was Rosetta Stone—Rose Etta Stone was how she spelled it, I learned later on. I don't read the Bible every night or nothing, but still, even I'd hearda the Rosetta Stone, but before I could think of the right way to ask her about it she asked me what's mine. Well, I said, and then I thought for a minute. My full name is Coretta Beech Tree Johnson, born Lewis, but you can forget about that right away, and about the Beech Tree too. That was just the sentimental idea of some old man who made his daughter give her daughter his mother's name, as if that might somehow honor a woman and a tradition that we the living had no knowledge of. I'd like to think this woman, Carved-Like-A-Beech-Tree, was a good woman, but for all I know she coulda had three eyes and a taste for the blood of young children, and I'd just as soon not carry that history around on my driver's license—and besides, who ever heard of a beech tree in Kansas? It seemed to me that I had about as much right to ask Rosa where she got her name as she had to ask where I got mine, and I wasn't ready for that yet, not so soon after Sawyer, and what I said was, Cora'll do just fine, thank you very much, and do you want gravy on your meat or just on your potatoes?

Sawyer left me his grandma's big house but nothing else. Everybody told me starting a café was a bad idea, what with Elaine Sumnertime's place over the road and Art Penny's down to Bigger Hill, but I figured most people I knew wouldn't mind saving a quarter here, fifty cents there, not to mention a whole lotta attitude, and by and large I was right. Still, a hundred and fifty people don't spend that much money eating out, and when I put up the Room For Rent sign folks said I was even crazier than when I opened the café. In a town with people trying to rent whole houses for a hundred dollars a month, who'd want to take a room in a house with a single mother and her four-year-old son? Well, thank you, Miss Rosetta Stone, for helping me prove them wrong again.

This is what she wrote on the little contract I had her sign:

Home Address: *none*

Length of Stay: ?

Age: N/A

Non-smoker.

At first she just lived here. Kept herself to herself. Bought a radio for her room and tuned it to the gospel station outta Bigger Hill. Mostly she knitted. Knitted enough blankets for a army hospital. Sometimes I stood outside her door, listening to the clack her needles made. My momma knit a lot when I was growing up, but the different thing about Rosa's knitting to my momma's was that Rosa could stitch in time to the music, which is some kinda feat if you ask me.

When it warmed up she started helping out in the café. No money, thanks, I just like the occupation. She taught me more than a few things about cooking: she knew more about Caribbean food than I knew there was to know, and she showed me how to use curry powder and cardamom and turmeric without making something that tasted like a tonic for the croup. Maybe I'd like it if she grew some herbs in the back garden? Sure, I said, no problem.

Now, there's a old dead hedge in the back yard. I guess it come in handy, kept the snowdrifts outta the back yard, give us some privacy, but it sure was ugly. Well, Rosa didn't just plant me some herbs, she planted morning glories in every color of the rainbow up and down that hedge, inside and out, and in weeks it was shot through with green for the first time in my memory, and then later with little bursts of flowers. Even my Sawyer, who don't like nothing except hot dogs, Coca-Cola, and Saturday morning cartoons, even Sawyer said Rosa done made the back yard a worthwhile place to be in.

Me, I just thought it looked pretty, like so much of what Rosa done. Like Rosa herself.

Rosa had planted just about everything which'll grow in the Kansas climate, and some things that don't too, basil and dill and rosemary and sage and thyme. She just used the little empty spaces in the garden. Me, I grew things like tomatoes and corn and potatoes, nice neat rows of useful vegetables planted in sensible rectangles of earth, but Rosa, she planted her herbs in little patterns, zigzags and spirals, and sometimes it looked like she just let the seeds fall from her hand where they may. I never really thought of a vegetable garden as being like pretty before, strong maybe, boisterous, and I'd always prided myself on a bit of a green thumb, but the thin greens of Rosa's herbs had offset my vegetables and so when she told me to lookit the garden one day I suddenly saw it all in a new light.

"Your herbs is coming up fine," I said. I said, "Where'd you learn so much about them? About herbs, I mean?"

That's when I learned you can ask Rosa any question except ones beginning with *where*. Later on I learned you can't ask her no questions that start with *when* either.

Home Address: *none*.

What Rosa did then, she didn't answer me. Instead she pulled a feathery sprig of dill outta the ground, and under cover of that blooming dead hedge she plaited a lock of my hair into a braid and wove that dill right in, and when she finished the braid lay against my cheek.

Length of Stay: *?*

Rosa put a hand on my cheek. One cheek felt her hand, the other felt wisps of dill brushing against my skin, and they both smelled the same, both smelled like sweet fresh dill, and there was a fainter smell too, of the dirt the dill'd been pulled from, and then there was an even fainter smell, and even though I can put a name on the smell I can't really describe it. The smell was Rosa.

Rosa said, "You got to live with something if you wanta understand it. Can't read about it," she said, "can't look it up in no encyclopedia, can't study it. You got to see it and feel it and smell it and hear and taste it too, you got to experience it with your natural senses."

Rosa had black eyes and black hair that was almost as kinky as mine, and the closest I can come to describing that smell of hers is to go back to my momma again. She was a Rochelle by birth, my momma, cousin to Webbie Greeving's own momma Emily, and when he was still alive Reverend Amias used to let her use a room in the church basement for her Saturday afternoon socials. It was a tiny room filled up with coffee and cakes and sweet fruits like strawberries and peaches, and black women, and as I breathed in that smell I wondered if Rosa was, you know . . . Rosa's skin was what they call olive, which don't mean green as much as it means it could go one way or the other. Well, it seems a funny thing to be shy about, but there you go.

I couldn't say nothing to Rosa. I just sort of nodded my head, and Rosa smiled.

She said, "If you watch how a plant grows, how it grows and how it don't grow too, eventually you'll find out what makes it grow best."

So now, in the summers, I'm happy. Flowers blooming, strong green vines bursting with heart-shaped leaves, the thin threads of Rosa's herbs holding our patchwork garden together. But come fall Grady Oconnor rototills the garden under, and come winter the hedge has a new layer of dead vines twisting in and out, pushing out like veins on a old white lady's legs. Come March, April, Rosa lays in her stock of next year's seeds, waiting for the thaw, and then I start to breathe easy. Just one time I told her I thought she was being a bit heavy-handed, and then she explained to me what faith was. Sometimes, she said, sometimes you believe in what you see, but real faith only comes when you realize the eyes are deceivers and you learn to believe for the sake of believing. For no reason at all. Well, that sounded so pretty I coulda just about sat down and cried—and I did start crying, but not cause I believed what she said. I cried because I didn't. I didn't have no faith. I only believed in what my eyes showed me. Sawyer, Rosa, the little bubbles on a pancake that tells you it's time to flip it over.

A five dollar bill will still buy dinner in my place, and so will five dollar bills, or five hundred cents in any combination you wanta give them to me.

I taught Sawyer. A clean plate is a happy plate.

Where there's smoke there's fire, that's what my momma taught me.

But I knew that wasn't what Rosa wanted to hear, and so I just smiled and I said her name. Rosa, I said, and that was all, that was enough, for that day. In those days the trouble was in the past—Eric Johnson, and the first Sawyer—and nobody knew about the trouble to come, Colin Nieman, and his little friend with the funny name. And Lucy Robinson. Again.

3.13

Colin

NONE OF GALATIA'S STREETS WAS PAVED, BUT THE packed earth which composed them seemed, if anything, even harder than asphalt. It formed a ridged surface as pleated as a washboard, and I was bouncing along one of these roads, Adams I think it was, East Adams, when a mound of earth dislodged itself from the road directly in front of me. I didn't have time to swerve. There was a thump, a stomach-churning lurch, and all at once *Die Walküre* was drowned out by a loud incessant squealing. I was out of the car in a moment, I saw her clearly, splayed across the road. My mind was buzzing with so many things: with Justin, just out of Bigger Hill's hospital, with impatience for the lab results that I believed would clear my name, with my novel, which had taken off since that night in the police station. My mind was filled with these other things, and what I saw first was not the body which actually lay on the road, but Lucy Robinson's body, her bruised pink flesh, her torn purple dress. The hallucination lasted only a moment; in a moment flesh turned into coarse hair, bruises into globs of dried mud, torn dress into the mottled markings ranging over the back and stomach and legs of a small floppy-eared sow. The sow was still squealing, a loud thin noise terrible to hear; her spasming front hooves still tried to drag her to safety, but her hind legs lay twisted and useless. Her back, obviously, was broken; but, even so, my relief that it wasn't a person—that it wasn't Lucy Robinson—was so great that I began laughing. Only two or three peals had escaped when a human voice, as loud and thin and desperate as the sow's, cut me off.

"What the *hell*'s so funny?"

The man who had spoken was coatless, and his heavy belly bounced up and down as he ran toward me; he glared at me malevolently, but before I could answer he shifted his gaze to the pig.

"Charlene!" he called, his tone softening. "Charlene, honey, what happened?" He fell to his knees and gingerly took her head in his arms. At his touch the pig, Charlene, stopped squealing, but her mouth hung open and her breath pulsed out of her in clouds of steam; her front hooves still twitched with an effort at flight. The man looked up at me. "You killed her! You killed my Charlene!"

The word *killed* came out *kilt*, and, for just a moment, I pictured that: the fat man in a skirt with Charlene naked in his arms, and then I pictured Charlene in the kilt with the fat man naked in her arms, and then I decided the scene before me was preferable to either imagined option. Despite myself, I chuckled one last time.

"*What's* so funny?"

"F-forgive me," I stuttered. My hands moved vaguely through the air, but the etiquette of pig killing was beyond my grasp. "She was lying in the road. I didn't see her. Please, forgive me."

The man spat at me. "She always lies in the road. She always lays right there!"

He pulled an arm from Charlene's trembling head and pointed at a depression beneath the Rover's engine. I glanced at the soft-edged hair-fringed hole, and when I turned back the man had bent his face over Charlene's. He was young, I saw then, barely twenty-five, although his hair was thinning and the patchy ginger stubble on his cheek was studded with gray. Those cheeks, I couldn't help notice, were rather jowly, his eyes small and piggish, and something that looked a lot like shit clumped on his boots. Nevertheless, the muscles beneath his yoked plaid shirt were big and round and solid, and given added bulk by a thick layer of fat. A large knife hung in an embossed leather sheath off his belt.

He looked up suddenly. "Darrell, Grady," the man called. "He hit Charlene!"

I turned and saw two men, one black, one white, sauntering toward us. Their coats were still unzipped, and the white man carried a lined denim jacket in his hand.

"Looks like he did," the white man said, his drawl as lingering as his walk. The black man just nodded, and then he put a hand over his mouth, but not before I'd seen a glimmer of a smile.

No one said anything then. It was quiet enough for me to hear the car stereo's *buh buh buh BUH buh, buh buh buh BUH buh,* and then Charlene squealed again, a long bubbly peal, terrible to hear.

"Just listen to her," her owner said to me. "Look what you done to her."

"Now, now, Howard," the white man said. "I'm sure it was a honest accident. This man is a stranger to Galatea. Can't expect him to know Charlene's habits."

The man pronounced *Howard* as *Haird: Howard* was *Haird, can't* was *cain't* and *habits* came out *doins*, and it was a lot easier to listen to his accent than to what he said, because the single glance he gave me belied any charity that might have been contained in his words. He handed Howard his jacket but Howard knocked it away.

"*Honest?*" Howard yelled. "*Stranger?* First he, he, he *steals* my Lucy from me, and now my Charlene. *Accident?*"

It was only when Howard mentioned Lucy's name that I realized the depth of the drama we were enacting; I realized that these men had, on some level, shared my vision of Lucy's battered body sprawled in front of my car. Still, no one responded to Howard's accusations. The black man seemed to be fascinated by the Rover's design, although his mouth was still hidden behind his hand, and the white man just stood between me and Howard for a moment, glancing back and forth between us with an almost metronomic regularity, and then his eyes settled on me, and a broad ungenuine smile split his face, revealing teeth browned by chewing tobacco. He wiped a hand on his pants and thrust it at me.

"Name's Darrell Jenkens. Two *r*'s, two *l*'s. That's Grady Oconnor," he added, jerking his thumb at the black man. "No 'postrophe. That's Howard Goertzen. And that's Charlene."

His hand was still extended; it seemed, if anything, even dirtier after he'd wiped it on his dusty pants, but I took it in mine.

He squeezed then, hard, and I squeezed back; he squeezed even harder, but I had studied martial arts with a Buddhist monk who could pulverize a cue ball with one hand while sipping tea with the other. Within my grasp Darrell Jenkens' knuckles popped with a sound like twisted bubble wrap, and the smile left his face.

"I'm Colin Nieman," I said. I didn't offer him any tips on spelling.

Darrell Jenkens was shaking his hand. "I know who you are."

"Please forgive me," I said again. "For hitting Charlene. But she *was* lying in the road."

Darrell Jenkens paused for a moment, and then he stuffed his hands in his coat pockets. I saw his eyes run up and down my body, taking in my navy wool jacket and the crisp white button-down shirt beneath it, my pressed chinos, my hatless and hairless head; he himself was tall, skinny, dirty, with a freckled complexion like a piece of paper spat on by the chaw whose juices rimed his lips. After a moment he shrugged again.

"Bound to happen," he said, and it wasn't immediately clear if he was talking about Charlene, or me, or something else. "Everybody said to Howard keep that hog outta the road."

"Darrell," Howard Goertzen called. "Darrell, look at her. My God, Darrell, she's dying."

Darrell Jenkens went to Howard Goertzen then, and, in a moment, Grady Oconnor—no 'postrophe—stepped up to me.

"Howard ain't got that many friends."

He worked hard to keep his voice steady, but he was clearly more amused than distressed by the situation. A sudden bout of squeals erupted from Charlene, but Grady Oconnor merely waited them out.

"Howard's daddy runs a pig farm westa town. Nice little operation. Charlene was a runt Howard took a liking to a couple-a years back, right around the time Lyle. Her momma woulda probably just ate her, but Howard took her away and bottle fed her, raised her up like a pet."

"Lyle?"

"Lyle was Howard's brother, joined the army. He died in that conflict in Iraq."

"The Gulf War?"

Grady nodded. "That'd be the one."

"And 'Charlene'?"

Grady was still nodding. "Yup. Charlene. I think he named her after that pig in the storybook."

"You mean *Charlotte's Web*?"

"That'd be the one."

"The pig was called Wilbur."

"Well. Howard don't read much."

"And the spider," I said. "The spider was called Charlotte."

"That's Howard for you."

"Grady Oconnor!" Howard's voice cut into our conversation. "Are you gonna stand there all day yakking with that *man* or are you gonna *do* something?"

Grady looked at me for a moment longer, and I saw an emotion, annoyance maybe, or something stronger, cloud his face, and then he turned to Howard.

"What you want me to do, Howard?" He turned back to me. "You got a gun in that vehicle?"

"A gun?"

"No use in the creature suffering."

Creature came out *critter* and *suffering* rhymed with *Bufferin*. I said that I didn't own a gun.

"Oh, *really*?" Grady replied, and what little trust I had invested in him vanished. "Cold out today," he said, and then he zipped his jacket.

It was cold, I suddenly noticed. Howard Goertzen, still coatless, was shivering beneath Charlene, and the spray of her breath had coalesced into a damp red-tinged stain on his pants. My ears were so cold I could feel my pulse beating in them.

Another faint echo of *Die Walküre*, and then a new sound, of gravel beneath the wheels of a car, followed by the short blast of a police siren. When Lawman Brown emerged from his cruiser, he presented a face as stolid, lined, and inexpressive as a born joist. He approached, one hand on his stomach, the other on the protruding handle of his gun; his stomach also protruded. He was humming "Leroy Brown" under his breath, a tune which I realized was somehow anthemic for him, and for an awful moment Jim Croce competed with Wagner, and then, mercifully, both Lawman Brown and the CD went quiet at the same time.

In New York, we had driven a Mercedes, a convertible; but when we moved I put it in a garage and bought a Range Rover, and it was the Rover's grille, a steel webbing that the dealer's brochure claimed had been tested against "Rommel the Desert Fox in the wastes of North Africa" that first compelled Lawman Brown's attention when he showed up on the scene. He affected not to notice Charlene, nor did he acknowledge me, or Howard or Darrell or Grady; instead, he ran a single gloved finger along one of the grille's steel plates, and when he had finished he nodded his head approvingly. Only then did he turn to us.

"So, gentlemen, what seems to be the problem?"

"What's the problem? What's the problem!" Howard Goertzen screamed. "This here"—his mouth twisted around words his brain could not fill in—"this here *man* done hit my Charlene."

Lawman Brown turned to me.

"Mr. Nieman."

"Sheriff Brown."

"You seem to have a knack for landing smack dab in the middle-a things, Mr. Nieman."

"In this case, Sheriff, it was Charlene. She was lying in the road."

I pointed at the hole beneath the Rover, but Lawman Brown kept his eyes on mine.

"Howard!" he called out. "Howard, was Charlene taking a nap in the middle-a East Adams again?"

As if I might have hit her on Jefferson, and then dragged her one block west.

"She always sleeps there, Lawman Brown, everybody knows that."

"My name, Howard, is Eustace. My title is Sheriff."

Grady Oconnor's hand rushed back to his mouth.

Howard Goertzen bent his cold-pinked cheeks over Charlene. "She was just waiting for me to finish up lunch."

There was a long silence then, in which all eyes were on Lawman Brown. I felt myself start to shiver and wished I'd grabbed my coat from the Rover. Lawman Brown's face might have been stiff, but his chest swelled a bit under our gaze. I assumed he was one of those self-important men who enjoy being the center of attention—which, in fact, he was—but the reason for his puffed-up chest was revealed a moment later, when a not-quite-silent burp caused the cheeks of his closed mouth to bulge out, and then his chest deflated as the stomach gases escaped his body in a long purse-lipped sigh.

At the end of his burp he pulled his gun from his holster. He didn't do it dramatically, but all the same I felt my spine stiffen, and I had to resist the urge to duck behind the Rover.

"Fraid there ain't much I can do for you, Howard," Lawman Brown said, turning to the man and the pig. "People done told you time and time again, busy street's no place for a napping hog."

Not one other car had driven by. *Busy*, I thought, must be a relative term.

"Aw, Lawman Brown."

The sheriff didn't correct him.

"Step away from there, Howard. It's time to put Charlene outta her misery. And whyn't you put your coat on before you freeze to death."

Howard Goertzen stared at Lawman Brown's gun for a moment, and then his eyes flicked to me, and to his coat, and then back to Lawman Brown.

"I'll get back, but only if you make him do it. Make him finish off what he started on."

The malevolence in Howard Goertzen's voice added a layer of meaning to his words. He was stroking Charlene's head tenderly, and I remembered then that someone, Divine or Wade or Webbie, had mentioned that he had been Lucy Robinson's leading suitor.

"I expect Howard has a point. You know how to operate a firearm, Mr. Nieman?"

"I've fired one before," I said. I held out my hand for Lawman Brown's gun.

Lawman Brown looked at my hand, and then, without comment, he walked to his cruiser and returned with a rifle. At no point did he reholster his pistol. As he handed me the rifle, the deer-hunting scene from *Beauty* flashed in my mind, and even as I tried to remember the actual incident, the words I had used to describe it overwhelmed the memory:

> *The gun went off and the deer was running and the deer was jumping and the deer was standing still as the gun went off, and the deer's throat burst and its life splattered across the forest floor, running, jumping, standing still, I was firing again and an antler was splintering off like a branch, an eye was exploding and I was running, jumping, standing still, the deer was mine and in my arms and I*

> *ripped open the seam of its throat and put my hands right inside and felt the tide of life pushing out and out, no shore of skin to contain it, to repel it, repel life, repel death, for a moment we fled death together, running, jumping, standing still, and then forever after it was just me, alone, the blood growing cold around my hands, night falling, the other deer running, jumping, but all of us standing still.*

Charlene seemed virtually dead, her eyes blinking continuously, her chest fluttering as rapidly as a bird's. I took a step toward her, and Howard Goertzen wiggled and rolled his fat body out of the way, grabbing his coat at the last minute. I held the rifle in one hand, finger on the trigger, the stock resting on my forearm and backed in the crook of my elbow, and even as Lawman Brown said, "Don't you think you oughta—" the shot rang out and a small bloodless hole appeared behind Charlene's ear and she died without a twitch. No blood came from the wound, but in place of her steaming breath a thin vapor trail floated up from the bullet hole.

When I turned to Lawman Brown, the rifle, of course, turned with me, and Lawman Brown jerked his pistol up and pointed it at me. I realized then that I had moved to a place where grown men still contemplated each other with guns in their hands.

I swiveled the rifle then, and presented it stock first to Lawman Brown. "It's a single-bolt action .22, Sheriff. It only takes one bullet."

Howard Goertzen looked stunned, and something that I hoped was merely Charlene's drool had stained the crotch of his pants. Darrell Jenkens busied himself brushing dirt off his pants, and the grin had vanished from Grady Oconnor's face.

Lawman Brown looked down at Charlene, and then, shaking his head slightly, he turned to me. "You wouldn't happen to've known Eddie Comedy, would you?"

I smiled, and shook my head, but I suddenly understood why Darrell Jenkens had spelled his name. He had spelled his name because he knew I was a writer, and he wanted to make sure I got it right in the book.

Two *r*'s, two *l*'s. No 'postrophe.

I guess he wanted to make sure I got Grady Oconnor's name right too.

3.14

Webbie

IT WAS IMPOSSIBLE FOR ME TO STAY SILENT IN THE face of Justin's silence, but I learned not to ask him questions when I spoke to him. Instead I spoke in statements: It's cold out there, I would say, or, The grocery store was having a special on rump roast, or, Wade says hi-lo. The limestone house was always neat but sometimes I made a token effort at straightening up. Sometimes I cooked for him, but usually Justin only picked at what I made. You have to eat, I would insist, until one day Colin came in while we were at the table.

"He already ate," he said.

"He did?"

Colin himself had bought groceries, and he began to put them away. "He eats every day," he said. "He hasn't given up eating, just speaking."

I didn't like the way Colin could say it so blandly, as if Justin had merely made a Lenten renunciation, and, angrily, I said, "Kill any pigs today?"

Colin looked up from his groceries. His smile was not unkind, nor was it full of mirth. "You know, Miss Greeving, I think I prefer you in Wade's presence. In Wade's house. Something about him seems to . . . subdue you."

"You leave Wade out of this."

The vehemence in my tone surprised even me, and Colin's smile widened in triumph. "No, Miss Greeving, I did not kill any pigs today. I ran five miles, and then I wrote two thousand words, and then I purchased groceries at the local food shop, a charming establishment which offers an entire range of generic products served up in chic black-and-white packaging—an apt metaphor, don't you think?—and I even picked up something in the butcher department labeled *beefalo* because it sounded interesting, although I'm not sure what it is."

At some point during Colin's little speech I had turned back to Justin, and when Colin finished, I said, "Look at him. He looks thin."

Colin's sigh was exasperated. "He *is* thin."

"He looks *dangerously* thin," I said, "and I don't see how you can make jokes—"

"He has *always* looked dangerously thin, Webbie. It's part of his appeal."

"His *appeal*? How can you be so callous?"

"I think the real question, Webbie, is how can you be so naive?" I started to answer him—to protest really—but Colin steamrolled right over me. "You know, Webbie, you really are a cliché. Just another small-town hick with an Ivy League diploma. You hold yourself so far above the people of your town, the white people *and* the black people, because of a silly little thing like a Columbia education, and yet you are as selective in what you will and will not know as they are."

There was something in Colin's words that struck me dumb, and it was all I could do to stammer out a "W-w-what?"

"Look at him, Webbie, *look at him*."

I didn't want to, but I felt I had to. I turned, and looked at Justin. But it was as if there was nothing there. Just, just . . . Justin Time, a made-up name attached to an unknown entity, a skinny cypher with fading bruises and faint scars all over his body.

"He's a *prostitute*, Webbie, a street hustler, an undernourished little kid with an overactive imagination given to melodramatic personal gestures, one of which was running away from what was probably an abusive family situation and so ending up on the streets of New York City, where he sold his ass to losers like me who just happen to be attracted to his type. That's all, Webbie, that's it. He's not a martyr or a saint, he's a dime a dozen. Fifty bucks an hour, to be precise."

Justin didn't move throughout Colin's speech, but out at the ends of my arms my hands were flying around like balloons on strings caught in a windstorm. "I, I, I," I stuttered. "I can*not* believe this."

"No, Webbie, you *will* not believe this. You choose not to. You can accept the fact that Divine is a prostitute because Divine is an uneducated nigger like you once were. But you think Justin's different. Justin talks like an educated man. Justin's *white*. But he's no different from Divine, Webbie, just better read. Why do you think the two of them can't stand each other? It's because *they're just the same*."

Finally he had given me something I could grab on to. "I thought it was because they were fighting over you."

"Me?" Colin smirked, but there was a nervous undercurrent to his voice. "There's nothing to fight over."

I noticed a small bruise on Colin's neck then, a love bite. I didn't think Justin had put it there.

"Really? I don't think Divine knows that."

Colin sighed. "Listen to me, Webbie, okay? Justin made a choice, a foolish choice, but a choice nonetheless, and it's time you recognized that. He can renounce it if he wants, but we can't do it for him."

I didn't say anything then. Colin stared at me for a moment, and then he resumed unpacking his groceries. At some point he took out a styrofoam tray of meat wrapped in cellophane. I shook my head.

"It's buffalo meat," I said, "buffalo mixed with ground beef. Beefalo." I shrugged. "I'm just trying to help."

Colin spoke softly. "And I'm sure Justin appreciates it." He smiled, and it would have been convincing if he hadn't seen where my eyes were focused, and pulled his shirt over the hickey on his neck.

"So," I said then. "How is Divine?"

Colin started to say something, and then he stopped. "I think it would be better if you didn't come over until Justin asks to see you. For everyone's sake."

He spoke in a neutral tone, but his eyes turned nervously to Justin, and I looked with him. Justin's gaze remained fixed on the unoccupied space between me and Colin. He still held his fork in his hand, and when no one spoke for several moments he put it in his mouth and pulled it out again. He chewed slowly, swallowed. There had been nothing on his fork.

3.15

Cora

HE WAS DRIPPING WET THE FIRST TIME I SAW HIM. HE was wearing gray sweatpants and a gray sweatshirt and some really expensive running shoes, so I figured that's why he was sweating fit to flood the plain at nine in the morning on the first day of December. I'd never seen him, like I said, but didn't nobody have to tell me who he was—and didn't nobody have to tell me he hadn't done it neither. Some things you just know about a person on sight.

Not much was said between us that first morning, but he come in the next morning, and the next, and the next. Then there was the weekend, and then he come in on Monday. I got to know him, I guess, got to know him in all the ways that matter, at least as far as I'm concerned: no bacon, no coffee, no hash browns or grits. Sometimes he had a couple-a poached eggs on dry wheat toast, but usually he just had the toast and half a grapefruit. No sugar on the grapefruit. And pink, please: ten times more vitamins than the yellow. From Grady I got the other part, the part about him being a writer, and being from New York, and being rich as Croesus. Grady even said he heard from Nettie Ferguson that he had a cocaine problem which I doubted cause I never heard me of a drug addict who could get up at six in the morning and run five miles without having a heart attack. And then too Grady told me about him and Reggie Packman, I mean, about him and Divine, and about that other one, the one with the funny name, sitting around in that funny room on top of the old Deacon house and never saying a word. Grady's a quiet one, but you figure out pretty quick he's got his ear to the ground. But none of that was my business, not if Grady was sneaking into that house at night and not what he seen in there if he did, and after a while I told Grady to keep his gossip to hisself. If Colin Nieman wanted to have breakfast in the café on the wrong side of the tracks, that was his business. His business was his, and mine was mine, and let's keep it that way.

Still and all, I guess I figured it out pretty quick. He was trying to get on with things. You know, live life as normal as possible. Not, like, pretending that nothing had happened, but not, like, letting the whole affair take him over—and I have to admit that knowing somebody was looking at my blood and stuff with a microscope give me the heebie-jeebies just thinking about it. I mean, they can tell what you eat and drink nowadays just by looking at a single drop of your blood, if you do any drugs, if you got any diseases, and I suppose they could tell if you'd held some girl down on a dirt road and had your way with her. Me, I'da been taking extra bacon, extra eggs, just to get through the waiting, and I had to hand it to him for making it through on half a grapefruit, no sugar. But I drew the line at skim milk in his coffee. There ain't no such thing as skim milk in Cora's Kitchen.

So that Monday I brought him his breakfast, if that's what you wanta call it.

"Mind if I sit down?"

He put down his book right away. "Please do."

"You take weekends off?"

"Excuse me?"

"You don't jog on the weekends?"

"Oh," he said. "I do, but not as early, and not as far. And never on Sundays."

"That's good," I said, "cause I'm closed on Sunday. Hey," I said, "you know what they call jogging around here?"

"Uh . . . ?"

"Running when you don't have to."

He seemed to like that. He laughed, and then he said, "Have you ever jogged?"

"You trying to be funny?"

"Just thought I should ask."

"If I jogged, my bosom'd be hanging down round my kneecaps by now. Anyways, I'm not the running type. I'm more the sitting-still type."

"I've been running for thirty years. Every morning, no matter where I am. I don't feel complete unless I do."

What I wanted to do then was ask him why in the world he decided to settle down here, but I didn't think that was my place. So all I said was "I feel the same way about a cuppa coffee myself. You wouldn't want to see me before I had my coffee."

"You wouldn't want to see me before I've had my run."

"Well, I wouldn't mind seeing you after you had a shower neither. No offense, Mr. Nieman, but you sure do *sweat*."

Rosa come in a little while later, carrying a flat pan of macaroni and cheese, made up but not baked yet, and she like to pour the whole pan down my skirt when she walked into the room because she was staring so hard at Colin.

"He ain't a Martian, girl," I whispered, but I was watching her careful. Rosa don't do things by accident. "Excuse me, Colin, but I believe you ain't met Rosa yet."

He looked up from his book. I'd like to tell you what book it was, but it was in Latin and I only knew that because he told me. "No," he said, "I don't believe I have."

"Well, this here's Miss Rosa Stone," I said. There was a funny silence then. I knew I was supposed to say something else, like, "She a good friend of mine," or, "She works here with me," but neither of these things was quite true. I watched Colin look back and forth between us once or twice, and then, I don't know how, but I could just tell: he knew.

He stood up, but before he could walk over to Rosa she set the macaroni and cheese down on the counter and walked over to him. "I'm very pleased to meet you, Mr. Nieman."

Well, I don't think I ever saw Rosa just walk up to somebody in four years of knowing her, and my jaw like to hit the floor.

"I'm so pleased to meet you, Miss Stone."

Rosa wiped her hand on her apron and shook his. "Please, call me Rosa." She was blushing fit to bust a blood vessel.

"I was just about to tell Colin that he should come in here for lunch or dinner sometime," I said. "He don't eat nothing for breakfast but a grapefruit and some toast."

"Oh, Cora's a beautiful cook, Mr. Nieman. You really should come by for lunch sometime."

She wasn't looking at him, I noticed then, she was looking down at his table. At his book.

Colin looked a little sheepish. "Actually, I don't eat lunch."

I laughed at that. "Well, Mr. Nieman, I sure hope you eat dinner."

"Yes, I do eat dinner. Usually."

"Well, maybe one of them usually nights you'll drop by and let me fix you a proper meal. A cook don't feel appreciated unless she's actually cooking for somebody."

"I will. I'll drop by soon. I promise."

"Dinner starts at five," I said. "Kitchen closes promptly at eight-thirty, but there's usually something warm till about nine." But I hardly heard myself speaking to him because I was watching Rosa. Her lips was moving as she looked down at Colin's book, moving slow, as if she was sounding out the words.

When Colin turned back to her, she jumped a little. "Oh, excuse me, Mr. Nieman," she said. She put a finger on the page, let it trail over the paper. "Such beautiful writing."

"You read Latin, Miss Stone?"

"Rosa," Rosa said, and she blushed. "I just meant the shape of the words. The way it looks on the page. Beautiful. Beautiful."

Later on, when Colin was gone, Rosa come back around the counter to put her mac and cheese in the oven, and I kind of used my body to keep her back there. The space behind the counter's not so narrow that two people can't pass by each other, but at least one person's gotta give a little.

"Girl," I said. "What gives?"

"What?" Rosa said. Her eyes dropped to the floor. "What you mean, what gives?"

"I *saw* you. You was reading that book. Not just admiring the way the words looked on the page. You was *reading* it."

"Cora, that book was in *Latin*."

"I know that. I know that very well. *Latin*. Why you think I'm asking. And don't tell me nothing about being no Catholic. Amen is one thing and virgins is something else."

"Virgil."

"What?"

"He was reading Virgil. He was reading about the founding of Rome."

"What does *that* have to do with anything?"

"Oh, Cora. I done told and told you, just don't ask me, okay. Don't ask, don't even wonder. It's easier that way, trust me."

"Easier for who? Me? Or you?"

"I just *said*," Rosa said, "don't ask." She took a deep breath. "This'll be done in forty-five minutes," she said, and it took me a moment to realize she meant the macaroni and cheese. And then she pushed past me, and I heard her feet running up the stairs, and the slam of the door on the room that she still paid me fifty dollars a month for.

Well, that slam took me back, so far back that what I had to do was sit down and let my head drop in my hands and push those tears back in my head before my whole brain leaked out. Sawyer'd slammed the door like that, not on the night he left, no, he'd sneaked out that night, but on another night, on the night he went to collect Eric Johnson's body. I mean, he was the boy's uncle, and Marsha, like I said, Marsha wasn't no good to Eric or nobody else. I remember Sawyer got a phone call from somebody, he wouldn't say who, he got a phone call and he took it and after he said hello he didn't say nothing for a real long time, and then he said I'll take care of it and he said goodbye, and then he hung the phone up and he held me for a long time. And then he left. When he come back it was nearly dawn and he smelled like sweat and dirt, he was filthy, that man, but he was so . . . well, *tired*'s not the right word, but it's as close as I can come, and Sawyer was so tired that he didn't even bother to wash or even undress, he just lay right down beside me, and this time I held him, for richer or for poorer, in sickness and in health, dirty or clean, I held my Sawyer while he cried and cried and cried. He didn't say nothing for a long time, he just cried. He didn't say nothing until he was done with crying, and then what he said was I buried him. Where no one won't find him, where no one won't ever mess with him again. Oh, my Sawyer. He had grave dirt on him and an ache in his bones that my own hands could feel, but even so he turned on me, all of the sudden and outta the blue, he rolled on top of me and I could feel him down there not hard but I could feel him through his pants, and what he said was You wanna know why I don't want no kids, Cora? You wanna know why? *That's* why! I tell you I was never so scared in my life as I was that night, I mean I hadn't said nothing and there was my man laying on top of me like a stranger, and I threw him off me and rolled over away from him and I heard him get outta bed behind me, heard him walk across the room and out the door. And it wasn't our door he slammed, but the door to the extra room, where he slept that night.

The door to Rosa's room.

Length of Stay: ?

The bell rang then, and I looked up, and I wouldn'ta been surprised to see Sawyer come back after all this time. Cause it felt like that. It felt like something, somebody, like Colin and Lucy Robinson and even somehow Rosa was bringing it all back, but what I wasn't sure, what I couldn't tell, is if they was taking me back there, or if, somehow, what seemed more frightening, they was bringing it all forward. The bell rang, but wasn't no one at the door. Only the wind, I thought, until I realized the bell was still ringing, until I realized it was the timer, and all it was telling me was that Rosa's macaroni and cheese was done, and I got up then, I turned the timer off, and I turned the oven off, and I took the macaroni and cheese outta the oven and set it on the counter, so it wouldn't burn. There wasn't nothing else I could do, about Sawyer or Eric Johnson, about Rosa, about Colin Nieman and Lucy Robinson. But I could make sure the macaroni and cheese didn't burn, and I did.

3.16

Colin

YOU COULD SEE HIM MAKING CHOICES. IN THE MORNINGS he would touch me when he woke up, sometimes even kiss my shoulder lightly, but if I said good morning he would stiffen momentarily, then relax and slip out of bed. The telephone made him jump; if I didn't answer it he would turn the answering machine's volume down all the way. He turned the television on once and then, after staring at it for a moment, turned the volume down on that as well. Sometimes I saw him handling CDs, flipping through their booklets, rolling the sharp edges of the disks along his palms, but he never turned the stereo on. Once I heard him humming. I was in my office and he was in the other room and I didn't know if he knew I was there. He hummed for nearly a minute, some pop song whose tune was familiar to me though I couldn't quite name it, and then, right before I could remember a few of the words to the song, he stopped. Oh, Justin, I thought, but I too didn't speak. I'll be done soon, Justin, soon I'll be done, and then, one way or another, we'll go. But first I must finish what I've started.

3.17

Divine

THIS TIME WHEN I COME OVER I DIDN'T KNOCK. I FIGured I wasn't a stranger no more and I let my own self in and I walked kind of quiet but not like on tiptoe or anything through the entrance hall and the hallway and towards the light that was coming out of Colin's study.

What I don't understand is, why live in a house with like twenty rooms in it when you spend all your time in just one, and that one smelling like moldy books to boot? I tell you what: if *I* lived in the old Deacon house I'd walk around a bit, I would.

Justin seemed to have his own room too, now that he was up and about, or up anyway, he wasn't really about. He spent all his time in that little room stuck up on top of the roof, Colin told me what it was called but I can't remember the name. I seen him up there sometimes, standing in a window and looking for all the world like old Mrs. Bates in that movie *Psycho*, who, I just want to remind you, who was fucking *dead*.

So, anyway, there was Colin, or I guess I should say there was Colin's desk, which was like ten feet long and five feet wide and so high that even Colin who was a damn sight taller than six feet had to like sit in an extra-tall chair just so that he could write at it, that desk, calling it a antique just don't do it justice, it was more like a statue or something, a—a *monument*, carved all over and inlaid with gold or something, well, gold paint at least, topped with a slab of marble and on top of the marble this sheet of blood-red leather laid right across the top of it, which the leather you could only see bits and pieces of cause it was almost completely covered by like stacks and stacks of paper, sometimes just two or three sheets in a stack, sometimes what looked to me like enough paper for two or three books, and in the center of all this paper there was the two typewriters, the electric one, shiny and silver and humming and shit, and the manual one, black and quiet, and in between them I could just make out the smooth top of Colin's head, which was laid down on the desk.

He was snoring.

I guess it hadn't never occurred to me before that Colin Nieman might have problems like the rest of us. Like I always thought there was only a couple of things you had to worry about in this life, like how are you gonna pay your bills and who's gonna keep you warm come nighttime, and these were things Colin Nieman with his money and his looks could more or less take care of in his sleep, so to speak. I mean, isn't that what that thing he read me was about? But then I guess there was the problem of what to do with the rest of the day, when you weren't writing checks I mean, or fucking. You know, Webbie went off to school and Wade paints and like that, and as I looked at Colin sleeping at his desk I realized he'd decided to fill his days with writing, which what I mean was, I didn't think it meant all that much to him, except as a way of fending off other things.

Colin's head popped up then, all of a sudden like. There was something like a scowl on his face and I wasn't sure if it showed up there before or after he saw me.

"Reggie," he said.

"Don't *even* go there," I said. "Don't put on your turn signal, don't even look down that road. My name is *Divine*."

Then Colin smiled, which wasn't particularly reassuring cause it didn't seem like his mood'd changed or nothing.

"Did you come to see me?"

"You don't see a hoe in my hand, do you? I ain't no field nigger come up to the Big House to say the back forty's all done. Did I come to 'see' you? Shit."

"Take your pants off."

"What?"

"Take your pants off, and turn around."

"Right down to business. A man after my own heart."

"I'm after your ass. Now take your pants off, and turn around, and shut up."

Well.

I shut up first, and then I turned around, and then I undid my pants and began pushing them down.

"Not all the way," Colin said. "There's good."

The waist of my pants was about to the middle of my thighs. There was some cold air on my legs there, but my ass was covered by my shirttails.

"Lift up your shirt. Just—there, that's good."

I noticed that the door was open then and I wanted to like shuffle forward and close it, but I figured that was pretty much outta the question. So I stood there, and waited, and hoped Miss Justin didn't decide that right now was a good time for him to come ask what did Colin want for dinner.

Like he *would.*

Cupola, I remembered then. *Cupola* was the word Colin used for the room where Justin spent all his time. Stay there, I prayed, stay in the cupola.

Then behind me I heard Colin's chair squeak as he moved. Here it comes, I thought, but instead of footsteps what I heard next was the sound of Colin's typewriter, and I have to tell you at the sound of that my hard-on disappeared like water in a desert, and I was left just kind of standing there in front of the open door and I still wanted to close it, not because I was afraid Justin might see me but because I was afraid he might see Colin, doing what he was doing to me, which was, well, which was nothing.

Behind me the typewriter went on making its awful racket, but Colin didn't say nothing at all, and what I thought about was that sack, that fancy cloth sack filled with paper, except the way I thought of it the sack already had the eye holes cut out of it and it stared up at Colin from the marble top of Colin's desk and Colin stared back down at it like it was human, like they was having a conversation, and then I realized—what they was talking about was me.

3.18

Webbie

MY CHILDREN, MY FATHER'S VOICE ECHOED THROUGH the house, *a thousand plagues have threatened our land. My children,* he called, *the land itself, as you know, the land is no easy companion: she tests us with the dry of drought and the wet of flood, she burns us with hot and freezes us with cold. Come hailstorm, come locust, come raging fire and tornado, this land holds us in the palm of her hand and feels free to close that fist upon us whenever she wants, to lock us in the grip of her fury.*

The telephone rang then, like some small mercy. When I answered it I mashed it to my ear, and I stuck my finger in my other ear to block out the sound of my father's voice.

"Hello?"

"Webbie."

"Wade."

In the pause before Wade spoke again, my father's voice pushed through my finger, *fought hard to get here*, I heard, *fought hard to tame this land and call it our own . . .*

"How have you been?" Wade said.

"Oh, you know. The Reverend's about to drive me crazy with all these sermons against the infidel, but otherwise."

"I haven't seen you in a while. Too long."

I didn't say anything immediately, but my silence only allowed my father's voice back in my head, *these enemies are as nothing compared to that which comes at us now . . .*

"Did he say something about enemies?"

"Oh, you know." I tried to laugh. "Christians always see the devil somewhere."

"Uh-huh." There was the briefest pause—a single word snuck through, *insidious*—and then Wade said again, "How have you been?"

"Oh, Wade, please don't ask me. I just . . . can't."

. . . the lion that dresses itself in the clothing of the lamb . . .

I looked down and noticed that my hand was on my breast. I wondered what that would look like to someone else, someone looking in through a window, someone who didn't know who I was talking to, or even someone who did.

"Webbie, I'm all alone here. Divine's never here now, he's always over there. And Colin and Justin, well, I mean, of course they never come over. And—oh, Webbie, please. I just look at these big empty sheets of canvas and all I want is someone to *talk* to."

. . . did not the cities of the plain fall into a perversity born of luxury . . .

"Talk," I repeated absently.

"Just talk, Webbie. Just . . . some food, some wine, a nice evening."

. . . straight path is the narrow path, and the only path to the Lord. Look not to the pleasures of this earth . . .

"Webbie?"

"Wade, I can't. I have to make dinner for Dad."

"It's two—"

"Lunch. A late lunch then."

I hung up then, just in time to hear my father say, *Cast away that which would tempt you, lest you would lose those treasures forever*, and then I hung there, caught by his words. What, I wondered, were my temptations, what were my treasures? It had been so long since I had felt anything besides the push and pull of these two men, Wade and my father. Which was the treasure, which the temptation? Or was that just a ludicrous construction, the attempt to fit two variables into an equation to which they didn't belong? I remembered what Colin had said, about the things I refused to know.

I looked down then, saw that my hand was still on my breast, and I jerked it away as though one or the other were on fire. Again, the dilemma: which was burning, which was the one burned?

My father hadn't resumed speaking, but I was still caught up in his words. The phone was next to the refrigerator, and on the refrigerator was a plastic-capped magnet which bore the inscription: *For the Lord so loved the world that he—* The rest of the quotation had been rubbed off by years of use, and it looked as though the Lord so loved the world that he gave me the notes my father fastened to the refrigerator with the magnet. For the Lord so loved the world that he *gave the bathroom a good cleaning, top to bottom*. For the Lord so loved the world that he *paid a visit to Alma Kiehler to see why she hadn't been to church last Sunday*. For the Lord so loved the world that he *laid out the blue suit with the red tie*. Today the Lord had so loved the world that he gave a list of ingredients for beef stew, and at the end of the list my father had written, "I grow weary of scavenging. If you are too tired to cook then perhaps you could prepare a pot of stew which will save you the trouble of seeing me for a few days."

Without giving myself time to reconsider, I turned the note over. "Leftovers tonight," I wrote, "or call one of the Church Ladies over. I won't be home until tomorrow."

Even as I was putting on my coat I thought, *home?* and before I left I went back into the kitchen, crossed out the word *home* and wrote *back* instead, and then I ran from the house to my car, and started it, and drove away. Not to Wade's house, not to Justin's. But I *was* going looking for a man. A black man, specifically. Colin was right. It was time I found out a few things.

I didn't sleep with anyone during my single year at Howard. The worldliness of the other students intimidated me, and their knowledge as well, and I chose to compete in the academic arena. But after I transferred to Columbia I settled into a groove. I made friends, I dated a succession of men. All of them had their strengths and weaknesses; none of them produced in me a feeling that I would like to think of as love, although I blame that failure more on myself than I do on them. Not one of the men was black, though, an omission I noted at the time but didn't worry about. There will be time, I told myself, and indeed there will be time.

But there wasn't time, then or now, not time to wait, not time to waste. When I left my father's house, when I left Galatia and Wade and Justin and, indeed, Lucy Robinson behind, I wanted to drive all the way to Kansas City, but I limited myself instead to Wichita, a listless sprawling city whose network of highways suggests a population of millions rather than the two hundred fifty thousand who actually live there. Among those thousands was a substantial black population, whole neighborhoods, parks, clubs, churches, street upon street of ancient clean Chryslers and Buicks and cared-for Caddys trolling over the ground like huge armored beetles. I had expected that I would go to a bar, I would listen to the music that my father owned but never played, Ella and Sarah and Mahalia, but as it turned out I didn't have to wait that long.

It was just after five when I saw a small park in which two black girls in long iridescent parkas punched a frozen tetherball with mittened hands. I bought a cup of coffee in a café from a waitress who seemed unperturbed by the fact that she didn't recognize me, and I sat down on a bench to watch the girls play. I took pleasure in the fact that I didn't know their names. In Galatia everyone knew everyone else's name, and their business. These children didn't even look at me.

"Pardon me, ma'am, but you wouldn't be expecting company by any chance?"

I looked up to see a big man, somewhat round in the middle but with very sharp edges. His skin was as creamy and smooth as the inside of a walnut shell, with a smattering of freckles on his cheekbones so dark and round that they might have been drawn there with a marker. Like me, he had a cup of coffee in his hand.

"I don't know anyone to expect."

"Then allow me to introduce myself," he said, and waited a moment, as if allowing me to refuse. "My name is Wallace Anderson." He extended his hand and I shook it.

"Webbie," I said, "Webbie Greeving." He held my hand until I had said my last name.

"Well, that's the prettiest name I heard since Christmas," he said, and we both laughed, and then something prompted me to tell him my whole name.

"William Edward Burghardt Greeving," I said. "A.—William Edward Burghardt Martina Greeving."

He just looked at me for a moment, and then he laughed and said, "Webbie. Like I said, a pretty name for a pretty lady." He took a sip from his coffee, chuckled again, and then, after a moment of deliberation, he pulled a small bottle from his coat. "You mind?"

I held out my cup. "I don't mind at all."

"So you not from the neighborhood?"

I laughed at him. "Do you recognize me?"

" 'S'a big neighborhood."

"I'm from up north. Galatia."

"Well, I'll be. I ain't never met no one from Galatia before."

"There aren't too many of us to meet."

"Well, that makes me all the more lucky, don't it? So few of you, so many of us, and me the privileged one."

He was turned toward me on the park bench, his knee inches away from mine. He talked casually. He asked me a little bit about Galatia, told me a little bit about the neighborhood, which was flat as a pancake griddle but still bore the name Tower Hill. When our coffee was gone we went back to the café for another and we shared a plate of roast beef and mashed potatoes and gravy. There was still tinsel and garland decorating the café, and a little light-strewn orange tree, like you see in Chinese restaurants in New York. After a while he stopped calling me Webbie and started calling me little lady, and then he just called me girl, and when we went back to his tiny house there was a proper Christmas tree, thin and thinly decorated, and dry. He called me sugar and honey and sweet thing there, and he mixed his drinks strong and didn't ask me why I had come to Wichita. His home was messy but not dirty, a bachelor pad, and there were eight-and-a-half-by-eleven-inch glossies of two teenaged girls on the mantel. I didn't ask him about them.

He pulled the thong from my hair and ran his fingers through it until it had relaxed and floated about my face in light wisps. I ran my fingers over the sides of his head, over the plain of his flat top. He smiled wide, showing a mouthful of strong white teeth.

"You shivering, little Webbie."

"It's been a while."

"That's a shame. Pretty lady like you shouldn't be kept waiting."

"There's no one to keep me waiting," I said, misunderstanding him, and he put a finger to my lips.

"Maybe you kept yourself waiting. What was you waiting for?"

"Me? I don't know that I was waiting for anything." But even as I said this I thought, My father's death. But that wasn't the truth, it was just anger. Wade, I thought, Justin, I thought, Lucy, I thought, and thought and thought and thought, and I closed my eyes.

I assumed he would kiss me but nothing happened. After a long pause he ran his fingertips lightly over my eyelids. "Where you going, pretty Webbie? Pretty baby, come back to me."

I opened my eyes. "What?"

"You don't have to close your eyes. Nothing you see is gonna scare you."

"How do you know?"

He chuckled, and put his fingers on my chest and unbuttoned just the top button of my shirt. "Because," he said, "I'm just gonna show you your own self right now." He unbuttoned another button. "You not scared of your own self, are you?"

"Of course I am," I said, and he laughed again.

"Well, don't worry. You got me tonight. You got Wallace Anderson to protect you from A. William Edward Burger Greeving, if that's what you need."

"You left out Martina."

"Oh, I'm watching out for her too. I'm watching out for alla you."

He slipped his hands between my shirt and my shoulder blades then, and used his strong thumbs to press into the muscle, and rub, first hurting them, then relaxing them. In a moment he had slipped the straps of my bra off my shoulders, and my bra slipped down just far enough to expose the tips of my nipples.

"No worries tonight," he said, rubbing again, "no troubles, only Webbie and Wallace, Wallace and Webbie."

I wanted to kiss him, to silence him, to speed him. I wanted to explain to him that I didn't want to be seduced by a black man, just fucked by one, I wanted to tell him that I didn't know why I wanted such a thing and that I didn't want to know either, that what I was doing here was not knowing. But it was all I could do to remain standing under the pressure of his thumbs. I looked down and saw that my hands were clenched in fists. It took all my strength to relax them, and as I did I felt the relaxation travel up my arms, through my kneaded shoulders, down into the rest of my body, and I sighed suddenly, loudly, deeply, and Wallace said, "There now, that's better, ain't it?" and I looked up at him and smiled, tentatively, a request, and he pulled me to him in a light hug. "There now," he said again, rubbing his big arms up and down my back. "Webbie's with Wallace tonight. Tonight Wallace'll worry about Webbie, so she don't have to."

3.19

Colin

BREAKFAST.

Cora's.

Grapefruit, coffee. No eggs—no, really—but thank you for offering.

I had finished *The Aeneid*, moved on—or moved back—to the *Iliad*. Before *The Aeneid* I had read the *Inferno*. You see that I had developed an interest in closed communities.

I didn't have Greek, so I read a translation.

I'd finished neither my grapefruit nor my reading when someone entered Cora's café. The bells on the door startled me; by the time I usually arrived, the "breakfast rush," as Cora called it, was long over, and only once or twice had a customer strayed into the café while I was there. Then, too, there was the fact that the door to Cora's was glass, and I suspected that most Galatians who saw a white head through it—particularly a head as recognizable as mine—would have turned away without coming in. At any rate, I always sat with my back to the door, so that I would not have to be an active participant in such a drama.

As I said, the bells rang, startling me, but I didn't turn around. I continued reading, but from the corner of my eye I could see that Cora had stopped working behind the counter, and stared at the door.

Then I heard the humming.

"Well," I said then, "if it isn't bad, bad, Lawman Brown."

Cora laughed. She laughed out loud, and even after she'd clapped a hand over her mouth giggles continued to leak from between her fingers.

"G'morning, Sheriff," she finally managed to say. "Can I get you a cuppa coffee?"

"No, thank you, Cora, I'll just be a second."

"And how bout you, Mrs. Krebs?"

"No, thank you kindly, Cora. I'm sure we'll only be a moment."

I turned then; it seemed to me that Rosemary Krebs was worth turning around for, although I pretended not to notice her right off.

"So, Sheriff, what can I do for you?"

Lawman Brown blinked. "Beg pardon, Mr. Nieman?"

"Oh, come now, Sheriff. You didn't just happen to drop by Cora's while I was here, did you?" I let my eyes stray to Rosemary Krebs', and then return to his. "I rather suspect you've come to make an announcement."

Lawman Brown seemed about to answer, when a heavy rapid tread sounded on the steps behind him. A shadow filled the door, then pushed it open, and Grady Oconnor rushed into the café, nearly toppling Rosemary Krebs in the process. He was panting, and he looked around the room, as if surprised to find it so filled, and then, nervously, he pulled his cap off his head and held it in his hands.

"Pardon me, ma'am," he said to Rosemary Krebs. "Morning, Cora," he said. "Morning, Sheriff, Mr. Nieman."

"Grady Oconnor, what you doing here at this hour?"

Grady swallowed before answering. "Calvin Brickley busted a axle on his tractor. He was so upset that he just sent me and DuWayne home for the day."

"And you thought you'd get you a early start on lunch?"

Grady looked down at his feet. "Bit early for lunch. But I wouldn't mind me a second breakfast."

"Mr. Nieman," Lawman Brown said, "Mr. Nieman, I got to be getting back to work."

"By all means, Sheriff. Please, get back."

Lawman Brown peered at me suspiciously, as if he was trying to decide if I was making fun of him. Beside him, Rosemary Krebs stared vacantly into space, and only a tapping foot betrayed her impatience. Grady Oconnor's eyes were still cast down, but it was impossible to tell if he was looking at his own feet or at Rosemary Krebs'.

"Mr. Nieman," Lawman Brown said again. "If you don't mind me stating your business in public . . ."

"Please, Sheriff, speak freely. I have nothing to hide. Nothing, at any rate, that you can reveal."

Cora laughed again, less loudly, but distinctly.

"It's about them tests, Mr. Nieman."

Cora's laughter broke off abruptly.

Grady Oconnor, I noticed, was bunching his hat in his hands.

The tempo of Rosemary Krebs' tapping increased, and the sound her foot made was the only sound in the room.

"Everything come out okay, Mr. Nieman."

" 'Okay'?"

"The samples we found. The blood and the tissue samples, they was mostly from Lucy Robinson, and your friend. The, the semen didn't match up to either of you."

"You're saying that I didn't rape Lucy Robinson."

"It would appear not, Mr. Nieman."

"And if we can trust appearances, Sheriff Brown, which we all know is a doubtful proposition, but if this once we decide to do so, then we can also assume that I didn't attack her either, or kidnap her, but that someone wearing my clothing did."

Grady Oconnor dropped his hat to the floor then; it landed within inches of Rosemary Krebs' tapping foot, which skipped one beat and then continued tapping. It seemed to me that her foot had attained the speed of a sewing machine's bobbin, and its staccato rhythm seemed to be pulling the fabric of the floor beneath her body and spewing it out somewhere behind her. Her face remained unreadable, however, and, after glancing at it, Grady Oconnor made no move to pick up his hat. Lawman Brown didn't answer me, and, finally, Cora spoke.

"Grady," she said, "pick up your damn hat. Eustace," she said, "answer the man. And Mrs. Krebs," she added in a cautious but firm tone, "I'ma have to ask you to stop that tapping before I take a cleaver to your foot."

Lawman Brown flushed, and flashed an angry look at Cora. I could see him considering whether to deliver his "my-title-is-sheriff" line, but before he could the ball of Rosemary Krebs' foot struck the floor with a resounding final splat, and she turned her face to me.

"What the sheriff is attempting to say, Mr. Nieman, is that your name has been cleared and you are now free to leave Galatea."

In a single darting movement, Grady bent over and picked up his hat.

"What I'm saying," Lawman Brown said, "is that anytime you wanta clear outta here, Mr. Nieman, I will personally send a few men over to help you pack up and get lost."

"Well, I thank you for your generous offer, Sheriff. But as it happens

I have some unfinished business of my own, and I have no immediate plans to leave Galatia."

Though I'd spoken to Lawman Brown I'd kept my eyes fixed on Rosemary Krebs. But it was Cora who spoke next.

"Unfinished business?" she said.

Although Lawman Brown was not the kind of person I liked to turn my back on—nor, for that matter, was Grady Oconnor, or Rosemary Krebs—I looked over at Cora, because her tone had not been particularly welcoming. It had, in fact, been hostile, and I saw that she regarded me with a slightly bewildered expression on her face.

"My—my book," I said, somewhat flustered by her reaction.

"Your book," she repeated. She tried to laugh. "You mean, that one on the table there?"

"I mean the one I'm writing, Cora. Cora, what *is* the matter?"

Cora had grabbed a dish towel and was kneading it in her hands. Her jaw worked, but no sound came out. Finally, she managed to spit out, "Why, that, that, that's perverse, Mr. Nieman. *Perverse*."

"Cora—"

"You shut up, Eustace, just shut up. And you," she said, turning back to me. "What you mean, you have to finish your book? They's a whole wide world out there, go finish your goddamn book somewhere else."

"But, Cora, it's Galatia that's inspiring me."

"Galatia, my ass. Ain't no such a thing as Galatia no more. Not since *him* and his boss come along. You say you writing bout Galatia, but what you writing bout is in your own head. So whyn't you take that head off and write about it somewhere else."

"Cora, I don't understand."

"No, you don't! So let me explain you, Mr. Nieman. We got a delicate balance going here, Mr. Nieman, a real delicate balance, and when you come along you threw it all outta whack. You come along and things just went to *hell*."

"But, Cora, Lawman Brown just said—"

"But Cora nothing! I never once thought you did what they said you did or I'da never let you sit down in my café. But as sure as I'm a Negress and that dwarf white bitch there think she some kinda old-time Massa I can tell you that whoever did rape poor Lucy Robinson did it cause *you* come here, and maybe if you leave you'll take your trouble off with you. We don't need *strangers* in this town, Mr. Nieman. Don't like em, don't need em, don't want em, so be gone with you."

I wanted, then, to see how Rosemary Krebs reacted to being called a bitch and a Massa, but just then the towel Cora was kneading in her hands ripped loudly in two. Cora looked at the two halves for a moment, and then she threw them in opposite directions. In the moment of silence that followed her action, Grady spoke.

"*I'll* take his head off, Cora. If you want."

Grady and Cora looked at each other, and for the very first time since I had moved there, I felt the palpable division between the races in Galatia, as the two black people in the room regarded each other as if the three white people who were also present simply did not exist.

When Cora spoke, her voice had quieted somewhat. "You shut up, Grady Oconnor," she said. "If they's one thing I can't stand it's a snoop and a gossip. You get yourself back to work."

Grady didn't move, and after a moment I spoke.

"Cora," I said, as gently as I could. "Surely you don't believe that your problems will disappear with me. I'm not the cause, Cora, I'm just being used as someone's catalyst."

Cora's back sagged, and her breath came in ragged gulps. Her tirade seemed to have exhausted her, and she leaned heavily on the counter.

"I don't know what that word means, Mr. Nieman."

"Catalyst," another voice said. The voice was Rosa's, and she stood in the doorway that led back to the kitchen, a bus tub of apples in her hand, and when she spoke again it was in a dry flat voice, as though she was reciting from memory. "A substance that can cause a change in the rate of a chemical reaction without itself being consumed in the reaction."

Cora looked up, a horrified expression on her face. Her hands reached about wildly, but there was nothing for her to grab. "Oh Rosa, honey, oh Rosa, I didn't mean *you*. I didn't mean *you* was a *stranger*." And then, all at once, she was sobbing.

Rosa kept her eyes on Cora's. "Mr. Nieman, Mrs. Krebs, Sheriff Brown, Mr. Oconnor." She said all our names carefully, as if she were reciting them as well, "I think you all should leave now."

She set her bus tub down and rolled up her sleeves.

"Well, Rosa—"

"Please, Sheriff." Rosa smiled, briefly, but she didn't turn away from Cora. "I'd hate to have to call the law on you."

She went to Cora then, without waiting to see if we would heed her, and she wrapped her thin arms around Cora's broad back. For one long moment no one moved or spoke; the four of us beyond the counter's periphery regarded the two clutching women within it, and the café was filled with Cora's sobbing and the smell of food. And then Rosemary Krebs turned to me, and when she spoke it was in the same automatic voice Rosa had used.

"Mr. Nieman," she said, and then she paused, and then she smiled. "It is a pleasure to know that we may continue to enjoy your company. Rosa, Cora, Grady," she added without looking at any of them, "good day. Eustace," she said, but she didn't add anything after his name. Still, he seemed to know what was expected of him, and, slowly, as if he wished to avoid disturbing the bells, he pulled open the door. The bells rang anyway.

3.20

Divine

HERE'S SOMETHING THAT CAN HAPPEN. YOU CAN PUT your car on a road round here, some two-lane rural highway that's straight as a arrow and if not as flat as a pancake then at least as flat as a omelet—a Western omelet say, with like here and there the bump of sausage or tomato or onion—and then you can just kinda go on autopilot, especially at night with like your only distraction being a pair of headlights way up ahead, flick to low beams, flick back to high, ease the seat back a little and put on the cruise control, you know what I'm saying, and you can, like, just find yourself tooling along one of these roads and shit, and before you know it an hour's gone by, two, three, and suddenly you realize you're in another state. In this case—I mean, if you was like starting out from Galatia—the state would like as not be Nebraska, which ain't all that different to Kansas, but you'd still notice little changes, I mean, shit, the mile markers start over if nothing else, and for just a while, until you turn around or decide to keep going, you have this like sense of yourself as a foreigner, a traveler, a stranger in a strange land, someone on the road *to* as opposed to on the road *from*. Well I tell you what. I thought about that. I thought about how easy it'd be to just drive and drive and keep on driving, fuck Colin and fuck Wade and fuck that creepy little Justin and all those other freaks back in Galatia. But, you know, Galatia's leash is only so long, and so after like maybe thirty minutes insteada three hours I turned, and then I turned again, and pretty soon I found myself at a stopping point, and I stopped. Cause, you know, I wasn't really the type to go nowhere. Stopping was just what I *did*.

Okay. So, some context. Colin, I guess, Colin'd had this big fight at Cora's after Lawman Brown had told him that those lab tests had cleared his name. I guess Colin wanted to stick around town but Cora thought he should clear on outta here. Anyway, that's what I heard from Blaine Getterling, who got it from Grady Oconnor, and Grady was there. But by the time Colin got to the old Deacon house he'd changed his mind, I guess, and by the time I got over there, which was like pretty late cause I'd been down to the Big M seeing if I could sniff up a trace of Ratboy and so anyway by the time I showed up at the old Deacon spread Colin had like completely packed up his office and shit, I mean all that paper that'd been on his desk was all like taped up in boxes and shit, and the typewriters too, and they all sat in this big old pile by the door.

The boxes had labels on them, things like *Version 1* and *The Abduction* and *The Dinner Party part 3*, but the message was pretty clear to me, and the message was: moving time. Which was fine with me, and I was all like, So when're we going? Which is when the shit hit the fan, cause Colin said in that way that only Colin Nieman can that "we" wasn't going nowhere, that "he" was going back to New York and that "he" was taking Justin with him, and that "I," if I was smart, would find me someplace better than Galatia to live. And then I asked him Well what about his novel, and he was all, Jesus, the daisy chain don't waste no time, and I said, You told Cora and them that you wasn't leaving till your novel was done, and he said, Yeah, well, I changed my mind. And then, you know, I guess he felt at least a little sorry for me cause he came over and was all like putting his arms around me and shit, and he was all like, The book's close enough to done, he was like, I can finish it anywhere now, it's time I went. Which is when I was all like, Yeah, well, fuck you two, and so anyway that's like the short version—the long version includes him like fucking me again, but who really gives a shit, right?

Certainly not Mr. Colin Nieman—which Grady told me means No-Man, and he ain't a man as far as I'm concerned. And Grady told me too that Colin is a cocaine user, and I told Grady I could believe it cause of some things I'd read, and I told Grady too that maybe Colin knew more about Lucy Robinson than he was letting on, which when I said that shit

I didn't mean anything against Colin, I was only trying to give Grady something to talk about, but afterwards, after I saw Colin, I got to hoping that Grady would talk *a lot*.

When I left Colin's I started for Wade's and then I changed my mind and started for the Big M and then I changed my mind again and started for Sloppy Joe's and then I changed my mind and decided to head outta town. Nowhere in particular, just out. North, to be specific.

One of the Urban Development Projects that dumb bitch Rosemary Krebs give up on pretty early was a public swimming pool. Like everything else in Galatea, the library and the school building and the police station, for a long time there was just some dumb-ass sign up in a vacant lot that said "Future Site of blah blah blah." In this case the sign said FUTURE SITE OF THE GALATEA MUNICIPAL SWIMMING POOL AND WATER AMUSEMENTS FACILITY, and the only reason I remember that shit word for word is cause it stuck around a good ten, twelve years, fading and blistering in the weather, until finally it just disappeared one night, along with the signs for the GALATEA MUNICIPAL MINIMALL AND SHOPPING CENTER and the GALATEA MUNICIPAL ZOO, PETTING *and* VIEWING. I mean, shit, wheie the bitch think she be, Southern California or some shit? And but anyway, I suppose that outta all them stupid shit projects she dreamed up, the swimming pool was the only one folks really missed, cause, you know, surface water's in fairly short supply around here, and not all that many folks can afford their own swimming pool. The preferred swimming hole—the one where I ended up on the night Colin told me he was leaving—was a good fifteen miles from town. People liked it cause it wasn't some stagnant-ass pond: it was a sharp bend in the Bow River that formed a nice deep pool about the size of a basketball court, and plus too there was several big old cottonwoods that shaded the hole in summer and, you know, provided a couple-a good limbs for tying rope swings to and all that shit.

And there was also this like one huge and absolutely ancient willow tree that legend has it was the father of the willows that grow in the park in Galatia, and legend also has it that this willow tree is the tree Eric Johnson was tied to.

It catches up with you. You know, the story.

But I wasn't thinking about Eric Johnson when I drove there. I was thinking about Lucy Robinson. Cause I guess the one thing I had that you could call a run-in with Lucy Robinson happened at this here swimming hole, which what basically happened is one day Ratboy drove me and him out here to go swimming and we found Howard Goertzen and

Darrell Jenkens and Eddie Comedy just about to get into something with Grady Oconnor and DuWayne Hicks and Melvin Cartwright, cause, you know, nobody was quite sure who owned the land the swimming hole was on, or in, I guess you'd say—the one thing people *was* sure of was that it wasn't Rosemary Krebs'—so basically it was first come first serve, and even though you coulda drowned half the town in there without noticing, the general rule was that white folks and black folks didn't go swimming at the same time, and plus there was the general belief that Eddie Comedy'd had *something* to do with the lynching of Eric Johnson, and there was the fact that Eddie'd been made quarterback of the high school football team when everybody knew that Melvin Cartwright could throw the ball about twice as far as Eddie could, and plus too Eddie Comedy ran like a girl to boot. So as you can imagine, things was pretty hot when me and Ratboy showed up and suddenly this white boy/black boy thing just kind of completely disappeared and was replaced by this straight boy/fag boy thing, and since Ratboy was never one to back down from a confrontation, I thought we was gonna get our asses whupped for sure. But then what happened was before anything could happen Myra Robinson showed up with a carful of pasty-faced girls, Lee Anne Atkins and Shelly Stadler and of course dear sweet little Miss Lucy Robinson, and then that was kind of it. Cause in the first place there's something about a woman's presence that tends to cool off fighting men, you know what I'm saying, especially if that woman is like a *mother* even if she only maybe ten years older than the men involved, and, on the other hand, the more important hand I guess you could say, on the hand you write with, there wasn't no black man in Galatia who was gonna even *admit* to noticing that the teenaged Lucy Robinson was in possession of a goodly set of T&A let alone stand around while she stripped down to a purple bikini and strutted down to the hole in little white plastic slip-ons and white-framed plastic sunglasses the size of Texas and calling out, Hi, *boys*. I mean, she-double-fucking-*it*. And so like Grady Oconnor and DuWayne Hicks and Melvin Cartwright and even me, yeah, even I told Myra that as a matter of fact we was done swimming, didn't really feel like swimming anyway, goddamn but I forgot I had a lotta work to do, and we left. Ratboy I have to say kind of didn't get it, and Myra, well, I've always been pretty amazed by what some folks, especially women, especially white women, can pretend they don't know.

It's always like that, see, first one thing and then another and then another. It's always Eddie Comedy and then it's Melvin Cartwright and then it's me and Ratboy but I suppose that in the end, around here anyway, it's always Lucy Robinson.

The first time I ever come here I was six. My daddy was in the water and my momma helped me get aholda the rope swing and pushed me high out over the water and my father and I was afraid to let go and I like to killed me and my momma both when I crashed back onto dry land.

That rope swing was still there. It had that stiff-slack look telephone wires get in the wintertime, and it was kind of shiny in the moonlight with frost. Whoever'd used it last had been a good neighbor, that's what my momma called being considerate, being a good neighbor, and they'd left the loose end of the swing looped around a shrub so it'd be easy to get at.

And I don't know, I guess I felt like I was playing catch up. There was Colin and Justin back in the old Deacon house *right now*, packing up to go, and then there was me, out at the swimming hole, and not only was it not even summer but it wasn't even that *year*, it was three, four years ago, it was ten, twelve years ago and it was like the faster I run to catch up the further back I fell in time.

It wasn't just that the situation was bigger than me. Everything was always bigger than me, shit, I was used to that. But this situation was just growing and growing, not around me but away from me, and I guess I had one-a those realizations that it'd always been growing away from me, that I just didn't matter, not to Colin, not to Wade, not, now that Ratboy was gone, not to anybody back in that stinky little town, which as far as I was concerned was really the whole world.

I remember my daddy saying I'll catch you and my momma saying I'll catch you if you don't want him to, and I remember coming home from school exactly two years and two weeks ago and finding the house empty of everything but the dead Christmas tree and the burned-out lightbulbs in the ceiling. They'd taken the ones that still worked.

Most of the top of the swimming hole was frozen, there was just this little like channel that cut down the center of it where the river was still running, and of course I guess I mean I know it was still running underneath the ice. Then there was leaves and twigs and a couple-a beer cans on the ice, kind of half frozen in place.

Something else I remembered: coming to the swimming hole one early and cold spring morning to find a few green sprouts of something growing in a pit of dirt that'd collected on a little iceberg that still hadn't melted away. That didn't seem particularly important then and it don't seem particularly important now, but all the same it was what I remembered.

A long skin of ice cracked off the rope when I grabbed it, and I thought about the rubber Colin hadn't worn when he fucked me.

Some branches rattled together when I gave the rope a testing tug.

My daddy explained it to me this way: you could swing out and you could swing back and nothing would happen, or you could swing out and drop in and that'd be that. Or you could just get in the car and go back home. He didn't give a shit.

My momma told me that spit freezes but tears don't cause-a the salt in them and low and behold she was right. She told me that another time, not the time I first came swimming here. My momma gave a shit but all the same, she said, she just couldn't take it, looking at her little boy and seeing what'd become of him.

The rope was tied to the willow tree.

As long as I'm being completely honest I suppose I should say that as I took a firm grip on the rope my clearest thought was that I wished that my underwear was clean, but then I supposed that the dirty water would fix that problem, make everything a nice and uniform and neutral shade of gray, and I thought it was a bit of a shame about my coat, a really nice shearling number I got Wade to give me last Christmas, but there you go. Next time I'd try to dress for the occasion.

I gave the rope one more testing tug and then I said out loud Quit stalling Divine and then I just grabbed on to the rope and up and jumped and all I really noticed was that the wind on my wet cheeks was fucking *cold* and I wanted it to stop and my daddy wasn't in the water and my momma wasn't waiting on dry land and now my only two choices was that I could drop in or I could swing back and I tried to think of something good to say as my last words and I couldn't although I did sort of wonder where *was* Webbie and I also kind of hoped, surprise surprise, that everything turned out okay for Lucy Robinson, and then insteada saying goodbye I just said Fuck it out loud and then I let go.

3.21

Webbie

SOMETIME ON THE SECOND DAY I SPENT WITH WALlace Anderson we were driving through Wichita, when we passed a public library. "Please, can we stop for a minute," I said to Wallace, and it seemed to me he used the bumpers of his huge old Cadillac to clear a parking space between two compacts that would have fit under the hood or in the trunk.

Years of part-time work at Columbia plus the two days a week I spent at Galatea's library meant that I didn't have to check a card catalog first; I went straight to the XXX's, criminology, and after a minute I chose a thick illustrated volume on organized crime called *Victims and the Mafia*. There something you tryna tell me? Wallace said then, in that artificially hushed tone which people who are unfamiliar with libraries use in them, and I jumped at his voice because I was so unused to being accompanied by someone that I had forgotten I was with him. I looked up at him and smiled but didn't say anything; and he turned from me to look at a poster of a chimpanzee wearing a dunce cap and holding a book upside down, and after a moment during which I assume he read the poster's caption he laughed once and then he turned back to me and shrugged, and put his hands in his pockets and said, You go on, you do what you got to do.

I'm still not sure what I was looking for. I'm not even sure if I found it. I had been caught by the word *victims* in the book's title; I just felt that I wanted to see photographs of "victims," and I turned page after page, looked at victim after victim, and I don't remember thinking of Lucy Robinson even once as I looked at those pictures. What I remember is a photograph of a man called Salvatore Genovese. Salvatore Genovese, the caption told me, had been skimming money from a bookmaking operation he ran for some syndicate or other in New York City, and when he was caught his punishment was to have his fingers cut off with the tool that Coach Carting used to clip locks left on lockers at the end of each school year. I don't know how to describe the hands in the picture because they didn't look like anything I had ever seen, not like the hock of a pig cooked in a pot of collard greens, not like the body of a cat hit by a car, certainly not like hands. Salvatore Genovese's punishers hadn't killed him, they said, but they claimed that in his pain he had thrown himself through a window six floors above the ground, and as proof of their innocence they said they would have opened the window if they'd wanted to throw him out. I stared at the picture, stared and stared at it. Salvatore's hands blurred into and out of focus before my eyes, so that sometimes they *did* look almost normal and at other times they seemed so unlike hands that they weren't threatening, but always they returned to their violently mangled state, and when, finally, Wallace took the book from me and closed it I saw that my hands were balled—no, not balled, but clenched, contorted even—into tight little fists. As Wallace slipped the book back into its empty niche on the shelf, I looked at my hands and willed them to open, but they would not. They were no more responsive than the hands in the picture had been, and as I stared at them I remembered an image from Colin's *Beast* of an old and senile woman who had lain with her hands curled into fists for so long that her fingernails had grown into her palms. No, I remembered then, not Colin's *Beast*, but Justin's, and I thought of Justin's mouth, closed like that woman's hands, and like my hands. My mind conjured an image of Justin's lips sealing and his teeth growing into the flesh of his jaws, and I felt something almost like shame then, because I had gone into the library thinking about Lucy Robinson and after just a few minutes my mind had abandoned her for Colin, for Justin, for me. Then Wallace was back and he put his big arms around me and I felt the flat open palms of his hands against the small of my back and the light drum of his fingertips there, and he said, "You don't got to tell me nothing you don't want to," and he just stood there, holding me lightly, and air slipped from his nose and entered the collar of my open coat and slipped inside my shirt and was cool against the sweat on my back. He said, "You take as long as you need," and I wondered then how something I *could not want* could feel so good.

I woke up in the middle of that night from a nightmare. I had been dreaming, not surprisingly, of mutilated hands, but the hands in my dream were black: the hands were mine. For a moment I was disoriented and even more afraid, but then, all at once, I remembered where I was. I recognized the knotty pine bureau with its shiny polyurethane veneer, dulled by dust and moonlight; I recognized the one hundred twelve caps emblazoned with various logos and advertisements that hung off pegs on one wall; I recognized Wallace. He slept naked. Before going to sleep we had had sex, and we had washed, and then he had tried to pull on a pair of baggy boxer shorts; but I'd put my leg between his as he'd pulled them up, and I used my foot to push the boxers back to the floor. Wallace had grinned at me and chuckled and pulled me to him in a tight bear hug, as though I'd done something miraculous.

Now he slept flat on his back, his stomach slightly rippled like a thick-skinned pudding, tight corkscrews of hairs scattered across the soft expanse of it, little slivers of chocolate. The sound of his breathing was deep and loud, although it wasn't a snore, but with each breath his stomach seemed to move not at all, as though unseen depths within him contained all that extra air. He slept with one hand in the space between his penis and navel, and I was struck by the contrast between the two skins, the rough chapped dry skin of his hands, pale-palmed and slightly freckled on top; and the almost absurdly delicate skin of his soft penis, which looked from this angle and in this light like the bottom of an infant's foot. Just looking at him was enough to bring to mind the feel of him, the hands that had run over my shoulders almost like sandpaper scraping away impurities, and the penis, which I had held in my hand, and inside me, and against my cheek, though Wallace hadn't let me put it in my mouth.

When I turned my head slightly I could see his face, his lips parted and damp, his cheeks round and covered with a day's growth of beard. His hair had gone a little nappy, and the lashes of his closed eyes were luxuriously long and thick, almost feminine. At some point during the evening I'd teased him about those long lashes, and he'd said that his momma once told him that the only two things that was girly about her boy Wallace was his eyelashes and his modesty, and he'd laughed a little at himself, and his eyes had fallen to the floor.

There was a faint smell in the room of what we had done. It was tangy and ripe, like the smell of something cooking.

My car keys were on top of the bureau. Wallace had folded my clothes for me and placed them in a drawer with his own. He was neat, he said, but not really clean, and when I asked him the difference he wrote my name in the dust on the otherwise bare top of the bureau.

Neat, he said, but not clean.

He spelled my name W-E-B-B-Y.

When the heating unit kicked in the whole house shuddered, but I wasn't startled. I was used to it already; the wall's rattle was like the rattle of a door closed in another room, announcing the arrival of a frequent if somewhat noisy neighbor.

I had made Wallace turn the heat up high, so that he would not feel the need for blankets or clothes.

I took Wallace's hand in mine.

I told myself that this wasn't why I'd come here.

I could not tell myself what *this* was.

I pulled Wallace's hand to my cheek and ran his knuckles over my skin, and Wallace murmured something in his sleep.

I don't know if they were actually words he murmured, but nevertheless I understood his meaning, and I relaxed into them and slept with them in my ears.

"You don't have to go back," Wallace was saying to me. He said, "You can stay." And, for another night, I did.

3.22

Lawman Brown

JUST ON THE OFF CHANCE HE'D FAXED A LINE TO SHERiff Peterson down to Bigger Hill, who'd investigated that attack out by the Big M oh it must be a couple-a three years ago at least. Which was still unsolved, Lawman Brown added to himself, although he didn't mention that in his note to old Petey. That'd been something and I mean something. The poor kid, Lawman Brown couldn't recall his name off the top of his head, although come to think of it maybe they'd never got a name off the kid? Anyway, the poor kid'd been hanging out by the Big M when it happened, which truth is, Petey had told Lawman Brown when it first happened, truth is the victim if you can call him that had been seen loitering in the parking lot behind the Big M on more than one occasion and you don't need a detective badge to figure out what that meant. Anyway the kid had been making his way back to that same shack where Eddie Comedy'd showed up in September—Lawman Brown didn't ask Petey in his note if he had any new info in the old attack but he did ask if he'd maybe gotten any leads on who mighta torched it a few weeks ago—and but anyway, what happened was the guy'd just rounded a corner and well Petey didn't even want to imagine how *tuckered out* the guy musta been, ha ha ha, when all of a sudden he came face to face with this like *enormous* man. Who, he said later, who this enormous man was eating something out of a can. Which was what the man used to hit him first: apparently the victim hadn't even blunk before the man brought the flat end of the can right down on the guy's forehead.

Creamed corn, according to forensics, and, well, what old Petey wanted to know was what kind of man walks around with a *can opener*?

After that the story got kind of hazy. The kid passed out from the creamed-corn blow, which was more or less a mercy, and he didn't wake up until three weeks later, in the hospital. When he did wake up he found he had something like thirty-seven, Lawman Brown thought that was the number, *thirty-seven* separate fractures in his arms and legs and fingers and toes, and the kid's pelvis had been stomped on till it cracked in half, and every one of his fingers had been like pulled from its socket and left hanging by the skin alone. A year after the attack and the kid had still been bedridden and it was all he could do to hold a spoon to feed himself soup, which was all he could eat on account of every last one of his teeth was gone and the two breaks in his jawbone never really healed right and no dentist was willing to do pro bono the kind of prosthetic work it would take to give the kid a working set of dentures.

But what made the whole thing kinda interesting, Petey told Lawman Brown, what made it interesting was that besides the extensive jaw damage and of course that first blow from the corn can there were no other injuries to the kid's head or torso except that fractured pelvis, which his pelvis was actually fractured *four* times and which was why the kid would probably never walk again, or at least not walk right. But there was nothing that you'd technically call life threatening about the kid's injuries, although of course there'd been the very real possibility that the kid coulda starved to death if a couple-a boys hadn't come across him two days later. Still, you couldn't really say that he'd been beat to death. If he'd died, that is, which he said he wished he had, when he could finally talk, sort of. He could sort of talk, Petey meant. He definitely wished he'd died.

The ring of the fax machine always made Lawman Brown jump. It wasn't something he used often enough to get used to, and half the time it was just Nettie's cousin anyway, what was her name, Betty, or Hettie, anyway it was something that rhymed with Nettie, she was this secretary in Kansas City who used her boss's phone bill to fax Nettie recipes and dress patterns and cartoons from the Sunday paper. But this time the pages that come through was for him, and it was from Petey, and it was a PhotoFit based on the injured guy's description of his attacker. The only thing Petey'd written on the page was "Bare in mind it was dark out and he was drunk." Lawman Brown bore that in mind, and he took a long time looking at the fax, and then he crumpled it up and threw it in the trash. Nettie called to him then, Eustace, she called, was that for me? and Lawman Brown called back, No, he called, it was just one of them little checkups the machine runs on itself, and Nettie called back, I *do* wish there was some way to turn that off, that beeping drives me round the *bend*, and Lawman Brown allowed as how he wished the same thing too, and then he picked the wadded fax up outta the trash can and shoved it in his pocket, and only then did he notice that a second page had come through, a second Photofit, and what this PhotoFit was was the kid as the police artist had figured he might've looked before he lost all his teeth and had his jaw twisted half off. Lawman Brown looked at the face, thin-lipped, buck-toothed, although how the police artist coulda guessed that he didn't know, the picture had a general ferrety look about it and the artist had even gone so far as to pencil in a couple-a zits on the guy's forehead, and Lawman

Brown could understand then why he'd got the nickname Ratboy. Petey's note with this PhotoFit was asking first of all if Lawman Brown might have any clue who the kid was, and the other thing he wrote was that the kid, who Lawman Brown figured musta been still in the hospital, the kid had managed to steal some insulin and shot hisself up with it six months ago and died and just between you and me, Petey's note said, that was probably just as well.

Lawman Brown wadded that page up too, stuffed it in his pocket with the first page, and it occurred to him as he did so that the man had done what he'd done to the kid, to Ratboy, to Lamoine Wiebe—well, Lawman Brown figured, it wouldn't do no one no good to know that now, and poor Carol Wiebe, he'd had enough grief from his one and only son already—and but anyway, at any rate, the man had done what he'd done to the kid in something like an hour, tops, and Lucy Robinson had been missing for going on two months now. Lawman Brown thought he would burn the two fax pages up when he got home. Until then he did his goddamnedest best, Pardon me, Lord, but he did everything he could not to think of what kind of shape Lucy Robinson might be in by now, which as it turned out didn't make no difference anyway, because he was going to find exactly what kind of shape she was in soon enough.

4

4.01

Sawyer Johnson

MY MOMMA SHE DRAGGIN ME LONG FASTER'N I WANNA be dragged along, cant hardly breathe but she draggin me faster'n faster. Its dark out, she say and I say I *know* that, and she say You hush now, and she say It past my bedtime, but when we come up to the police station she let up a little, I think to let me catch my breath but when I look up she just starin at the building, the windows is open and I can hear voices shouting, cant hear what they sayin but I can hear em shouting and then my Momma starts up again with the dragging, even faster, I can't even find the breath to ask her slow down and her fingernails cuttin right into my wrist, she call down to me don't you *never* go out past dark without me or you end up like that, she say you end up just a voice in a room.

4.02

Howard Goertzen

THE DARK MOUND OF IT WAS LIKE A LESION IN THE road. Ten years ago Lucy Robertson had stood in this very same intersection in a dirty and torn white dress and screamed for help because of what that white nigger'd done to her, and now there was just the dress, not the white lace one she wore when she was seven years old but the purple stretchy velvet one she'd looked so cute in at Rosemary Krebs' dance the other night, when she was with that little pansy boy from New York City, and Howard Goertzen put gloves on before he rolled up the dress, and he had a sense that rolling it up wouldn't do no good in the same way that rolling up an unrolled roll of toilet paper doesn't do no good, and then he drove to the station house and he gave the bundle to Lawman Brown and he watched as Lawman Brown re-unrolled the dress on a steel examination table. There was something fundamentally lifeless in the way the dress moved beneath Lawman Brown's gloved fingers, as though some essence it had contained once was gone now, and Howard Goertzen had to swallow the gorge that was rising in his throat, and when, finally, he could speak again, he could only say, "Aw gee," and when the dress was fully extended and as flat as it could go he said, "Aw, aw gee," again, and nothing else. The dress was so badly shredded that the strips of its fabric showed up against the silver surface of the table like a dark maze. It was frayed, flayed even, as though it had been whipped as in whipped-with-a-whip whipped from her body, and it seemed to be decaying under the rot of mud and blood and other stains that coated it, and Howard Goertzen heard Lawman Brown say, "It looks like somebody threw it in a washing machine with a loada broken glass," and there was the gorge again, and Howard Goertzen swallowed it back down again, and he said, "And Lucy, it looks like he threw Lucy in there too." In the other room Nettie Ferguson could be heard saying, "I'm saying he *said* he was gay, said it, just like that," and then Howard Goertzen said, "I was just driving by, to look at the spot where, you know, where Charlene died. And there it was, right in the same place, right on the corner-a East Adams and First. Right where that bastard killed her."

4.03

Nettie Ferguson

IT WAS A WHITE PLASTIC BAG WITH THE WORD ZABAR'S

written on it in big orangy-brown capital letters, and didn't nobody have to tell nobody where it come from. "That just *sounds* like New York City to me," Eustace said when he saw it. "Zay-bar's," he said, and then he said, "Yup. *Jew* York City," and if the situation hadn't been so serious and if Myra Robinson hadn't been standing right there Nettie Ferguson woulda allowed herself a chuckle at Eustace's joke, but as it was he remained stiff and formal in front of Myra Robinson and so Nettie Ferguson did too, she was standing behind Myra Robinson but she remained as stiff and formal as Eustace while meanwhile Myra Robinson stood there shaking and holding the bag by its knotted plastic handles, which the bag, Nettie had noticed when Myra first come into the station house, the bag was filled with something dark and fluffy and weightless apparently, a big ball rustling in front of her stomach in Myra Robinson's shaking hands and Myra Robinson herself looking a bit like a big rustling ball in front of the hulking form of T. V. Daniels—gosh darn but that boy could *eat*—his body dwarfing hers the way she dwarfed the bag, and between the two of them Nettie Ferguson couldn't hardly even see the bag let alone begin to guess what mighta been in it. Now T.V. cleared his throat and said, "I found it in her mailbox," his voice the voice of the tall lanky boy he used to be, Nettie Ferguson oughta know, she used to babysit for him way back when when her Horace was alive, and when Nettie Ferguson looked at T.V. now what she saw was a little reed of a boy trapped underneath layer upon layer upon layer of fat, it was sad, Nettie thought, it was a shame really, when he was a boy he used to watch that *Mickey Mouse Club* show every single day and when the closing theme song came on he'd be so caught up in it that he'd get up in front of the TV and dance around real slow and pretty and Nettie Ferguson just could *not* imagine what T.V. would look like if that song came on right now. At T.V.'s words Myra Robinson made a choking noise and Nettie saw Eustace reach out and take the bag away from her before she dropped it. "There there," Eustace said as soothingly as he knew how, which wasn't very much, even he woulda had to admit it, Eustace Brown didn't really know from soothing. "Now now," he tried again, Eustace tried again—one of the things Nettie Ferguson had learned from her bird's-eye point of view on more than a few criminal investigations was the need for specificness of detail—"Now now," the Sheriff of Cadavera County said to the distressed mother of the missing person, Myra Robinson, "I'm sure it ain't nothing. It don't hardly weigh enough to be nothing, but let's just have us a little look-see to be sure," and then Nettie Ferguson saw him make a little experimental tug at the knots, which resisted his fingers, and she nodded her head approvingly when Eustace said, "Hey, Myra, you ain't happened to of run across Reginald Packman lately?" because she knew that what Eustace was doing was distracting her, distracting Myra Robinson, in order to reduce her state of agitation. "Been looking for him for a few weeks now," Eustace went on. "Can't seem to find him nowhere." Myra Robinson looked at Eustace as though he'd spoken Spanish or something. "What?" she said. "Who?" "Reginald," Eustace said, his fingers pulling harder at the knots, "Packman," he finished, still trying without success to work the knotted handles free of each other. There was a long moment of silence then, until T. V. Daniels said in a weak, in a sort of strained, quiet voice, "Divine," and Myra Robinson repeated, "Divine?" She was looking down at the bag Eustace was still working on as though T. V. were telling her that Reginald Packman—*Divine!*—were in that bag, and Eustace was prying at the knot with his key now—boy, Nettie Ferguson was thinking, that bag don't weigh nothing, does it—and then Myra Robinson said, "No, no, no Divine," as if he didn't even exist, and a moment later T.V. said real quiet, "No one's seen Divine in a dog's age," and Nettie Ferguson herself was just about to ask T.V. why he was so well acquainted with Reginald Packman's comings and goings but just then the handles suddenly snapped free of each other and the bag spat forth some of its contents into the air and all over Eustace's desk in a thin but almost corporeal cloud. "What the hay?" Eustace said, and T. V. Daniels put his hand over his nose like he thought it was poison gas or something but Myra Robinson was already sobbing and screaming and clutching at clumps of the stuff, and it took Nettie Ferguson, trying to extricate the chain of her glasses from the buttons of her blouse, a moment to understand what she was saying. "My baby" was what Myra Robinson was sobbing. "My baby, my baby, my baby. Your hair!" and all the sudden Nettie Ferguson found herself in need of something to lean on and she put a hand down and felt it land on the familiar comforting shape of the telephone, which when all the sudden it rang scared Nettie Ferguson so much that she fainted clean away.

4.04

Lawman Brown

T. V. DANIELS COME IN WITH A STACK OF THEM. "I thought it was odd," he said, wheezing, "all them red flags up. Everybody in town don't usually mail a letter on the same day." There was like a moment, every time Lawman Brown saw T. V. Daniels, that he had to stop a minute and process just how *fat* the guy was, like say the number "seven hundred and thirty-one" didn't really mean nothing—the number being the number Donnie Miller had given him, Donnie Miller who worked at the grain elevator and who, he said, had weighed T. V. Daniels the same way he weighed a load of wheat, namely, by weighing T. V. Daniels' lopsided car with T. V. Daniels in it, and then weighing it again, still lopsided but empty this time—but anyway this number didn't really mean nothing to Lawman Brown, but what did mean something was how Nettie Ferguson had had to haul herself up, complaining about her arthritis every step of the way, to unlock the second half of the double door so T. V. Daniels could like get *in* the building, and it was only after processing this that Lawman Brown took the handful of pictures from T. V. Daniels—the pictures having the same relationship to T. V. Daniels' hand as postage stamps have to most other people's hands. Then he was all business. He shooed Nettie back to her phone and leafed through the pictures slowly, Polaroids, by the looka them, and after a minute he threw them onto his desk and he said to T.V., "Polaroids." "Kodak, actually. It says so on the back." Lawman Brown scowled at T.V. "Why you bothering me with these? They ain't nothing." T.V. hesitated a moment, and then he sifted through the pictures and pulled one out. "Lookit that one," he said, and Lawman Brown squinted, and he saw nosy Nettie Ferguson trying to see what he was seeing, and he turned his body a little and put on his glasses, squinted again, and then he said, "Is that a hand?" and T.V. nodded, and Lawman Brown said, "Well, all I gotta say is that somebody should learn to focus, is all I have to say," and then T.V. cleared his throat and said, "Um, Sheriff Brown," which secretly annoyed Lawman Brown, he liked people to call him Lawman Brown so he could tell them to call him Sheriff Brown, but he liked to be called Lawman Brown first, "Sheriff Brown," T. V. Daniels was saying, in that high thin trapped voice of his, "most of em, I mean, well, most of em are all the same color?" Nettie Ferguson punched like maybe three keys on her typewriter. Lawman Brown squinted at T.V. over the thick horn-rimmed top of his nonbifocal lenses. "Meaning?" T.V. ran his hands over the fulminatiousnessness of his stomach, which took a long time, and when he finished he said, "I think they're pictures of some . . . body," at which point Nettie Ferguson's old Royal Electric produced the distinct sound of several keys all striking each other rather than the paper, and at the same time Lawman Brown slapped his forehead and said, "Lord a-mighty! He's dismembered her!" "No, no," T.V. said now, "it's just the pictures. She's whole. It's just the pictures that're bits and pieces," he said, and then he began clearing away the mess of dirty napkins and plastic forks and styrofoam coffee cups with solidified inches of white-veined coffee stuff in them and spreading out the pictures on Lawman Brown's desk, and as he worked he said, "Here's her hand, see, and this one, I think, this one's her wrist, and I think this is her forearm," and so on, piece by piece, he began putting them together, until finally Lawman Brown put a hand on T.V.'s hand and stopped him. Nettie Ferguson was staring outright now, and he glared at her until she picked up the phone and held it absently to her ear, and then he said to T.V. in his best neutral-slash-accusatory tone, "You seem to know just how these here things go together," and T. V. Daniels performed a sort of upper body wiggle-jiggle-and-shake it took Lawman Brown a moment to recognize as a shrug, and he, T.V., he said, "they got numbers on the back of em." Before either of em could say anything else, the door chimed and Matthew Edwards, who had complained in the past that T.V. didn't always make it all the way down the Damar-Palco road to his house (and mailbox), Matthew Edwards walked hesitantly into the station house with a little white-rimmed black rectangle held in one hand, and he tipped his hat hi-lo to Lawman Brown and flashed a look at T. V. Daniels, but before he could say anything his eyes dropped to the vaguely fish-shaped assortment of pictures on Lawman Brown's desk, and he stared at the single picture they made and very slowly he added his own piece to the puzzle that had become Lucy Robinson's body.

4.05

Cora's Kitchen, Sumnertime's Café, and Sloppy Joe's Pool Hall

ALMOST EVERYBODY SAID THE SAME THING: WASN'T the first time Myra Robinson wandered up and down the streets of Galatea in the middle of the night, drunk and carrying on in a state of what Rosemary Krebs had once called "partial undress." Of course, usually she sang, and of course usually when she was in a state of partial undress the temperature wasn't hovering right around the freezing mark, that'd be zero degrees Celsius but your average folks around here didn't have much truck with the metric system, which is to say that they tended to think in terms of like thirty-two, thirty-three degrees Fahrenheit, and given the temperature and a recent and rather unexpected thunderstorm Galatea's dirt roads were in a soupy semifrozen state, like the Jolly Green Giant's broccoli-n-cheddar mix taken out of the freezer but not fully defrosted yet, and folks figured this had something to do with the fact that Myra Robinson—who as Faith Jackson just had to tell Reverend Greeving she didn't *even* know where you could buy a nightgown like that around here but you sure couldn't buy it out of the Sears catalog that was for sure—Myra Robinson wasn't singing but was making little like screaming noises, which also seemed understandable, given the temperature, and recent circumstances. Not much had happened recently to make Myra Robinson sing. She wandered Galatea's snow-sogged streets, sobbing, crying out sometimes, and always making a funny keening noise, *keening* being the word Matthew Edwards used, Matthew Edwards who claimed to be part Comanche or Chickasaw or some such, and when Yankee Carting asked Matthew Edwards what the hay keening was Matthew Edwards said it was the sound a squaw made right before she threw herself on her brave's funeral pyre, and even before Yankee could ask what a pyre was Matthew Edwards said, fire, funeral fire. Myra had a coat on, open, over her nightgown, and she hugged a little black box to her chest. Afterwards folks admitted they worried about her catching pneumonia but no one really thought about frostbite because that nightgown with its little fake fur ruffs at cuff and hem and neckline—was that *waist*line you said? Darrell Jenkens said with a wicked grin out to Sloppy Joe's—that nightgown dragged on the ground behind Myra Robinson like something out of a old black-and-white movie and who woulda thought she didn't have no shoes on under there, and, well, besides, people assured each other, everybody knows you can't talk sense to a drunk, which, if we're going to be brutally honest, is what Myra Robinson just in fact *is*, and Lucy or no Lucy nobody in Cadavera County, which had been a dry county until the mid-eighties, that's the nineteen eighties, had much sympathy for a single mother with a drinking problem and a nightgown whose neckline showed off her bellybutton. And so it was only when she wandered back out of town again, toward her house, then past it, and on toward what certain folks persisted in referring to as the old Deacon house and what other certain folks liked to call the limestone house and what only Wade Painter and Rosemary Krebs called Colin Nieman's house, it was only then that someone came to her aid and it was the new man, the man whose, ahem, *friend*, had been present at the scene of the crime, the man whose coat had been found there and whose bag had contained Lucy Robinson's hair and whose Polaroid or was it a Kodak had taken all those pictures—well how much more evidence do you need, was what Vera Gatlinger had to say, I mean *really*—it was the man who owned the house, Colin Nieman himself. Well, good for him, T. V. Daniels was heard to say at Sumnertime's—T.V. who said the pictures was taken by a Kodak—in a tone of voice that didn't sound like it wished him well at all, but anyway by the time Colin Nieman found her the tape in the tape recorder she was carrying—it was his tape recorder, wouldn't you know it—had run out, and Myra Robinson was by that time as quiet as a church mouse, and when Colin Nieman got her inside of that big old mausoleum, oh excuse me, Grady Oconnor laughed at Cora's Kitchen, that *mansion*, when Colin Nieman got her inside his house and into the light he saw then that she didn't have no shoes on and her feet looked so terrible that he just picked her up and carried her to his truck and drove her straight to the hospital down to Bigger Hill, which as you can imagine Rosemary Krebs mentioned to Pastor Little that if Galatea had its own hospital then perhaps something more could have been done for poor Myra Robinson's feet. It was only later, as he was driving home from the hospital, it was only then that Colin Nieman remembered the tape recorder, which sat now on the passenger seat, and this Nettie Ferguson had it straight from the horse's mouth that Colin Nieman pressed the eject button on the tape recorder and a tape popped out and Colin Nieman slipped said tape into the car stereo which Nettie couldn't remember the brand name of but she said she was pretty sure that it wasn't even Japanese, it was *German*, which after a significant pause she sniffed and said well that tells you how much it cost and a few other things too, and Colin Nieman rewound the tape back to its beginning in his expensive German car stereo in his expensive

British jeep-type vehicle and then, when it got there, it switched into play mode automatically, which DuWayne Hicks said his R.C.A. car stereo would do too, and it was made right here in the U.S. of A., as the A. in R.C.A. let you know, and when you remember that Colin Nieman hadn't heard Myra Robinson wandering the streets earlier then you can maybe understand why he drove his car into the ditch, because the car stereo speakers spat out nothing but screaming, not a woman's screams but a girl's, not Myra's, but Lucy's, and in the dead silence at Sumnertime's that followed this last revelation Howard Goertzen allowed as how it seemed to him that Colin Nieman probably woulda drove his vehicle into the ditch anyway because Colin Nieman had already demonstrated with fatal-to-Charlene effect that he wasn't exactly the world's most accomplished driver, which is to say that he seemed real good at going forward but not so good when it came to stopping, that was all Howard Goertzen had to say, and then Elaine Sumner said that if it was okay with everyone she was just going to make a fresh pot of coffee and serve everybody a slice of that apple pie they could all smell because it seemed to her that a body could use something a little sweet and a little stimulating after a story like that, on the house, Elaine Sumner said, moving her big hips in and out and in between the little tables in her café, and she added too that she sure hoped the groundhog saw his shadow tomorrow because she for one and she didn't think she was the only one but she for one was going to buy whatever her Mary Kay account executive said was her spring colors because she could not N-O-T *not* take one more day of this winter, not one.

4.06

Lawman Brown

NOW WHEN MYRA ROBINSON WALKED SHE ROLLICKED back and forth in that way she'd had ever since the tape showed up on her front porch and she'd gone out for her little midnight stroll in the slush. The doctors'd managed to save her feet but she had no feeling in them, nothing, she said, it was like her legs stopped at her ankles and she was walking on air, and she was perpetually pitching back and forth and side to side and having to use her hands for balance, which today as she made her way through the station house door she was carrying a fairly smallish box, and when she pitched forward the box rattled, not in any unusual or ominous way, all sorts of things could rattle although off the top of his head Lawman Brown couldn't think of anything, not one thing in the world that would rattle inside a cardboard box, and for no reason at all the blood ran cold in his veins. The doctors had given Myra orthopedic shoes which looked kind of like jackboots with a steel exoskeleton running up the ankle, and they clanked and clumped something awful when she walked. She pitched and stumbled into the station house, past Nettie Ferguson's desk, who by this time Nettie Ferguson pretended not even to notice when Myra Robinson came into the station house, and as she threw the rattling box on Lawman Brown's desk she, Myra, she was saying, "Oh God oh God oh God oh God," and Lawman Brown, already put off his feed by the sound of the box and Myra's clippety-clop of a footstep, Lawman Brown said, "Now, now, Myra, calm down," but Myra just went on saying, "Oh God oh God oh God oh God," and then, finally, she took a breath, a wheezing wobbling breath—Myra hated to sit down because standing back up tended to be a ordeal—and she said, "Oh, Lawman Brown, I just know it's something terrible this time, terrible, terrible, terrible." Lawman Brown was so frazzled that it didn't even occur to him to tell Myra Robinson that his name was Eustace and his title was Sheriff, and instead, tentatively, he picked up the box. There were no markings on it which he could see. It was plain brown cardboard, clumsily taped shut, about the size of a loaf of bread, and "Please," Myra was saying, and swaying like a stalk of wheat in a heavy wind, "please, just open it and get it over with. Just open it. Just tell me what is it." "Now let's not be hasty, Myra," Lawman Brown said, recovering himself a little, "we don't want to get ourselves into trouble here," at which point Myra shouted, "What do you think, Eustace, it's a bomb or something? It don't weigh a *pound*, for Christ's sake. It weighs less than a little bird—" "Myra, please," Lawman Brown just had to interject, "your lang—" "Just open the damn thing!" Myra screamed. "—gwage," Lawman Brown continued, setting the box back down on his desk and drawing himself up to his full height. "And I'll thank you to afford me the respect and title my position is afforded." He stood there, unconsciously swaying in sync with Myra's swaying, but then he out and out stepped back when Myra teetered forward and put her face right in his and said, "Listen, Eustace Rumpford Brown, I was at school when you was just the fat doughnut-eating son of a sharecropper who spent four years butt-warming the bench of a football team that didn't even have eleven players, and if you don't open that box right now I swear to Christ I'm going to climb on top of your desk if I have to flap my arms and *fly* to get there, and I'm going to take such a big and smelly shit all over your precious collection of stained napkins and picnic silverware that you won't be able to get rid of the smell for a month!" Somewhere in the interval between the word *shit* and the word *silverware* Lawman Brown concluded that dignity was no longer really an issue here and compliance was the cheapest option available to him, and so he pulled out his pocketknife, which he had half a mind to stick in Myra Robinson's larynx box for calling him a bench warmer, he was a *alternate* and it said so right in the yearbook, and he slit the box down the center with a vigorous stroke and ripped the box flaps open so roughly that whatever was inside went spewing into the air and bounced on his desk and on the floor with a sound like falling marbles, and the first thing Lawman Brown thought of was Myra's reference to birds, and he tried to tell himself that what he was looking at was little speckled blue eggs and not, as he knew they were, Lucy Robinson's fingertips. "Dear Jesus," he said, and Myra Robinson said nothing, and behind her Nettie Ferguson was saying, "Eustace? What is it, Eustace?" and Lawman Brown tried to shake his head but the movement brought the bile to his throat, and he ran toward the restroom, and behind him he heard Nettie Ferguson scream, and the uneven clompety-clomp-clomp of several of Myra's footsteps, and then the heavy wet-flour-sack sound of her body falling to the floor.

4.07

Winda Bottomly

THE THING WAS, SHE DIDN'T REALLY WANT NOBODY TO know it, but the thing was old Winda Bottomly couldn't read. Didn't really bother her none, not really, not too often, she had the TV at home and just about the only thing else she ever did was go to church and by this time in her long, long life—one husband, two kids, all three of em gone now—she'd memorized every last song in the hymnal and Reverend Abraham, who was one of the few people who knew her secret, Reverend Abraham always made a point of having some nice young boy or girl from the grade school speak out the Scripture reading for the week, and not just for her benefit neither: there was more than one person in Galatia who'd never learned to read, and don't you think the phenomenon was confined to the east side of the grain elevator neither. Oh, and Cora's. Winda Bottomly went to Cora's, but there wasn't no need for reading there: your nose could tell you what was on the menu just fine. Be that as it may, it was Winda Bottomly who found the sign. It was the first day of spring, and Winda had made a point of tending to her husband's grave every year for the past 'leven years on the first day of spring, the kids, well, the kids hadn't died around here and the powers that be, in one case a no-good husband and in another the U.S. Marine Corps, hadn't seen fit to send em back for a proper burial, but "I put him to sleep in the winter," Winda told her friends, "and I wake him up in the spring," and this year she had awakened early and she had made her way out to the graveyard before sunrise because it was something to see, the sun spreading its infinite grace over the prairie, creeping along on its red-tipped fingertips over the just-turned-green fields of wheat and touching, finally, the shiny dome of the bald bluff, and afterwards, after the sun'd come up and Winda had combed the grass clean over William's grave and planted this year's plant, a white lily this year, for peace, it was after she'd done all that that Winda Bottomly made her way back to town and it was then that she saw it. To her it was just a scrawl on the white wall of Rosemary Krebs' grain elevator, a tangle of black spray-painted lines with a couple-a red splotches off to the right, but, illiterate or no, Winda Bottomly recognized writing when she saw it. Immediately she thought of Webbie Greeving. That woulda been the person to get, Winda Bottomly thought, in the first place Webbie knew about Winda, and in the second Webbie was the kinda person who didn't just read something, she told you what it meant—but no one had seen hide nor hair of Webbie Greeving since just after this all started, and besides, it occurred to Winda Bottomly, the only person liable to be up that early, in town, was Cora, and so it was to Cora's she went, but who answered the door was that white woman, Miss Rosetta Stone, she called herself, which Winda Bottomly was pretty sure was a fake name she'd stole from the Good Book. Winda didn't dislike Rosa, no, she wouldn't go that far, but she sure didn't trust her, and when Rosa told Winda that Cora was sleeping in this morning and if it pleased Winda okay Rosa would come with her and look at whatever it was she wanted looked at, Winda looked at her suspiciously but couldn't see no way around it. And so off they went, Winda and Rosa, not exactly arm in arm, not exactly buddy-buddy, Rosa not asking what Winda was doing up so early and Winda not asking Rosa what Cora was doing in bed so late, and then, when they had got smack dab in front of the grain elevator and there was the words staring them right in the face Winda just stood there and waited, because she didn't want to admit to some white woman she didn't even know that she couldn't read, but Rosa, instead, I don't know, instead of reading the words out loud or whatever it was that Winda had imagined she'd do, Rosetta Stone let some sound out of her mouth that sounded unholy to Winda Bottomly, and then she struck out at Winda Bottomly, hit her right in the shoulder she did, and she screamed, "Why you bring me here!" and then she run off, and so it wasn't until some three hours later when Faith Jackson herself called up Winda to ask her if she'd seen it that Winda Bottomly found out that what was written on the wall of the grain elevator was just two words: FIND ME!, it read, and the red marks off to the side, Faith Jackson told her, those red marks was a explanation point.

5

5.01

Justin

I'M STILL HERE.

5.02

Divine

THE WATER WASN'T COLD.

5.03

Colin

FOUR WEEKS AND FOUR DAYS AFTER I BEGAN THE LATEST

version of my novel, which is to say, thirty-two days after Lucy Robinson was kidnapped, I finished it. I finished it in the afternoon, after my morning quarrel with Cora and before my evening quarrel with Divine; in between those two events I managed, finally, to write the scene which led up to and concluded with the last line that had been eluding me for over twenty years, and as soon as I finished typing it I packed the whole thing up, the handwritten manuscript, the various pen-scratched typed copies, and the final, finished version, into several cardboard boxes, and I was still packing many hours later, when I got the call from Wade, telling me about Divine. I will admit that for a moment I thought of ignoring his summons; what more could I do, I asked myself, hadn't I already done enough? But eventually reason—I was going to say compassion, but I don't think, really, that it was compassion—won out, and I left my boxes behind, went to see what aid I could give to Divine, or, failing that, to Wade. I was gone for less than an hour—what *could* I do, after all; hadn't I already done enough?—but still, it was time enough: when I returned to the limestone house, my manuscript was gone.

5.04

Webbie

ON THE MORNING OF OUR EIGHTH DAY I LEFT HIM. HE was easy to leave. He was just a large dark figure, arms and legs sprawled across white sheets that had gone yellow from too many washings. He snored as I dressed, snored as I wrote *Thank you* in the light coating of dust on his mantel beneath the smiling pictures of the two girls whose names I still did not know, snored as I opened the front door and put the morning paper on the couch. Everything was fine until then; everything, I mean, made sense—far too much sense—but as soon as I left his house I got lost. I knew where the corner grocery was, I knew the café that made the best ribs and the café that made the best pie, and I knew the way to the incredibly long and narrow cinema whose tiny screen seemed no larger than a television's when you sat all the way in the back row, where we had sat, but still, I got lost because I wasn't looking for any of those things.

I was looking for my car. It took me nearly an hour to find it, and as I wandered his neighborhood I watched for him nervously. I didn't know how I would explain myself to him should he find me, should my feet betray me and lead me back to his house. How could I tell his stubbled face and bumpy flattop that I had only wanted to know what they would feel like, how could I tell him that even after seven days of cooking and eating with him, of watching TV, of laundry and vacuuming and not one but two new ties, after seven days of all that I would still remember not him but the *feel* of him, the little spiraling hairs of his stomach pressing into mine, the broad soft fullness of his lips sucking on my skin. How could I tell him I was ashamed, not of him or of what I had done with him, but of myself, of the way I had thought of him. I had succumbed finally, after all these years: I had thought of him as black before I had thought of him as a man.

And then, when I found my car, I also found a note tucked under the windshield wiper. I thought it was a ticket at first—it was tucked into a clear plastic envelope in the way that parking violations are, to protect them from rain and snow—but when I pulled the paper out and unfolded it I found only seven words written there. *My name is Wallace Anderson,* the note read. *Goodbye Webbie.*

5.05

Justin

ABANDONMENT IS IMPOSSIBLE. MEMORY PERSISTS, DEspite all the odds, despite all our efforts. Amnesia is like the color black: it effaces by inclusion. Excluding nothing, no one thing can come to prominence. And so I return to my abandoned beginning, my false start: *If it's after midnight it's my birthday.* If it's after midnight then I have somehow managed to live for twenty-one years, and now I embark on my twenty-second. For the past five of those years Colin has orbited me like the moon orbits a planet, and what seems like years and years before Colin I orbited another man like a planet orbits a sun. But now I declare myself to be a comet, a celestial body with its own path, neither dependent upon nor depended on by anything else. This book is a telescope. Look through it; look for me: my bright and shining eye, my halo, my tail, stretching out behind me. You might view that tail years after I've passed by; I might have imploded, exploded, collided with something else and disintegrated, I might have run out of gas or, who knows, I might be blazing still, but in any case my tail lingers on, fading, but fading so gradually that you'll never know if what you see is real, or merely a shadow burned into your eye.

5.06

Divine

THEN IT WAS COLD. GOD*DAMN* BUT IT WAS COLD. I guess it musta took a second for the water to soak through my clothes or something. I mean I let go-a the rope, I heard the ice break, I knew the water had to be *cold* if there was *ice* on top of it, but all the same there was a good long moment before I felt it, felt the cold or even felt the wet for that matter. For a second I just felt suspended, loose and slippery and all over the place like a jellyfish, and then but suddenly then the cold of the water pushed—no, not pushed, *squeezed*, it squeezed through my clothes like a vise grip, and my like arms and legs snapped shut and I rolled into a ball and fell head over heels and I just sank like a stone. I mean I tell you what: it was like the devil's hand reached up outta hell and pulled me straight to his bosom. But he don't scare me, the devil, or the thought of hell. In the space of three years I'd lost Ratboy, I'd lost my parents and Wade and now I'd lost Colin Nieman, I'd even lost the name I was born with, and somewhere in there it seemed like I'd lost my soul too. If Satan wanted a piece-a my ass, well, he was just gonna have to take his place in line is all I have to say, cause I can't give him what don't belong to me no more.

5.07

Colin

MYRA ROBINSON HAD HOLED UP IN HER HOUSE SINCE the February night on which she had destroyed her feet. Divine had it from T. V. Daniels that after the box containing Lucy's severed fingertips had appeared she no longer dared open her mailbox; she never answered her phone either, and one day in late spring I called her, only to find that it had been disconnected. Later that afternoon I drove past her house and noticed that her car was fast disappearing under a tangle of quick-growing itch ivy, and when I saw that I made an arrangement with Vera Gatlinger at the I.G.A. to have groceries delivered to Myra's home, and after a little hemming and hawing Vera let me know that Myra had already made arrangements with Joe Brznski, the proprietor of Sloppy Joe's, to receive a bottle of Jack Daniel's every Monday. Joe and Vera and T.V. were the only people in Galatia who had any occasion to visit Myra—certainly Lawman Brown, who had made absolutely no headway on the case, avoided her house—and they all told the same story to anyone who asked: Myra was doing nothing. Absolutely nothing. She sat in an odd electronic rocking chair that Bea had given her, her lifeless feet suspended on the footrest in their orthopedic boots, and if anyone dared mention Lucy's name to her she would smile brightly and mumble something about someone named Angela; she would accept the whiskey or the food or the mail that was offered her, and even as she vacantly drank or ate or read she would ask her benefactors if they knew her beautiful Angela, her angel, her little gift from God.

Well. I didn't manufacture a new name for my missing book, but I was, all the same, possessed by the same inertia which had taken over Myra's life. Whoever had stolen my novel had taken not just the final version but all the manuscripts and notes and dribs and drabs that had led up to it, leaving me with not one single physical reminder of what I had written. For a week after it disappeared I could not even get out of bed—I suspect that had as much to do with what happened to Divine, and with the fact that I was also no longer welcome at Cora's or Wade's or anywhere else in town—but when seven days of bed rest had done nothing more than put ten pounds around my waist, I got up, I took my morning run, I made my own coffee and took my place at my desk, and then I did nothing.

For eight or ten or twelve hours a day, for five months, all through the bitterness of winter and the blandness of spring and the beginning of summer, I did nothing. Oh, I suppose I didn't just sit there. While it was still cold I would build a lovely fire in the fireplace; the room's bookshelves had been filled with thousands of leather-bound worm-eaten volumes when we'd moved in, and it was these I burned. At first I checked the books to make sure the pages inside were actually ruined, but after a while I just grabbed them indiscriminately and threw them into the flames with a little malevolent laugh. The damp bindings and mushy pages didn't burn all that well, so keeping the fire alive took some effort; often I would have to prime the flames with a few fresh, crisp, dry—and blank, I must tell you, painfully blank—sheets of my own writing paper.

Then spring came, a tiny two-week affair in April which yielded almost immediately to the listless ninety-degree days of an early Kansas summer, and when it grew too warm for a fire I found other things to do with my time, other invented tasks that would take me out from behind my desk, where I started each morning by typing the words *The last line of this story is inevitable*, and where I ended each evening by typing the words *I never saw him again*. That was all I typed, each day for *five* months, because even though I could recall each and every scene that had occurred in my novel with the sort of precise detail with which victims of car crashes remember the last few moments before their accidents—I felt the enveloping warmth that surrounded the narrator's body as he swam in Otto's healing sphere; felt, deep in the pit of my stomach, his terror when he discovers the pyramid of discarded books—I still could not remember a single one of the *words* I had used to describe these scenes, and it seemed to me that unless I could exactly duplicate my missing manuscript then I would have . . . what? I would have failed. Failed what or failed whom I didn't know, and so I sat there, taunted by those first and last sentences, lost in a silence as labyrinthine as Myra's and as vacant as Justin's, until finally night fell, and under cover of darkness Divine would emerge from wherever he had been hiding in the house or the fields like a copper-colored cocoa-buttered ghost. Divine. He coiled his fragrant, flexible arms around me like a memory, kissed me softly atop my big bald useless head, he cooed sweet nothings in my ears with the softened sweetened voice of the dead, and then, for the duration of the night at least, I let myself get lost in him.

5.08

Webbie

THIN, FRAIL, SWEATING, THE TINY FORM OF ROSEMARY Krebs leaned into an overfilled grocery cart. She was so caught up in her struggle that she was oblivious to the eyes of the three or four other women in the grocery store, who all watched her with amused and slightly spiteful smiles on their faces, and I was no exception.

I had been back in Galatia for less than an hour. I was buying the ingredients for the winter stew my father had asked me to make the week before.

Rosemary Krebs had made the mistake of wearing a cream-colored silk suit to do her shopping, and she was sweating so profusely that faint stains were visible at her underarms and the small of her back, and a fur stole hung off one shoulder like a misstuck tail. Her low heels gave her feet no purchase on the I.G.A.'s linoleum floor, slick with melted snow, and sometimes her legs slipped about so wildly that she seemed like a two-tailed spermatozoon.

She seemed to sense eyes on her, and she looked up suddenly. Seeing me, she released her cart and straightened to her full height; the cart's handle came to her sternum. She was panting slightly, but still managed to speak in her soft even voice. "Webbie Greeving," she said, "good evening."

Sometimes you know things you don't know you know. Sometimes you do things and you don't know the reason why. "Would you like a hand?" I heard myself saying, and my own expression must have been as surprised as Rosemary Krebs'.

"Beg pardon?"

"It looked like you were struggling."

I had come close to her. I could smell her perfume, and, barely, her sweat. I thought, This is what the Mayor smells after they fuck. Some part of me—not my mind—remembered Wallace when I thought that, and I shook myself slightly.

Rosemary Krebs waited for my spell to pass and when it did she was smiling her politic smile, and I doubted that she and her husband had ever fucked. "A lady doesn't struggle, Webbie, although sometimes a lady does have . . . difficulties."

"Yes, well," I said, and then, catching sight of my father's stew ingredients in my own cart, I said, "If you're done shopping, perha—I mean, maybe you'd let me push your cart up to Vera."

Within her tiny chest Rosemary Krebs' shrunken heart beat a dozen strokes; my own heart seemed to beat slower and slower, until finally she spoke.

"Why, thank you, Webbie. That would be most appreciated."

Vera looked at me as if I'd grown a third eye *and* a second nose as I wheeled Rosemary Krebs' cart to her register, Rosemary Krebs a step in front of me, like a good Muslim leading his wife. Without asking, I began to unload Rosemary Krebs' groceries onto the conveyor belt, and Vera, after a further speechless pause, began to ring them up.

"Sure is a lotta groceries, Mrs. Krebs," I said.

"Phyneas and I are entertaining at the weekend. A belated New Year's festivity, if you know what I mean."

I put a head of broccoli on the belt.

"Belated?"

Rosemary Krebs' smile was nearly beatific. "After the fact," she said.

I put another head of broccoli on the belt, a handful of spring onions.

"I declare, Mrs. Krebs," I said, and then, for good measure, I said it again. "I *de*-clare, Mrs. Krebs, you are the busiest woman this town has never seen. What with all your community service and the Development Fund and the regular business of taking care-a a man, it's a wonder you find the time to throw so many parties."

"It *is* difficult," Rosemary Krebs conceded, as if forced to do so.

"And the food," I said. "Mmmm-mmmm good."

"Well, we women just have to be a bit more resourceful than our menfolk." She laughed briefly, and when I looked up I saw that she looked not at me but at Vera, but Vera wasn't having any of it. She blindly punched numbers into the cash register and stared at me over the top of her reading glasses, and I returned her gaze but kept my face as neutral as I could.

"Vera," I said, "when did pot roast get up to twenty-five dollars a pound?"

Rosemary Krebs looked alarmed. "Excuse me?"

Vera started visibly, then busily scanned the long tape hanging from the register. "I'm sure it's just a keying error, Mrs. Krebs."

"Two-fifty I think is the price," I said, and as Vera voided out the sale I gave Mrs. Krebs a knowing smile. The cart was unloaded by then, and I moved to the other end of the checkout counter. "Do you like paper and plastic, Mrs. Krebs? Or just plastic?"

"Just paper," Rosemary Krebs said, her thin voice filled with authority. "And I always double-bag."

"Of course."

Rosemary Krebs leafed through the television supplement idly, indolently, sometimes glancing at her watch or at the other women in the store while I filled her cart with brown-bagged groceries. Vera was ringing up Tamara Atkins, Lee Anne's mother, and Rosemary Krebs and I faced each other over her cart.

"Mrs. Krebs," I said hesitantly, "I don't wish to seem forward . . ."

I let my words trail off, and Rosemary Krebs, her voice as quiet and eager as a fisherman testing a nibble on a line, said, "Yes?"

"Well, I know you've been, you been looking for someone to, um, to do some work for you. Around your house, I mean."

Again, Rosemary Krebs allowed herself only the one word, but a slight tremor in her voice added an extra syllable. "Ye-es."

"Well, truth is, taking care of, care-a my . . . daddy don't take up nearly all my time, and, well, Christmas time always lets me know that I could sure use some extra pocket money just like everybody else."

A trace of suspicion limned Rosemary Krebs' face. "I thought you worked down to the municipal library."

"That's volunteer work actually," I said, and waved a hand. "Besides, those books ain't going nowhere. Not round here anyway."

Rosemary Krebs paused a moment. In a tone of mild reproach she said, "You shouldn't underestimate the power of the written word, Webbie. It can change your life." I just smiled at her while the cogs and wheels whirred in her brain, and at length she spoke in a voice that rang out above the cash register's renewed clanging. "Webbie Greeving, are you asking me for a job?"

Vera stopped ringing again, and this time she turned and stared openly. Tamara Atkins, less bold, searched for a penny at the bottom of her voluminous purse.

"Why, yes, ma'am, I do believe I am."

Rosemary Krebs peered at me intently, incredulously, her face animated by suspicion—and also by a delight so undisguised that it took all my effort to keep the loathing out of my own expression.

After a moment she shook her head as if to clear it. "My goodness, just look at the time. It's nearly the Sabbath. Hardly the time to discuss business." Her voice had changed suddenly, slipping into the tones that generations of her foremothers must have used when they addressed their maids and slaves. "Webbie, why don't you drop by my house Monday morning, and we'll discuss this further."

"Eleven o'clock all right, Mrs. Krebs?"

"Eleven o'clock would be fine."

She put her hands on her cart then, attempted to turn it. It didn't budge. Slipping quickly between her and the cart, I turned it around. Rosemary Krebs was already walking toward the door, and to her back I said, "Allow me."

5.09

Justin

ONLY AN INFANT CAN BE AMONG PEOPLE AND BE SILENT, and even then it must tolerate the big-toothed mouths of adults cooing words and half-words and quarter-words over its head: "ma-ma, ma-ma," "da-da, da-da," "coo-coo, coo-coo," "ca-ca, ca-ca." But even if you stop talking that doesn't mean you stop thinking. In truth, that's what I wanted to do, and in the first few weeks after the attack, when the memory of it wouldn't go away, and the sights and sounds and smells of it wouldn't go away, and when, especially, the words wouldn't go away—the words my mind added to the too-silent scene, the words I used, as if to write the scene out in my head—I almost repented of my vow, because after I found that I couldn't swallow the words then I wanted to spit them out. But I knew it would do no good, it would make no difference. Words hadn't saved my mother, hadn't stopped my father, words hadn't kept me innocent or restored health or life to any of my dying or dead friends, and I knew that even if I had been able to speak on that icy road, to reason or shout or just to beg, it wouldn't have saved Lucy. And don't tell me that isn't what words are meant to do. What else are they for? I tell you: if I could have found the words to fix things, I would have spoken them. It's not that I *wouldn't* speak: it's just that I no longer knew what to say.

5.10

Divine

SOMEHOW I THINK I MANAGED TO GIVE THE IMPRESSION that I was like *in love* with Colin Nieman, or well at least that I wanted to be in love with him. Well, I didn't. I wasn't. I'm not. I mean, whatever I am, I am not now and never was in love with Colin Nieman. But what I did want, back then anyway, when I still wanted things, what I wanted was for him to love me—what I wanted to do was *make* him love me. Colin was a lot of things, he was beautiful especially, God you can't imagine how beautiful he was, beautiful and talented and on top of it all he was rich, and despite what I said to him he was a pretty good lay, and for a while I thought he was my ticket outta Galatia. But the one thing he never was and never coulda been was my lover. I mean I guess I could see how someone could love him, but I didn't. I don't. And I won't, not ever, cause that prize belongs to Ratboy.

Ratboy.

He was five feet five inches tall and if he jumped up and down he could just push the scale over one twenty, but he walked with the bowlegged swagger of a horse-breakin' cowboy twice his size, and if he even *thought* someone was looking at him funny he'd attack, just like a rat, he told me, hand, hand, foot, foot, *tooth*. In two years I never saw him win a fight—I never saw him even come close—but I never saw him run away neither. He might be all covered in bruises and blood and barely able to stand or see to swing a punch, but it was always like the other guy who left first, leaving Ratboy kinda wobbling there, yelling with what was lefta his voice, "Yeah, that's it, you pussy, you run away before I *really* get mad." I don't think I ever saw him without a black eye or dried blood under his nose or a bruise on his body that felt like a orange buried beneath his skin, and then too there was the white scar in the pink of his upper lip from where somebody or other'd introduced his face to the open edge of his locker door. It almost looked like a harelip scar, that scar did, but Ratboy wore each and every one-a his marks with pride. "I sure taught him," he'd say as I washed out his cuts, sprayed a little Bactine onto the open flesh. "He won't bother us no more." He wouldn't never let me put a Band-Aid on him. "I want em to see my wounds of war," he said. "I want em all to know what I go through, just for you."

His real name was Lamoine Wiebe but no one ever called him that. For a long time people called him Dwebey, or just Dwebe, but then somebody or other said that he had kind of a rodent look around the face, kind of a ferret face, kind of a rat's, and then I don't know if it was somebody else or if it was Lamoine hisself but pretty soon everybody including Lamoine was calling Lamoine Ratboy.

Ratboy.

My hero.

I was only twelve when it all started, and he was sixteen, but even then I knew he was crazy as a loon. That didn't mean he wasn't still my hero, and my lover too.

5.11

Colin

HE WOULDN'T TELL ANYONE WHAT HAPPENED. HE wouldn't, I should say, tell me or Wade: he wouldn't tell us how it was that he drove away from my house early on a January evening wearing a brown and white shearling jacket, a long-sleeved white T-shirt, thin skin-tight black pants, white socks, and black slip-on shoes; and showed up in the early morning hours at Wade's house, bereft of jacket and shoes—and, as well, of his car—the remainder of his clothing soaked through with ice-cold water and muddied to a uniform grayish brown. The gel had been doused from his bleached hair, which had dried by the time I arrived and floated off his head in an airy eerie light-filled afro; it ringed his face like a halo when I arrived, and vibrated as he shivered violently on a chair. Wade had got his clothes off him by then, dried him with a towel, covered him with a heavy blanket; the heat was turned up so high that it slammed into me like a wall when I came through the door. His face was streaked with trails of dirt and water; grit was packed under his fingernails, which were wrapped tight around a cup of steaming liquid that he refused to drink, and he refused also to speak, or even to look at us. His lips and the hollows beneath his eyes were still blue, and he stared at a spot that wasn't in the room. He shook and shivered and shimmered even, seemed almost to be fading away, until finally I pried his cup from his clutching fingers and laid him down on the couch and tucked the blanket deep under the cushion to hold in the warmth, and hold him in place. Wade retreated to a corner as soon as I arrived, a stricken, helpless look on his face, and he stayed there until Divine had fallen asleep, and I looked at him then, across the expanse of Divine's body—it was not to be the last time I looked at Wade in such a manner—and on that first occasion I said, He'll be okay, which is not what I said the second time I put Divine's body between mine and Wade's. When I returned home, as I said, my novel was gone.

Like me, Divine stayed in bed for a week. His silence was not as complete as Justin's, but all the same he refused to tell either me or Wade what had happened. I specify us, because I suspected there was one person Divine did tell: the person to whom he spent the next seven days writing a single letter. Wade said that Divine stole one of his sketch pads—Wade used that word; he used the word *stole*—and he propped it on his knees in bed, and he wrote so slowly and carefully that, according to Wade, it was almost possible to believe he was drawing on the pages, not writing on them. Every so often he ripped a page from the pad and crumpled it up, and these he stuffed in his pillowcase and guarded carefully until, a week after he'd taken to bed, he got out of it. In one hand, Wade told me, he had a single page filled with tiny writing; in the other he had the pillowcase stuffed with his abandoned efforts. He put the former in an envelope, sealed it, addressed it, never once let go of it; he put the latter in a barrel in the back yard and burned them, pillowcase and all. He bathed, groomed, dressed himself, and then he took his letter and Wade's car and left Wade's house. He and the car showed up at the limestone house sometime later, but the letter was already gone. He let himself in and made his way to my bedroom, where, smiling mischievously, he did a little striptease for me. He started out silent, but as he danced and stripped he began humming, and then mumbling a little, under his breath, and then singing, and by the time he was naked he was shouting at the top of the lungs. The song he shouted was the "Battle Hymn of the Republic," each and every verse of it, and when, several hours later, I asked him why he had chosen that song of all songs, he said that it was the only song he knew all the way through, and when I asked him why he knew it all the way through he said, Cause it's Reverend Abraham's favorite song, that's why.

5.12

Webbie

YOU ENTER A BUILDING, AN OFFICE, A RESTAURANT, A house, differently as an employee than as a guest. With the exception of the limestone house, compared to which it seemed like nothing more than a prettified farmhouse, the Krebs home was the largest and most opulent in or around Galatia—it was twice as large as my father's—but in my three or four visits I'd never taken too much notice of it. Usually when I entered that house I was thinking about how quickly I could leave, and after I began working for Rosemary Krebs I still thought about that, but I also thought about how much time I would have to myself while I was inside, and in order to get that time alone I had first to earn Rosemary Krebs' trust.

Trust is the wrong word—so is *earn* for that matter—because Rosemary Krebs wasn't the kind of woman to trust a domestic, let alone a black domestic. Faith? Confidence? I don't know; *trust* will have to do. Words slipped away from me when I was around Rosemary Krebs; it was almost frightening, in fact, how easily they vanished. Couldn't come across like no uppity nigger, could I, with book learnin and too much attitude? For all Rosemary Krebs could tell, the only words I knew were "Yes, Mrs. Krebs" and "No, Mrs. Krebs," although soon enough I settled into "Yes'm" and "Nome" in my best "I-don't-know-nothing-bout-birthing-no-babies" mode. Rosemary Krebs seemed not to notice. I suppose, to her, that was just the way a maid talked.

On that first Monday she opened the front door for me. It took her a long time to open the door, and I realized as I waited that I should have gone to the back door, that servants did not use the front entrance. The bland curves of her face wore an expression that was ever so slightly strained, impatient. She looked at her watch and then she directed me to a tiny room at the back of the house, into which a spindly chair, thin dresser, and narrow bed had been crammed. The bed bothered me. Did she think I was moving in? A black blouse and skirt hung from a peg on the wall. They were old and well-worn but had been made from good heavy cotton, and the apron and cap that accompanied them were fringed with handmade lace; they seemed to me not just antique but anachronistic, and after I had changed into the uniform I surveyed myself in the mirror that hung on the back of the door. I had thought that I would look like an impostor, at best an actress, but I did not. In some way the room and the uniform and the old flecked mirror were more than me, and I looked like a maid.

When I reported back to Rosemary Krebs, she handed me a feather duster, and then she led me through the rooms on the first and second floors, explaining what needed to be done to each room, and when, and where, and how.

"Of course," she said, when we had finished, "this house was built by Phyneas' family."

I wasn't sure what she meant by *of course*, but I just said, "Yes, Mrs. Krebs."

She was silent for a moment, and then she sighed. "Well," she said, "I did what I could."

A reply seemed to be expected, so I said, "Yes, Mrs. Krebs," again.

She scrutinized me then, so hard that I thought I had given something away. But after a moment she only said, "Please arrive in your uniform and ready for work at ten o'clock. And Webbie?"

"Yes, Mrs. Krebs?"

"For the future, may I suggest nylons." There was no question in her voice, and I didn't answer. "White," she said, "no seam. A seam, my mother always said, is unseemly."

I smiled at her mother's wisdom—I sensed that I had not yet earned the privilege of laughter—and that, then, was that.

5.13

Justin

BY MAY, WADE'S YARD WAS A RIOT. A SPRINKLER SYSTEM on a timer kept it wet all the time, but that was the only care he took with it. Bright green Bermuda grass lay flat, too long and heavy to support itself, and when a breeze blew the grass shimmered silver. A lone catalpa was in the process of shedding mushy white blooms, the barbed wire fence—a pasture's fence, not a yard's—was green with arrow-leaved vines, morning glories perhaps, or maybe some of the local itch ivy, and bedraggled roses rested against the walls of the house. Through it all the wool of a cottonwood stand flew through the air like snow, but the house itself remained spare, white, square, silent.

No one answered when I knocked. I knocked again; again no one answered. Then I went back to the studio. I hadn't been there since our first visit to the town. It's hard to call it a studio when it so obviously was what it was: a house. An unloved house, which, for all the enforced sterility of the building Wade actually lived in, was not a feeling that that cube gave off. The screen door whined a reproach as I opened it, the wooden door flinched when I knocked, each of Wade's footsteps was an audible sore point on the staircase, and when, finally, he opened the door, he regarded me for a long time with an expression that looked very much like regret on his face. His eyes were very clear, but the rest of him was coated in pale dust. Eventually, he spoke.

"I suppose talking to you is pointless, but I'm not very good at mime. Do you want to come in?" He stepped aside and I stepped inside. Wade and the house smelled alike, smelled as he had when I first met him, only more strongly. The chemical odor was almost narcotic, and I found myself inhaling deeply. "I should probably open a window, you're not used to this," Wade said, but then, after watching me for a reaction, he said, "Ah, why bother. You know how to open a window."

He left me then. It surprised me, shocked me even. I don't know what I'd expected, but I hadn't expected him to turn his back on me. I wandered the rooms for a little while, looked at all of his beautiful, beautiful paintings. I wondered if he ever made a mistake, or if he threw his mistakes away, or if the sheer abundance of canvases rendered any flaws unnoticeable, like flowers in a garden. I wandered the first floor, made my way to the second. One room was locked. Supplies, I thought. I avoided the room Wade was in, but soon enough he came out. I expected him to address me, but he just walked past me into the room adjacent to the one he'd been working in, and after a while I realized he had merely shifted locations, and then, without knowing what else to do, I followed him.

The room was small. It gave off the feeling of a nursery, the extra bedroom. All the paintings in it were white, touched only occasionally by color. "This is an amazing room in the winter," Wade said out loud, and I nearly jumped. "That tree there"—he pointed at a large maple perhaps twenty feet from the window—"sometimes gets covered with snow, and the light it reflects is almost blinding. White," he said, "seemed the only color. But now it's spring." He paused; he looked at the white square on the easel. The paint was clotted and rutted, like a busy dirt road a few hours after a blizzard. With a sigh, Wade dipped his brush into a dirty can; it came out dark; it laid a thin green vertical line near the center of the canvas. A second dip, a second line, this one horizontal and bisecting the first. Wade looked at the green cross, and then he looked at me. He shrugged his shoulders. "So," he said. "Now it's spring."

5.14

Divine

THE FIRST THING YOU GOT TO UNDERSTAND IN ORDER to understand the secret of Ratboy's success is that the dick bone is connected to the brain bone in teenage boys, and the second thing that you got to realize is that the dick bone always wins out over the brain bone, and the third thing is that, for teenage boys, every issue is a dick-bone issue.

Ratboy used to make a mint of beating other boys at pinball, is what I'm trying to say.

This might sound surprising, given that there's like only about five thousand souls down to Bigger Hill, and only, like, a quarter of those folks are kids, and outta all them only a few hundred of their parents ever let them hang out at Arcadia. I mean, you'd think word woulda gotten round that Ratboy was the best damn pinball player ever, and in fact word *did* get round, and that's why Ratboy made so much money. A teenage boy, see, a good all-American red-blooded virgin-fucking teenage boy, he can never resist a challenge, and especially not from some skinny runt with a split lip and a girlfriend who looks pretty suspiciously like a boy. That's the nature of the dickbone. The fact that most of the boys who hung out to Arcadia had pimples and wore glasses and the closest they ever got to a naked virgin was a look in the bathroom mirror only made it worse for them. Arcadia was, like, the closest thing they had to a football field, and they really really *really* wanted to be champion. But they never had a chance, cause Ratboy was hands-down the best pinball player in alla Cadavera County, and the one time we drove down to Wichita he was the best pinball player in Wichita too, and I'm sure he's the best pinball player wherever he is now, if he can still find a machine to play on.

Whenever I could I'd go with him to Bigger Hill, to Arcadia. There was hundreds of machines there, Arcadia was like the size of a basketball court and they had everything from those stupid games where like a ground squirrel pops its head out the hole and you got to hit it with this like one-ounce plastic bat, to, like, foosball and pinball and every possible video game there was in existence then. Western Kansas maya been a little slow in other ways, movies always took a couple extra months to make it in from one coast or the other and I mean let's not even get started on *fashion*, but video games we was always right up on, the latest, the greatest, and the best. But Ratboy always went past alla them, "modern decadence" I remember he once called video games, and he went straight to the back to the little dusty corner where a half dozen pinball machines sat around, mostly I think to fill up a space that'd be empty otherwise, and he changed one dollar and one dollar only, and lined up the quarters on the machine. In all my time with him I never saw him change a second dollar, even when they upped the price to fifty cents.

The secret is in the hips is what Ratboy used to say.

"It's all about thrust," Ratboy said, and he popped his pelvis against the machine. Lights flashed, explosions boomed. I heard a whoop and realized it was my own.

"That's right, baby," Ratboy said. "You cheer for me. You cheer for your man."

Eventually a crowd gathered round. Someone would pass by, glance at the oddball, the pinball player, notice the score or maybe the number of credits he had coming to him or maybe the fact that he didn't seem to lose a ball, ever. The machine's pop as it gave him a free game almost always brought someone over, and if all else failed then I'd go round Arcadia and stump for him myself, because in the first place Ratboy liked playing to a crowd, and in the second place the best way to make sure some freckle-faced redhead redneck would make a five-dollar bet was to make sure all his friends was watching. Ratboy said he played best that way, and the one time I said I never saw him play bad, ever, he chucked me on the chin and called me sweet-tart, which was one-a his names for me. Sometimes when the crowd around him had passed to that special level of silence which is like how teenagers show their awe, Ratboy would stop midgame. He'd catch the shiny steel ball with the left flipper in midfall—always the left flipper, cause I always stood on the right side-a the machine—and with his left hand holding the flipper up and holding the ball in place, he'd reach out and put his right hand on my neck and pull me over to him and give me a kiss, a big one or a little one, tongue or no tongue, it don't matter, a kiss is still a kiss, goodbye is still goodbye. "This here's Reggie," Ratboy'd say to his audience. "Reggie brings me luck." Without taking his eyes or his right hand off me, he'd snap the flipper button with his left hand and there'd be lights and explosions, and then the electronic crack as the machine gave him a free game would shut up any noise the crowd mighta made at his display of Q.P.D.A. Me, I never honored them with a glance. I couldn't look away from Ratboy even if I'd wanted to, and I waited for the quiet moment after the machine had settled down. In the quiet moment Ratboy always said, "I couldn't do it without Reggie," and even though I knew there was something wrong with what he was saying I was never quite sure what, although I guess now I know. The plain truth was that he *could*. He could do it without me. They all could.

5.15

Colin

HE SLEPT OVER THAT FIRST NIGHT. I WON'T SAY THAT he feigned sleep, but it did seem to me forced: I shook him once or twice, but he would *not* wake up. He had curled his arms around my waist and clasped his hands together to hold them there, and the breath coming from his open mouth coalesced on my abdomen and left a little puddle of water there. I lay awake, trying to decide what to do, but soon enough a choice was made for me: Justin came in. He didn't actually come in; he only stood in the doorway, a stick-thin silent figure dwarfed by the door frame's outlandish dimensions, and when I first noticed him I had the impression that he had been standing there for hours, innocuous, unnoticed, not watching us, not even waiting for us to finish, just standing there. "Justin," I said, but of course he didn't answer. There were only snores from Divine, the puddle of breath on my skin, and, when I spoke, a half word that my stomach seemed to have shook out of him. At the sound, I looked down at Divine, and when I looked back at the door,

Justin had gone. I don't know where he slept that night; at any rate, he never slept with me again. So it went: first he stopped speaking to me, and then he stopped sleeping with me, and then he began spending all his time at Wade's. Early in May I discovered a pillow and a blanket on the floor of Justin's cupola. I say *discovered,* but what I mean is that I spied them through the door's keyhole, because Justin never left the room unlocked. After that I didn't worry so much, knowing that during the day he was in Wade's concrete bunker, and at night he slept within the citadel of the limestone house. Perhaps I was just relieved to have one less thing to worry about. I didn't worry about Justin, but instead turned my attention to Divine.

Clothed or not, his was a naked soul. He sat at my feet if I wouldn't let him in my lap; he followed along behind me like a devoted dog. If I was within his sight he stared at me constantly; neither magazine nor television nor nuclear explosion could shift his gaze, and if I met his eyes even for a moment he started talking. Let's go, is what he said most often, let's just go, and my reply was always the same: "I can't go."

"That's a loada malarkey," he said one day.

" 'Malarkey'?" I said.

Divine ducked the question. "You can go anytime you want," he said. "Nothing's holding you here."

"You've changed," I said. "Before your . . . accident, you would never have used the word *malarkey*. You would have said a load of bullshit, or a load of fucking bullshit, or a motherfucking load of motherfucking fucking—"

"All *right* already," Divine said. He shrugged; he waited; he shrugged again, but refused to look at me. "Can't we just go?"

I didn't answer him. I sat at my desk, my hands on my typewriter, open and unmoving, like a Buddha's. Today's sheet of paper stared at me, crested as it always was with the words *The last line of this story is inevitable*. Divine sat beside the typewriter, and, with one finger, without looking at me, he traced a line from my right hand, up my arm, around my shoulders, down my other arm, to my left hand. His body followed his hand; he slid off my desk and walked in a slow arc around my body.

"No one won't stop us," he said again, when he'd finished. He hovered behind me, his fingers kneading my shoulders. "They'd be just as happy to get ridda us."

"I can't go," I said again, and then, as an afterthought, I added, "until it's found."

And then I typed the words, but what came out was: *I can't leave until she's found.*

"They ain't never gonna find nothing," Divine said. "Lawman Brown couldn't find his own heinie to wipe it, or his own hand to wipe it with."

" 'Heinie,' " I repeated, but my eyes were staring at the words I'd typed. I was realizing something I hadn't really known until I'd typed them: that I could not, in fact, leave until she was found. A nauseating ball of guilt formed in my stomach then, and for a moment I thought I might actually vomit. How could it have happened that Lucy Robinson had been displaced by a few pieces of paper?

Divine's hands had gone slack on my shoulders; I wasn't even sure if they were still on my shoulders, until, after a long silent moment, I felt them float off me. Divine emerged from behind me, made his way to the side of my desk; he walked with an exaggerated slowness, and I knew he did it so that I would have plenty of time to look at his ass, and I admit it: I looked at his ass. I had seen it so many times that it lacked any power to arouse me. I don't think, in fact, that it had ever really aroused me. It wasn't Divine's *ass* I was fucking.

When he reached the side of my desk he turned around and slipped his hip onto the desk. "I'm not so sure I understand," he said quietly. There was a smile on his face as he spoke, and it was an awful smile, a clown's smile, having nothing to do with the expression in his eyes, just as the tone of his voice had nothing to do with his words. His expression and his tone were both full of uncertainty, fear even—whether of me or of something else I didn't know—but, at any rate, all Divine seemed to know to do with his fear was to say, "Maybe you should explain it to me," his voice as hollow and empty as that of a porn star who thought neither of his line nor of the coming scene, but of the hit of cocaine he'd be able to take as soon as both were over.

I looked down at my typewriter.

The last line of this story is inevitable.

One of Divine's legs began to swing back and forth.

I can't leave until she's found.

"You think it's sexy, don't you? You sit there with your tight pants and swinging leg and you think maybe I'll just bend you over my desk and fuck you?"

The tempo of Divine's leg swing increased, but he didn't say anything. I was still shouting though, shouting words that seemed as distant from my thoughts as Divine's swinging leg seemed from his.

"Well, come on then, let's do it. Turn around and drop your pants.

You want a little rape fantasy? You want me to tie you up, stuff a sock in your mouth?" I grabbed his hand then, jerked him toward me. "Right here, Divine." I threw him, chest first, onto the desk, heard his chin bang against the typewriter.

"Ow!"

"Am I hurting you, Divine? Of course I'm hurting you. You *want* me to hurt you, don't you?" I grabbed his hair then, used it to point his face in the direction of the paper in the typewriter. "Read," I said. "Read out loud."

"What?"

"Read!"

Divine's voice shook. "The last line of this story is inev, inevitable."

"Not that!" I jerked at the page, pulled it halfway from the typewriter, pointed at the second line there. I was bent over him with my groin pressed against his ass. "That!"

Divine panted and trembled. He started to speak, but nothing came out except a choked cough. He licked his lips, tried again. "I, I can't leave until she's found." He was still for a moment, and then, very suddenly, very quietly, he started crying. I could feel his sobs in my fingers, which were still entangled in his hair.

"Very good," I said, the anger gone from both my voice and my body. I released his hair. I stroked it once, just once, smoothed it as much as the gel-stiffened strands would let me. Divine's body quivered under mine but he kept his sobbing silent, and neither he nor I reacted when the phone rang.

The last line of this story is inevitable.

The phone rang again.

I can't leave until she's found.

The phone rang one more time.

It was a perverse urge that made me reach over and around Divine's body. I put my hands on the typewriter and I began to type the words that always ended my day. *I never saw,* I began, but I stopped, because I didn't know what pronoun I should use. *Him? Her? It?*

The machine clicked on. There was a long empty moment of the tape recording silent air, and then an unidentifiable throat cleared itself, and Lawman Brown's drone filled the room. "Colin Nieman," he said, "Sheriff Brown here." There was a pause, and then he said, "I think we found something here, Mr. Nieman." Another, longer pause, this one filled with what sounded like rustling pages. "I never saw him again," Lawman Brown said. "If that sounds familiar, Mr. Nieman, then I guess you maybe wanta come on down to the station."

I got home a few hours later. Divine was asleep on the couch. His cheeks were puffy and grimy and he'd obviously run his fingers violently through his hair because it now puffed around on his head in the same golden afro I'd seen that night in Wade's house. Under one arm, I held a wrinkled and slightly muddy sheaf of pages, but it was complete, it was my novel, it was the final version and it was all there.

Divine didn't awaken when I turned the light on, and he didn't awaken as I set the recovered pages on my desk. Like almost everything else—like all those other parts of Lucy Robinson's body—they had showed up in Myra Robinson's mailbox, and T. V. Daniels had found them on his afternoon delivery. T.V. said that Myra hadn't received any mail for days, though, not even a catalog, and of course she never mailed anything out, so the manuscript could have been there for a week or more.

The crumpled sheet of paper was still in my typewriter. *The last line of this story is inevitable, I can't leave until she's found, I never saw,* and Divine didn't awaken when I pulled it from the typewriter and laid it atop my novel. He didn't awaken as I started a fire in the fireplace with a few blank sheets of stationery and a tattered titleless volume I pulled from the shelves, and he didn't wake up as, one by one, I fed the pages of my novel to the fire. Dozens of opening lines flashed past my eyes before disappearing in a blaze of fire and a column of smoke, *The last line of this story is inevitable, Most people have seven holes in their head, I offered you a truncated version, A steel shutter scrolled open, It happened in an alley, When I awakened,* but Divine didn't awaken, it seemed nothing could wake him, and when, finally, I had finished destroying the thing I had made, I joined him on the couch, and I lay there listening to the fire burning out behind me and I tried to find words for what I was thinking, but the only thing that came to me was a cliché.

Up in smoke, I thought. It's all gone up in smoke.

5.16

Webbie

OBSEQUIOUSNESS PAID OFF SOONER THAN I EXPECTED. Rosemary Krebs was a busy woman who, like a businessman, preferred to conduct her affairs out of the house, and one week after I began working for her she presented me with a key which, she told me, would only open the back door, and thereafter she resumed working out of the Municipal Annex, which is how she referred to the PortaShak behind the police station. The office there was ostensibly the Mayor's, but he, when he wasn't out pressing the flesh or tending to the imagined needs of his town, preferred, like a housewife, to do his business at home, where he was easy to keep track of because he always shut himself up in his little office on the third floor, loudly declaiming something he called his "stump speech," and even when he left his office to use the bathroom or raid the refrigerator he continued speaking, and a trail of "working together"s and "sharing our strength"s marked his path through the house like the bleep of a radar icon.

The Krebs house—Rosemary Krebs once referred to it as "Eustace's family seat," which made it sound, to me, like a communal toilet—was a manifestation of Victorian grandiosity, not as old as it looked but in worse shape than it should have been, given its age. It was divided into far too many heavily draped rooms stuffed with furniture that might best be called "pioneer baroque." Everything that could be braided was tasseled, and every surface that could be abraded was carved into representations of Greek and Christian parables. They were scored into the legs and sides and surfaces of couches and tables and armoires to such a degree that dusting became a sort of history lesson, or, more accurately, a lesson in morality: the Lord can invade your body with impunity, as a tongue of flame or a swan; defy God and the whale will swallow you whole or the world be placed atop your shoulders; love yourself too much and your beauty will be rendered into the fragile and impermanent form of a flower.

In addition to her love of ornament, Rosemary Krebs, along with her other Southern peculiarities, was a staunch believer in displaying anything that even hinted of family history, prestige, or, failing that, simple wealth. Crystal, silver, porcelain figurines: Rosemary Krebs had them all, and she had them all out, and arranged in patterns that rivaled the displayed objects for intricacy and elaboration. What's more, she had the history of each piece memorized: if, in her presence, I picked up a silver spoon to polish it,

Rosemary Krebs would lose her eyes in a distant gaze and say, "My Aunt Carolinia, my mother's sister, a Hoovier until the day she died"—a spinster in other words—"first brought that spoon into her house, long before Daddy ruined us." If I responded to what she was saying with a group of words arranged in a comprehensible sentence—if, in other words, I spoke to her—Rosemary Krebs would immediately silence herself, but if I continued to work obsequiously, proffering only a "yes'm," then she would continue to talk for a while, offering me some ostensibly notable chapter in her family history, yet always, with comments like "before Daddy ruined us," hinting at the sordid, which, I suppose, in that grand Southern tradition, Rosemary Krebs preferred to think of as tragic. At any rate, I annotate all her possessions not just because they were ostentatious and vulgar, but because they were impossible to clean. After a week in her house I was able to respect Rosemary Krebs on at least one front: anyone who kept that house as immaculate as it had been, and still managed to meddle in everyone's business, was a resourceful person indeed.

Still, it was hard to imagine that in such a house, where as much as possible was placed front and center, anything could be hidden, but the more I became acquainted with Rosemary Krebs' endless collection of bric-a-brac, the more convinced I became that all this display was just an elaborate mask, and the true face of Rosemary Krebs' house had yet to be seen. The basement and the attic, when I finally managed to penetrate them, were as fruitless as I'd expected them to be, yielding only the usual assortment of old hooped dresses and pictures of a plantation house flanked by live oak draped in Spanish moss. The four-pillared Greek revival porch of the plantation house was the forerunner of the porch Rosemary Krebs had added to Phyneas Krebs' house when she took possession of it; the dresses, I later learned, were a source of chagrin to Rosemary Krebs, who confided in me that all of the Hoovier women had worn each other's clothes, but no amount of tailoring could scale them down to her small frame. In addition to the pictures and the dresses there were chests and crates—cardboard boxes weren't good enough for even discarded Hoovier heirlooms—full of tchotchkes, most of them broken, the individual fragments wrapped in tissue or packed with straw. Still, a winter's worth of searching yielded nothing more incriminating than an exchange of almost erotic letters, many spiked with verse, between the young Rosemary and her father on the occasion of each other's birthday, a charged correspondence which terminated sometime after her seventeenth birthday.

It was the Mayor who finally pointed me in the right direction. I walked in on him one day in the library, and I was so surprised that I gasped, not at encountering him, but at the open volume in his hands. I suspected Phyneas Krebs' reading to be confined to the three books on his office desk—*Winning Big in Small Town Politics, How to Be an Effective Leader*, and *Everything I Need to Know I Learned in Kindergarten*—and, as well, the inscription carved on his headboard: *For God so loved the world.* The craftsman had carved the words big, and just like the magnet on my father's refrigerator, the rest of John 3:16 had been elided in the Krebs bedroom—as had, I realized, the words in the book the Mayor held. He snapped it shut, but not before I saw that it was hollow, and then he grinned sheepishly as he shoved one closed hand in his pocket and replaced the book on the shelf with the other. He stood there awkwardly for a moment, the grin still plastered on his face, and then he cleared his throat.

"Say, Webbie," he said. "Say, could I maybe ask you a question?"

I smiled at him, but my eyes were noting the book he had just placed back on the shelves. "Of course," I said when I had located it, and then I added, "Sir."

"Now, correct me if I'm wrong, Webbie, but you are acquainted with Mr. Nieman, aren't you?"

My smile faded. "Acquainted, yes. I wouldn't say I knew him well."

"Well, yes, I mean, no. I mean, I didn't mean to imply that you knew him, I mean, *well*."

I smiled again.

"Anyway, I was wondering if you maybe knew . . ."

I ran the feathers of my duster over the palm of my hand, as if I were eager to return to work. "Yes?" I prompted.

"Well, I mean, well," he stuttered, and then he spat out, "Was he *really* a revolutionary?"

I felt my smile stiffen on my face. "Beg pardon, Mr. Mayor?"

"It's just that, you know, Eustace had that copya Mr. Nieman's book down to the station house the other day, and I kinda snuck me a peek."

"I'm sorry, sir, I still don't understand. Did Colin, did Mr. Nieman claim to be a revolutionary in his novel?"

"Well, now, that's just what I'm not sure of. I mean, everybody's been saying he was writing about Galatea and all, but, you know, when I picked this book up all I saw was stuff about the desert and the ocean. And then there was this stuff about, like, tattoos and eye contacts and steroids and stuff, none-a which I ever seen Mr. Nieman have, or, or use, or whatever, but then this guy Mr. Nieman was writing about was a writer himself and so, well, I . . ." He looked at me with an expression of genuine fear on his face. "You don't think he's got something like that going on here?"

"Something like . . ."

"I mean, there *is* an election coming up."

It was a long moment before I trusted myself to speak without laughing, and even then I had to address his shoes, which shuffled nervously under my gaze. "Well, sir, I should think Mr. Nieman has more than enough on his plate right now, without . . ." I allowed the sentence to remain unfinished.

"You think?" the Mayor said.

"I do, sir."

"Well. Well then." He giggled a little bit, and I risked a look at his face, and when my eyes met his he giggled again, and then he said, "Well, I guess I oughta be getting on with things. You're doing a real nice job, by the way, I never seen Rosemary so happy since you come to work." He mumbled a farewell then, and stumbled from the room.

"Thank you, Mr. Mayor," I called behind him. "You have a good afternoon." When, a moment later, I heard the front door close, I ran to the shelves.

The book the Mayor had held turned out to be an ancient encyclopedia volume whose eviscerated innards had been stuffed with cash. I replaced the book immediately—money I didn't need; I had cashed my paychecks only to allay any suspicions Rosemary Krebs might have—and then I set to cleaning. I chuckled under my breath every once in a while as I worked, sometimes at the thought of the hollow book on the shelves, sometimes at the Mayor's notion of Colin Nieman as some kind of revolutionary sent to foment political strife in Galatia. What, I wondered, was his book about—but as soon as I asked myself that question I rushed back to the shelves. The book that contained the Mayor's stash was labeled *M–Money*, and I suddenly found myself pulling other books off the shelves—well, it was foolish of me to think they ever *read* them, wasn't it?—and as I worked I remembered that these books, like virtually all the furniture in the house, had originated not with Phyneas Krebs' family but with his wife's. It took fewer than a dozen attempts before I found another hollow tome, a leather-bound copy of *Moby-Dick* within which were several pearl-topped hatpins. I thought pearls, as sea things, formed the connection to *Moby-Dick*, but then I realized that the pins, like my father's collection of canes, were ivory, and I was willing to wager that, like the corsets in the basement, the ivory was whalebone.

In the next few weeks I discovered that Rosemary Krebs' mania for display was matched by an even greater mania for hiding, and, like any obsession, it seemed to have far more to do with action than object. In the same way that T. V. Daniels ate anything placed in front of him, be it TV dinner or T-bone steak, Rosemary Krebs hid anything she could find a place for, as long as she could devise a suitable system of correspondences between the object and the place in which she hid it. Thus, the Mayor's extra cash was stashed in a volume marked money—which, by the way, remained there, suggesting to me that the Mayor hadn't mentioned our encounter to his wife, or that he had and she was testing my honesty. I soon discovered that the primary function of all the ornate carving on Rosemary Krebs' furniture wasn't beauty, or parable, or even, as Wade suggested, distraction, but the concealment of hidden springs and buttons that provided access to the compartments that were scattered throughout the house. Guests sipping iced tea in the sitting room had no idea that their elbows rested inches above a bound folio of lace swatches, each intricate square an ivoried hint of a dress, a veil, a glove never worn; the armrest which concealed the lace was carved with a relief of Arachne, first weaving at her loom, then being transformed into a spider for her excessive pride. Dinner guests passed their plates over a cache of blueprints, grandiose versions of the town library, a civic center, a hospital, and even more grand designs for a mayoral mansion, a county courthouse, a mall, a Burger King. In a matter of weeks, once I knew what I was looking for, I had found dozens of hidden things: thimbles, earrings, letters, a bullwhip, dried flowers, a plastic doll, a stack of old 78s. Most of these objects were so thickly covered in dust I knew they hadn't been touched in years, and most, as I have already noted, seemed to be worthless, hidden not for their sake, but for the sake of hiding itself. Behind a panel in a closet door—the panel was carved with a blank scroll of parchment—I found an ancient quill, its nib stained with dark, dried ink. Beneath the false bottom of a porcelain vase enameled with Chinese dragons I found a cache of wooden matches in boxes which bore the names of European hotels. Someone should have told Rosemary Krebs that dragons didn't breathe fire in Chinese mythology. At the bottom of an umbrella stand—an umbrella stand, in western Kansas, with an average annual rainfall of twenty-two inches—I found what was perhaps the most poignant hidden treasure, a bottle half filled with water, stoppered and sealed with wax. A curling yellowed label had been tied to the bottle with a piece of string, the words on it, written with a broad-nibbed fountain pen whose ink, like blood, had faded to a light reddish brown:

R.—
Rainfall, tenth birthday.
—E.

"E," I should mention at this juncture, was Eminent King, Rosemary Krebs' father, although, at the time I found the vial, that was about all I knew about him.

So many things: tiny books hidden inside larger ones, a marble nestled in a tin of tea so old that it had disintegrated into a powder as fine as ground peppercorns. Photographs. Fall leaves, still so bright they seemed painted. The ivory bishop to an ancient chess set, his face cracked and blackened with age just like a real man's. So many things, and all, as far as I could tell, completely useless to me, meaningless; they left me clueless, if I may use a loaded term, but even so I kept digging, convinced that among all the useless bits and bobs and trinkets there must be at least one real treasure. But as the months passed I came to doubt that I would ever find anything of value, and I grew sick of breathing in the fumes of ammonia-laced water and burning my hands with the caustic polish Rosemary Krebs had me apply weekly to her silver, and it became harder and harder to look down at her tiny, birdlike feet tapping on the parquet floor that I had swept, mopped, and waxed on my hands and knees, muttering "Yes'm" and "Nome" and resisting the urge to pop her with the scrub brush I held in my hand, and then, finally, unexpectedly, perseverance paid off. Perhaps *perseverance* isn't the right word; perhaps I should just say that dumb luck and a lack of any other options led me to it, the second most important thing I was to find in my long, odd search for Lucy Robinson, although by that point I wasn't quite sure what I was looking for. My searching had taken on some of the qualities of Rosemary Krebs' hiding: it was just something I did, because I had nothing else to do.

It was in her bedroom. It was, in fact, in her bed. It occurred to me one day that the *o* in the word *God* carved in the headboard was rather suspiciously oval, eyelike I mean, or egglike, and it only took a single firm push to open the door to a small compartment that contained a fat Bible, which, in place of the books of Deuteronomy and Exodus, contained a slim volume filled with Rosemary Krebs' own law and her own journeys: her diary. It was an odd account, beginning when she was seventeen and continuing sporadically for over twenty-five years, until shortly after Kenosha burned down and Galatea was founded. It was this diary, and the clipped brittle anecdotes that Rosemary Krebs occasionally related to me, that enabled me to create a cohesive narrative line. It was an odd story, complete in and of itself, and yet taking me, on its own, absolutely nowhere. The metaphor that comes to mind is that of a railroad track: Rosemary Krebs' history was a single rail, and even as I laid it I knew that there was a second track I had not yet begun. I worked in fits and starts, stealing glimpses at the diary whenever I changed the bed linen or cleaned the bathroom in the master bedroom, and I assembled the evidence as I had in my days as an historian, on note cards that I ordered and reordered as the sequence of events became clear to me, and that I, like Rosemary Krebs, kept hidden from prying eyes. And as I worked I remembered Justin's comment about humanity's need to reveal itself through written confession. Nothing is ever written down solely for the eye of the writer, he'd said: it's always intended for a larger audience. And that, I realized as I made my own notes, was as true of me as it was of Rosemary Krebs.

5.17

Justin

HE PUT ME TO WORK. HE SHOWED ME HOW TO MAKE A stretcher, pull canvas over it, prime the canvas, paint it. I shouldn't say that he put me to work: he taught me to paint. "I'm not an art director," he said. "I'm not an idea man. And I'm not old either. I do my own work." The stretchers I built, I used, rickety things, as shaky as the strokes I laid on them. Wade gave me paint and brushes, an easel, a place out of direct sunlight, but after that I was left on my own, and, since I didn't know what to do, I tried to emulate Wade. I used the same colors he did, pulled and pushed and daubed with the brush as he did, but my canvases just looked like a wall painted by an epileptic. Wade never criticized the things I painted, but sometimes he would criticize the way I made them; reshaping my hand around a brush, he would say, "Gently, gently, it's a paintbrush, it's *paint*, not a needle and thread."

One day a flickering shape outside the window distracted me. It was a bird, but it moved so quickly and stayed for such a short time that I had no idea what kind of bird, and, unbidden, an image of the walls of the cupola sprang into my head. On a corner of my canvas not already discolored I tried to copy one of the birds from the cupola's walls, a meadowlark, magenta-backed and lavender-bellied and speckled all over with neon-green dots. Those were the colors the original painter had chosen; I, with the colors Wade had mixed, merely did my best to re-create them. As I finished I remembered that one of the meadowlark's trailing feet had clutched a vine that looked a lot like seaweed, and I added it at the last moment. I stepped back and looked at my lopsided creation. I thought that, like a bee, it shouldn't have been able to fly, but it did. Then I realized Wade was staring at my painting.

"That's good," he said, very quietly, very strangely, and, in spite of myself, I blushed. Wade stood silently for a moment, and then he drew a thin-tipped paintbrush from a mason jar and dabbed it in a dark smear on his palette. He stepped up to my bird and with a few deft gestures corrected its form slightly. At first I just thought he was making it look more like *a* bird, but as he worked I realized he was making it look more like *the* bird, the bird on the wall of the cupola. When he'd finished he stepped back. "Bea must have taken good care of that room, for the murals to be intact. They weren't very sturdy to begin with." He smiled. "Yankee Carting's TruValue doesn't exactly make their plaster from the same materials the Romans favored." He looked at the painting when he spoke. "I must have been fifteen or sixteen when I painted that. Bea was in her late sixties, Hank was already dead. It was the first time I was ever paid for my work. Well, no," he corrected himself, "no, it was the second." He paused, sighed; he didn't tell me what had been the first time he was paid for a painting. "Bea was vague" is what he said. "All she wanted were birds, all they had to do was fly heavenward. 'Heavenward,' she said, 'toward Henry.' " He stopped again. This time he went to the mason jar, picked up another brush, a flat one perhaps a half inch wide. He whited its bristles. "It must be fading now," he said. "Faking. I mean flaking. Is it flaking?" He looked at me but I didn't move. "Ah, I forgot," he said, smiling slightly. "Justin doesn't talk. Justin doesn't even nod his head. Is it flaking, Justin, like this?" He stabbed at the painting; what was amazing, I thought, was that in a single, seemingly violent gesture he managed to produce a mark that looked like the flaking plaster of the room. "I had this idea," Wade said, "not a bad idea for a fifteen-year-old, that the lark trailing a piece of seaweed would be a Plains version of the dove carrying the olive branch back to Noah on the ark. Proof, you know, that somewhere, out there, there was water." He laughed. "And she already had the ark, too. Who knew?"

As he said that I remembered the gap in the cedar hedge that had allowed me to see clearly the fire which consumed Noah Deacon's ark, and I wanted to tell Wade that whoever Bea had been, whatever she had known, she had known about the landlocked boat on her property. But I didn't tell him, and Wade continued speaking. "Now, I suppose, now that dream must be flaking off in chips and pieces, falling to the floor in a little spray of dust. Falling hellward." As he spoke he stabbed again and again at the bird, and it disappeared in flecks of white. "Soon it will be gone, won't it? Maybe I'll outlast it, maybe I won't, but you certainly will." He stabbed and stabbed. "Soon the wall will be bare again, a hint of faded color here and there, and then what will you have to look at? Will you look at this, Justin?" He jerked his brush at the obscured blob on the canvas, and when I didn't follow his brush with my eyes he turned my head for me with a hand that stank of paint. "What will you see in it, Justin? Will you try to see that lost bird, or perhaps the real bird, the one that was sacrificed to make that mural? Or will you look for the only thing it can really show you?"

He stopped suddenly. "Oh, Justin, don't cry." I stiffened, sniffled; I hadn't realized I was crying. I had been thinking of the remnants of Colin's latest novel that I found in the fireplace in his office, and I had been thinking of an earlier attempt at that novel, one which I had destroyed myself, and now I was crying. After a moment of hesitation Wade took his hand off my cheek, and then, slowly, tenderly, he put it back on. The smell of paint was stronger on him than it was on me, and I relaxed against his hand. Wade took my relaxation as an invitation, and his arms enfolded me and pulled me against his body. His hold was awkward, the hold of a man who knew how to embrace someone, but not how to give them a hug, and his voice, when it came, was right in my ear, almost painfully loud.

"The first time I was paid for painting I was thirteen. I won a statewide competition to repair the mural of John Brown in the Capitol Building in Topeka. Do you know that mural, Justin? Do you—oh." He laughed a little, his hot wet breath dampening my ear. "It's very famous, that mural, very silly but very famous. John Brown stands there in his buckskins, a rifle in one hand, a Bible in the other, and a fierce, fierce look of determination on his face. He doesn't look like a liberator at all, he looks like a crazy man, which, at the end of the day, is what he was. But at the time he didn't look like much of anything because the paint he had been created from had never been properly fixed, and the humidity was causing it to peel off in flakes like a sycamore trunk shedding its bark. For some reason our local politicians decided that it would be a good thing if a Kansan did the repairs, and, as I said, they held a competition and I won. The competition was anonymous, and I think everyone was a little surprised to find out that the winner was only thirteen, but then they decided it made for even better publicity. I was photographed with half the state senators, with the governor even. I can't remember his name, but I pretended to shake his hand for something like twenty minutes while the cameras flashed, and then they put me up on top of a scaffold, just like Michelangelo, I thought at the time, just like Michelangelo, and they left me alone. Well." He laughed again; his grip had softened as he'd spoken, and the fingers of his left hand were idly scratching the small of my back. "I don't know why I'm telling you this," he said. He sighed. "I did an okay job. I didn't do anything wrong. But I was thirteen. I thought of myself as some kind of young radical, although, really, I was then and have remained a reactionary. What I mean is, I put my own slogan on John Brown's Bible before I finished. I painted *John Brown was right*, and as soon as I had, I painted over it, but it's up there still, underneath a nice thick coat of vellum-colored brown and these fake hieroglyphics meant to represent letters but which are nothing more than little swirls and hatchmarks and dots and dashes. *John Brown was right*. I thought of it as my own contribution to history. Oh, Justin," he said, his voice changing suddenly, becoming deeper and more desperate. "Don't end up like me," he said, "please don't end up like me." His breath caught in his throat and he stopped, and I knew that I should have spoken. But I said nothing, and Wade said nothing, and after a moment he let go of me and picked up a wide flat paintbrush and with a few deft strokes he painted over the bird, over the canvas and over the words he had written on John Brown's body and over me, and left behind nothing but a smooth slick sheen of white.

5.18

Divine

THE FIRST TIME WAS IN HIS DADDY'S BARN. I WAS

twelve, he was sixteen, we was in a empty stall between this old gray gelding that was just about ready to take its final walk to the glue factory and some sow nursing next year's breakfast bacon. I'd known him for one week, seven whole days.

Ratboy said, "I wanna tell you how it is between us." He turned me toward him, took me by the shoulders. I was taller than him by a hair, but I bent my knees a little so he wouldn't be self-conscious. He said, "You're a faggot and I'm a faggot lover, and that's just the way it is. People like us, people who fit, we got to stick together."

I'd been called a faggot before, but I'd never heard of a faggot lover, and even as I accepted his definition of me—so it *is* true is what I remember thinking—I waited for him to tell me what a faggot lover was, what *he* was. And it's not like I didn't know about sex or nothing, it just never occurred to me that *they* might enjoy doing it themselves, as opposed to doing it to me, and I was right in the middle of some kinda thought like that when Ratboy just leaned forward and kissed me. Instinct or something made me bend my knees lower, so my head was beneath his. The position was so awkward that I started to lose my balance, but Ratboy just caught holda me and held me up with a strong arm—I maya been taller than him but I weighed less cause there wasn't really nothing that you could call muscle on my body yet. Later on Ratboy said that was one-a the things he liked about me, but that day he just pulled his lips from mine long enough to say, "I'll always catch you, if you wanna fall."

And then he pushed me down in the hay.

So. His Daddy's barn, his Daddy's bed, his bed, his car, on blankets in fields. We never did make it out to Noah's ark, I guess I couldn't bring myself to bring a white person there or something, but we did it a couple-a times in the Cave of the Bellystones—Lawman Brown maya put some lock on there but it was a pretty simple thing to unscrew the hinges the lock was nailed to and open the door that way, and judging from the cans of food and used rubbers and stuff that me and Ratboy found there, we was hardly the only ones doing it. Once we did it in the locker room, the other boys gone but Coach Carting still whistling some stupid song to himself in the shower. "Hey, Water Boy," I remember Ratboy said that time. "Ratboy wants a drink."

Finally, my house. My parents was on a day trip to Hutchinson—my Daddy, among many other stupid acts, bought hisself a Japanese car, and Hutch was the closest he could take it for a tune-up, which, as you might expect, it needed fairly regular. My momma went for the shopping, such as it was, at the mall.

Ratboy and me cut school right after first period. I let us in the back door, the kitchen door, and right away he pushed me down on the linoleum. "Every single room" was what he whispered in my ear.

I blew him in the kitchen. He did me the first time over the dining room table, my nose right in the pepper shaker. We 69'd in the living room, all the way through *Family Feud*, and we just made a mess out of my room is all I can say. In the bathroom we got all clean again, and then he took me into my parents' room. There was just something about *defiling* that he liked to do. He was naked, dripping from the shower, and he fell on the bed, flat on his back, bounced up off it back on his feet. "That's a good box springs," he said. The outline of his wet body showed up on the white bedspread.

Ratboy opened up drawers one by one until he found the one with my momma's underwear. My momma was a small woman, you understand, which is one-a the reasons why she only had me—another was the fact that she didn't like sweating, and it's pretty hard to make a baby at either end of the process without sweating. I wasn't exactly a big boy, and the long and short of it is that all her things fit me, pretty much, Ratboy used a little toilet paper to fill out the sag in the bra, and he showed me how to tuck, and there I was: high heels, white nylons, garter belt, black panties (lace in front, just a string in back, Momma, who knew?). The bra was a little pointy push-up thing with about a inch of padding sewn right in, which surprised me, cause I always thought my momma's cleavage was natural, and the wig, the color of what Cora likes to call dirty honey, which is to say the unfiltered stuff, smelled like dust all around my head. My lips was as red and blurry as cherry pie filling, and Ratboy just looked at me and said, "Baby, you look divine."

So there.

I watched him in the mirror. It was the first time there'd been a mirror—believe me, if you'd ever seen Carol Wiebe you'd know why there wasn't no mirror in that house. Ratboy, kissing me all over, then me kissing him, or rather him making me kiss him, him moving my face from place to place on his body, the little quiver in his butt cheeks when he did me, the straw nest of his hair after my fingers had messed it up, the wig coming off in his hand. Afterwards we spooned back to front, and in the mirror I could see the pale outline of him all around my body like a glow, and little red blurs on my skin where his kisses had transferred my lipstick back to me.

He pointed to the mirror. "I bet you never knew your parents liked to watch themselves fuck, did you?"

"You the first white person ever been in this house."

"I bet they was watching themselves as they made you. I bet they was saying, We gonna make the prettiest little black boy the world never seen."

"I don't know if they'd be more upset if they found out I was doing it with a boy in they bed, or if they found out I was doing it with a white boy."

"In they bed," Ratboy said.

". . ."

"And that black boy's gonna be so pretty, they was saying, so pretty that no one'll be able to resist his charms."

"I guess I'd be surprised to find out my parents ever had that much to say to each other in they whole lives, but *you* certainly do have a way of saying things."

"I have a way of saying things?"

"Whatever you say sounds like the truth. 'N if it ain't true, you make it true."

My momma and daddy, they was so stupid. They thought I dressed up some girl in my momma's lingerie and diddled her on they bed. As if. My daddy grabbed me by the hair and drug me into his room and pointed at the outline of a body on the crinkled bedspread. "And what is *that*, young sir?" is what he screamed at me, and me, I could only look at it and after what Ratboy and me'd said and done, I mean, how could I lie? My momma was standing in the doorway with her arms crossed over what I now knew was a manufactured bosom, kinda biting her lip and frowning, and I looked at her and I looked at my daddy and I said, "That's Ratboy," and I fastened my eyes on Ratboy's shadow, left behind just like Peter Pan's, cause let me tell you: nothing holds a water stain like cheap satin. My momma kinda caught her breath in her throat and my daddy just stood there dumbstruck for about two minutes, and then real slow he pulled his belt from his pants and pulled my pants offa me, and my momma said, "Aw, Ronnie, don't hurt the boy," but as it turned out my daddy never beat me. Instead, he saw the love bites there, other little pieces-a Ratboy left behind, left on me, and I think he was still willing to give me the benefit of the doubt but there was no way he could deny the smile that was spread across my face. My daddy dropped the belt on the floor and barely made it into the bathroom before he started puking, and me, I didn't even have the good sense to pull up my pants and hightail it outta there. I stood stock-still, staring at Ratboy's outline on the bed, and then when I looked over at my momma I understood for the first time just what Ratboy's power was. My momma was still like in the same position she'd been in before, but she'd kinda shrunk a little too. It was like suddenly there was one more thing in the world, and it took up space at her expense.

Sometime after that my daddy caught us holding hands, and he walked right up to us and punched Ratboy so hard I heard something go *snap!* He was on the ground for a good long time while I just stood there, frozen, and my daddy stood there, spit dripping off his lips, and then, before me or my daddy knew what was happening, Ratboy was up off the ground and he had aholda one-a those lengths-a two-by-four that always happen to be around when you need one, and he whupped my father so hard upside the head that he knocked him out cold. Then he took my hand again, and we walked away.

So I guess Ratboy did actually win one fight.

We slept in his car for a week, and then Lawman Brown put Ratboy in jail for another week, and I went home. My daddy tied my hands to the bedpost and he whaled on me with his belt for ninety-seven minutes straight—I watched the clock the whole time cause my momma had turned the bedspread facedown—and then finally my daddy dislocated his shoulder and for the next two weeks not only did he have a bruise the shape and pretty near the size-a the state of Kansas on his cheek, but he had his arm in a sling too. And I wasn't as bad hurt as you might think because my daddy didn't take down my pants. He started to, but then he changed his mind.

5.19

Colin

I MIGHT HAVE WANTED MY NOVEL TO DISAPPEAR, BUT someone else did not. Just days after I burned the first recovered copy, a second one showed up. It was a photocopy of the original manuscript, and it showed up in Howard Goertzen's mailbox. Howard didn't give the manuscript to Lawman Brown; he called me himself, and when I arrived at his father's pig farm I found it waiting for me in a box filled not just with my novel, but also with a good helping of pig shit. I took it home, where I doused both box and contents with gasoline, and burned the whole thing on the obsidian moat that surrounded the limestone house, but a few days later another copy surfaced. Literally: it was sealed in plastic and floated in the tank at the base of the windmill in Galatia's park, and it was found by none other than Reverend Greeving and his Church Ladies on their way to Sunday-morning services. One of the Church Ladies delivered it to me personally; which one it was I wasn't sure, but she stood on my porch and blinked her eyes against the Thursday-afternoon sunlight and glanced occasionally to her right and left, as if looking for the two women who usually flanked her. "The Reverend just asked me to tell you that he finds your reading of the Scriptures a might peculiar" is all she said to me, and then she turned and carefully picked her way across the rocks to her car.

And so it went: another half dozen copies of my novel showed up here and there; no one else had the gumption or the inclination to deal with me personally, but instead used the intermediary of Lawman Brown, and I took each progressively more deteriorated photocopy he procured for me, and burned it, and waited for another to appear. At some point, as I watched my novel disintegrate into ashes for the fourth or fifth time in as many weeks, I was reminded of the story of the phoenix, and after that I dug out my paper shredder and used that to destroy the returned copies instead. I could have used scissors, but there was a reason why I didn't use scissors—a reason why I owned the paper shredder in the first place. But the shredded pages only reminded me of the first novel I'd ever lost, and so, in the end, I dug a hole in the obsidian and buried them there, one at a time, week after week, until, as suddenly as the stolen copies had begun appearing, they stopped.

I wasn't surprised. The point had been made, I supposed, the objective reached: the objective being, as far as I could tell, that everyone in Galatia should know what sort of things I had written about them, and about myself. By the time the pirated copies of my novel stopped showing up, rumors about town had it that I was a junkie, a prostitute, a spy, a terrorist even, a mad scientist, a nymphomaniac, and, of course, a jewel thief. The erroneous conflation between author and character seemed to me so obvious as to be comic; and yet it made no sense. I was here; I existed; the details of my biography and of my character were readily available, but still people found it necessary to invent one outlandish story after another to explain my presence. But as soon as Lucy Robinson disappeared, so did all talk of her. On most days it was easy to believe she had never existed, or that she had died long ago and was best forgotten, and even as her kidnapper provided us with clue after clue, if not to her whereabouts then at least to her continued suffering, less and less was said about her. But it occurred to me, as well, that what was happening to both of us, to me and to Lucy Robinson, was in some ways the same thing. Both of us were being effaced, I by lies, she by silence. It felt in some way as if she *had* died, and I had come back as her ghost, to haunt Galatia. And that only strengthened my resolve that I *would* haunt Lucy's town until she was exhumed, or I was exorcised. If that was all I could do for her, I would do it faithfully, and as well as I could.

5.20

Webbie

DADDY RUINED EVERYTHING.

This was the first line seventeen-year-old Rosemary King wrote in her diary, which, as first lines go, was as catchy as any Colin ever spouted off for his novel—his missing novel, I suppose I should say.

For an entire week that was all I had to go on, *Daddy ruined everything*, because no sooner had I cracked the brittle spine of Rosemary Krebs' diary than I heard the distinctive tap-tap-tap of her hard-heeled shoes on the stairs. They were my best defense, those floors, old, slightly warped, and hollow: even a footstep as light as Rosemary Krebs' echoed throughout the house.

Eventually I gained access to the bedroom again, and to the secret compartment in the headboard, and I was able to learn that the man Rosemary Krebs had once called Daddy had been born Justice Eminent King, called Judge by his family, Emmet by his friends, and His Eminence by the local newspaper. This last is the most telling detail. In the young Rosemary King's words: "Momma always said there were two kinds of people who should never refer to a Southern gentleman by his Christian name: a Negro who don't work in his house and a newspaper reporter—and even if the Negro does work in his house he can only use his employer's Christian name with permission, and only if he calls him Mister first." It is perhaps gratuitous to mention that the *i* of "Mister" seemed to have been inked over an *a*, but I mention it anyway, if only for sake of accuracy. At any rate, Rosemary King's point seemed to be that it was the fault of the gentleman himself if such a thing happened, for only a man who lost the respect of his peers would be so abused, and, in the case of Judge King, one didn't have to look too far to find his vices: Rosemary had set them off in a neat numbered column on the second page of her diary.

Vice's
1. *Gambling*
2. *Liquor*
3. *Loose women*

Under the heading *Borderline* she had written *Too much vetiver* and *Too long of hair*, and under the heading *Questionable* she had written *String ties*.

Loose, I soon realized, was in this case a euphemism for *black*.

Judge King's courtroom was hereditary, like his home, Seven Oaks—or the Seven Deadly Sins, as the paper called it, when it wasn't just calling it King's Castle—and as a result most of his time was spent perfecting the art of leisure, in the pursuit of which he managed to gamble and drink up what remained of the family's antebellum fortune. When Rosemary King was eleven, Seven Oaks was sold at a bankruptcy auction, the big house bulldozed and cotton planted in its place, and the defrocked justice took his wife and daughter to live with a "minor cousin," a spinster called Aunt Syrene, "a woman too loathsome to contemplate, let alone describe."

Aunt Syrene lived an hour west of Wichita, in Hutchinson. "Like cattle," Rosemary wrote, "she had been driven across the country." Her diary was sketchy about the years they spent with Aunt Syrene, but she describes the house as "good-sized but shabby," stuffed with Aunt Syrene's junk and "packing crates in which the treasures Momma herself had salvaged from Seven Oaks were lodged like gold in the silt of a miner's pan." Worst of all, though, was the fact that the house was located in a neighborhood which, like her father's passion for vetiver cologne and long hair and string ties—the picture that comes to mind all too clearly is that of Colonel Sanders—was "borderline." "Why, one morning," Rosemary recorded, "I went to the corner store to fetch Momma some fresh eggs and lemon, and I walked past two darker skinned women who were talking to each other—*and they weren't speaking English*!"

Aunt Syrene's flood of male callers was matched only by Judge King's tendency to dine out. "June 17: Daddy dined out; Momma taken to her bed; another dinner alone with Aunt S. In a transparent effort to hide the fact that she was drinking—she caught me sniffing her glass last week—Aunt S. poured her gin into her *soup* and spooned it up with none too steady a hand. The soup was tomato and Aunt Syrene's dress white (if you can believe *that*!). The stains told their own story." Still, the teenaged Rosemary seemed to have lost none of her admiration or love for her father, and even though these diary entries were written years after that love had disappeared, its shadow could still be felt in her words. "He was a King, after all, and married to a Hoovier, and the King path was noted for its bumps and detours but always it had ended up smooth again, and sure, and in the right place, and I believed it would lead us back to a decent place once again."

Rosemary's mother, the Hoovier—Rosemary refers to her once as Rubella, but I find it hard to believe that she actually bore such a name—remained a silent figure throughout these years, but the one thing that was clear was that Rosemary reserved her true contempt for her. Mrs. King liked a fried egg sandwich in the morning, a weakness bred in her by her black nanny. She "forebore" lunch but served tea: cucumber and cress sandwiches and a silver pot of Earl Gray. "Momma always put a pitcher of milk on the Fall of Troy tea tray, though she, of course, only used lemon, and she decided who would be invited back for a second visit based on whether or not they poured milk into their tea like a commoner, which meant that we soon took tea by ourselves, with only the occasional company, if you can call it that, of Eleanor Vanderbilt, an old woman not nearly as grand as her name made her out to be—and who, as it turned out, was unable to properly digest lactose. Dairy, apparently, made her flatulent, and so, unfortunately, did tea, and soon enough it was just Momma and me."

Still, despite these refinements, Mrs. King was a failed woman. Aunt Syrene, on the other hand, was simply a fallen woman, not worthy of the attention that contempt would entail, and Judge King did the only thing required of a gentleman: "He never left the house dirty or drunk, and if he ever came home in either of these states he made sure that none of his womenfolk saw him that way." Any other faults he had, then, were too minor to mention, and they were, besides, his wife's responsibility:

according to the code Rosemary had learned from her mother herself, it was a wife's only responsibility—to preserve her husband's appearance in society, which in turn preserved her own, and her family's—and Mrs. King's inability to do so made her, in the eyes of the young Rosemary, not a fallen, but a failed woman. "My mother neither smoke nor drank nor ever admitted to being hungry in front of someone who wasn't a relative, and her response to a dirty glass in the parlor, even after we were forced to let our last servant go, was to ring a bell. All of these efforts to maintain her own dignity were as naught, however, for she could not maintain her husband's, and, as she herself taught me, a wife's dignity at the expense of her husband's was a thing as useless as a sail without a mast to hang it on."

Just as I was closing the diary to go and scrub Rosemary Krebs' toilet, I glimpsed a couple of words—*mistress* was one of them and another *indiscreet*—and I was eager to see just what such words could imply in the context of the King family. But it was nearly three weeks before I found out: two days after I read the passages I have just relayed, Lucy Robinson's fingertips showed up, and for the next ten days neither Phyneas nor Rosemary Krebs, nor anyone else in Galatia, did much of anything. It seemed that only the farmers and I still worked each day, and I almost lost my will—not to mention my mind—waiting for the day that Rosemary Krebs would return to work. What I did lose was Lucy Robinson. On some level I actually resented her for stealing the show as she always did, as though the severing of her fingertips were a sort of grandstanding on her part; and I could hardly contain my anger at Rosemary Krebs for loitering in her own house, or my excitement when she returned to work. As it happened, Phyneas Krebs was also out of the house that afternoon, and so I was able to read, unmolested, for nearly an hour.

There were dozens of entries after the last one I had read, each one shorter and more enervated than the last, detailing the humdrum daily details of existence in the King household. Mrs. King spent more and more of her time in her bed; Judge King spent more and more of his time away from it; Aunt Syrene got into whatever bed she could; and young Rosemary, just graduated from high school, drifted among the three of them, serving tea as best she could, and guarding what little remained of the Hoovier and King family heirlooms from her father and her aunt's plundering. It seemed as if this state of affairs could have been perpetuated indefinitely, or at least until Rosemary had married into better circumstances, but her father finally, "and, I suppose now,"

Rosemary Krebs wrote years later, "inevitably broke through the final barrier: he was indiscreet." Or, rather, his mistress was indiscreet. She came to the King house in the middle of the night and called out to Eminent King with "coarse endearments," but the first person she succeeded in awakening was Rosemary. "I curse the urge that drove me to the window," she wrote, "but, like Eve, I allowed myself to be tempted by the husky, exotic tones emanating from Aunt Syrene's lawn. As if the voice hadn't made it clear to me: not even white trash could call out filth like that. But my eyes confirmed the horror. Daddy was carrying on with a"—and here, in the heavy blot appended to the tail end of the pen stroke on the letter *a*, I could almost feel Rosemary King's struggle to find the willpower to write the word—"a Negress." Eventually her father emerged onto the lawn, and, after an encounter which Rosemary "could not watch but could not look away from," he sent the woman away. I wasn't surprised, when I checked the date of the entry, to find out that Rosemary saw her father's mistress less than a month after her seventeenth birthday—the last birthday for which she and her father ever exchanged cards.

There was a gap after this scene; the shorn stubs of three pages protruded from the diary's spine like the stump of an amputated limb; and then the next entry, dated some six months later, indicates that, rather than transfer her loyalties from father to mother, Rosemary chose to redirect them outside the house. "He is as tall as I am small" is the first complete sentence to appear after the missing pages, and I knew immediately that she must be referring to Phyneas Krebs; I call it the first complete sentence because there was also a fragment at the top of the page, which, like a bodiless tail, seemed to spasm about on the page: "is what I can do." Of her future husband, Rosemary King wrote, "I have no illusions as to his capabilities. He is a silly man. But he doesn't drink or smoke, and when he does he has the good sense to lie about it. He refers to his Daddy's farm as a ranch, and, most importantly, he is a believer. And I won't have to change my monogram." There was a courtship, ostensibly of Rosemary by Phyneas, but clearly orchestrated by her. There was an engagement. There was, finally, a wedding, which seems to have been a travesty on all fronts. Not only did Rosemary have to wear a store-bought dress, but Aunt Syrene, having discovered the hereditary Hoovier gown, wore it herself. According to Rosemary's diary, Phyneas' father only washed "what skin showed beyond his suit, which, being ill-fitting, was quite a bit." The bridegroom's mother cinched in her waist with a belt rather than a corset or girdle, making her look "like a sack of flower dumped on a stool. Unfortunately, unlike a sack of flower, she possessed the ability to speak." Judge King burped aloud during her vows, and Mrs. King spilled champagne on her dress during the reception. It was Aunt Syrene who caught the bouquet; she tucked one yellow rose through a moth-eaten hole in the lace at her cleavage and tossed the rest of the flowers in the trash.

In what was, I think, the only conscious act of sentimentality ever recorded in her diary, Rosemary King retrieved a single petal from one of the flowers—a yellow rose, gone dingy and brown by the time I saw it—and pressed it in with the page, and it was a similar, albeit more hostile urge, that caused me to pull the petal from the page and crumble it to dust before replacing it and returning to work.

5.21

Justin

WADE UNLOCKED THE DOOR SLOWLY, PUSHED IT OPEN, let me enter first. The room was small, dim, shaded by the wide leaves of a grapevine that scaled the outer wall of the house. I thought at first that the window was also shrouded by a thin white blind, but then I realized that sheets of paper had been taped to the panes. "A long time ago," Wade told my back, "this was my room." Now, it seemed, it had become Divine's: hundreds of drawings of him covered every surface of the room, even the floor. The inside of the door, when Wade closed it, was covered; the papers taped to the window were also drawings, and the setting sun came through them and through the hollow outlines of Divine's body that were drawn on the paper. There was something so repulsively pornographic about the pictures that I found it impossible to look directly at them. Even in those which didn't reveal Divine's face, just his hand or his foot, he still seemed to be staring out at his viewers, and the pictured limb was offered as an instrument for sexual gratification, although whether that offering was Wade's or Divine's was impossible to tell.

I looked at Wade then; he looked nervously back at me. "Right," he said. He said, "You don't have to take your clothes off, but that *is* the usual way." Then he sat on the floor and busied himself settling a hard-backed pad on his knees, sharpening pencils—the shavings, and his feet, and my feet, smudged the drawings of Divine beneath us—and when he stood up he seemed surprised to find me standing in the same position as before. He hesitated a moment, then walked over to me, and then he awkwardly undressed me. I was wearing only a short-sleeved button-down shirt and a pair of loose shorts, so the process wasn't that difficult, and when my clothes were off me Wade pushed a little on my shoulder, not pushed really, but pressed, guided, and I sat in the swath of light from the window.

Wade looked at me for a long time, and, to avoid his eyes, I looked at the pictures on the wall. Despite myself, I realized what Wade was doing, and what he was going to do. Before Wade ever started that first drawing of me I could see the changing face of the room, could imagine like pictures of me covering like pictures of Divine. As I sat naked in the middle of the room, I wondered which part of Divine would be effaced by which part of me. My neck? My thigh? Would he start with my penis, or with my face? Would he first draw a picture of my entire body and then dismantle me, or would he assemble me limb by limb, get to know me piece by piece?

"Could you cross your arms, um . . ." His voice trailed off. He leaned into me, and as delicately as a girl might arrange her doll on her bed he arranged me for his picture. I moved in his hands, felt his warm fingertips against my wrists, my cheek, my thigh. When he was done he sat down again, and I didn't look at him. I couldn't. I thought that if I looked at him, his eyes would draw words out of me. He sat still for a moment, and then I heard him say, "Divine always, he always looked at me," and then I heard his pencil begin to scratch on the paper. It sounded vaguely familiar, but it took me a moment to realize that it sounded like Colin at work, pushing a pen over paper. I shivered.

"Are you cold?" No, Wade, I'm not. After a moment, Wade said, "Silly question," and his pen resumed scratching. I closed my eyes, to avoid Divine's. "Please don't," Wade said, but I ignored him. "Justin?" I continued to ignore him. After a moment Wade's scratching continued. I felt it on my skin, as though he were tattooing me, but I sat still. A long time later, Wade shook me, and I opened my eyes. "Done," he said. The hand that shook me was smeared with lead dust. "You fell asleep?" he said, as if he were not quite sure. He handed me my shorts. "I didn't find any underwear?" In answer, I took my shorts and put them on. My eyes flickered to his pad. It was open but bare, and at the sight I shivered. Had I become invisible? "I put it up," Wade said. He waved a hand at the walls, and my eye scanned them quickly but I couldn't find myself. Wade put his arms around me in another of his awkward embraces. His bones were close to his skin and they pressed against me like, I thought, like pencils, or the stems of paintbrushes. "Thank you," he said. He stepped back from me. "It's my private vice." My eyes rested on a picture of Divine clutching his erect penis. Did Wade expect me to do that? "Imagine," Wade said, "me, still doing life drawing. Well," he chuckled, "I guess I can trust you to keep my secret."

5.22

Divine

THINGS CHANGED AFTER RATBOY'S WEEK IN JAIL. WE'D been going together for a year: he was seventeen and I was thirteen and I'd just started high school and he'd just dropped out and now he was talking about getting the hell outta Galatia for good and always. And that's when he started going to the Big M.

Ratboy didn't tell me what was up at first. Just one day I come outta school to meet him like I always did and he wasn't there, which kinda fucked me up but good cause I'd had me some words with this doofus called Merle Potter and I was counting on Ratboy to either like kick Merle's ass or get me outta there in his car, and instead Merle, who was this great big but sorta doughy boy with crossed eyes that were set like half a inch apart in his face, Merle drug me behind the gym and he said I had a choice between one of two things making repeated contact with my mouth, which one of them was his fist and the other was his dick, and I said well can I see the dick so I know which is bigger? And can I just say too that I hope he's learned a little self-control in the years since then or else he better find a wife who can come in like thirty seconds because I like didn't even have time to *decide* what my attitude was like gonna be toward this. I mean, this boy added a whole nother dimension to the word *premature ejaculation*.

So anyway late that day Ratboy found me at what by then had become our usual place: the top of the grain elevator. You'd be surprised: right there in the exact center of everything, and for a year no one had ever once caught us going up or coming down, which Galatia's—excuse me, Gala*tea*'s grain elevator does have a covered ladder instead of a exposed one like mosta them, but still: I mean, we had to park on the street and walk across the highway and everything, and it wasn't like there was any place to *hide* once you got up top. So. It musta been about eleven o'clock, maybe midnight, before Ratboy come over the side of the elevator. He had a kind of sheepy—sheeply? sheeplike?—smile on his face and I like made up my mind to stay mad at him but I never could, not with Ratboy, he just sat hisself down next to me and put a arm around my shoulders and gave me the littlest tenderest kiss on the cheek and right away all my anger melted into a little puddle at my feet. And right away too I knew what he'd been up to cause I could smell it on his breath, could smell it all over him really, and I thought well shit, maybe I *should* be mad at him but then what had I just been up to?

He had a fresh black eye, but that was so not unusual I didn't ask him about it.

And then Ratboy he pulled a wad of wrinkled bills outta his jeans pocket which the money he gave to me and said could I count it, and I did and it come to something like a hundred and ten bucks or something like that.

And even though no one had ever sat me down and like *explained* the concept of hustling to me I still knew what he'd gone and done and I said, "How many?"

And Ratboy said, "Just three."

And I did some math and I said, "Three's not bad."

"There was more, but I bought me a good dinner."

"More than three?"

"More money. But I ate at the Big M."

"You was out to the Big M?"

"That's where I met them."

"The three?"

"In the parking lot."

". . ."

"Hey, little baby," Ratboy said in his most tenderest special voice, and the arm that was around my shoulders squeezed me tight. "Is that tears I see? You crying on me?"

I tried to keep my voice steady but I didn't have much luck. "You gonna leave me. You gonna keep doing this till you got enough money to take off and then you gonna fly the coop."

"Hey," Ratboy said again, his voice sweet and tender as stewed meat, his arm tight as a vise around my shoulders. "Hey hey hey. Hey hey hey hey *hey*-yay," which the way he said it sounded like a lady cat getting fucked in the middle of the night and despite myself I giggled a little.

"Who you think you're talking to anyway? Huh? This is Ratboy here, this ain't no Merle Potter."

"Duh," I said, but then I looked up at his eye. "Merle did that?"

"You should see Merle."

Merle Potter's left *leg* was about the same size as Ratboy, and everyone knew how his parents had paid for him to take tae-kwon-do classes down to Bigger Hill to improve his self-esteem on accounta his being plump and cross-eyed. Ratboy woulda been lucky to land a punch.

I said, "Aw, you tired of cleaning up after me."

Ratboy did the thing with the hey-hey-*hey*-yays again, and this time as he did it he shook me with his arm till my head wobbled back and forth like a Weeble.

"What I am is tired of this *piss* hole of a town."

"See. I told you."

"Which is why I'm gonna make us enough money to get us outta here."

"Us?"

"I gave *you* the money, didn't I?"

I looked down at the cash in my hands. "You giving this to me?"

"For safekeeping. You know how . . . impulsive I can be."

He smiled when he said *impulsive*—and he took his hand off my shoulder too, and he undid his belt buckle.

"Yeah, I know. You pretty impulsive."

He was pushing his pants down then, and I kinda swallowed. We'd made out and stuff up there, but we'd never like, you know, *done it*, right under the eyes of God.

"Reckless," he said.

"Yeah, you that too. You reckless."

He was pulling his dick out.

"Wild."

"Wild."

And then he was standing up and walking over toward the edge of the grain elevator and I was saying Ratboy? but he just kinda shot me a look that I didn't understand and kept on walking toward the edge of the grain elevator, or shuffling I guess you'd say, his pants down around his ankles and his butt hanging out down below his shirt and even in the dark I could tell that there was like some dark grubby smears on his mighty white butt cheeks that looked for all the world like someone'd been *digging* at him, but I didn't ask him about that cause for like one awful minute I thought he was gonna jump.

"Ratboy!"

He reached the edge of the platform and then he stopped, which I have to tell you made me breathe a sigh of relief, and then I started laughing because I realized he was peeing, he was actually taking a leak on Galatea—and I mean, yeah, he was peeing off the west side-a the elevator. There was maybe just the littlest bit of a breeze and it blew Ratboy's pee off to one side-a him and broke it up into little tiny drops that sparkled just a bit in the moonlight and it was just like, you know? what? the littlest bit *eerie* I guess you'd have to say, watching him pee, because without his pee hitting anything like water or dirt or a tree it didn't make no sound, no sound at all, which I guess I'd always sorta thought, I mean well not *thought* but just took it for granted sort of, the sound a guy makes when he takes a leak. Without that sound, and with his pee sparkling in little drops in the moonlight, he coulda been pouring just about anything down on the town, I mean like a magic potion or fairy dust or what do they call them? pennies from heaven? and a part of me believed, or wanted to believe, that Ratboy really was taking the first step toward taking us away from there, he was making Galatea disappear, he was making it *not exist anymore*, which for some reason I knew had to happen if we was ever really gonna leave.

When he finished he stood there for a minute without pulling his pants up, and then he cupped his hands around his mouth and he shouted, "Fuck you, town!"

"Fuck you!" I yelled, but from where I was, cause standing near the edge of the elevator always made me dizzy.

Ratboy turned back to me.

He looked down at his dick.

"Well," he said, and he shook the last few drops of pee from it. "Since it's already out . . ."

After that Ratboy went to the Big M three-four times a week. Hustling turned out to be kind of like drugs: the first time is the best and after that you spend most of your time just trying to make do. I don't think he ever turned another hundred-dollar day, except, well, except this one other time, but sometimes he made fifty, sixty bucks and he refused to leave the Big M until he had at least twenty-five, and, you know, it added up, and in a couple-a months I had a thousand dollars in a envelope which I kept duct-taped to the bottom of a dresser drawer, but Ratboy said it just wasn't enough.

" 'T'san expensive world out there" is what he said.

Well, it was getting toward wintertime by then, and Ratboy was sick a lotta the time what with always standing around outside in the cold, I guess, and plus too there was the fact that his Daddy'd gone and kicked him out and he refused to spend any money on a motel room, he give it all to me and slept in his car, in the daytime, and he just like ate whatever it was he could scrounge up, a bag of chips or a can of corn maybe, cream corn I remember, Ratboy said he ate it right outta the can. It got to where he was down to the Big M practically every night, coughing or sniffling or whatever, but he said it was okay cause mosta those guys never noticed anything that was going on above the level of his belt. He said this to me when I saw him that maybe one time a week when he snuck over to my house to give me money. We hardly ever met up toppa the grain elevator no more, Ratboy said it was because it was just too cold up there but I sorta figured out it was because he was too dog tired to climb up the ladder, and I couldn't even remember the last time we'd done it ourselves. By then his eyes were puffy and always had dark circles under them what from always being out all night, and, you know, he wasn't really getting into fights around Galatia no more cause he was never around but he was still showing up with bruises on him, they seemed to like to hit him in the face especially, or on his butt.

And so anyway Ratboy said it's an expensive world out there, and I said, "But what's it costing *you*?"

"Aw, don't you worry about me. I can handle it just fine."

And I was fourteen then, and he was eighteen, and then too Ratboy'd gone to some pretty big trouble to make sure I was the town faggot and I was getting beat up and other stuff on a pretty regular basis and nobody wasn't giving *me* no money, that's for damn sure, and I said, "And well then but what about *me*?"

At first Ratboy looked like he was gonna get pretty p.o.'d, but then he took a couple-a deep breaths and it passed, and he said, "What a*bout* you?"

And I said, "You never got time for me no more. I'm lucky if I see you once a week."

And Ratboy he just shrugged his shoulders and he turned a little bit away from me, I'd managed to get him up the grain elevator, which it seemed to take him hours to make it up that ladder, and his profile was just like a dark outline where there wasn't no stars, and when he opened his mouth to speak it was like he was spitting out the stars I could see behind him, or maybe eating them up.

And after a really long time Ratboy said, "There's some sick fucks out there," he said, and after a even longer time he said, "I shouldn't be touching you right now. Not with what I got all over me."

And this time I didn't say what about what was all over me cause there was something in Ratboy's face that let me know it just wasn't the same thing, cause . . . cause why? Cause the bottom line was that I was doing something which the truth was I liked to do even if I wasn't doing it with people I liked doing it with, and Ratboy, he didn't even like what he was doing but he was still doing it—doing it *for me*—and I guess I maybe wonder if that's what the difference between a faggot and a faggot lover is, which, and I just have to say this shouldn't come as no big surprise, which I had an idea that Colin Nieman would know the answer to.

5.23

Colin

ON THE FIRST DAY OF SUMMER, ROSEMARY KREBS called.

"Mr. Nieman," she said on the phone, "I wondered if you were free to meet with me?" She asked me to her office in town; I told her she would have to come to the house. When she resisted, I insisted, but she suddenly relented and said, "That would be good. I haven't seen the inside of the limestone house in many years."

I had not actually seen her since January, in Cora's, and when I opened the door I was struck anew by her size. She was no bigger than a ten-year-old girl; her glazed hairdo was her largest feature.

She handed me a bag without speaking, and I didn't have to open it to know what it contained.

Inside the house she made no attempt to hide her wandering eyes. "Perhaps you'd like a tour," I said, and she nodded her head. Without waiting, she led me from room to room, and at some point I noticed that she looked not at what I had done to the house, but at the house itself, the detail of a molding, the thickness of a wall. At one end of the second floor hallway, she stood in the window and surveyed the property through one of the carefully positioned gaps in the hedge.

"Donald Deacon called that cedar break Stonehedge," she said after a long pause.

"He did?" I said. "I didn't know."

"No," she said. "You wouldn't. Perhaps," she added, "perhaps we might go for a stroll. I am eager to see how Kendan Regier is running the place for you."

There was just the slightest pause between the word *place* and the words *for you*.

"He seems to be doing a fine job," I said.

"Well then. A constitutional is always nice, yes?"

No was obviously not the answer she was looking for, so I smiled and said, "After you."

Outside, she said, "The Deacon spread was always different from the other farms around here, more of a, a ranch really, than a farm.

For a moment, I could have sworn she was going to say *plantation*.

"Most farmers have scattered holdings, a few fields around the house, a few here and there across the county. In some ways it makes for a nice system. It keeps one from becoming too isolated, which can be a danger of farm life."

"But you," I said. "Your"—I paused—"holdings"—I paused again—"aren't exactly scattered."

She stopped walking and turned her head up to look me in the eye. Her gaze was steady, level I want to say, leveling, and I mean that literally: it was as if I had become as small as she was. She nodded then, turned without speaking, and started walking again.

I followed her crunching footsteps off the stones of the yard. Her shoes were low-heeled things, but her gait was almost perfectly smooth, as if she were walking on nothing more ungainly than a deep pile carpet. Once off the stones, she did, however, point to them and ask, "Are you going to leave this?"

"For a while anyway. It's quite beautiful. In its own way."

Her voice slipped into a clipped, almost acerbic tone. "A Giacometti statue is quite beautiful," she said, surprising me. "In its own way. But I wouldn't want one hanging in my parlor." She smiled slightly, and her voice resumed its normal light drawl. "I should expect it makes the heat even worse," she said, a transplanted Southerner once again, and she waved one of her hands at the shimmering lines of the heat mirage that danced over the expanse of black stones.

"I should think that's what Bea had in mind."

"To accentuate the heat?"

"To accentuate the mirage."

Rosemary Krebs offered me half a smile and a something that might have been called a snort if it had come from a nose less refined than her own, and then she turned and resumed walking. Her stride was firm and purposeful and I followed along behind her, admiring her careful steps, the way her arms remained primly at her sides rather than, as mine were doing, moving from side to side to help me maintain balance on the uneven ground. At the top of a hill was a barbed wire fence, and she turned and walked, knowledgeably, I thought, to a gate a hundred yards away. On the other side of the fence, ankle-high green wheat grew from slightly moist crumbly soil. About a mile away a huge sprinkling apparatus elevated on daddy long legs–type stilts sprayed water over a field. Rosemary Krebs walked carefully between two rows of wheat for a minute or two, until she reached the top of a small rise. In the valley, nothing but sky had been visible; here, the tops of the trees in Galatia's park could be seen, and the steeple of Abraham Greeving's church, and the bluffs beyond. In the opposite direction, the remains of Kenosha were made manifest by a dark cloud clinging to the ground. Rosemary Krebs turned herself around in a full circle where we stood, taking all this in, and something in the sight of her stopped me. I stood a dozen paces behind and below her and looked up at her tiny form. It seemed to tower above the landscape, and the only comparison I could think of was borrowed, from Stevens, from his poem about that jar in Tennessee, and the line that came to mind was of the jar taking dominion everywhere.

Rosemary Krebs cleared her throat, summoning me from my thoughts and to her side. "I doubt you have ever stood here before, have you, Mr. Nieman."

I looked around for a moment, as if I might be able to distinguish this spot from any other on the featureless prairie, and then I shrugged. "I doubt it."

"This spot is the highest point between the Bare Bluff and Kenosha. When Kenosha was still . . . extant, this was the only place where you could stand and see both towns. My daddy brought me to the seashore once, when I was just a little girl, and years later, when I first stood here, I thought that the line of Kenosha's grain elevator looked like the tip of a cresting wave on the horizon."

I looked at the cloud again. Nothing like a wave was visible. A storm maybe, although it seemed to me that that was just projection on my part. I looked down at Rosemary Krebs, who looked up at me expectantly. But I said nothing, and after a moment she turned from me, and her voice, when it came, was dramatically quietened.

"I had always planned on giving this to Lucy Robinson."

"How could you give her something that wasn't yours?"

"For a wedding present. Just the money, of course, nothing against the terms of Bea's will. I intended to give her the money and she would buy it herself, and I had intended also to leave her my own land. Galatea would have been Lucy's, Mr. Nieman. All of it. My dream would have been realized in her. But it seems now that that will never happen."

In the distance the sprinkling apparatus seemed to shut itself off, and I remember wondering if it had been shut off for my benefit. This may seem like the height of paranoia, or it may seem like a logical reaction after the events of the past eight months. More than a few random acts had been committed for my benefit. And I remember also hoping that the sprinkler would turn back on, but it did not turn back on.

"Mrs. Krebs," I said, and then I stopped. I cleared my throat noisily. "I just want you to know that I am very sorry about what's happened."

"I believe that you are, Mr. Nieman. Unlike Eustace Brown, I don't feel the need to project false guilt on someone just because that person and I happen to have different lifestyles. There are things for God to judge, and things for man to judge, and I find it prudent to leave celestial matters to their proper sphere."

"I suppose I should thank you for that."

"Don't thank me, Mr. Nieman. I am not your friend, and do not want to be. But neither do I consider you an enemy. An adversary perhaps," she said, and then she turned around. She looked at me, her blue eyes made gray by the harsh sunlight. "I cannot buy this land, Mr. Nieman, but I can lease it, for a year, a century, forever. It depends on you, and you alone. You could leave. You could take Justin and leave."

"I could leave now."

"But you won't, Mr. Nieman. You haven't, and I must confess I do wonder why is that? I thought at first it was your missing manuscript, but that would no longer seem to be a consideration."

I shrugged.

"Why *do* you stay, Mr. Nieman? What are you waiting for?"

I said, as simply as I could, "I am waiting for Lucy Robinson." I said, "I can't leave until she's found."

A look of horror crossed Rosemary Krebs' face for the tiniest moment—not terror, not fear, but some kind of deep revulsion, and it occurred to me for the first time that some people did not want Lucy Robinson found. And then, when she spoke next, I realized that she, too, had read my book before she returned it to me.

"Ah," she said, and there wasn't a trace of sympathy in her voice. "You are waiting to find yourself."

5.24

Webbie

ROSEMARY KREBS MOVED TO KENOSHA THE DAY AFTER her marriage to Phyneas Krebs, taking with her all of the Hoovier and King family heirlooms, but leaving behind, permanently, it seemed, the Hooviers and the Kings: no mention is ever made of her father, mother, and aunt again, not even the dates of their deaths; for all I know, they could be alive still.

The Krebs house was, even when Rosemary Krebs first took up residency there, closer to Galatia than to Kenosha—"an interesting geographic peculiarity which Phyneas had somehow failed to mention"—but Rosemary Krebs, like the rest of the Krebs family, conducted her business and social affairs in Kenosha. But Kenosha was an old small poor plains town, qualities which conspired to make it, in Rosemary Krebs' phrase, "in some ways more Southern than the South itself." All of her efforts to join what passed for society there were completely rebuffed, primarily because she possessed, in her own words, "only two attributes: breeding, and the Krebs family money, and both of these things were despised in a town that had neither." To make matters worse, Phyneas' pet name for her had somehow managed to escape the walls of their bedroom, and, though no one ever called her by it to her face, she heard it often enough whispered in rooms or shouted in streets behind her back. The Krebses had honeymooned in Maryland; the nickname was Crabcake. "Or Crablet. Sometimes he calls me his little crablet, and then indeed I wished I possessed a shell, so that I could crawl inside it—and away from him, and his misbegotten town."

But she persisted. Her efforts were aided by the early death of her father-in-law, giving her, through Phyneas, control of the ranch, and it was she who, at twenty-one, had the foresight to drill their first oil wells, and it was she who persuaded Phyneas to use the proceeds thereof to open Kenosha's first and only bank, and, a few years later, a second branch in Galatia. It was she who began remortgaging the farms which bordered the Krebs ranch, and, a few years later, repossessing them and adding them to the Krebs spread. She toyed with the idea of giving the ranch a name, but, in a rare attempt at humor, wrote, "What would I call it? The Seven Cottonwoods? The Seven Withered Elms?" She considered the idea of calling it Seven Fields for some time, but ultimately rejected the idea as too "abstract." She wasn't yet twenty-five when she wrote: "I want a single field, a huge field as wide as these barren plains, stretching from one ugly end of this horizon to the other. I want to be able to turn myself around in a circle and see nothing that isn't mine."

Time passed; months, sometimes years lapsed between diary entries. "My ledgers are my diary now": the single line entry for 1969. It seemed that, however insignificant Kenosha's resources, and however much Rosemary Krebs managed to increase her own, this tiny town and its denizens still possessed the power of condemnation or approval over Rosemary Krebs, who seemed to want not merely their approval, or their acceptance, but to be above the level of such base judgments entirely. The single most telling line she wrote about Kenosha was "It is their autonomy I despise: they move about like ants who have no discipline, no queen." And so she hatched a plan, a plan that seems to come from a fairy tale rather than a history, a plan by which Kenosha would be not just effaced but erased, and a new town drawn in its place, and as I read those lines I suddenly remembered the platter I used to serve Rosemary Krebs' tea each afternoon. The platter contained the single reference to the *Iliad* that I had come across in the Krebs house, and on its enameled surface Troy's walls were toppled, bodies strewn about, smoke thick in the air, and the effect of the scene was made somehow more gruesome by the fact that it was rendered in the swirling blue lines of a *faux* Wedgwood pastoral. In the scene, Achilles stands atop the Trojan Horse with one sandaled foot on the fallen body of Paris; one hand holds his sword, the other Helen. Beneath them, the conquered city is in flames, and even as I thought of that I heard a door close downstairs, and I was only able to glance at the first line of the next entry before returning the diary to its hiding place: *Kenosha*, the line read, *has got to go.*

5.25

Justin

I MADE SOME DINNER,'' WADE SAID ONE EVENING. ''A big pot of spring stew, all the early vegetables. Well," he said then, "it's Cora's recipe, but I made it. Okay," he admitted, as if I had challenged him, "she made it up for me and I just brought it home. I would've made it, but she said the recipe was a secret." He smiled a little, almost goofily. "Anyway, I hope you'll join me."

He fed me. If I still spoke, what I would have said was that the stew looked a bit like one of Wade's paintings, and tasted just as good.

Afterward he gave me his bellystone. "Please," he said, "I know how much you loved it." I thought it odd that he used the past tense, as if, without words, I was now without feeling.

Wade, artful seducer. You kissed me with lips that tasted of coriander and paint dust. I thought, Tomorrow you will draw my face. Tomorrow you will draw my dick. Tomorrow you will draw a complete portrait of my body.

You ran your fingertips over my eyelids, shutting them. You said, "Sshh."

Wade, you devil you. Who would've guessed that you moaned like a teenaged boy. You pawed at me, managed to pull a few strands of my hair out as you pulled my shirt off. "Oh, you're so beautiful," you said, as if you'd never seen me naked before. You sucked as if for milk at my nipples, and I thought for some reason of Webbie, of my first meal here, and her hand on her breast.

There were no mishaps that night. You were sweet, and clumsiness kept you from being too tender. I wasn't surprised that you didn't use a condom, but I was surprised that I let you. I was surprised at your penis, at its durability, though after several hours it just seemed like another one of your limbs, flesh wrapped over bone, hardness its natural, its only state. I watched you sometimes, as you went about your business. A man like you, in ecstasy, must have served as an early model for paintings of Jesus. There were even faint smears of red paint over your heart where you had idly scratched yourself earlier in the day. When your eyes opened they didn't see me, but that didn't surprise me: I wasn't in this house, I was in your parents' house. I wasn't in this bedroom: I was in your bedroom, the bedroom you had slept in as you grew up. But where were you, Wade, where did you lose yourself? Were you trying to take me there? Part of me wants you to take me there, but I know I can't go. Wade, you and me and Colin and Divine—were they fucking at the very moment we were?—and Webbie, and Rosemary Krebs, and Abraham Greeving, and Myra Robinson, we're all alike, with just the tiniest differences. But you, Wade, you stand just outside our circle, even farther than me. For you have gone where we all long to go. You have gone mad.

5.26

Divine

HE COME THROUGH MY WINDOW ONE NIGHT AND HE just sat in my room for one whole hour and cried. He didn't say nothing, didn't hardly make a sound, but while he cried he pulled the biggest wad of money outta his pocket he ever made, it was all singles I saw after a moment, and one by one he unwadded them and laid them in as neat as possible a stack on the bed between us and I don't know why but I knew to count them out loud, a whisper so's I wouldn't wake up my folks but out loud, and Ratboy cried and I counted one-two-three and so on and along about twenty-five or thirty my eyes'd got used to the dark and then I noticed these like little marks on his arm where it stuck outta his shirt, they was maybe red but I couldn't really tell cause the light was off, and along about fifty or so I realized the little marks was cigarette burns and right when I hit one hundred I had a picture in my mind of more or less exactly what musta happened, one-two-three-four-five-etc., except Ratboy he couldn'ta said "et cetera," he'da had to count all the way up to a hundred, 1, 2, 3, 4, 5, etc.

After that night Ratboy just started leaving the money for me. It was all I could do to catch a glimpse of him coming or going. Sometimes he'd leave a note with the money, usually the notes just said *You know I love you* but one time I remember Ratboy wrote down a p.s. which was *You know what surprises me is most people don't ever seem surprised.*

In the meantime, in the middle-a all this, I was still in school. I was fourteen by then and I was a freshman and I was fast, and I mean *fast*, which seemed like a genetic accident more than anything else. My parents'd told me I was gonna have to go out for a sport and come spring I'd already skipped basketball cause I'm short and football cause I'm small and so track was all that was left for me cause I hope you don't think I was gonna play *tennis*. And then like there I was, first day of practice, and what Coach Carting did was he lined us all up freshmen, sophomores, juniors, and seniors, and he said, I remember exactly, he said *The one lesson in life that I can teach you is that somebody always wins and somebody always loses*, and then he fired a gun which I swear was loaded up into the air and the next thing I remember was that the first person to cross the finish line was me.

The last person was Merle Potter, which is a fact that only means something to me right now. I mean, why *didn't* I just run away from him?

And I guess that raises the question of why didn't I run away from them all? Not just back then, but later on too. Why didn't I run away from that man out to Noah's ark, and from Wade, and from Colin? And why, when I did I run from them, why did I just run here, to the bottom of the swimming hole? I mean, I was scareda them, sure, but I guess when it comes right down to it, I was more scareda what I might run into than what I shoulda been running away from. And. So. And. But. And. Anyway.

The long and short of it was that I'd won my first race and Coach Carting put me on the team and then on impulse when I won my first invitational I went out and bought a pair of spikes.

I bought them with some-a the money I was holding for Ratboy.

The money we was gonna use to get away.

In some ways I didn't believe in the whole idea of it anymore. I mean, there was a *lot* of money under my drawer—under three different drawers actually, cause it wouldn't fit under just one or even two, and it seemed like if we couldn't get along on what was there then what in the world *would* it take for us to get along? And in some ways I didn't even believe in him anymore, in Ratboy I mean, he was kinda like the tooth fairy except I didn't have to give him nothing and he still paid off, and a whole lot better. I guess maybe I did believe in him, cause I sure as shit believed in his money. I guess maybe what I'm trying to say is I took him for granted.

"The issue," Ratboy said, "is respect."

Which is what he said when I showed him the spikes and after it'd come out how I paid for them.

I didn't say nothing to him cause I knew even before he said it that I'd done wrong. I'd done *him* wrong.

"I guess you can run mighty far in those shoes."

He picked one-a them up then. The burns on his wrist was kind of faded by then, it just looked like he'd maybe had chicken pox or something, like a month or so ago.

He dropped the shoe on the floor.

"Mighty far."

He dropped what money was in his pocket next to the shoe.

And then he climbed out the window.

I never seen him since.

Something happened then—in the swimming hole, I mean, not in my bedroom. Nothing ever happened in my bedroom after that. Nothing at all. I'd been falling forever it seemed, for months and years and centuries, that when my feet finally touched the bottom of the swimming hole it was like a shock went all the way through me, and alla the sudden I was planted ankle deep in this what felt like ice cold diarrhea and what I remembered was my socks, I was wearing white socks which really didn't go with what I had on, and I thought, They never gonna come clean now.

But one more thing. My theory. Before I give up the ghost. About what happened. To Ratboy.

Okay. Deep breath.

Ha, ha.

Okay.

I don't think he run off, see. I don't think he left me. I think someone took him.

We'd been through too much—aw, what am I saying, *he'd* been through too much to just throw in the towel like that. I mean, Ratboy just wasn't a quitter. And I mean he didn't even take the *money*. But then I don't know, cause the money always seemed more about me than about him.

One time, this was pretty early in his Big M days, I asked him if he liked it even a little bit. And it's not just that he said he didn't like it—it's that he wouldn't even say it. He wouldn't even say what he was doing let alone that he didn't like it. He just said, Like what? and I said, You know, and I put my hand on his ass, and he right away rolled off his stomach and onto his back and he stared up at the stars, which when you was laying down on top of the grain elevator the stars was absolutely the only thing you could see, and after a while he said How much we got? and I said Two hundred and seventy-six dollars, or whatever it was then, and then Ratboy rolled toward me, but just until he was on his side, he kept his ass turned away from me, and he said, Soon, he said, We almost there, and I remember I said, We almost where, and he said, We almost gone.

Which just leaves one thing I guess.

The money, I mean. There's always the money.

The money I left taped to the bottom of those three dresser drawers. I never touched another cent of it, I never even took it out to count it and see how much was there. I mean, I'm only human, I make mistakes just like anybody else but I try never to make the same mistake twice, and if Ratboy did come back then I wanted him to see that every last goddamn dollar bill that he'd slaved for was still there waiting for him.

Except that it's not.

It's with my parents.

Who took it when they packed up and moved out in the middle of the day cause they couldn't really kick me out cause there was no place in Galatia that was far enough away that it wouldn't be like I was still living in their house. I don't know if they found the money when they moved or not, though I figure they didn't cause they'da left some sign if they had, my momma and daddy was both greedy in they own ways and even if it was just that they'd stopped into Cora's and bought a dessert in the middle of the day I'da found out if they'd had any extra money.

My feet was in that goddamn ice-cold muck.

The only thing about losing the money that bothered me was that the money was all I had left to remind me of Ratboy, and even though it wasn't even where I looked at it, still, it was where I thought of it all the time, and so thought of Ratboy, and after that I didn't think of him as often, or in the same way.

Black pants, white socks, black shoes, and that ice-cold muck.

For a few months after my parents left, the few months before I made Wade's acquaintance, I still slept in our house. I slept in my bedroom. In the carpet on the floor the marks of where my bed and my dresser and my chair'd been was still there, and I used to sleep in between the four dots that marked the place where my bed'd been, and I used to go over to the four dots that marked the dresser's spot and pretend to open it in the morning and choose my clothes, even though the only clothes I had was the clothes on my back. Not that any of this has any bearing on anything else. I'm just saying, is all.

I'm just saying that falling had been its own reward and once I reached bottom there seemed like nothing else to do but keep going, so I pushed, which of course sent me going back up, and the one thing that I did realize as I reached my hands out for the starry surface of the swimming hole was that in this case, in my case, going up was no different than going down. I realized that I could freeze to death in a desert just as well as in the arctic, I could fall a thousand miles without ever taking my feet off the ground, and it seemed to me that if I was going to drown I might as well drown on dry land, drown on air.

5.27

Colin

ROSEMARY KREBS HAD ALMOST CONVINCED ME THAT she was telling the truth about her love for the land, but unfortunately for her she kept on talking; eventually her words acquired the false tone of a political speech and then I began to tune her out. We walked aimlessly; I tried to steer us in the direction of the limestone house, but the truth was I had no idea where it was. I tried to use the sun for direction but it was almost directly overhead, and, too, I realized that even if I could have used it to establish the points of the compass for me, I still would have had no idea which way to walk. At one point, however, Rosemary Krebs said something about "natural and archaeological resources," and then in a flash of inspiration so unexpected that it struck me like a blow, I realized where Lucy was being held.

I could barely keep my voice level when I spoke.

"Um, Rosemary?"

"*Par*don me, Mr. Nieman."

"Excuse me—Mrs. Krebs. But isn't the cave around here somewhere?"

"The cave?"

"Of the Bellystones?"

She paused then, an equivocal expression on her face.

"Mrs. Krebs, *please*. It's a matter of some urgency."

She didn't have to look around to get her bearings. She pointed, down the hill we stood on and to the west. "I do believe it's over there. Just beyond the next rise."

I turned and started walking immediately, and after a moment I heard her steps behind me. "Mr. Nieman," she called, "may I inquire as to your sudden interest in the cave. I mean, I take it from your inquiry that you've yet to make a visit there."

"I'm sure you'll understand me when I say that the events of the past eight months have pushed sightseeing to the back of my mind."

". . ."

"Did you happen to see the pictures, Mrs. Krebs?"

". . ."

"Of Lucy. The ones T. V. Daniels found in February."

". . ."

"In the pictures Lucy appears to be lying on bare soil. Lawman Brown thought perhaps she was in an unfinished basement somewhere in Galatia."

"Well, many of the older homes in town *do* have fruit cellars and—"

"—and one of the things you promised everyone who moved to Galatea from Kenosha was a full finished basement, the better to hold the groundwater which seeped into it each spring."

". . ."

"At any rate, Lucy was not found in either a fruit cellar or a basement."

". . ."

"Now, it's my understanding that the Cave of the Bellystones is in fact a manmade space. An excavation, a dig, a, a—"

"It's a hole in the ground, Mr. Nieman, approximately twenty-one feet by twelve feet by five."

"Exactly!"

"Not that I've been down there myself."

"Of course you haven't."

". . ."

"Mrs. Krebs, has *anybody* thought to check the cave since Lucy was taken?"

"By anybody I assume you mean Sheriff Brown or, perhaps, the Mayor."

"What I mean is, it's right *here*. Less than two miles from town, less than a mile from the site of the abduction. It's right—"

"—here, Mr. Nieman. It's right here."

We had crested the hill then—the rise, as Rosemary Krebs more accurately named it—and there, below us, in a gravelly valley, was the entrance to the cave. The sudden sight of a building after miles and hours of nothing but grass and sky, even one as rudimentary as that tiny plank-sided cone, was somehow silencing, and Rosemary Krebs and I stood together for a moment, just staring. Then Rosemary Krebs cleared her throat.

"Perhaps once a century," she said, "the spring rains are so heavy that the south fork of the Solomon River jumps its banks and the flood waters travel a route that cuts across the western edge of Galatea and passes directly through this little valley here. The last time it happened was more than a hundred and twenty-five years ago, and when the waters retreated the cave's entrance was discovered. It had been underground until that time, no one knows for sure how long, probably buried by the same process which later uncovered it. Phyneas"—she paused, and cleared her throat again—"the Mayor had the housing erected some years ago, both to ensure the integrity of the original structure and to safeguard against children falling down the shaftway."

There was something forced about this speech as well, although it took me a moment to realize that she was merely telling it because she was stalling. She didn't want to go down there.

"Do you have a key," I said then.

". . ."

"On you, I mean."

Rosemary Krebs sighed. "Yes."

"What a fortuitous occurrence. May I borrow it?"

Rosemary Krebs reached into a pocket of her suit and pulled out a single key. "Mr. Nieman," she said as I advanced on the shack, "would it be logical to suggest that if the cave is still locked then it is doubtful that anyone is inside it?"

"Look at this."

". . ."

"Here," I said, "and here, and here."

"Are they—"

"Footprints. Very large footprints."

"I can see that, Mr. Nieman. What I meant was, are they yours?"

". . ."

"Although," she went on, "I would assume they are not, as they appear to be quite old, and you have said that this is your first time here."

"Mrs. Krebs," I said then, "at the bottom of most padlocks there is a serial number. If you write away to the maker of the lock"—I fingered the large silver thing that held the door to the cave closed—"in this case, Master, they will send you a new key."

"That seems to me a labor-intensive plan to gain access to a shack in the middle of a field. He could have just clipped it."

"He *clipped* her fingers, Mrs. Krebs, because he wanted that act to be discovered. I expect he desired some element of secrecy in his lair. Although for all we know he could have clipped this lock and replaced it with one of his own."

I fit the key to its slot then, and it slipped into the lock smoothly; a quarter turn, and the bolt clicked free of the body of the lock.

Rosemary Krebs cleared her throat. "But he didn't."

"But he didn't," I said, and then I said, "Mrs. Krebs, is this lock opened regularly?"

"To the best of my knowledge, it's not been opened in eight years, unless Eustace—"

"Because it opened very smoothly for something that's been exposed to the elements for so many years."

". . ."

"I'm just saying."

After a moment I took the lock from the clasp. Humidity had caused the door to swell and stick in its frame, and I had to jerk on it in order to open it, and, as soon as it had, a fetid stench rushed from the cave.

"Jesus Christ!" I said.

"Oh dear Lord," Rosemary Krebs said at the same time. She put a hand to her nose—but, I noted, she didn't step away from the cave.

As soon as the smell hit my nostrils, I found myself strangely calm.

Whatever was producing that smell was dead, and, for whatever reason, I was pretty sure that Lucy Robinson was not yet dead.

"Pardon me," I said, pulling my T-shirt off. I bunched it up and pressed it to my nose.

"Mr. Nieman—"

I removed the shirt from my nose. "I'm going to have a look around."

"Mr. Nieman, don't be foolhardy. We should contact Sheriff Brown."

"With all due respect, Mrs. Krebs, *that* would be foolhardy."

Rosemary Krebs almost smiled.

"Is this your flashlight?"

". . ."

"It was hanging here. Did you perhaps leave it here when you erected the shed?"

Rosemary Krebs shook her head.

I clicked the flashlight on and a bright beam of light stabbed into the shed.

I noticed that the flashlight had a light coating of dust on it, and noticed also that the dust turned muddy on contact with my sweaty hand.

"For the record," I said, "I am leaving fingerprints on this flashlight now, and not at some point in the past."

"Of course you are."

I looked back at Rosemary Krebs. One of her tiny hands covered her nose and mouth, but her eyes were bright and unreadable.

"If I start to scream," I said, "run."

"And if you don't?"

"Then run faster."

I admit that there was something satisfying in saying these words, in evoking the pulpy narrative of a horror movie. Real crisis! Real danger! Here we go!

We stopped talking then, which was a good thing, because each bite of a word brought a mouthful of that stink into my body, and I was ready to vomit. I managed to tie my shirt around my head in an inadequate sort of cozy, and then, the flashlight pulsing its way ahead of me, I headed into the cave.

A little spiral pathway wended into what seemed like nothing more than a pile of smooth round stones; in just seconds I had twisted out of the sunlight and into darkness, and I noticed that many of the stones seemed slightly crystalline in nature, and they reflected my light in dizzying, almost hypnotic flecks of color. But any archaeological curiosity I had was cut short by the sudden end of the path. The flashlight showed me a gnarled and nobbled post sticking out of a smooth-edged hole in the ground. If anything, the stench was worse than ever. The flashlight had a looped strap at the end of it wide enough to fit around my hand, and I hung it from my wrist, grabbed the pole, and started down. At some point in the past—in another life, it seemed—Justin had told me that Webbie had told him that the shaft was only a dozen feet long, and so I just slid its length, figuring that if anyone *was* down there, that surprise would be my only advantage. But I really couldn't believe that anyone could have lived with that stench for any length of time, and remain sane.

My feet struck soft earth. I took a step back from the pole and even as my shoulders and head struck the roof of the cave my feet crunched against something metallic; in a moment the flashlight showed me an empty can, the kind that vegetables come in, its label just a charred remainder, and for a moment I was distracted by the can's shape, how its alternating bands of ribbing and smoothness looked exactly like a truck-stop rubber. It occurred to me, too, that the label had been burned off because the food in it had been cooked right in the can, and in a moment the flashlight's beam had found a half dozen other cans and the remains of a fire, all fairly close to the shaftway. Farther away, more cans, all empty, all with the labels burned off, and, as well, several shapeless brown masses I thought at first were rodent carcasses but then realized were the swollen shapes of books that had at some point been soaked in water, cheap drugstore paperbacks most of them, many of which had been shredded and fed to the fire. For a moment I was held by that: the arrangement of the few elements, cans, fire, waterlogged books, and, indeed, the cave itself struck me as somehow deliberate, deliberately symbolic, and I could easily imagine him reading by the light of a fire made with the pages of the books he was literally consuming, and eating the food he cooked in the flames.

He. Him. We spoke of him almost familiarly, as if we knew him.

The flashlight's beam passed over the niches in the wall Justin had also told me about. I thought at first that they had collapsed or been partially filled in, but I realized that a box had been placed in each of them, and even in the dim light I recognized them as boxes that Justin and I had used to move. The one nearest me had the word *Copper* written on its side; it had contained a bowl made of beaten copper that Justin had picked up when we went to Cairo, a bowl etched with fake hieroglyphics which, we had been told, contained a spell granting immortality to whoever mixed a certain potion in the bowl. One of the spell's ingredients, I remember, was a liter of human blood, and I remember Justin whispering to me his surprise that the ancient Egyptians had been familiar with the metric system.

"Mr. Nieman?" Rosemary Krebs' voice was faint but clear. "Are you okay?"

"I'm fine, Mrs. Krebs. Everything's fine."

In fact I didn't quite believe that. It occurred to me that even more pieces of Lucy Robinson could be in those boxes—that she could in fact be dead, that she could be what I was smelling. I couldn't bring myself to examine the boxes immediately, and so I cast the flashlight's beam over the rest of the cave—twenty-one by twelve by five, as Rosemary Krebs had told me—and it was in the farthest corner of the room that I saw it: a cloth-draped mound.

He hadn't gone to any trouble to disguise it beyond the blanket, and, whatever it was, it was too small to be Lucy Robinson. At least I hoped it was.

I picked my way to the mound. Maybe I had been conditioned by the movies, but I expected something—the hiss of snakes or rats, a concealed stake-bottomed pit in the earth, a trip wire loosing a fatal arrow—to make my descent into the enemy's trap more dangerous. But the only sound was my own breathing and my footsteps; my greatest obstacle was the sharp edges of the lids of opened cans of vegetables. At one point I tripped over something buried in the dirt: a pair of boots, my boots. I had no doubt that they would match the prints outside, and on the road where Lucy Robinson was first taken. I went on then, slowly, walking nearly doubled over; still, soon enough I was at the mound, and I used my thumb and forefinger to fling the blanket away. I'd like to say the stench grew suddenly stronger but it already infused every cubic inch of the space in the cave, and the only dramatic element in my action was a faint squelching noise that I suspected was the ripping of rotting flesh.

The thing under the blanket had been dead for a long, long time. Stringy gelatinous flesh hung off a skeleton whose white bones showed through in more than a few places. In a moment I made out the cloven hooves—a calf?—and then I saw the slightly snoutish shape remaining to the nose and I realized it was a pig. In another moment I noted the broken ribs on its right side, and then I shone the flashlight directly on the skull and I saw the hole on the right side of the skull.

Charlene.

I stared at her for a moment, but she had no secrets to tell me.

Howard Goertzen?

Lucy's suitor?

Charlene?

It occurred to me that it had been Howard Goertzen who found her dress, on the corner of Adams and First.

It occurred to me also that Howard Goertzen was a short man, but he was fat as well, and that his feet in my boots would leave deep footprints.

For some reason, it seemed necessary to cover her body again, and I manipulated the stiff sticky blanket gingerly. Something shiny flashed when I lifted it. I paused; I debated. Then I reached for it.

It was a piece of paper; I held it only by the edges. It was a card actually—not a business card, but a calling card. My calling card. My name stared up at me.

Colin Nieman.

After a moment I turned the card over.

I^{k}n w you w^{o}uld l^{oo}k h r f^{o}r answ rs.

The line was taken from *The Beast*, from Justin's book. The message had even been typed with my typewriter, the one I had discarded after throwing it at Justin.

Justin.

It occurred to me that just about anyone wearing my boots would leave deep footprints in mud.

For some reason I was possessed of the urge not just to destroy the card but to destroy it by *eating* it, and that thought, finally, brought up the gorge that had been building in my throat for the past ten minutes. I managed to turn to avoid Charlene, and I threw up all over the empty cans of food and waterlogged books, and then, slowly, carefully, I slipped the card in a pocket—*my* card, *my* pocket, with the message that I was sure had been written to me and not about me. I made my way back to the surface and to my house. Not my house, but *the* house, *a* house, a house that belonged neither to me nor to Rosemary Krebs, but to the unknown man—no one could convince me that piggy little Howard Goertzen possessed either the brains or the willpower to commit such an act—the nameless man who had claimed not just Lucy Robinson's but, I now realized, all our lives.

5.28

Webbie

GENE ZWEMMER WORKED AS HARD AS POSSIBLE AT BEing Kenosha's town drunk. He "reported for his first day of work today," Rosemary Krebs wrote in her diary on May 13, 1973, "smelling like he'd gone swimming in the pool hall rather than drinking in it." His reputation carried even to Galatia, and he could often be found at Sloppy Joe's when the liquor wasn't cheap enough in Kenosha. He was a short man with a mouth that hung continually half open, like a door slowly working its way loose of its hinges; he was bald as well, but sported nearly a foot of facial hair, a sort of woven vertical place mat that displayed the crumbs of his most recent meal. This beard was also stained to a nameless noncolor, neither brown nor yellow nor orange, from the perpetual cigarette that, lit or unlit, always dangled off his lower lip. No one was quite sure if he had a home or not; if he did, he never made it back there at night, and the morning sun found him more often than not curled up under someone's shade tree or porch swing or in the back of their pickup, the matted mass of his beard flipped up over his face to keep the light out of his eyes.

This was the person whom Rosemary Krebs hired to be her handyman.

She never described him in her diary as I have, but immediately after Kenosha burned down a few pictures of him ran in various papers around the state, and as Kenosha's surviving families settled in Galatea, they pooled their lore about the man who had, depending on how you looked at it, either killed their dreams or given birth to new ones for them, and they stored it someplace deep in their minds, crammed in there with stories about Buffalo Bill and Paul Bunyan and Mother Goose. But all Rosemary Krebs had written about Gene Zwemmer was that "he was less than a man. He was just an appetite, and what I saw in his eyes convinced me that I was justified in doing what I was doing." The date on that entry was May 28, 1974, the very day that Kenosha was consumed by fire, and even though I believe that reconstructions make for poor, for dishonest history, I still found myself unable to prevent my imagination from seizing hold of that morning and shining its bright light on all the corners that the extant records left in shadow. And this isn't a history, after all, it's not even a story: it's just an excuse.

Every day for two weeks the thermometer had pushed past ninety by noontime. Not a cloud in the sky, nothing more than a memory of a breeze. Still, spring had been early and wet that year, and harvest was nearly half over already. It was a fast crop but for the same reason it was a poor crop; yields were low, prices poor, and tempers in general were as hot as the weather. What a body could use was a nice calming drink, is what Gene Zwemmer was thinking to himself, something ice-cold but burning like fire all the way down. He was thinking of vodka—thinking of it, because the pool hall didn't open till three—but what he ended up with, quite unexpectedly, was whiskey.

He was driving to work. He drove slow. He drove, in fact, at no more than ten miles per hour, and even glasses-wearing grandmas who still regarded automobiles as something of a novelty sped past him in their dusty LTDs and Crown Victorias. But one thing Gene Zwemmer had never done is he'd never hurt a soul in his life. School was out and children were about and his weren't exactly the fastest reflexes in the world. He drove slow, all the way to Galatia, to Rosemary Krebs' overgrown doll house.

She was waiting for him on the back porch. That was something Gene Zwemmer didn't really care for: she wouldn't never let him use the front door, she always made him come round back. Not that he ever actually got to use the door: she didn't let him in her house at all, but even in the dead of winter came outside in one of her tiny, tidy gray skirt suits to give him his chores for the day.

But this morning—well, it was probably after noon by then—this afternoon she was standing on the back porch, and she gave him a little wave as he drove up, and she smiled at him as he made his way up to those rickety steps. He put his hand on the step railing but didn't mount them. Never was a big fan of steps, Gene Zwemmer. Preferred nice flat level ground. Never saw a pool hall with steps, did you?

Rosemary Krebs stood at the top of the steps, and the extra height allowed her to look down on Gene.

"Morning, Gene," she said.

"Morning, Mrs. Krebs."

"And how are you this morning, Gene?"

"I'm fine, Mrs. Krebs, thank you for asking." A pause, a squint. " 'N' you, Mrs. Krebs?"

"Couldn't be better, Gene, couldn't be better. Gene," she said, "would you like to step inside for a moment?"

"Step?"

"Inside, Gene. Step inside."

Well. Well, well.

Gene Zwemmer tightened his grip on the railing, and, carefully, he made his way up the four steps. Going up wasn't so bad anyway. Going down though. Well, he'd cross that bridge when he come to it.

The back door led through a little mud room into the kitchen. There was all the usual stuff in the kitchen—sink, stove, fridge—plus a whole lot more. Long-stemmed crystal glassware hung upside down off racks like you see in fancy bars—on TV; there were no fancy bars in Kenosha—and dish towels didn't dangle off drawer pulls but were, instead, draped neatly over dish towel–sized towel rods. A dozen cutting boards hung off one wall, and an enormous butcher block sat on the counter beneath them, so studded with knife handles that it looked like a magician's prop to Gene. The last thing Gene noticed, before he noticed the table, was the nineteen white teacups that hung on hooks off one wall; there was a twentieth hook, and Gene wondered if its teacup was dirty or busted. It was busted, Gene: it had been broken before Rosemary Krebs ever took up residence in Phyneas Krebs' house, and if Gene had pulled on the hook a little hole would have opened up in the wall, revealing the three fragments that, if glued together, would have formed the twentieth teacup.

Then he noticed the table, and on the table sat a large brown envelope, a box of cigars, a bottle of Jack Daniel's, and two glasses, facedown. Of all the items that caught his eye, it was the presence of a second glass that captivated his attention. Why, Mrs. Krebs? Who knew?

"Do you know what today is, Gene?"

"Tuesday?"

"Ho-ho, Gene. Yes, it's Tuesday. But do you know what else it is?"

He wiped his brow. "Hot?"

"Yes, it's certainly hot, Gene. Gene," she said, reaching out and turning one of the glasses face up. "It's our anniversary, Gene."

"Um, you and Phyn—you and Mr. Krebs, ma'am?"

"No, Gene, you and I. One year, Gene, we've been working together for one full year today."

In fact, it had been one year and two weeks, but Rosemary Krebs had had to wait for the harvest to come in.

Gene Zwemmer didn't say anything. He had never held a job for an entire year in his life, but he'd never tried to either. It didn't strike him as something particularly worthwhile, or worth noting, especially not with a bottle of Mr. Jack Daniel's himself. He noticed that the seal had not even been broken yet.

"Anniversaries are a big affair where I come from, Gene. In the South."

"Georgia, ma'am." Gene Zwemmer had heard more than once that Rosemary Krebs was from Georgia.

"That's right, Gene. Georgia." She reached for the bottle, but her hand stopped in midair before touching it. "Ah, would you? My . . . hands," she said, and waggled her fingers at him, as if that meant something.

He reached for the bottle slowly, waiting for something to slap him down, but nothing did, and the hardness of the glass neck in his hand convinced him that he wasn't dreaming either. Rosemary Krebs didn't say anything as he opened the bottle, and you could hear the paper seal tear as he twisted the cap off. He set the cap on the table, but he didn't pour.

"Gene," Rosemary Krebs said. She smiled, and then, after a long pause, she turned the second glass over. "I just thought we should mark the occasion?"

"Ma'am . . ."

"With a toast," Rosemary Krebs said. "To a successful year, and to all the successes ahead."

"Ma'am."

"Perhaps you would be so kind as to do the honors."

"Ma'am?"

She didn't say anything then. Just nudged the glasses.

"Ma'am!"

Gene Zwemmer grabbed for the bottle, then slowed himself down as he poured. Wasn't any of Rosemary Krebs' business knowing that him and Mr. Jack Daniel's wasn't regular drinking buddies.

He held up his glass. "To Lynchburg."

Rosemary Krebs' fingers were curled around her glass, but she didn't pick it up. "Pardon?"

"Lynchburg, ma'am." Gene Zwemmer pointed at the bottle. "Lynchburg, Virginia, home of the Jack Daniel's distillery. In the South, ma'am."

His hand trembled a little as he held his glass in the air, waiting for Rosemary Krebs to pick up hers.

"Oh, of course. Lynchburg."

"Ma'am." Gene Zwemmer made a one-handed toasting gesture with his glass. "To Lynchburg, ma'am. To the South."

Rosemary Krebs smiled again. She lifted her glass and touched it lightly to Gene's.

"To Lynchburg," she said. "To the South."

Gene Zwemmer nodded. "Bottoms up," he said, or thought, he

wasn't quite sure, and then the drink was gone. His eyes closed as the liquor hit his throat. Coarse as honey, sweet as sandpaper, he thought, and when he opened his eyes he saw that Rosemary Krebs' glass was also empty, and he saw too, with that crystal vision that only good alcohol will give you, the forming of seven tiny beads of sweat on her upper lip. Her eyes were wide, her nostrils flared, and he could hear her breath gushing in and out of them. A long moment after that, he heard her swallow.

"Well well well, ma'am," he said. "We-he-hell."

Rosemary Krebs smiled without showing her teeth. She didn't say anything.

Gene Zwemmer poured them each a second glass.

A third.

She held up her hand at the fourth, but motioned for him to go on without her, and as he poured and smelled and sipped and savored—what, he wondered, what wonders would their second anniversary hold, their third, fourth, fifth?—Rosemary Krebs pushed her hands through thick cotton air to the box of cigars. She flipped its lid open as though it were either very heavy or very delicate, and she regarded the brown cellophaned tubes with a mysterious smile on her face before she finally picked one up.

She held it end to end between two fingertips.

"It . . . looks . . . just . . . like . . . a . . . turd."

"Ma'am?"

"Like a turd, Gene, like a long neat chunk of shit, like—"

No, I thought to myself. *No, she didn't say that.*

Well. I too had read a copy of Colin's novel. No one in Galatia had escaped that plague.

"No celebration is ever complete without a cigar" is what she said, and, a little addled by drink, she placed it right in Gene Zwemmer's never-quite-closed mouth.

"Ma'am?"

The lighter was in the pocket of her jacket, a fancy thing made of smoky glass through which Gene Zwemmer stared dumbly at a bubble of air floating in lighter fluid. She struck it, and a tongue of flame burst from its top, and she held it to the end of his cigar. Her hands wobbled a little, making it hard for him to get a light off the flame, or to read the letters that had been etched into the glass of the lighter, but eventually the end of his cigar glowed red six inches in front of his face and he had made out the inscription.

J.F.K.

"Pardon me, ma'am. But that wouldn't be the late president's lighter, would it?"

"What?"

Rosemary Krebs would have been startled by a comment so far from the matter at hand. She would have looked at the lighter for a moment, and then, I suppose, then she would have seen Gene Zwemmer's error, and she would have laughed.

"J.E.K.," she explained. "Justice Eminent King." She paused for a moment, and then she pressed the lighter into his hand, the one that wasn't still curled around his empty glass. "It was my father's," she clarified. "But, seeing as neither Phyneas nor myself smoke . . ." She folded his fingers closed over the lighter, patted them, withdrew her hand.

With her own hands, with both of them, she poured him a fifth glass of whiskey.

"Ma'am," Gene Zwemmer said. He took the cigar out of his mouth long enough to drink, and then he put it back in. "Ma'am."

Rosemary Krebs tapped the envelope on the table.

"Just one little errand today, Gene. If you don't mind."

"Ma'am?"

"If you could just drop this off with Bruce Hennessy down to the grain elevator?"

When he left, the lighter was in his pocket and the cigar was in his mouth, the envelope full of reports and the box full of cigars and the upright bottle still half full of what Lynchburg and Mr. Jack Daniel's did best were pyramided on his folded arms.

Rosemary Krebs remained seated when he stood up. She pressed her palms flat against the table and her tiny little bottom lifted perhaps an inch above her seat, but then it sank back down again, and she remained in her chair. She didn't bid him good day.

The steps were something he hadn't reckoned on, and the glowing tip of the cigar, five inches now, five inches in front of his eyes and filling them with smoke, just made it worse. But it was his anniversary, and damned if he was going to fall down four measly steps on his anniversary. Still, the glowing tip of his cigar skewed his perspective, and he wavered at the top of the steps.

He closed his eyes finally, closed his eyes and trusted his feet, and took the steps as a young child would: one (and one), two (and two), three (and three), four (and four), and he was on the ground.

He was in his car.

He decided to drive back through Galatia to get to Kenosha. It wasn't every day he got to drive with a cigar in his mouth and a bottle of his personal lord and savior Mr. Jack Daniel's held safe and sound between his legs.

Nigger families did the things that nigger families did: rocked on porches with rinds of watermelon at their feet while pickaninnies ran without no shoes on through litter-strewn grassless yards, and Gene Zwemmer smiled at them all, the glowing tip of his cigar still a good four inches from his bent lips.

Nice park though.

He was through Galatia.

Kenosha came over the horizon so slowly that it seemed to be climbing up out of a hole. The grain elevator appeared first, a long row of uniform white columns. The land seemed to pull back from it like a lip exposing shiny white teeth.

He held the bottle between his legs.

He held the cigar in his mouth.

He held the steering wheel with both hands, because Gene Zwemmer had never hurt a soul in his life.

School's out, children about.

He smelled the dusty air that clung to the elevator. Dry and dusty and settling on his skin, that air, even under his clothes even, that dust could get anywhere. It got in his eyes, and, what with the smoke coming off the end of his cigar, three inches now, only three inches from the tip of his nose, he figured he'd better slow it down.

He eased right up on the scales, right beneath a hundred thousand bushels of wheat, a million million kernels of the stuff, a trillion particles of wheat dust floating all around him.

There was something wrong with this picture, he thought.

What was wrong with this picture? he thought.

He thought, and to help himself think he took a deep breath.

The tip of his cigar was so close to his face that he felt its heat on his cheeks as he inhaled. It opened up like a third eye, a bright red and pulsing orb.

If this works, I will take it as a divine sign, Rosemary Krebs was writing in her diary at just that moment.

I imagine the air glowing around Gene Zwemmer's face, sizzling, sparking like a struck flint, sparkling like the glowsticks children twirl on the Fourth of July—Independence Day in the rest of the country, but here, in Galatea, Founders' Day.

It was a small book, Rosemary Krebs' diary, but there were still a hundred pages after the one on which that sentence appeared. But she never filled those pages. She only wrote one more line, and then she hid her story—her confession, Justin would have called it; and somewhere in Colin's novel, I remembered, he also referred to that book as a confession—and left it there forever. Apparently one sign from God was enough, and she didn't tempt fate by asking for a second.

His beard went first, three decades' worth of greasy food going up in a single viscous black cloud. The fancy glass lighter with its etched *J.E.K.* exploded over his heart, the bottle of Jack Daniel's blew off his genitals, the gas tank in his truck took off both legs at the ankles—all trivial injuries, really, given the fireball that was about to reduce Gene Zwemmer to a half dozen pieces of charcoal.

The air is burning was Gene Zwemmer's last thought. The air is burning, the sky is falling, and everything has gone up in smoke. The last sentence of Rosemary Krebs' diary read, *This is the craziest thing I ever heard tell of*, and for the first time in my life I found myself in complete agreement with her.

6

6.01

Myra

MY NAME IS MYRA ROBINSON BUT THAT'S NOT IMPORtant. This is all about Lucy and don't let nobody tell you different. Found or missing, spoiled or pure: Lucy.

My daughter.

Lucy.

Now shut up and listen, cause I'm gonna tell you how it is—how it is and how it was and how it all came to be.

6.02

Wade

SUMMER WAS AS HOT AS WINTER WAS COLD.

It always is, in Kansas, but every year it comes as no less of a surprise. In other states fall is a warning and spring a time of happy preparation, but here in the heart of the country we have no such luxuries. It's cold until it's hot, and then it's hot until it's cold. Both seasons offer their own pleasures and their own miseries, and though most people reckon winter a worse time than summer, I would reckon that those people are not from Kansas.

Here, heat kills as much as cold.

Here, fewer people have access to the mercy of an air conditioner than to some form of heating, be it forced air or woodstove or the animal comfort of several bodies in one bed.

Here, each winter, Kansans come as close to hibernating as do any people, and there is a pleasure in that, or at least a relief. What do most people long for, but to sleep?

But that winter, the winter that Colin and Justin came to us and Lucy was taken away, offered no relief, for Lucy Robinson's true abductor did much to keep Galatea on the jump simply by remaining absolutely anonymous even as he reminded us that somewhere, out there, Lucy Robinson suffered at his hands.

Lucy's dress.

Lucy's hair.

Lucy's screams.

Lucy's fingers.

Find me.

In the midst of this Layton Buzzard packed up his wife and son and moved away from Galatea. Roman List and his wife Stacy weren't long in following.

On the white wall of his own house, Roman List spraypainted the words GONE AWAY in red letters ten feet high.

On the other side of Highway 9, Bruce Cardinal, a single man, left the house his family had lived in since the turn of the century. There was even talk that old Rochelle Getterling, ninety if she was a day and widowed more than half her years, was going to move in with her newly widowed sister somewhere down South.

Before he left Bruce Cardinal took an ax and destroyed the inside of his house. Every stick of furniture, every wall, chopped into kindling. Inspired, perhaps, by Roman List, he too left a note: *Not for you.*

It was a wonder, people said, that he didn't just burn it down.

Gone away.

Not for you.

So, when the snow melted, there was a reason for the world to look a little shrunk.

It had.

The warmth, when it came, seemed unwanted, and most people continued with their winter sluggishness. The sun shone for its own reasons, and the farmers went back to work because the sun did, but everyone else still seemed in that daze of cold.

Sometimes, as the days grew warmer and warmer, I longed to feel winter's daze of cold. But the urge to paint is a hot urge: the smell of paint is a hot smell, its touch is liquid and hot, even after it dries. I painted, and painted and painted.

I painted and Colin wrote and Justin was silent.

Other people had their lives, but we had our art.

Justin, especially, had his art.

6.03

Myra

TRY TO IMAGINE US. TRY TO IMAGINE THE FIRE. PERCY Tomkins who went all the way through school with me, he was in that Iraqi war and he said he never saw nothing to equal it.

The fire was like a tidal wave. It was a solid wall twice as tall as a house and giving way to a cloud of smoke that stretched up past seeing, and it *ran*, I tell you, it ran through town. I don't suppose any of those who died knew what hit them, because it was one-a those things where you either got away or you didn't. There weren't any close shaves. There wasn't enough time. No one alive today who was alive then has burn scars or anything like that. If you were close enough to wonder what was going on, then you were close enough to die without finding out.

Nineteen years old, my first apartment. Half a duplex with a back yard and a blighted elm tree all my own, a window air conditioner working overtime to keep it cool inside.

I was baking cookies.

If you ask me now what I was doing baking cookies in the middle of a May afternoon, I couldn't tell you. Maybe I was making cookies for Stan, I don't know. What I do know is this: making cookies saved my life, or at least my sight.

The oven was directly opposite the sink, and above the sink was a window that looked in the general direction of the grain elevator. I say general, because the elevator was two miles away and you couldn't even see it from the window. It wasn't like I ever thought, The grain elevator's thataway.

There was a window in the oven door too, and I was bent over, watching my cookies. If you were looking in through the window over the sink you'd have seen my butt, a few cookies and one pregnancy thinner than it is now.

It was my butt that took the glass when the window blew in.

I heard the explosion first. Luckily I wasn't a girl with fast reflexes—those didn't come until motherhood—because otherwise I'da turned around and caught the glass in my face. As it was, I jumped a little, and then I yelped as I felt that hot air pulse into the room. It seemed to move slowly, almost lazylike, and I could feel it boil around my skin like hot water. I don't even remember the window busting in. What I remember is the eerie sensation of my clothes and my hair floating up in that hot air. It felt just like a hand, that air, except it managed to touch every part of me at once.

I suppose I shoulda been scared, but I wasn't, not right away. Instead I thought, *This* is what I've been waiting for, and I wasn't thinking of Stan.

I still don't know who I was thinking of.

6.04

Webbie

SOMETIMES I WONDERED WHAT WALLACE WOULD THINK of me in my maid's uniform. Both of them covered my body: both seemed to retain their own identity, while I vanished beneath them. Wallace was a big man, and when he lay atop me I could feel his skin covering all the spare parts of me. And he knew this too. "Nothing can get at you now," he whispered in my ear, *nuthin kin git atchoo now*, "without it goes through me first," and the way he said *me* made his body sound more formidable than any ancient city's walls. I suppose my maid's uniform offered some kind of protection as well. Once I had put it on, it shrouded me; its magic was so potent that the disguise continued even after I took it off. I was no longer Webbie Greeving, an independent college-educated feisty female; I was Rosemary Krebs' maid.

But after I had completed her diary, my work in her house seemed to be done. I knew that I had found what I needed to find in that house, and after that my uniform did nothing more than chafe my skin, and so did my father's epithet. I had never before heard my father use the term *nigger*, not even to place it in a white man's mouth; even in sermons when he preached against an "urban mode of communication"—you can't imagine how my father *hated* rap music—he wouldn't use the word, but instead spoke of the folly of attempting to reclaim the terms of prejudice and hate. I knew my father's anger had as much to do with Rosemary Krebs as with me; he regarded her as he would the she-beast mother of the Antichrist, and the fact that she was childless only added to his suspicion. His hatred of her was so great that the mere mention of her name sent him into flying fits of anger. For forty years he had been Galatia's high priest, a mantle he had inherited from five previous generations—an uninterrupted chain that was longer, he had pointed out to me, than many a dynasty in Europe. He would never admit it—well, he probably would, actually—but my father saw himself as something of a benevolent despot; by his mind alone were decisions made, by his hand actions taken, and if this situation was undemocratic it was also for the common good, and no one ever complained. Some people left—a lot of people left—but that was to be expected. Rural life wasn't exactly the wave of the future. But those who remained behind enjoyed the benefits of living in a small conservative Christian community—and, of course, the closest thing to freedom from white people that this country could offer.

Rosemary Krebs changed all that, and she did it against my father's will, did it without even consulting him. When Rosemary Krebs' construction crews arrived a few weeks after the fire in Kenosha, my father, flush with the successes of the far-off Civil Rights movement, led the town against her. He wrote letters to the state government, and, when that failed, he held a sit-in on Rosemary Krebs' land. She ordered her bulldozers to plow on, bodies or no bodies, and faced with the advancing plows my father and his flock scattered like sheep.

Of all the memories I have of that time, the clearest is of my father continually pacing, the house, the pulpit, the streets of Galatia, and railing against "that wicked woman, that wicked, wicked woman." I had never met that woman, or seen her from less than a half mile away, but what I didn't realize was that my father hadn't either. Rosemary Krebs' Galatea had destroyed my father's town, but her refusal to even speak to him wounded his pride even more. She treated him as white folks treated niggers in the reconstructed South—she ignored him—and her strategy worked. Fury blinded my father and robbed him of his effectiveness, though I suppose Rosemary Krebs would have been successful anyway. Nothing she did was illegal—nothing she did in Galatia anyway, and I'm not really sure that anything she did in Kenosha was actually against the law either. She bought a man a drink. She gave him a cigar.

This is the craziest thing I ever heard tell of.

It was more than a year after the construction of Galatea began before she paid a visit to my father. I don't know why she finally came, nor why she waited so long; maybe it took that much time for her to gain the information she needed. Most of her cheap ugly houses were finished and filled by then; a few people, not rich, but with insurance money or the ability to secure a loan, were building nicer homes. The I.G.A. and TruValue were nearing completion, and Silas Brecken, who used to run Galatia's general store, was already talking about closing up shop to cut his losses. She came on a Saturday, without calling first; the fact that my father was home that afternoon, though he was usually out on Saturdays, has since led me to wonder if she was having our home watched.

The woman who rang the doorbell was significantly shorter than me. She wore a brown shiny suit, and a three-stranded choker of pearls encircled her throat. She couldn't really look down on me, but I could feel the gesture in her eyes. "Good afternoon," she said. "Is your father at home this afternoon?"

I nodded my head, staring in wonder at her tiny wrists, her bird legs, the big globe of hair fixed around her head and glowing with an eerie blue light against the bright noon sun.

"Do you think I could speak to him?"

I nodded again, but still didn't move. The little woman clucked her lips.

"Is something the matter?"

"Why, you ain't no bigger than a scarecrow!"

I hadn't meant to be rude, but Rosemary Krebs flushed deeply. She leaned close to me and whispered, "Where I come from little girls are punished for speaking so rudely. Now go and get your father before I tell him what a wicked child you've been."

"I'm sorry."

"Go," she hissed, and I ran up the stairs.

A few minutes later, I sneaked down the stairs behind my father. Rosemary Krebs had let herself into the house, and she stood in the living room. Her eyes looked only at the stairs, and then at my father, as if none of the room's furnishings merited her attention.

"Good afternoon, Mr. Greeving," I heard her say. "My name is Rosemary Krebs."

"I know your name." My father, white shirtsleeves rolled up to his forearms, regarded the Bible he still held in one hand. "Most people call me Reverend."

"Forgive me for disturbing you from your studies, Mr. Greeving. I thought perhaps it was time that we met."

"I'm surprised you didn't just call me up to the big house." He took one step farther down the stairs, but that was all. "It's always something when Massa comes out to the shacks."

Rosemary Krebs nodded at the Bible in my father's hands. "I'm sorry to disturb you from your studies, Mr. Greeving. I'll try to take up as little of your time as possible." The tiny woman in our living room spoke as if she were reciting lines she had no stake in. The only person, it seemed, who would benefit from believing her was my father.

"You already took up too mucha my time, Mrs. Krebs. Now, if you don't mind, I have a sermon to prepare."

But Rosemary Krebs stood her ground. "Your manner is most commanding, like all the great preachers and leaders of your people, Mr. Greeving. May I ask where you studied?"

My father's volume lessened only slightly. "Excuse me?"

"Where you received your degree, Mr. Greeving. Excuse me—Reverend. What seminary you attended."

I couldn't see my father's face, but his shoulders sagged, just a little. He was silent for a moment, and then he turned his head and saw me. His face had fallen too. "Get on out of here," he said.

"Daddy?"

"Go on, get over to Charity Getterling's, or go find Coretta Lewis to play with. Me and the white lady got business to discuss."

As I ran past Rosemary Krebs she looked down on me and smiled—not vindictively, but triumphantly, and she seemed somehow much taller than she had five minutes earlier—and, though I didn't know what else would transpire in my absence, I knew that she would tell my father that I had been rude to her, and sure enough when I returned my father threatened to wash my mouth out with soap if I ever even spoke to that woman again, and then he sent me to bed without supper. It seemed to me then that he was punishing himself as well, because he also didn't eat. He paced the floor of the Archive all night and all the next day, surrounded by thousands of pieces of paper whose only purpose was to give his town legitimacy, the legitimacy of history. But one piece of paper was missing from that collection, and though its absence seems trivial compared to all the other things that were happening, I still feel my father's pain, for I suffer the same lack: my father, like me, did not have a diploma. His only claim to the name *Reverend* was self-made, just as my claim on the name *historian* was, and, as we both learned the hard way, such claims are just not good enough.

6.05

Myra

IN MY HEAD IT'S ALL HAPPENING AT THE SAME TIME, Kenosha and the fire and Eric Johnson and Stan going off, and then Lucy.

Lucy's birth.

What can I say. She came quick. Labor lasted two hours, tops.

I remember it two ways. I remember this awful pressure in me, like someone was filling me with boiling water, filling me up past the point of bursting, filling and filling till I prayed I would just explode.

And I remember a light. I remember being in this light, wrapped up in it like in a blanket, this light was soft and warm and held me up and held me together even, just like skin, and while I was in this light time disappeared.

And then the two memories come together.

The light moved inside of me with a rush. It was right then, I know, right then that Lucy Robinson became the person she is today.

And then the pressure forced the light out of me. I swear it was coming out my eyes and mouth and nose, out of my pores, and of course it was coming out of me down there.

So I named her Lucy. We'd been thinking of Mary—Stan and my's mothers was both named Mary—but Lucy. The light. Lucy.

Her tiny hands was in tiny fists when they handed her to me, and she was screaming and carrying on like birth was some great wrong we'd done to her. I remember wanting to count her fingers and toes, the way you do, I wanted to make sure she was all there because I had a funny feeling she'd left part of herself behind, inside me.

In fact, she'd took out something extra.

I pulled at the little fingers of her right hand, one by one. One two three four five. Her left hand, one two three four five.

There was something in her left hand.

By then Lucy's mouth had found my nipple and the doctor had done his job and gone to write out the bill and the nurses was busy with this and that. Stan was on his way from the waiting room.

There was a pebble in Lucy's hand. A tiny black stone no bigger than her baby fingertip.

I took that pebble. I never told nobody about it. Part of me wanted to swallow it, send it back where it come from, but I knew it'd just come out again, and if it didn't then it'd just cause problems. So I kept it, and when I went home I put it in the little cedar chest where later on I put the first lock of her hair and her first lost tooth and the pink blanket my mother started knitting for her the night she was born.

The very last thing I put in that chest was one patent leather shoe.

When Stan left that chest was the one thing he took with him.

6.06

Justin

THERE WERE PERHAPS A DOZEN DIFFERENT WAYS I could walk between the limestone house and Wade's, but only two or three of these routes also avoided Galatea. I don't know why I didn't like to walk through town, but every time I approached it I felt like the little girl in *We Have Always Lived in the Castle*, a fallen aristocrat forced to endure the evil whisperings of simpleminded villagers. No one whispered at me in Galatea; a few people stared, but no one even pointed. People only speculate when they don't know the truth, and everyone in town knew the truth about Colin and me, and Colin and Divine, and Divine and Wade, and Wade and me. In that respect, I think, they were a step ahead of Colin and Divine and Wade and me.

I preferred to walk home from Wade's at night. "Stay," he would whisper, but I would get up and get dressed and leave. Sometimes I passed Divine on my way out of Wade's. He would stand in a room with the snarl of a poodle whose domain has been invaded. Sometimes I passed Divine when I arrived at home. Then his head would fall, and he would slink out of my way like a cat caught on the prowl. But usually we passed each other somewhere on the plain, he driving, I walking: Divine, like me, didn't like to pass through town.

Sometimes darkness offers an illusion of vulnerability, sometimes of safety. When I was a child I was terrified of the dark, and when I lived on the streets I avoided daylight like a vampire. Now I take what each day and each night offers. One night a lone bull followed me for a mile, the three strands of a barbed wire fence all that separated me from two thousand pounds of restless flesh. One night a barn owl sat on a fencepost and watched me come and go: only its head turned, one hundred eighty degrees, and in the moonlight it appeared completely white and neutral. Rabbits sprang from beneath my feet, startling me with their own fear, dogs barked and rustled chains or came quietly whining for a scratch on the nose, or the thin rank trail of a skunk coiled around me in the air. Sometimes branches broke in one of the small stands of soft-wooded fast-growing trees that punctuated fields, and this is the only time I grew truly frightened. I told myself that it was a dog, or a clumsy deer, and I made myself walk slowly, steadily on. I would not run.

Sometimes a car passed me. If it came from behind I did nothing; if it came from in front I lowered my face against its headlights. Every once in a while a car would slow inquisitively, but usually they sped past me. Here, when it's dark, most people are sleeping, and those that aren't are on their way to bed, and not much deters them from their destination. But one night headlights caught me from behind; a moment later engine noises and crunching gravel reached my ears. The vehicle itself took a long time to reach me, and I realized without turning that it was slowing down, coming slower and slower, and at some point I realized that it had slowed to my pace, and it was following me. My shadow was so elongated that it seemed to stretch right to the horizon, but that was the only thing I could see.

I turned. The lights were high and square: a truck. It stopped. A moment later the engine shut off, and then, with a flash, four lights mounted on the grille shot a wide bolt of light down the road, spilling into the fields, silvering the ripening wheat that swayed in a breeze. I heard the doors squeak open but I could see nothing beyond the wall of light. I heard footsteps, more than one set. Eventually three shapes walked in front of the light, all of them rendered eerily thin, long-limbed and big-headed, like space aliens, and I knew even before they spoke who they were.

"Well, whata we got here?" Darrell Jenkens' voice drawled.

"Looks like we got us a stray cat," Howard Goertzen's voice answered him.

"A tomcat out on the prowl," Grady Oconnor's voice said.

"A tabby cat's more like it," Darrell Jenkens said. "A pussy cat. Here, pussy, pussy, pussy. What'sa matter pussy, cat got your tongue?" The laughter of three beer-thickened voices bounced off each other like balls in a lottery machine, spilling misfortune and misanthropy out into the night.

"Looks like a pig killer is what it looks like to me," Howard Goertzen said then.

"Looks like a hitchhiker is what it looks like," Darrell Jenkens said.

"Pig killer."

"Aw, Howard, don't let's get started on this pig-killing business again," Darrell Jenkens' voice cut in, annoyed.

"Darrell! You said my name! You weren't supposed to say my name."

"Well, idiot, who's calling who stupid?"

"But Char—"

"Howard!" *Haird!*

There was a fleshy thud then, and then a moment of silence, and then Darrell Jenkens' voice said, "And besides, it was the other one who killed your Charlene."

"One's just the same as the oth—" Howard Goertzen began, but Darrell Jenkens cut him off with another "Howard." A moment later Grady Oconnor's voice resumed the conversation. "Don't it know," he said in slow measured tones, "that hitchhiking's illegal in the state of Kansas?"

For the first time I wondered if I should be afraid. I had never been called an *it* before.

"Perhaps we oughta be making a citizen's arrest. On behalf of the good people of Galatea," Darrell Jenkens said.

"For the gooda the people," Grady Oconnor answered him.

Howard Goertzen's sulking was inaudible, but it felt like a hot breeze on a summer day that leaves your skin covered in a film of sweat.

"Well then," Darrell Jenkens said, "that sounds like an idea then. No need to wake up Lawman Brown for a trifling matter like this. This ain't nothing a grown man can't deal with himself."

6.07

Myra

MY LUCY. FOUR YEARS OLD, SKIN LIKE IVORY, HAIR LIKE ebony, just like in that song. She had seven white dresses, one for each day of the week, each one prettier than the last. Come Sunday she looked like a little bride. She sat in church next to me and Stan, her patent leather slip-ons surfing above the floor, white gloves, white socks, a flowered hat on her head, fancier than Easter.

When the collection bowl came around she wouldn't drop Stan's five-dollar bill in, she insisted that we put it in one of those envelopes that say "Gift of" on them.

Only one woman in town used those envelopes. They were only there because she insisted on them. Everybody else felt they were just a way of making it look like you were giving a lot of money when in reality you were slipping in a pittance. Better to just drop in singles and swirl them around a little—and besides, Nettie Ferguson counted the offering each week for Pastor Little, so it was no secret how much Rosemary Krebs put in her envelope.

Then again, maybe that was the point.

Her envelope was always all the way on the bottom of the collection bowl because she sat all the way up in the front pew. From where we sat she was just a pair of shoulders and a cone of hair, both steel gray and just as rigid. Lucy kept her eyes on Rosemary Krebs' hair throughout the sermon. God may have worked miracles in the past but Rosemary Krebs took her to the mall each weekend, and from an early age Lucy valued the tangible over the insubstantial, especially if it had lace at the collar.

Seven white dresses, fancier than Easter.

Oh, I don't blame her. That's one of my beliefs: never blame the child when the fault is her elders'.

Stan and I used to nudge her, Go say hi-lo to Mrs. Krebs, Maybe Mrs. Krebs would like it if you brought her some of these cookies I just baked, Why don't you read the Sears catalog over to Mrs. Krebs' house. By the time I thought someone was overdoing it, either me and Stan, or Rosemary Krebs, or Lucy, it was too late.

She called it mentoring. Lucy revealed a lot of potential, she said, she had no children, there were certain supplemental advantages she could offer Lucy that perhaps Stan and I might find it difficult to procure, and like that.

By then I just wanted to tell her to stay the fuck away from my daughter, but Stan, hey, Stan paid the bills, and he knew just how much we owed at the First National Bank of Rosemary Krebs.

Life ain't easy being the number two plumber in a town the size of Galatea, only so many clogged sinks and backed-up toilets to go around.

He advocated caution.

When he said that I knew he'd been talking to her—the only thing Stan ever "advocated" was another round of drinks at Sloppy Joe's—and all I said was that if I got even a *hint* of something funny going on up at that fake plantation house I'd rip that beehive off her head and shove it up where the sun don't shine. But in the meantime Lucy was smiling and Lord knows we could use the extra money we saved on dresses and toys.

Beer ain't cheap at a case a day.

Old Henry was dead by then, I was working for Bea and she wasn't in the best of health, she took up a lot of my time. Stan was hardly working, and, drunk, he wasn't exactly the best babysitter. What could I say?

Well, I suppose I could've said no, but the point was that I didn't.

6.08

Justin

THE SMELL OF SHIT BEGAN TO GROW STRONGER, AND I realized soon enough that it came from outside the El Camino. A few corrugated tin buildings appeared, a small silo covered in asphalt shingles, a rickety rambling farmhouse with a porch swing half hanging by one chain. Howard Goertzen parked the El Camino next to a series of rank fenced-in lots. It was his father's pig farm. As we climbed from the El Camino I cast a single look at Grady Oconnor. I don't know if it communicated anything—I certainly hadn't meant to invest it with meaning—but he held a hand out to help me down, and then, when I was on the ground, he turned away.

They led me into one of the tin buildings. Inside the shit smelled stale and fresh at the same time, and sweet as well, the air fetid and hot. A cold light snapped on, glinting off the mud-stained black-and-white backs of a hundred pigs. They rustled in the sudden light. A single narrow lane led between the pens, and we walked down it until we were in the middle of the barn. Darrell Jenkens leaned against the slats of a fence, while Howard Goertzen and Grady Oconnor stood, a few feet apart from him and each other. Grady Oconnor looked at his feet, and Darrell Jenkens and Howard Goertzen nursed beers.

"True what they say, Howard," Darrell Jenkens said eventually. *Haird.*

"Bout what?" Howard Goertzen said.

"Bout a hog'll eat just about anything?"

"Just about," Howard Goertzen said. "The only thing I know that'll eat what a hog won't is a billy goat."

"You got any billy goats?"

"Nope."

"Then I guess hogs'll have to do."

"Guess so."

There was a bit of silence, and then Howard Goertzen let out a chuckle he'd been suppressing since we walked into the barn.

"Hey Grady," he said.

Grady Oconnor looked up. "Yeah?"

"What'd you and the pussy talk about back there?"

Grady looked at me, back at Howard Goertzen. "Nothing," he said. "He don't talk."

"Yeah, that's right, I forgot. He don't talk. He don't say nothing."

"He don't even shake his head," Grady Oconnor said.

"Come again?" Howard Goertzen said.

"You ask him a question, yes or no, he don't even shake his head."

"That so?" He turned to me. "That so, pussy?" I just looked at him. "Well, shit, Grady, I guess you're right. He don't even shake his head."

"I'll be damned," Darrell Jenkens said.

Howard Goertzen let out a guffaw then, and said, "I wonder if he'd talk if I did *this*." He was beside me suddenly, his beer can dropped on the cement floor. He lifted me in his meaty arms and dropped me on top of a fencepost. It rammed into my tailbone, and I sat there, quivering slightly, until I hooked a foot through a slat and regained my balance.

"Nope," Darrell Jenkens said. "He didn't talk. Moved his leg there, but he didn't talk."

"Sure didn't," Howard Goertzen said. Grady Oconnor lit another cigarette.

"How about this?" Howard Goertzen said, and he poked me in the chest. I fell back, my torso depending over the pigpen, but my foot through the slat kept me from falling in. Beneath me, the pigs rustled a little.

"Nope," Darrell Jenkens said.

"And this?" Howard Goertzen said. He pushed me this time, and I grabbed at the fence and pulled myself back up.

"He grabbed the fence," Darrell Jenkens said. "That's something."

"It's something," Howard Goertzen said. "But he didn't talk. You know what I think?"

"What do you think, Howard?" *Haird.*

"I think that a man that don't talk ain't really a man. Ain't no better than a pig." He kicked the fence hard then, and the pigs closest to it jumped and jostled away from it.

"Oughta be in with the pigs," Grady Oconnor said, without looking up from his feet.

"Only seems fair," Howard Goertzen said. "We eat them, why shouldn't they eat us." He looked me right in the eye. "You kill them," he said, still, apparently, conflating me with Colin. "They kill you. Fair's fair."

The pigs were tightly packed, and had almost to climb over each other to move. I felt a coarse hide rub against my ankle. Howard Goertzen kicked the fence again, pushed me at almost the same time. I fell off the post, my knees hooked over the top rail of the fence, my foot still caught in the slats. My arms swung wildly for a moment before catching on to the top rail, but I didn't pull myself back up. I hung there, and the ammonia fumes were so strong that my eyes watered, and I coughed when I breathed.

"What was that?" Darrell Jenkens said. "He say something?"

"That was just a cough," Howard Jenkens. "He ain't said nothing."

"He don't say nothing," Grady Oconnor said. "He don't even shake his head." He looked up then, and, slowly but purposefully, he walked over to me and Howard Goertzen and he grabbed my shirtfront and pulled me up and forward. He pulled so hard that I pitched toward him, and my foot, still caught in the slats, tripped me, and he stepped out of my way and let me fall to the floor. I stayed there. My face faced Grady Oconnor's and Howard Goertzen's boots; Darrell Jenkens was somewhere behind me. Grady Oconnor wore pointy toed black cowboy boots, and Howard wore heavy Sears-issue light brown workboots, the suede kind that had become so popular among Chelsea clones in recent years. No one seemed to notice my little smile.

"That's enough, Howard," Grady Oconnor was saying somewhere above me. He said the word with two syllables. He said *Howard.*

Above me, Howard Goertzen's voice assumed a nasty edge it hadn't possessed when he was speaking to me. "Aw, Grady, I'm just getting started," he said, and as he spoke it finally occurred to me that he hated Grady Oconnor, really hated him, as in, hated him because of something, and that something was probably the fact that he was black.

When Grady Oconnor answered him, I realized that the feeling was mutual. "The boy's gonna get his hand bit off, Howard, and you gonna get our asses throwed in jail."

"Ain't no crime against hassling a faggot," Darrell Jenkens said now. I heard him heave himself off the fence, heard the sound of his approaching footsteps. One of his boots kicked my shoulder as he stepped over me, a rounded toe, like Howard Goertzen's, though when his foot had made its way past me I saw that his boots were black, not brown. I wasn't sure if the kick was intentional or not; a cold liquid which my nose told me was beer splashed on my shoulder just after the boot hit my shoulder. Darrell Jenkens stopped when he was on the other side of me; he turned. He prodded my ribs with one of his boots until I rolled over onto my back. "Lookit that," he slurred. "He ain't no better than a dog. He's worse than a dog even. Least a dog knows when to bite."

Above me, stalactites of dust hung from the rafters that ran across the width of the building. They swayed back and forth, just barely, as if somewhere above me there was the slightest hint of a breeze. There was no breeze on the floor.

Grady Oconnor seemed at a loss. He looked down at me with eyes that pleaded for me to speak, or fight back, or at least get up.

Darrell Jenkens' boot knocked against the side of my head. He staggered a little, when one of his feet was off the floor. As the boot landed heavily on the floor, I saw the faint imprint of yellow letters written on the front, right above the sole. *Steel Toe.*

"What's going on, Grady?" Darrell Jenkens said. "You acting like you're sweet on him or something."

Howard Goertzen laughed, and, as his body shook, the fence he was leaning against creaked. Beyond him, the hogs rustled in their pen. "You sweet on this faggot, Grady? I'll be goddamned, you think you know somebody, and then you find out he's sweet on a faggot."

"I ain't sweet on him," Grady Oconnor said, but he looked at me when he spoke, and his eyes pleaded with mine to do something.

Above the rafters the corrugated tin roof cathedraled up and away from me. The barn's lights hung at a point between the rafters and the roof, and everything above them was invisible. Below the lights, the tin was shiny, almost white, but above them it seemed to cant off into darkness. What was it Myra had said at Rosemary Krebs' dance? Everything in this town is loaded with double meanings. Everything means something. But Myra hadn't gone far enough. It wasn't just that everything meant something: it all meant too much.

"If you ain't sweet on him then why you making goo-goo eyes at him?" Howard Goertzen's voice.

"I ain't *sweet* on him," Grady Oconnor said. There was a hint of disgust in the way he said *sweet,* and I knew that whatever chance I had of escaping violence was just about to pass.

"Prove it," Howard Goertzen said. He laughed again, just a little, and the fence squeaked under him, just a little, and the hogs rustled behind him, just a little.

"I ain't got to prove nothing to you," Grady Oconnor said. "You don't know I'm straight up by now, that's your problem."

"I ain't got a problem," Howard Goertzen said. "You got a problem, Darrell?" *Darl.*

"I ain't got a problem, Howard." *Haird.*

"Well," Howard Goertzen said, "seems to me the only person with a problem is the one lying on the floor of my Daddy's barn."

The black above the lights had an empty open beckoning quality about it, as if, if I could fly, I could fly into it and it would take me. It would let me in.

"Like, *this* would be a problem," Darrell Jenkens said, and when he said the word *this* his boot swayed forward and by the time he said the word *problem* his boot was slamming into the side of my stomach, and I folded up and around it reflexively, folding so tightly that I trapped his leg in my folded body. The sound of my ribs cracking could be heard up and down the length of the barn, or at least I imagined it could, and after the sound was gone I heard Howard Goertzen's quiet laugh. "*Damn,* Darrell," he said. "I bet that hurt."

6.09

Myra

AFTERWARDS THEY HAD TO PICK GLASS FROM THE kitchen window out of my butt with something that looked like a big tweezers or a little forceps. It took eight hours and two doctors, and after the first hour the first doctor hooked me up to a Valium drip to stop me squirming around, and everything got kind of hazy after that. The only thing I really remember—at least it feels like a memory, though it feels kinda like a dream too, but then it all feels like a dream—I remember asking the second doctor if I was going to have like, unsightly scars, you know, on my backside, and the second doctor clinked the tweezer-forceps thing down on one-a those steel trays and laid one of his hands in its cold rubber glove on my burning ass and told me *Not if I can help it*, and then he laughed a little and said *At any rate it's nothing anyone'll notice after you've had your first baby.*

Well. Here is something I can tell you for sure. Don't wait to realize your past is important until after it's already past. Because I'll tell you: once it's gone it's gone, and if you didn't take no precautions against forgetting it then you will. No matter how precious you thought it was at the time. Bits and pieces, that's all you'll have left, slivers as tiny as the glass that doctor pulled out of my skin. Bits and pieces that when you put them together don't necessarily make up what it was had been taken apart. That's as good as I can put it. *Write it down.* Maybe I say that because of knowing Colin and Justin. But I say it. *Write it down now.*

6.10

Webbie

ON THE FIRST FRIDAY AFTER I HAD FINISHED ASSEMbling Rosemary Krebs' story, I picked up the key to the Archive. For me, it was all in the key and the lock: in all the years I had been alive my father had never left the Archive unlocked, but since I was five I could have, at any time, taken that key from its corkboard peg in the kitchen and opened that door. But it took me nearly thirty years to do that. The key was small and cool in my hand; it didn't burn me as I'd half thought it would, though I clutched it so tightly on my way up the stairs that it bit into my palm. It slipped into the lock easily, turned almost noiselessly. The door was quiet too; only the lights hummed a little, and their fluorescent glare, combined with the dusty smell of the room, reminded me of a barn loft, a place where old discarded objects acquire some kind of value based on their mystery, objects which, under examination, always turn out to be junk. I hoped that junk was all I'd find there.

Time slipped away from me once I began searching. Within a few minutes I wasn't looking for evidence of any shameful moment in Galatia's history, but was instead enthralled by a small but bustling community. In those hours in the Archive I felt my father's love for his town, and his fierce hatred of Rosemary Krebs for spoiling it: for the first time I realized that there had been something to spoil, although both the dates on these pictures and my own memory told me that what I was looking at had been gone long before Rosemary Krebs' tractors broke ground west of Highway 9.

When I found them, it was a shock. I didn't even realize I was in the Johnson family file. There had been an Alessander first; he had moved here and married Constance Getterling; they had two daughters, Blithe, who moved away, and Belinda, who married one of the Deacon boys, and a son, Samuwell, whose wife, Cherry Estevez, had come with her family to work in the fields. Samuwell and Cherry were the parents of Sawyer and Marsha. Sawyer had married Cora, of course, and fathered another Sawyer, and took off. Marsha had never married; she'd been engaged to Hally Taylor, whose death in a drunk-driving accident I could dimly recall. Everyone had assumed that Hally was Eric's father, but the dates on the notarized copies of Hally's death certificate and Eric's birth certificate were nearly eleven months apart. I wasn't surprised: that same everyone had also maintained that grief had made Marsha crazy and her craziness was what made Eric come out of her the way he had. At any rate, Marsha never really got it together after Hally's death, and Eric more or less ran wild from the time he could run, and now I found myself looking at what remained of his thumbs, wrapped up in a white embroidered handkerchief with the monogram *R.K.* on it, which in turn had been ensconced in a sealed Ziploc baggie with my father's handwriting on it.

My father had written *Eric Johnson's thumbs* on the bag.

The stained handkerchief was spread open, the shriveled parcels of bone and thready skin were still in my hand, when I heard the back door slam. I could have put them back, I suppose, closed the file, locked up the Archive before my father made it up in the chair lift, but I couldn't have beaten him to the kitchen with the key. And the key and these bones were tantamount to the same thing, I understood that much immediately: if I had claimed the one I would have claimed the other. In my father's eyes there could have been no difference.

So I sat there. I listened to my father stamp around the ground floor for a few moments, and then I heard the long slow whine of the chair lift as it carried him upstairs. He thumped down the hall, he appeared in the doorway. He looked at me briefly, noted what I held, and then he went to a cabinet I hadn't yet opened and he pulled from it a decanter and a glass. He carried these with some difficulty to his oak desk, sat on the leather chair behind it. The air in the Archive was so dry that as soon as my father unstoppered the bottle I could smell the alcohol.

"Whiskey?" I said then. "This room is full of surprises."

"Scotch," my father clarified. "Single malt." The high white collar of his shirt pushed at his cheeks, giving him a single thin jowl that ringed his face like Lincoln's beard. He sipped at the Scotch and grimaced, and for a moment a second line of flesh framed his face like a cowl.

I held out my hand, the hand that contained Rosemary Krebs' handkerchief and Eric Johnson's thumbs. "Is Eric Johnson alive?"

"I have no idea."

"You have no idea? Then what are these?"

My father sipped and grimaced; the cowl slipped forward and then slipped back. "Those are his thumbs," my father said, and I was about to prod him further when he went on. "In one of those drawers I have locks of your and your mother's hair that are just as substantial as those sticks you hold in your hand. Nevertheless, I know that your mother is dead and you are alive, not by evidence of those locks, but because I buried your mother in the ground and I am confronted by your face each day of my life." He sipped again, but didn't grimace this time. "Not all evidence is conclusive, daughter. Even the Bible would not be sufficient proof of the existence of God if we didn't see His presence in our lives. Now put those down. They, and you, have made your point."

I looked at the thumbs one last time, then wrapped them up in the handkerchief. "I'm keeping them."

"As you will. Certainly I cannot stop you." My father shrugged his right side, as if to emphasize his physical infirmity. "You are going to take them to Lawman Brown, I suppose."

I nodded.

"You should know before you speak to him that it was he who gave them to me."

I blinked. "You expect me to believe that."

My father drank. "I do."

"Then why didn't you do something?"

"Do . . . ?"

"Take them down to Sheriff Peterson in Bigger Hill, the Highway Patrol, anywhere."

My father made an arc through the air with his half-finished drink. The arc seemed to circumscribe Galatia, Galatea, Bigger Hill, Kansas, the world.

"They might have found Eric Johnson," I went on. "They might have found who lynched him."

"What would have been the point in finding the boy? To bring him back here, so that he could continue to hate, and be hated, and attack another white girl, or perhaps a black one? Finding him, I think, would have been a service neither to him nor to Galatia. And as to the men who lynched him, no outside investigator is needed. Mobs may hide their faces with masks, but they tend not to be so fastidious with their voices, and their trucks, and their shoes. Fifty-five men and boys tied Eric Johnson to that tree. Forty-seven white men and eight black men. If you'd kept on with your searches rather than allowing your attention and your imagination to be captured by a powerful but ultimately impotent symbol, you would have found their names written on a sheet of paper. Although," my father said, and sipped again, "the majority of those names have become nothing more than symbols as well. Only two of Eric Johnson's lynchers still live among us. All the rest have gone."

In fact there was only one, but we wouldn't know that for a few more minutes.

I could guess one of the names. "Lawman Brown?"

He nodded.

"And how can you—you, a champion of African-Americans—live with that?"

"The crime is his, not mine. And as long as he and I both know that, he is much more useful as sheriff than in jail."

"I can't believe I'm having this conversation. You sound more like a big-city politician than a small-town preacher."

"You have always been too easily swayed by appearances, daughter. Galatia *is* a city. It is as modern as New York or Chicago or Los Angeles, and if you are displeased by this state of affairs then you can blame your

. . . employer. I would have been content to remain an anachronism, the spiritual leader of an ever-shrinking flock, but she dragged Galatia into the twentieth century. She gave us what we never had before: a race problem. She gave us fiscal crises. She gave us brokered deals, urban development projects, capital funds drives. I preferred church socials myself, nothing more serious than spiked punch to deal with, and the food was always better, but some things would appear to be irretrievably lost. If I may be so vulgar," he said, and paused, and refilled his glass, and drank from it, "we have as much chance of regaining those halcyon days as Eric Johnson, living or dead, has of regaining his thumbs. But, as Mrs. Krebs is fond of saying, you can't stop progress."

"And where," I said, when my father had finished speaking. "Where does the welfare of Lucy Robinson figure into all of this?"

For the first time that evening my father seemed surprised. "What does she have to do with this?"

Despite my father's earlier admonishment, I could only brandish the parcel in my hand. "Do you think it's just a coincidence that *she* was the one who was chosen?"

My father looked at me for a long time, and then his eyes dropped to my hand, and then they raised themselves again and met mine. "No," he said in a level voice, "I don't. I think that whoever would have accompanied young Justin Time"—he said the name without even a hint of irony—"would have been, as you put it, chosen."

As my father had spoken I'd felt a change in the room. I wasn't sure if it was in him or in me, or in the atmosphere of the Archive itself, so long sealed, now, for the first time, breathing freely, but as I looked at it the figure behind the desk seemed to retreat from me, and I felt myself sliding backward also. I could see in front of me all of the things I'd done over the past few months, all my discoveries undiscovered and waiting for me to uncover them, and I realized that they made no difference, no difference at all.

"You said black men. Black men helped lynch Eric Johnson."

"Eight."

"Did you—?"

My father held up his hand, and the gesture actually relieved me. I don't think I could have borne the idea of my father in a Klan robe.

He put his hand down. "I would like to tell you that those men did what they did because Eric Johnson had stolen from them, or bullied their children, or even because of what happened to the girl. But I am afraid that their reason is the same as that of their white counterparts: they helped lynch Eric Johnson because of the color of his skin, and the blame for that sentiment I also lay at Rosemary Krebs' feet."

The explanation was too easy. I knew it, and he did too: after a moment his eyes dropped to his desk. He reached for his glass, saw that it was empty, and put his hand in his lap.

"You're her crony," I said. "You're her lackey. You're her flunky." House nigger, he had called me when I told him I was going to work for her, but he was merely a fool.

My father allowed himself to smile. "Use the word. You know you want to."

I only stared at him.

He shrugged. When he spoke his voice was unperturbed. "We keep each other honest."

"Honest? By whose reckoning? It looks to me that you both lie like dogs."

"Dogs do not lie. Dogs do not speak."

"Don't obfuscate."

My father shrugged again. "You may choose to see it as lying, or obfuscating. I prefer to think of myself as her shadow."

I nearly laughed aloud. "That might be the most shocking thing that's come out of your mouth all evening."

"I didn't say I chose the role. All I can do is play it for the good of Galatia."

"And what is the good of Galatia?"

"To continue on as we have, without further intervention from the outside world."

"And again I ask you," I stammered, "*where* does Lucy Robinson figure into all of this?"

This time my father didn't flinch. "She is not my responsibility, daughter. She is not one of mine."

We were saved by the telephone. My father answered it cordially, but almost immediately his tone and his face wrinkled in distaste, and he held the phone out to me. "It's for you," he said. "Apparently something has happened, yet again, to your little friend."

I held my hand over the receiver. "Who—"

"Howard Goertzen," my father said, and, though that hadn't been the question I'd been asking him, I suddenly knew the name of one of the other men who had helped lynch Eric Johnson.

6.11

Myra

THE FIRST TIME I HEARD ABOUT ANGELA I DIDN'T GIVE it too much currency. Lucy was five then, I think, she was playing with her birthday present from Rosemary Krebs: a dollhouse so big we had to keep it outside. Turrets, balconies, drawbridges, barred windows, real stucco on the walls, its own moat that you filled up with a garden hose. It was a castle, not a dollhouse, a palace for a princess. It was so big Lucy could fit inside it. One whole wall was a door, and Lucy used to slip inside and sit there all day in one of her white dresses.

She made Stan buy her a little chair so she wouldn't soil—she used the word *soil*—her white dress in the dirt, which prompted Stan to say that every gift Rosemary Krebs bought Lucy ended up costing *us* money. Still, he bought Lucy the cutest little white chair with blue flowers painted on it, and when he gave it to her, he said, "Here you go, Princess. Here's your throne."

Perched on her chair and sealed inside her dollhouse, Lucy told us, "This is a magic fairy castle. When I'm inside it I'm invisible."

This is how a five-year-old says Don't bug me.

Stan and I nodded, when she was inside the dollhouse we pretended we couldn't see her. Lucy, Lucy, we called, where are you, Lucy? and then we'd wander away.

But indulging her had some funny effects. For one thing, it made it easier for us to ignore her, which isn't something that comes naturally to a parent. For another, Lucy started believing the stories she was telling.

I told Stan, put the dollhouse in the shade of the two catalpas that grow in the back yard so it wouldn't get too hot for Lucy. I told him, I can see the headline: SLEEPING BEAUTY IS DEAD—GALATEA'S PRINCESS DIES OF HEAT STROKE. It just wouldn't do.

Trees are on the short side around here, so that's also where the clothesline is.

What I mean is, I wasn't spying. I was hanging clothes up to dry.

"My name is Angela," I heard from inside the castle. "I live in the most beautiful house in the world. From the outside it looks just like any other house, but on the inside there are lots and lots and lots of rooms, and in every room there is a secret surprise, and all of the surprises are for me."

She went on talking but by then I was out of hearing range. I was hanging sheets, and they do tend to move you down the line.

At the time I wasn't bothered.

What child doesn't tell herself stories?

Who hasn't toyed with the idea of changing their name?

Angela.

For a little while in high school I tried to get people to call me Maria—Muh-rye-a—instead of Myra, but it never caught on.

I remember there was a breeze blowing, so hot and so dry that it seemed to pass over your skin like a cotton ball run the wrong way up stubbly legs, and I was remembering that other hot wind, and my daydream of a lover who touched me everywhere at once.

I remember that the little prickly itch I'd had in my butt ever since the fire was particularly bad that day.

Little snatches of Lucy's words came to me on the breeze. ". . . little chest . . . magic mirror . . . silver tiara."

I remember wondering where a five-year-old learned the word *tiara*.

6.12

Justin

DARRELL JENKENS HAD THROWN UP AND FALLEN DOWN.

Howard Goertzen and Grady Oconnor seemed to have done nothing during the entire time it took him to throw up and fall down, and I realized they must be very, very drunk.

Now the fence creaked under the weight of Howard Goertzen's shifting body, the hogs rustled, and Howard Goertzen said quietly, "Uh, Darrell, you okay?"

Darrell Jenkens breathed heavily. In a moment, I thought, he'll start to snore.

"Hey Grady," Howard Goertzen said.

"Yup?" Grady Oconnor said.

"Grady, Darrell fell down."

"Looks like it," Grady Oconnor said.

Howard Goertzen started to laugh, accompanied by the squeaking fence and rustling hogs. "Hey Grady."

"Yup?"

"Grady, Darrell fell down! He fell *down*!"

"You just said that, Howard."

"I mean, he fell down in his own *puke*." His laughter was punctuated by hiccups now, and with each *hic* the fence squealed beneath his weight and the hogs had come to a kind of slow boil. As I rolled my eyes toward Howard Goertzen I saw him drop his beer can. It was a deliberate act, I saw, not an accident.

"Hey"—*hic*—"Grady?"

"What is it now, Howard?"

"I dropped my"—*hic*—"my beer, Grady."

"Hey Howard?"

Something in Grady Oconnor's voice pulled my eyes to him. I realized that he had said *Haird*.

Grady Oconnor was holding a shovel in his hands.

"Yeah Grady?" Howard said. He hiccuped loudly, and seemed mesmerized by the thin stream of beer pulsing from his dropped can.

Darrell Jenkens started snoring.

"Darrell's"—*hic*—"snoring, Grady."

"Howard." *Haird.*

I wondered where Grady Oconnor had got the shovel, and then I wondered if that really mattered.

"Yeah Grady?" Between his laughter and beer-slurred hiccuping voice, Grady Oconnor's name came out sounding like a slightly diphthonged *Gray*.

"Howard," Grady Oconnor said, moving toward Howard Goertzen, the shovel in both his hands, "Howard, just once in your motherfucking honky cracker fish-white life, Howard, I want you to *shut the fuck up*."

Haird. Haird, Haird, Haird.

Grady Oconnor jammed the handle of the shovel into Howard Goertzen's stomach. Laughter, punctuated by a hiccup, segued abruptly into an oomph, and then Howard Goertzen joined Darrell Jenkens and me in the vomit club, and through it all the fence produced a long protesting squeak and the hogs jumped and jostled and squealed.

Grady Oconnor rammed Howard Goertzen's stomach again, and this time the only sound came from the fence and the hogs. The fence didn't squeak, though: the top rail cracked and then, with a splintering noise, it broke under the weight of Howard Goertzen's ass. I saw Howard Goertzen's purple face as he fell backward into the hog pen, his mouth opening and closing but no sound coming out. He seemed to be chewing on air, and then his face disappeared as he fell the rest of the way into the pen.

The hogs were jumping about wildly now, the fence vibrating here and there where they bounced off it, and through their squeals I heard what sounded like tearing.

No sound came from Howard Goertzen, or from Grady Oconnor. Darrell Jenkens' snores had grown slightly louder.

The hogs' squealing took on a different tone now. It wasn't panicked as much as it was greedy. Some of the hogs seemed to have grown head and shoulders above the others, but then I realized they must be standing on Howard Goertzen.

After a long pause, Grady Oconnor walked over to the corrugated tin wall of the building and leaned the shovel slowly, quietly, against the wall. It stood there, next to another shovel, and a rake.

As Grady Oconnor walked back toward me where I still lay on the floor I heard, for the first time, another sound, and as it filled in another layer of space next to the sound of Grady Oconnor's footsteps and Darrell Jenkens' snores and the tearing of the hogs, I realized it had been there all along.

Grady Oconnor didn't meet my eyes when he bent over to pick me up. He struggled under my weight, heaved me onto his shoulder, nearly fell over. He didn't say anything, but his breath came hot and loud and fast.

Outside it was raining. The sound, I realized, had been the rain beating on the tin ceiling of the building.

"Sweet Jesus," Grady Oconnor said as he laid me in the back of his own truck. "Sweet Jesus."

He didn't seem to be talking to me.

6.13

Myra

I HAD TO FIGHT MY WAY THROUGH THE CROWD. PEOple was pressed together like they was in a basement watching a cockfight. The kitten Shelly Stadler held in her arms was yowling fit to wake the dead, but Lucy was louder. When I finally pushed my way to her I saw that she was standing in her own little space, her eyes closed and her hands balled in fists just like they'd been when she was born. Her white dress was dirty and one of her patent leather shoes was missing. Her mouth was open and one long scream was coming out of it. Every once in a while she stopped, heaved, gasped, and then she started up again. When I got to her I swept her up in my arms. Her mouth closed like a trapdoor, and she just kind of hung in my arms, shivering.

I felt everyone staring at me, waiting for me to ask the question.

What happened.

I waited until Lucy calmed down a little. I stroked her hair and her back and her arms.

"Lucy," I said, "what's the matter?"

She didn't answer me for a long time. I just kept stroking her hair and back and arms.

Finally she spoke.

"He touched me."

My blood ran cold. I didn't ask where. I didn't ask how. But I remember thinking that the little girl I held in my arms couldn't be my daughter.

"Who touched you, honey?"

Again she didn't answer for a long time. Again I just kept stroking her hair and back and arms. As if I could turn her back into Lucy.

I felt her shift in my arms. Her head turned, then her whole body. She spoke in a clear loud voice.

She spoke to the crowd.

"The white nigger," she said.

6.14

Cora

SIX O'CLOCK IN THE A.M. GRADY OCONNOR KNOCKING at my door. He had to knock twice and knock loud before I heard him through the drumble of raindrops and sleep swirling around my head. I wasn't even halfway through my first cup of coffee yet, which means that like *hearing* was a foreign concept to me, let alone something as complicated as opening the door, and Rosa'd gone back upstairs to get a shower in. I have to tell you that when I did finally hear somebody knocking at that hour my heart jumped right up into my throat and I raised the blind slowly and then I had to look at Grady Oconnor double because I thought, she did it again. She knew to close the blinds the night before.

Grady kinda sidewaysed in, and I was locking the door behind him before I realized I was doing it, *cha-thunk*, and the first thing I noticed was that Grady was carrying his cap in his hands and his clothes was dry but his hair was damp, which, at that hour, on half a cup of coffee, and with it raining outside, I couldn't make sense out of. Grady's head hung so low he coulda kicked it with his own feet, and I saw that he had on his newest and cleanest paira pants and a long-sleeved shirt with pearly snaps disappearing into the valley his shiny belt made in his belly. He wasn't dressed for the fields is what I'm saying. That was for sure.

"Why, Grady Oconnor," I said, "you look like you on your way to church."

"No ma'am," he said, and there was enough in the way he said them two words to make me catch my breath all over again.

When my chest had stopped fluttering I said, "Why don't you come on in, sit down. You a little early for breakfast but maybe I can fry you a egg?"

"I'm not hungry, ma'am."

"First off, you drop this ma'am business. And then you best tell me what's up."

Grady's hands like to rip his cap in half they was pulling on it so bad. "Kendall Hendricks got me going all the way down to Wichita today, to pick up parts for that new combine-a his. I done told him he shouldn'ta bought no International Harvester machine, they unreliable and you can't get no parts for them anywhere in a hundred miles." He put his cap down suddenly, pushed it away from him. "Thinking of making a day trip of it," he said. "Got me a buddy lives down to Wichita." He said, very slow, "Won't be back till at least tomorrow. Probably maybe Sunday. Probably."

While he spoke I poured him a cup of coffee. His hands shook so much that the cup rattled on the saucer like it was set on top of the washing machine. I couldn't do nothing bout his hands, so I put a couple-a napkins between his cup and saucer, and then, when it was quiet in the café, I said, "You got anything needs taken care of while you gone, Grady?"

He looked up at me then, with eyes that were shiny bright and scared. "Cora," he said, "you got to tell that man to get outta town. Just go. Never mind about no Rosemary Krebs or Lawman Brown or Lucy Robinson. Just tell him to get-*go*." He continued staring at me for a good long moment after he'd spoken, and then he jerked his head away and went back to staring at his coffee.

I took a drink of my own coffee. Sometimes Rosa put a little mocha syrup in the bottom of the cup, just a little, and she don't stir it in, so it settles down there and waits for me. What that means is that I don't taste it until I'm getting to the end of the cup of coffee, by which time she's usually in the shower. It suddenly flashed on me: Grady just come from the shower. That's why his hair was wet and his clothes was dry when he come in from the rain. That's what was so strange. Grady Oconnor always showered in the evening cause his momma Starling worked as a nurse's aide in the hospital down to Bigger Hill and she had to be in at 7 a.m., and then his daddy George always had a shower right after, before he went out to the fields, and there was barely enough hot water for two quick showers in that house and nowhere near enough for three, and I just knew in that way everybody knows everything about everyone else in a small town that Grady Oconnor always took his shower before he went to bed, and all the sudden I was scared again.

Now I tasted Rosa's mocha, a thick sweet chocolaty trail on my tongue, with thinner acidy streams of coffee on either side, and when, finally, the last of the sweetness had left my tongue, I said, "What happened, Grady?" and then I finished the cup of coffee Rosa'd made for me.

"Nothing's happened," he sorta whispered. "Not yet. But something's gonna. Something's gonna snap, something's just gonna go bang." He didn't say bang loud the way you might expect. He said it quiet: *bang*.

"Grady—"

"I was working with DuWayne Hicks last week, helping him move some cattle. You know how DuWayne's daddy Jim got that dog, that shepherd-lab mix with the floppy ears and kinda sloped hindquarters?

Well, that dog was acting a little ornery yesterday, singled out a calf and started nipping at it, nothing serious, nothing that a good swift kick in the you-know-where wouldn'ta fixed. But DuWayne, he just shot it. Didn't say nothing to me, didn't even shout at the dog first. He just shot it and left it in the ditch and when we got back to the house he told his daddy that the dog run out under the wheels of that man's funny jeep-type truck with the big grille in front."

"What you getting at, Gra—"

"With a *shotgun*, Cora. He shot that dog with a shotgun, at close range."

There were brown speckles at the bottom of my coffee cup, dark brown speckles of coffee grounds and light brown almost glittering speckles of caramelized mocha. Almost glittering, but not quite.

Grady was looking into the cup in his hands, and then he pushed back his chair and stood up. "I should get going. Long trip to Wichita."

"Sunday," I said back to him.

"Late," he said.

"Don't forget your umbrella."

"Ma'am?"

"Your clothes was dry when I let you in. Your clothes was dry but your hair was wet, so I figured you must have left a umbrella outside."

"Oh," Grady said. "Yes, ma'am."

I didn't bother to correct him, and I didn't stop him either when he pulled a dollar bill from his pocket and left it on the counter, and I didn't stop him when he walked to the door, unlocked it himself, and walked on outside. As soon as he was gone I run a sinkful of hot soapy water to wash them two coffee cups, and when I was done with that I took the bus tub full of salt and pepper and Tabasco shakers and set them on the tables for the breakfast crowd.

6.15

Myra

MY NAME IS ANGELA."

I was tucking Lucy into bed.

"I live in the most beautiful house in the world with my mother, who is a fairy princess. My father is an ogre who only comes out of the forest at night. He has seven arms and seven legs and seven eyes, and he is so ugly that my mother had to turn him into a candle. She lit him, and he burned up, and now we don't ever see him no more."

She slept with a smile on her face, and her left hand curled into a fist.

6.16

Divine

I FOUND HIM. IT WAS ABOUT FIVE IN THE MORNING, that time of the day when the moon and the sun are both in the sky. I was only just creeping outta bed, still stiff and sore and sneaking through the house, and I was thinking that Justin must be making little moony faces up in his garret when I got outside and saw him lying just inside the hedge.

When I first laid eyes on him I thought he was sleeping. "Well well well," I said out loud, "seems like Miss Thing *does* let her hair down every once in a while." But then I got up close and I saw a big bruise on his cheek. His eye was just starting to swell and turn black, and I figured they couldn'ta been beating on him more than two hours ago.

Then: "What the hell—"

The voice came from behind me, and I turned and saw Colin. How can I describe it? For a moment I was as happy as I'd ever been since Ratboy, because I believed he'd followed me, but the next minute he was charging across the yard in just a pair of running shorts, barefoot and wincing on the sharp wet rocks, and even as he shoved by me so hard that he knocked me to the ground I knew he'd just been waiting for me to leave so he could get up.

Then he was next to Justin. He kneeled down beside him, he took his head in his hands, stroked his hair, he *cried*, goddammit, he cried, even though Justin was waking up and it was clear that he wasn't hurt too bad. When Colin finally looked at me it was only to yell, "Don't just stand there, you idiot! Go get the car!"

6.17

Myra

ABOUT ALL I COULD DO AFTER MY FEET GOT FROSTBIT was sit. So I sat. Almost all I did was sit. Oh, I got up every once in a while, like when that box with what Lawman Brown thought was robin's eggs showed up, but mostly all I did was sit.

Blue nail polish. I told her it didn't match her dress but did she listen? Some things I will *not* take responsibility for.

It wasn't that I couldn't walk. I could walk. I could wobble and tipple-topple my way along, but I simply could *not* bear the sensation walking gave me, the tingle that started just below my knees and turned into this sort of eerie nothingness just above my feet. It was like my feet wasn't there, and when I walked I felt like I wasn't touching the earth, and it was *that* I couldn't take. Some people wanted to fly and they invented airplanes and space rockets and science fiction, but me, I was always happy enough to stand in one place and look just as far as the horizon let me see. Me, I was always a flat-earther. I believed that if you went far enough then you would indeed drop off the edge of the world, and after my feet went it felt like I was falling off that edge every time I stood up and took a step in any direction.

So I sat. I sat and rocked. Usually I thought about my Lucy, but sometimes, sometimes I thought about Rosemary Krebs, and, like I did with Lucy, I imagined her at a distant age, oh, seventeen I guess, I guess I made her Lucy's age, smoothed away the lines on her face and painted her hair black and injected a little bit of flesh into her titties and hips, and there she was, Rosemary Krebs, or whatever her last name was then, seventeen years old and as tiny as a nymphet, dressed always in a white dress like she later on bought for Lucy, and for some reason when I thought of this little girl Rosemary the one thing I thought of was her pregnant. Yes, I gave Rosemary Krebs a baby, and, I guess, a lover, I gave her hot sweating blushing cheeks and bloodstained sheets and a thousand sighs and gasps and tears, and then, every time, I took her baby away from her. I was her mother, the mother what said, I don't *think* so, little miss, and I sent that baby out into the world like a letter without a destinated or a return address, Moses in a basket of rushes, floating down the river.

It made it easier, that way. I could almost forgive her, that way, for taking Lucy away from me. Cause she did: even the Lucy I held in my head, the shiny little girl who memorized "Swanee River" when she was just five years old, that little girl was Rosemary Krebs' more than she was mine. Rosemary Krebs took her from me with dresses and candy and big promises. She stood her on the highest hill between here and Kenosha and said, Everything you see will be yours. She nurtured the greedy soul that lived inside Lucy just like it lives inside everyone, you, me, and every eleven, twelve, thirteen-year-old girl with no daddy and a mother with nothing more to offer than a drinking problem and a little savings account that'll maybe see her through two years at a community college, which as someone once told me is just about enough education to teach you what you don't know and don't have and never will. Rosemary Krebs nurtured that greedy soul in Lucy until it took her over, grew up in her and ate her up, and all I could think of sometimes as I rocked and rocked was one of those freaky tomatoes or pumpkins or cucumbers you see at the State Fair down to Hutchinson, mutant vegetables grown up as big as a house, and what you always see is their grower standing by them with a blue ribbon and a proud smile of ownership, but what you never hear of is anyone actually *eating* these vegetables, making a thousand gallons of spaghetti sauce, or a pumpkin pie the size of a wagon wheel, or just a plain old salad, tossed in a swimming pool and served with a couple-a rowboat oars.

6.18

Colin

DIVINE SULKED IN A CORNER OF THE WAITING ROOM. I felt a pang of regret for the way I'd barked at him earlier, but before I could say anything Webbie and Wade burst through the doors.

"Just bruises," I said. "One cracked rib."

"Who did it?" Webbie said.

I shrugged.

"Was it—"

"No," I said.

"How do you know?" Wade said. There was concern in his voice. There was also aggression.

"I know," I said. And then I added, "After six years, I know."

"Is he awake?" Webbie said quickly. "I want to see him."

"See what? See his bruises? Let him rest."

"I just want him to know we're here," she said. "In case he needs anything."

"Needs what?" I said. "He's in a hospital."

"Now look here, Colin—" Wade began, but Webbie cut him off.

"Don't," she said. "Just don't." She put a hand on Wade's shoulder and pulled him toward the door. He held back for a moment, looking at me intently, challenging me. I was about to take up his challenge when I noticed there was paint on him, not just on the clothes he'd thrown on but on his skin, and I remembered I had seen the same paint on Justin this morning, on his skin as well, as well as on his clothes, and I turned from Wade and walked quickly to Divine and put my hand on his shoulder.

Wade spoke again.

"Do you even *know* what you're doing here?" he said.

I turned. I left my hand on Divine's shoulder, and turned to Wade. He was standing in the doorway of the waiting room. Webbie stood just behind him. There was about Wade the air of a man who wanted to play a trump card, or make a revelation, or hurt me.

He definitely wanted to hurt me.

Divine's shoulder was warm under mine, and loose. I kneaded it, back and forth.

"Do I know what I'm doing here?"

"In Galatea," Wade said.

"In Galatia."

"Do you know how you *found* this place?"

"I found this place because Yonah told me about it. He told me it was interesting."

"Yonah didn't send you here because Galatea is interesting."

"Galatea isn't interesting?"

"Ga*la*tia," Divine said softly. I noticed that his shoulder was tight now, and warmer than it had been. Hot.

"Yonah sent you here to find out what I was doing."

"What *are* you doing?"

"Yonah sent you here to find out if I was *painting*."

I smiled. "Are you painting?"

"If Yonah sent you here," Wade said, his voice rising with frustration, "it means that he probably didn't even like you."

"Ah," I said. "Yonah *didn't* like me."

Wade blinked. "Yonah didn't like you?"

"Yonah didn't like me."

"Wade," Webbie said.

"You're hurting my shoulder," Divine said.

I let go of Divine's shoulder.

"Yonah liked Justin," I said.

Divine put my hand back on his shoulder.

"Yonah liked Justin," Wade said.

I began to knead Divine's shoulder again.

"Yonah thought *you* would like Justin."

"I like Justin."

I smiled again. "Yonah was right."

Webbie pushed Wade out of the doorway and re-entered the room. She looked from me to Wade, and then she looked, briefly, at Divine, and then she looked back at me.

"Are you two finished now? Are you quite finished?"

It was this point that Divine started laughing.

"Webbie's upset," he said.

Webbie started to say something but Divine cut her off.

"Webbie's *jealous*."

"Webbie's jealous?" Wade said.

Divine squeezed the wrist of the hand that was squeezing his shoulder. His fingernails dug into my skin.

"Cause no one ain't fighting over *her*. That's why Webbie jealous. Cause she all *alone*."

There was silence after Divine spoke, an awful, an unbearable silence, and I said again, "Yonah liked Justin." I said, "He liked him, he said, because he had nothing to fear from him."

6.19

Myra

THERE WAS A LOT OF MOMENTUM AND CONFUSION AFter Lucy spoke. You'd expect there would be. The air was thick with dust, and people was pushing and shoving at each other as if Eric Johnson might turn out to be one of them.

But in my arms Lucy didn't move. Her body was rigid, her stare fixed. I let my eyes follow hers.

Lucy was looking at Stan.

People were calling out for guns and knives and ropes and tripping over each other in their haste to get on with things, but Stan stood as still as Lucy, and stared back into her eyes.

He touched me.

The white nigger.

Stan blinked, and saw me looking at him, and he blinked again, and then, like the others, he was gone.

6.20

Thelma Goertzen

THERE WAS A SHOT IN THE MORNING AIR AND THEN

the rooster crowed and then there was another shot. There was sausage on the stove but I turned it off and ran outside and there was another shot. There was mud and puddles in the yard and another shot and the rooster crowed again and the hogs was still in the night barn and screaming and then there was another shot. There was Lyle in the night barn and five dead hogs in the pen and another shot and six and a vibration that like to knock me down and the hogs screaming and the dust and the semiautomatic .22 rifle with the twenty-round clip and the two spare clips in Lyle's pocket and another shot and seven and the vibration and there was blood coming out of Lyle's ears and the yard and the mud and the puddles and the phone in the kitchen and Nettie Ferguson and Lawman Brown and another shot and the puddles and the mud and the yard and another shot and too many dead hogs to count and piles of something brown and chunky on the cement floor beer cans another shot the brown was vomit and the beer cans was only two and the dead hogs too many to count and the screams and another shot and the vibration and the blood coming from Lyle's ears and Howard nowhere around and then but then and then there was Howard's boots in the hog pen and the dead hogs and another shot and the screams and another shot and the screams and another shot and the vibration that did knock me off my feet and the blood on Lyle's blue-shaved cheek and shirt collar and another shot and Howard's boots in the hog pen and another shot and there was something holding Howard's boots together. There was another shot. There was Howard's boots and there was Howard's boots and there was Howard's boots still laced up to the ankle and there was something holding them together and there was another shot and the vibration and the silent fall of a clip to the ground and the silent snap of another clip into place and another shot and Howard's boots and Lyle's blood and something warm on my neck and the sight and smoke and jerk of another shot and another shot and another shot and the dead hogs and the live hogs and Lyle's blood and Howard's boots and another shot and the vomit and the beer cans and another shot and then there was no live hogs and no sound and Lyle never even turned to look at me and Howard's boots and Lyle's gun and Lyle's mouth and Lyle's gun and then there was another shot.

6.21

Myra

THE DAY AFTER LUCY WAS BORN A NURSE COME INTO my room and said she wanted to apologize to me. She said they'd just changed the lightbulb in Labor and Delivery, they was right in the middle of the operation when I come in. She said I was already at eleven and a half and there wasn't no time to put the cover back on the light.

One of them industrial strength fluorescent coils, she said the light was.

She said the way I stared at that light it musta burned holes right in my eyes.

6.22

Wade

THE SIGHT OF THE WAITING ROOM, WITH ITS GLASS-enclosed posters of meadows, strong fathers, smiling mothers, safe infants, all given brutal prominence by pulsing and humming fluorescent lights, had almost undone me. Thank God Webbie was there, or I think Colin and I would have brawled. Afterward, though, after we left, I felt strange and excited, elated almost, but then I was just as suddenly tired, exhausted, as the adrenaline rush seeped out of my body. For the first time in months I didn't paint, but went instead, as soon as I got home, back to bed, and I stayed there all day.

But the next day I painted. There was nothing else to do: I couldn't exactly call Justin to see how he was, or pay a visit to him. I couldn't call Webbie either. At one point during the drive home she called Colin "that fucking cueball cracker faggot from New York City," and we shared a laugh, and then she asked me, quietly, why I wasn't looking for Lucy Robinson, but I don't think she liked my answer, and after that we drove on in silence. So: my studio.

My hand shook so badly that I began wondering if I could find a way to incorporate this stutter stroke onto the canvas, but before I could resolve the dilemma I heard a creak on the floorboard behind me. I turned; it was Justin.

He wore a tank top and shorts. It was what he wore most summer days, but today his bare skin was dappled with blue and purple and black bruises that were almost obscenely pretty. I wanted to embrace him but the bruises held me in check. I stammered a hello, and I almost imagined that he answered. But he only turned around, and I followed his slightly limping form to what used to be Divine's room. He waited while I unlocked the door, and then he shucked his shirt and shorts and walked—already barefoot, I noticed then, his feet unbruised but nevertheless painted black by three miles of rain-dampened roads—to the middle of the room, and lowered himself carefully to the floor. His limbs were as clear and distinct as pencil lines; drawing them seemed almost beside the point. Still, he sat there, obviously waiting, and, for the first time, he didn't close his eyes.

6.23

Myra

THE DOCTOR THAT COME UP FROM BIGGER HILL wasn't a regular pediatrician. He asked me to leave the room while he looked at Lucy, but I wouldn't.

I pulled Lucy's one shoe and her tights and panties off myself.

She just lay there while the doctor lifted up her dress and opened her legs and turned her from one side to the other.

He held one of those little penlights.

Both his hands were busy, so he held it in his mouth.

For the first time I looked at the line between my daughter's legs like I looked at my own: as something that men would take a interest in. I suppose I'd thought she was too young to be a woman yet, too young to be a girl even. I'd thought she was only a child, but now I realize: boys learn how to be boys, but girls are *born* that way.

I was still holding Lucy's shoe in my hand, and I used my shirttail to rub the dirt off it.

The doctor was quick and a little rough, which later on I decided was probably better than nice but slow.

When he was finished he took the light outta his mouth. He licked a line of drool from his lips and said that there didn't appear to have been any recent penetration.

He asked me if there was any need to examine her from the other side. It took me a moment to figure out what he meant—it took me a moment to get past the word *recent*—and then I just shook my head no.

With my permission he gave Lucy something to help her sleep.

He never once asked me where my husband was.

My husband who was tying Eric Johnson to a tree.

6.24

Webbie

I SAW HIM COMING DOWN THE ROAD. HE WALKED slowly, with a bit of a limp, and at first I thought he was naked. But he was only carrying his shirt, and his khaki shorts were as dirty as his skin was tanned. A crescent of a bruise still ringed his eye, a small lump bubbled at the base of his rib cage, and, though it pained me to see these marks on him, I think that if they hadn't been there I would have run away from him, because, as he approached, he seemed the most inviolable person I had ever encountered, not so much a person as a walking skin, a single solid uninterrupted expanse with no way in or out. It was the mouth, of course, the mouth that was always closed.

But I didn't run away; instead, I linked my arm through his and fell in step with him. "I think I've been looking for you," I said. "If you don't mind, I'd like to show you something." I felt the muscles of his arm shiver just a little, but he didn't resist. That didn't mean anything: he never resisted. "You're tan," I said then, trying to relax him. I touched his shoulder. "It looks good on you." We walked slowly; I steered us toward town, toward Galatia—the real Galatia, my father's Galatia. "I used to sunbathe when I was a kid. I had to do it away from home because the Reverend thought a bathing suit was inappropriate attire for a young lady, but I used to end up black as a plum." I paused. Every time I paused I waited for him to say something. I knew he wouldn't but it just seemed absurd, the two of us walking along, only one of us talking. We had had such wonderful conversations together.

Then my pause had gone on too long, and I didn't know how to restart the conversation. Conversation: I allowed myself to chuckle, but said nothing, and we walked into Galatia in silence. The warmth and weight of Justin's arm on mine made me conscious not just of him but of the town around me. Its typical torpor had deepened into something else, something subdued, repressed really. There were no cars on the road, absolutely none, no one tending a lawn or hanging out the washing; though summer vacation had started almost a month ago, I didn't see any children or even hear the sounds of their play; the Founders' Day picnic was only a few weeks away, but there had been no preparation so far, no decorations, no flyers requesting donations of food or drink. There were four or five newly empty houses, and their vacancies seemed to have tipped the balance against Galatia. Real estate signs, whimsical to the point of absurdity, swayed in the hot afternoon breeze. The words on the signs read FOR SALE but their creaks and rattles said, *Gone.*

In the park it was suddenly cooler, and I heard myself breathe an *aaah.* The thick air of dissolution and abandonment didn't quite penetrate here: the grass beneath the willows was as thick and green as it ever was, the occasional patches of bare soil damp and sticky on the soles of my shoes. Justin slipped his arm from mine and wandered a few feet away from me. His face wore a dazed expression, but there was a small smile on his lips as he walked beneath the dangling lines of the willows. He stretched his arms out and the strands slipped over them lightly as he walked. His feet made squelching noises in the mud. His shirt slipped from the waistband of his shorts and fell to the ground behind him, but he didn't seem to notice.

"Justin," I said, and he turned suddenly. His eyes were fixed on mine, his arms still stretched out. His mouth was still closed. I started to point out his shirt but the sight of his mouth stopped me. And then, I don't know why, but some perversity moved me to say, "I used to hate this park. I only came here when the Reverend sent me, when I was going to be punished. He used to make me pick my own switches from these trees. But—" I stopped suddenly, lowered my eyes from Justin's fixed stare. I continued speaking, looking at his feet. "But when I came back to take care of him, that all changed. I realized that he couldn't switch me no more. Anymore. Now I love it here. I come here all the time. I find it all the more beautiful, for being a reclaimed, a reprieved place."

I looked up at him again. His arms had lowered slightly, not as if from fatigue, but from age, in the same way that an old barn begins to sag with age. "Oh, Justin," I said, "Justin, he's alive. Eric Johnson is alive. Do you know who Eric Johnson is, Justin? You know, I know you do. Myra told you. He's alive, Justin, he didn't die on that tree. He fell off, Justin. He—" I dug into my pocket. "Justin," I said, "these are his thumbs."

I heard my words in my ears, and almost laughed at their absurdity. *These are his thumbs.*

A ray of sunlight mercilessly made its way through the willow's foliage. It found the bag in my outstretched hand, glinting off it, rendering its contents invisible. It looked like a bag of drugs.

As I'd spoken Justin's arms had fallen, slowly, then more rapidly. As I'd finished they'd tapped slightly, inaudibly, against his sides. His head fell a little, his back bowed. The lump beneath his rib cage bubbled like something ready to burst. Without looking at me again, he turned and began to walk away.

"Justin," I called. "Justin, please, I'm sorry."

The mud pulled at his feet, but he continued walking. The water table was so high that puddles formed in his footprints, and it looked as though he were walking on water.

"Justin, please, I don't know why I told you. Please. I won't bring it up again."

He was in the sunlight now. I saw for the first time another bruise, on his thigh. It didn't seem like the mark of an attacker, but a lover. I remembered Wallace then, and my arm, which had been extended, fell to my side.

"Justin," I tried one last time. "I just needed someone to talk to. Not to answer me," I said, though by this time he was out of earshot. "Just to talk to."

I watched him until he turned a corner. After he was gone his abandoned shirt caught my eye, and I put my parcel back in my pocket and retrieved the shirt from the mud. I looked at it blankly for a moment, and then I carried it to the well to wash the mud from it.

The tank water was dark and laced with moss, but it smelled clean and fresh, and I dropped the shirt into it. A glint distracted me. I thought it was a goldfish at first, but then I realized it was just a little thing, a stoppered vial, and I fished it out. The shirt unrolled itself and settled to the bottom of the tank. The vial was partially filled with pink liquid.

When I was in graduate school the last boy I'd dated had been called Karl Louis. He was white, not black, a scholar rather than a sprinter, with a soft pale belly covered in coarse hair and big book-grasping page-turning hands that handled my body in the same straightforward manner. He would stroke my hair, he would pull my clothes off, he would fondle me, face first, then neck, then breasts, stomach, and vagina: one thing always led to another with Karl, and when his hands had arrived at their destination he would part my thighs and enter me. There was no place for the detour of contraception in this plan, no condom or diaphragm, and the pill made me ill; inevitably, I suppose, I missed a period, and then another. Perhaps if it had happened while Karl was still at school things would have turned out differently. But he had, like me, just passed his orals, and he was taking a two-year appointment in Edinburgh where he also planned to complete his Ph.D. on an obscure Scottish poet. I should remember the poet's name, but I do not.

The design hadn't really changed in a decade: someone in Galatia was pregnant. I chuckled; I forgot about Justin's shirt. I walked home with the vial in my hand, and it was only when I reached into my pocket for my keys and my hand brushed against the slick plastic package that contained Eric Johnson's thumbs that I realized *who* was going to have a baby.

6.25

Myra

THE MEN TRIED TO FIGHT THE FIRE WITH BUCKETS AND sandbags and long lines of garden hoses from houses just outside of town, but the women and children seemed to know that the war was over as soon as it started.

Kenosha was gone.

We watched it burn, a long thin line of mothers, daughters, sisters, nieces standing just beyond the western curve of town.

There wasn't much of a wind, but what wind was blowing blew due east.

For the first time in my life I understood the expression "up in smoke." People's lives—their houses and cars and clothes and furniture and geraniums and life savings, and half a dozen souls—floated up into the air in flakes of gray ash and a cloud so thin that it almost didn't seem dangerous.

A half dozen dogs ran in and out of people's legs, barking and crying and carrying on. Something about that fire drove those dogs crazy, and one by one they took off over the fields. To the best of my knowledge they was never seen again.

Except for one.

One dog, it looked like a yellow lab although its fur had been burnt almost black, this one dog kept on skirting around the edge of town. It stayed halfway between the people and the burning buildings.

Some children, I remember, kept calling the dog. "Here, Boner, here, Boner," they pleaded, and at the time all I thought was, What an *awful* name for a dog.

The dog whined and growled, turned its head from the fire to the children and back again. It lay down, stood up. Froth dripped from its mouth like it had rabies.

"Here, Boner," the kids called, "c'mon, boy."

Even a few hundred feet away the heat of the fire felt worse than the worst sunburn you ever had.

The dog vomited, then ate what come up. It looked at the children, barked at them, not in warning, it seemed, but in invitation.

And then it ran into the fire.

The children screamed, and one little girl even darted after it. A woman lunged forward, grabbed the girl by her ponytail, pulled the both of them to the ground.

When that woman grabbed her daughter I had a hot flash all over my body, a flash of that hot air, the air that held me all over like a lover—and like a mother, I realized—and it's that woman's hand I feel now, and the hair in her grasp, when I think of Lucy.

I remember Stan found me later on and he kind of looked me up and down and he said, You okay? and I said, I'm okay, considering. He said, Considering that we lost everything? and I was remembering that mother's hold on her daughter's hair when I said, We didn't have nothing to lose. Not really, I said. Not yet.

6.26

Wade

ASLEEP, JUSTIN'S STILLNESS DISAPPEARED. HE TWITCHED, he shivered, he rolled from side to side, consumed by nightmares that seemed to thunder through his entire body. But if I touched him, the part of him that I touched would stop moving: my hand on his arm would still that arm, my hand on his head would still his head. But the rest of him remained in motion. He was like a snake, run over by a car, its crushed head stuck to the asphalt but its tail twitching furiously. It was as though the pieces of his body were no longer connected—as if, in his dreams, he was dismembering himself. Sometimes I wanted to know what haunted his sleep but usually I did not, for fear that it would invade mine.

My dreams were already full of invaders. My dreams were full of me, and a man named Yonah Schimmel. My dreams were full of people who did not exist anymore.

The concept of time has never meant much to me under the best of circumstances, and these could hardly be labeled the best of circumstances. Why *not* slip back into the past or forward into the future, why not slip sideways into a past that never existed? Why not? Because I could not.

Memory is like a river; remembering is like swimming. For some people it is like floating. For Myra Robinson it was like floating, a never-ending buoyancy that replaced the need for firmer, sterner ground. For others—for Justin—it was like drowning, a sinking so deep that the water became all, and, in becoming all, became nothing. But for most of us, for me and Divine and Webbie Greeving, it was simply like swimming, a harder or easier task depending upon one's condition, one's conditioning. For me, swimming had always been laborious, and I would never venture out except in the calmest water. Suffice it to say that that water, that river, the river in which lurked my memories of Yonah Schimmel, was not at all calm, and, though I wanted to swim further, I could only make my way to the point at which I felt the current's pull, its offer of floating, of drowning. I *wanted* to feel it but I didn't want to give in to it: I didn't want to drown or to float; I didn't even want to swim. I suppose you could say that I only wanted to wade.

It's not that I want to hide things from you, or even from myself. There is, in fact, nothing to hide. Or, put another way, there is nothing to tell. Once, a quarter century ago, I spent the better part of two years sleeping next to someone who slept as Justin slept, with uneasy dreams played out upon his twitching limbs, limbs which I stilled with my own nervous hands.

In one version of our meeting, Yonah said that I entered his gallery: I went in looking for a lover, he said, and I came out with a dealer. In fact I did not come out.

In another version of our meeting Yonah had me crawling around on all fours at a pornographic theater, wide open at front and back for whatever would enter me, desperate, he said, crying out to be filled. But in that version Yonah did not mention nor did he even seem to realize that he was the one who filled me.

In my favorite version of our meeting, Yonah said that he was walking by my studio one summer night and he noticed me painting through the open windows, and he stepped back and saw me painting under artificial lights and he . . .

At that point in the telling he was distracted, and so I never learned what he did and I never learned how we met. At any rate I never once painted at night.

The first time that Justin spent the night beside me I sat up and watched him sleep. I sat up and I watched him and I used my hands to still his twitching parts as I had once used them to still Yonah's, and at some point I found myself using my finger to trace imaginary drawings on his body, but I never once painted at night.

It was always the meeting that mattered to Yonah, never what came after, never what came at the end. I never heard Yonah tell stories of our parting, of that disastrous morning after when *I* tried to fuck *him*. To the best of my knowledge he never told any.

I have made those stories up myself. Over the years I have made up many different stories from the same events, and, like Colin Nieman, I have recorded more than a few versions of these stories. But, as things stand now, one version rises above the rest.

Gone away.

Not for you.

6.27

Myra

MY NAME IS ANGELA. I LIVE IN THE MOST BEAUTIFUL house in the world with my mother, a fairy princess who gave me a magic pony named Blue. Blue's hooves are the color of turquoise and his eyes are the color of the hottest part of a flame; his body is the color of the ocean and his mane and tail are the color of the sky. When I ride him I use neither saddle nor bridle, trusting to the steadiness of his girth between my legs and his neck between my arms, and to my mother, who would never give me a present that would hurt me. One morning I woke up and the sun was shining through the windows in all four walls of my room, and I thought, What a beautiful day for a ride! and I put on my Wednesday white dress and I went to Blue's bedroom. Blue was already awake and awaiting me, and I hopped up on him and we jumped out the window and were off. Blue ran and ran and ran, and his mane flipped about my eyes like clouds. I heard his hooves far below me, clattering with the sound of a speeding train, plop-plopping like frogs' bodies into a pond, tinkling like breaking glass, and we rode on and on, past forests and rivers and mountains, until Blue started running so fast I could see nothing but his mane in my eyes, and then I closed my eyes and just concentrated on the movement of my pony's body working beneath mine, and when I opened my eyes it was dark, so dark, and then I was frightened. But Blue had been a gift from my mother, and he told me not to be afraid. I felt his body turn beneath mine, and he told me that he would get me home, and when he stopped speaking I realized his hooves were making no sound at all, and I looked down and saw only stars far below us, but Blue told me it was only a lake, reflecting the bottom of the sky. Then I grew cold in the dark, but Blue's mane wrapped about me like the warmest blanket, and he ran and ran and ran through the night until suddenly we were in a forest of tree trunks so tall and so black that even their shadows were solid and had to be dodged, but Blue's mane was warm around my body and even twisting and turning to avoid the trees and their shadows his gait was smooth as pond water on a windless day, and I found that I was excited and no longer afraid. In front of me I saw a glow, and I thought perhaps it was Blue's eyes, lighting our way, but I peeked ahead and saw that it was the lights of our house, and then we were out of the forest and jumping back through the window of Blue's bedroom and landing in his soft straw bed. I rubbed Blue all over with a coarse cloth, wiping the sweat from his ears and flanks and sorting the burrs from his tail, and then I gave him a kiss between his glowing eyes and rushed back to bed. The sun was streaming full through the windows, and I had only just slipped under the blankets when the door opened and my mother came in, and smiled, and kissed me, and ran her fingers through my hair. When they came away I saw that they were threaded with a single blue strand, and we both looked at it, and laughed, and even as my mother braided the strand into a necklace for me she asked me *Was I going to stay in bed all day?*

6.28

Webbie

ROSEMARY KREBS HAD TOLD ME THAT THE KEY SHE gave me only worked on the back door of her house, but it worked on the front door as well. I had merely never tried it; but when I went to her house to return the handkerchief that Eric Johnson's thumbs had been wrapped in, I went to the front door, because I had also gone there to quit. I had meant to knock, but then, on impulse, I took my key from my pocket and tried it in the door, and, of course, it worked.

She was waiting for me on the other side of the door. She looked me up and down in my street clothes, and then she said, "You're fired."

I dumped my uniform at her feet. "I already quit," I said. I held out the handkerchief Eric Johnson's thumbs had been wrapped in. It was empty now, and stained, and slightly stiff. "I think this belongs to you."

Rosemary Krebs did not look at the handkerchief. "One day, Miss Greeving, you will realize that the true privilege of possession is being able to refuse what is rightfully yours."

She stepped back then, and I started to step in, but she closed the door in my face.

6.29

Myra

WHEN HE COME HOME THAT NIGHT HIS CLOTHES WAS soaked through with sweat and he stunk like a man with a night's sleep on him after a long day fucking some other woman. I'd say that my stomach was in my mouth, but it couldn't have gotten past my heart, which was in my throat.

I sat at the table with Lucy's shiny shoe in front of me.

Stan come in and closed the door behind him. His chest was moving up and down. Then he spoke.

"She lost a shoe too?"

"She lost a shoe."

"It don't matter, I guess. Mrs. Krebs'll buy her another pair."

"She don't need to."

"Well, I guess we can buy our own daughter shoes."

I shook my head. "This is her lost shoe."

Stan didn't say nothing.

"She's wearing her other shoe."

Stan still didn't say nothing.

"She wanted to wear it to bed. A clean white dress, and her one black shoe."

Stan spoke. "I don't understand," he said.

"She wanted to wear her shoe to bed."

"But she lost—"

"*This* is her lost shoe."

"I don't under—"

"*This* is the lost shoe. I found it in the dirty clothes hamper."

"Myra," Stan said, "what are you trying to say?"

"I'm just saying," I said. "Nobody didn't find it in the street. Nobody found it in *Galatia*. It was in the dirty clothes hamper, all wrapped up in a towel."

"You—"

"I was washing her dress."

"You was washing her dress."

"And I found her shoe."

There was a long pause. Then:

"I still don't understand."

"No, Stan," I said, "no, Stan, I expect you don't. I expect the whereabouts of your daughter's supposedly missing shoe mean nothing to you, or the smell of beer on your daughter's dress, or the fact that you got a stink on you, a stink on you, Stan, and I gotta tell you that you make me *sick*."

"Myra—"

"I can't even bring myself to say it, Stan. I can't make my mouth form the *words*."

"Myra, *I don't understand*."

"Don't tell me you don't understand. You don't *want* to understand."

"No, I don't—"

"You don't want *me* to understand. Well I think I understand plenty." I stood up. I clutched Lucy's shoe in my hand. "And I think you understand a lot more than I do." For the first time I let myself look him in the eye. "Cause if you didn't understand I suppose you'd break my jaw. I suppose that's what any decent man would do in your position."

"Is that what you want, Myra? A beating? You want me to break your jaw?"

"Yeah, Stan, that's what I want. I want you to beat the truth out of me."

I stood there, holding Lucy's shoe. Stan stood, still sweating, still putting out stink. Finally I spoke.

"I'm going to bed."

Stan showered before coming in, and he put on a T-shirt and a pair of undershorts before climbing in beside me.

Proof, if you ask me, what more proof do you need.

I turned my back to him. I held Lucy's shoe to my chest.

Angela.

I was beginning to see the need for an Angela.

In the middle of the night the phone rang. I remember hearing it and thinking, This is what I've been waiting for. Stan took the call in the other room, and after he hung up he got dressed and then he went out again.

That's when they finished what they'd started.

That's when they killed the boy.

6.30

Colin

I WAS LOST. I WAS TRAPPED INSIDE THE RETAINING wall of a lost city, a Troy, a Pompeii, a Babylon—and then a shout pierced the night. Again. It was unintelligible. It was, perhaps, not even a word, but it came from above me, and to me, in any language, it could only have been my name. I leaped from bed, surprised to see my naked body beneath my head; behind me, Divine's sleepy voice murmured, "Baby?" The door of the cupola was locked and solid, and all I could do was pound against it. "Justin!" I yelled, but the door yielded only silence. I stopped hitting the door with my hand then, and instead laid my head against it, and it was only when I felt the cold coarse grain of the door's wood against the top of my head that I saw the muddy footprints on the stairs, huge footprints, the size and shape of paddles or propellers, one track of footprints only, and that track led down the stairs, and I started pounding on the door again, but the door returned nothing to me except the sound of my own voice.

6.31

Myra

THE NEXT MORNING WHEN I WENT INTO LUCY'S ROOM and said *Lucy honey it's time to wake up* she stretched out her arms and legs like she was some sweet little princess, she smiled bright and she said *My name is Angela.* Well I kind of lost it. I drug her out of bed by her hair and I ripped that one shoe and that wrinkled white dress off her and I threw her into the bathroom and washed out her mouth with soap and I said to her *If I ever hear of Angela again!* Then I burned all seven white dresses in the back yard, and that one shoe, and I said *From now on Lucy's clothes'll have to do. And Lucy's name. For Lucy.*

Afterwards I put the shoe from the dirty clothes hamper into the cedar chest with the stone she was born holding and her first lock of hair and her first lost tooth and the pink blanket my mother started knitting the night she was born.

That's what Stan took with him when he took off next year.

One stone.

One tooth.

One blanket.

And one black shoe.

He left the hair behind, scattered around the bottom of the chest. Like a lot of brunettes Lucy was born blond and it was only later that her hair went dark, and I suppose Stan thought it was just loose packing material.

And Lucy. He left Lucy behind too. Sawyer Johnson took off at the same time Stan did, leaving Cora alone with their baby, just like Stan did with me and Lucy. One time when I was out walking with Lucy I walked past Cora Johnson walking with her son, and neither of us stopped and said hi-lo or waved or even looked at each other.

Proof, I tell you. What more proof do you need?

The way I see it only two people could've put that shoe in the hamper: Lucy or Stan. You tell me which is worse.

And I'll tell you this: Lucy never once asked where did Stan go. And neither did I.

Cause nobody asks questions like that in Galatea. Cause all those questions, *Where did* and *Who said* and *What about* always lead back to the one big question *Why*, and nobody around here even pretends to know the answer to that one. Or to want to know.

Sometimes it's okay, not knowing if you're right. At least you don't know you're wrong. Colin said it's in the space between those two sentences that every writer tells his story, and I said Okay, yeah, I get it, but what I think now is that's not the truth. What I think now is there's no point in telling lies, unless you actually believe what you're saying, and I tell you what: I believe it all.

7

7.01

T. V. Daniels

IT WAS ONE OF THOSE FRIDAY NIGHTS WHEN THE ACtual effort of getting out of his clothes and the dim premonitory fear of the effort it would take to get back into them in the morning was simply too much for him to confront, and so he lowered himself, still fully dressed, onto the stack of five flattened mattresses that he used for a bed, and fell asleep. In the morning he ate the first strips of bacon straight from the pan, before they were fully cooked; it was something he had done so many times before that he only gave each forkful of bacon a single shake to get the grease off it before stuffing it in his mouth. When the bacon was gone he cracked a dozen eggs into the pan, and he swirled the whole mess around until it reached the consistency and color of curdled café con leche—the color came from the half inch of bacon grease—at which point he began to eat the mixture straight out of the skillet. The last bits of egg were crispy filaments, like burned spiderwebs, and they crunched between his teeth but refused to actually break up, so he washed them down with a gallon of milk.

He did not drink coffee, because coffee upset his stomach.

After he had eaten he went to the bathroom and he opened his shirt and pants but didn't peel them off, and he swathed his underarms and genitals with a roll-on antiperspirant and deodorant and then he refastened his clothes. He shaved by touch—he had taken all the mirrors out of the house after his mother died last spring—and then he combed his hair straight back from his forehead, and then he gargled. He poured himself a cup full of Listerine and swirled it around in his mouth while he counted silently and slowly to one hundred, and then he swallowed the Listerine. The Listerine gave him a hot tingling buzz in his toes and fingertips, which made the effort of retying his left shoelace almost surreal—he hadn't taken his shoes off last night, but the left one had come untied—and at the last he gave up on a bow and just knotted the fuckers, and then he drove the two blocks to the post office to pick up the mail for the morning delivery. He didn't treat the mail he sent any different from the mail he received, didn't sort it out or deliver it first or last; he put it in his box when he got to it on his route, and so it wasn't until lunchtime that he discovered Divine's sideview mirror in his mailbox.

Even before he opened the flap he knew something was there, because the red flag was up and he hadn't put any mail out that morning. He didn't treat his own mail any different than anyone else's, and when he had a letter to mail he put it in his box and put the red flag up so that he'd know to pick it up on his morning rounds.

He knew it was Divine's sideview mirror, because Divine's driver's-side door was what he generally looked at when he ran into Divine out to Sloppy Joe's, and even a year after it had broken off he remembered what the mirror had looked like, and that it was gone.

It never occurred to him that Divine might have put the mirror in his mailbox.

He put the mirror on the seat beside him with the glass facing away from him, and for the rest of the day the mirror caught the sunlight and cast a shadow which slowly wandered the hull of his U.S.P.S. delivery vehicle. There was nothing unusual about the reflection—it was solid, its outline smooth and oval—and it wasn't until the end of the day, when he picked the mirror up to take it into his house, that he accidentally caught a glimpse of the glass, and he saw three things. He saw first of all that it was cracked, and then he saw that his own face was simply too wide to fit within the glass's borders, and then he saw with almost unnatural clarity four fully formed fingerprints, and after a long look at his bisected, dissected, blurred profile, he wiped the mirror off on his stomach and, chuckling quietly, waddled into his house. Normally on a Saturday evening he made a point of drawing all the curtains and taking off his clothes and washing them and himself; normally he remained naked until Monday morning, and he took his meals in bed, holding his food in the serving platter–sized depression that formed at the intersection of his sternum and breasts whenever he was lying down, but that night he kept his clothes on, because he would not be staying in all day tomorrow. He would be going out. It occurred to him that he would have had to forgo that pleasure anyway, because tomorrow was the Founders' Day picnic, but tell you the truth he'd been thinking of skipping the picnic anyway, because he didn't really like to eat in public anymore.

Like everyone else in town, he supposed that he knew something needed doing. But it wasn't until he looked at the part of his face he could see in the cracked sideview mirror that'd come off Divine's car that he realized he was the one to do it. How about that?

7.02

Wade

SUNDAY MORNING.

Seven a.m.

Founders' Day.

I walked that morning, as I walked every morning, from the house I had built to the house my parents had built. A tang of smoke limned the air, an invisible but savory trail that made my mouth water. It was the smell of barbecuing pork, seeping out of its closed pit and making its way to my house over two miles away. Or it was my imagination, which seems just as likely an option, given that the smoke would have had to drift against the wind to get here.

The path that led from my back door to my parents' front door was as straight and narrow as any road that Pastor Little or Reverend Abraham might preach about; it looked in fact like a cow path, a thin grassless depression barely twelve inches wide, and it took me perhaps sixty seconds to walk that path, every day, usually just once each way. Over the years I had turned that walk into a kind of trance experience, a way of emptying my head of all distracting thoughts so that for the rest of the day nothing would interrupt the connection that flowed between my eye and my hand.

As I walked I stared down at the dirt, looking at the shapes there, at the whorls of dewdrops and the helix of a snake track and the glint of tiny quartzite pebbles reflecting the sunlight, and, here and there, the faint traces of my own footprints from yesterday and the days before.

This is what passed through my head in the last moment before my outstretched hand reached my studio door, and then it was there, my hand, and I grasped the knob and turned it, and I was just about to go inside, to go out of the world, to paint, when my eyes were distracted by a flash of light on the porch railing.

7.03

Divine

THAT MORNING I WOKE UP IN COLIN'S BED. BY THEN I knew everything, the dusty white limestone walls and the oil paintings that hung on them, big dark things filled with saints and martyrs, the only brightness the halos that surrounded their heads and the gilt frames that surrounded the paintings. Closer to home I knew the four bedposts that crowded in on the corners of my eyes, each eight foot tall, thick as a punter's leg and just as muscled, well, carved I guess, or maybe *gnarled* is the best word: those bedposts looked like something Katharine Hepburn had been at with a knife in her shaking hands and a blindfold on to boot, and to tell you the truth they kinda gave me the creeps. Right at the point where the bedposts rose above the mattress there was a raw ring around each one, and I tell you what: it don't take a police detective or a practicing pervert to know what a rope burn looks like. Colin told me that his bed was a hundred and fifty years old and started out life on a coffee plantation in Guatemala, so there was every possibility that the rope burns was there long before Colin like took possession of the bed, or was born even, but still, I didn't ask him about them. Some things I figured I was better off not knowing.

A lotta things I figured I was better off not knowing.

Actually, I think it mighta been a banana plantation, if that makes any difference.

So anyway, that morning I woke up.

Founders' Day, no less. Independence Day everywhere else in the world, July the Fourth, but Founders' Day in Galatea, Kansas, Republic of Rosemary Krebs.

I knew everything by then, like I said, I didn't note it all down fresh. It was kind of just like *there,* like the air you breathe—like poison gas or the smell of roses, take your pick.

Colin was sleeping. How his mental alarm clock knew not to wake him up on Sundays was a mystery to me, when every other day of the week his eyes popped open right on the stroke of six. But it was after eight, and there was a pair of blue jays shrieking at each other outside the open window, and Colin's breath was still moving into and out of his big broad chest in the even pattern of sleep. The sheets was white and made of silk, and they had bunched up around Colin's legs, outlining them like, like, like I don't know, like casts I want to say, or like condoms, there was something hard and soft in the impression they give off, and for just a moment, I have to tell you, I *ached* with knowing everything I wasn't and Colin Nieman was. One of his feet was sticking out at the bottom of the bed and the lines of the bones in his toes was as clean and straight and strong as the spoke-thingies of a brand new rake, and I couldn't even *look* at his face. They say that the Lord makes some people and then He breaks the mold, but with Colin I had the sense that he broke the mold hisself, that he broke outta it, kicked and punched his way into this world and then calmly brushed his mother's dust off him and stole the heart of everyone that looked upon his serpent's smile.

Tines. The spoke-thingies on a rake are called tines.

I slipped outta bed then, dressed in the hallway so as not to wake him. The halls in the limestone house had this way of never quite reaching their destination: there always seemed to be a little room right before the one you wanted, foyers and vestibules and nooks and antechambers, and that morning it seemed I made my way through every goddamn last one of them until finally I was outside and went around to my car.

Which didn't start.

Dead as a goddamn doorknob it was, and already hot enough to fry a egg—or the back of your thighs—on those fucking vinyl seats.

I tried the key again. The only noise my car made was a bleat like a half-dead cow getting stabbed at by a cattle prod. I saw that the gas gauge was way down below E, which that's when I started to worry a little, cause I coulda swore I'd filled the tank up last night. But you know, things had got a little blurry by then, maybe I was thinkinga the night before, or the night before that, or sometime last month. Or maybe I'd just drove myself outta gas last night, who knows. But I was pretty sure I'd filled it up last night.

There wasn't no use sitting there waiting to die of heatstroke, so I got outta the car, but it was hardly any cooler in the open air: those shiny black stones, which still bore the nice neat *tine* lines of yesterday's raking, was like the top of a hot griddle, and after like two seconds of standing there I went back inside to think about what to do next. Then my choice was kind of made for me, because I ran into Colin inside. He was padding down the hall on the way to his office, wearing nothing but a pair of jockey shorts. He had a cup of coffee in one hand, and the little notebook he kept on his bedside table in the other, and one-a his thick black fountain pens stuck outta his mouth like a cigar.

The first thing I thought was that he'd just been waiting for me to leave so he could get up and set to writing, and when he looked up and saw me I knew I was right.

But then his mouth twisted around the pen in a big and kind of crooked smile, and he set his coffee and notebook down, and he took the pen outta his mouth and flicked it as though shaking ashes from a real cigar.

"My little chickadee," he said. "Back so soon?"

"My car won't start."

He was on me immediately, pulling me to him in a hug that was too tight to be real. "Well, it would seem your misfortune is my good luck."

I pushed back, but not too far. Not all the way out of his arms. "I got things to do."

"Things?"

"Stuff."

"Stuff?"

"I was just coming in for a glass of water before I walk on ho—before I walk on over to Wade's."

Colin looked me up and down for a minute. I could see him weighing his choices, what would be the quickest way for him to get me outta his hair without seeming too rude.

Well, I guess he don't got no hair, but you see what I mean.

It occurred to me, as Colin stood there with his thoughts kind of whirling around behind his eyes like a slot machine, that he cared for me just enough to feel guilty about hurting me. That was something, I guess, it was better than nothing. It wasn't the jackpot, but it was a payoff.

Atlantic City was one-a the places I wanted Colin to take me. Atlantic City, and Vegas, and what's it called, Monarchy, where Princess Grace lives. Lived.

Colin burped then, or hiccuped, it was silent, but the smell of stomach gases laced with fresh coffee filled my nose.

Damn, but he made a good pot of coffee.

He took a deep breath.

"I'll drive you," he said.

"Thanks," I said. "I can walk."

"I don't want you walking. There are too many deserted stretches on the road between here and Wade's."

"Ain't gonna be no deserted stretches-a road today. It's Founders' Day. Everybody and their grandma's gonna be out today."

"All the more reason for me to drive you."

"You let Justin walk."

"Justin lets Justin walk. I don't *let* Justin do anything."

He turned before I could say anything else and jogged to the stairs and up to his bedroom. I suppose I coulda run off, but what woulda been the point? There was only one way to Wade's, only one direct route anyway, and Colin woulda just caught up with me. In a minute he was back, dressed in shorts and a tank top and his running shoes. The top of his head was shiny with suntan lotion, and as we crunched our way across those shiny black stones to his car I couldn't help but reach up and rub the oil all the way into his skin, and even as I did it I had a feeling that he'd meant for me to do it.

"So," I said, "now I know why you don't never get sunburned."

A beep cut through the hot air as Colin flicked off the car alarm.

"Stick with me long enough," he said, "and you'll learn all my secrets."

I didn't laugh at that, though I probably shoulda.

Obsidian, I was remembering, was the name of the shiny black stones surrounding the limestone house, and Monaco was the name of the country where Princess Grace lived before she died, and I think that it actually was a coffee plantation in Guatemala where Colin's bed come from. Not that any of that mattered.

"Yeah," I said as I climbed into the car, "I bet I will."

7.04

Webbie

I WATCHED HIM DURING THE SERVICE. I WATCHED HIM

watching my father—watching the right honorable Reverend Abraham Greeving, preaching up a storm as he always did on the Sunday closest to Founders' Day. It was the one service of the year I actually tried to attend, just because I enjoyed the sight of my father so riled up, but I had planned to skip this year's performance because, given the context, I knew it would be hard to find anything amusing in the empty judgment and condemnation delivered from Galatia's pulpit. But that morning, after handing my father off to Faith and Hope and Charity, I found myself alone in our house; there was only my sore shoulder, and the Archive and Eric Johnson's thumbs and Lucy Robinson's pregnancy test, to keep me company, and on the mantel in the living room sat the halved bellystone Justin had fondled so long ago. That bellystone—and to the thumbs, and the pregnancy test, and the Archive, and the ten high stone steps on our front porch: they seemed to me just so many overdetermined symbols of life in Galatia, laden with meaning and yet completely devoid of signification, of an ability to affect things, to effect change, and, standing in my father's house with the faint smell of smoke coming in through the windows, I found it too easy to believe that I was just one more irrelevant item on that growing list. So I went to church. It was that or the Founders' Day barbecue. I went, I now realize, along with every other person who attended services that morning, to hear my father speak out against the very impotence we all felt. I don't suppose any of us expected my father's words to actually change anything, but at least there was camaraderie—*fellowship* is the word the other parishioners would have used—fellowship, and a few good songs.

He sat still for the duration of the service, almost rigidly still, his back just slightly bowed and his arms by his sides, his face set in a pose of studied attentiveness, eyebrows slightly raised, lips slightly parted, and after staring at him for a long moment I recognized his expression as one that I had cultivated during those long childhood years of twice-weekly churchgoing: that was the face that fooled my father into thinking I was paying attention.

Today I didn't pretend. I might have come to church to listen to the sermon, but as soon as I saw Wallace I took no notice of my father, and after a while I ignored Wallace as well. Instead I found myself imagining him on the morning I'd left him. What did I know about him, except his manner in bed and the fact that his response to hunger pangs at any time of the day or night was to fry up some bacon and eggs? Nothing else. But all the same I knew he wasn't the kind of man to wander his own house naked when he was alone. The curtains were all open, there were neighbors, family might drop by; if nothing else there were the pictures of the two girls on the mantel. At the very least he would pull on boxer shorts and a T-shirt and a pair of socks. In the kitchen, coffee, breakfast. While bacon was sizzling in a skillet he would retrieve the newspaper from the front porch. Still outside, even in the winter, he would scratch his stomach and fix himself in his boxer shorts while he glanced at the headlines, and then, suddenly noticing the cold, he would rush back inside and crack a couple of eggs in with the bacon. In five years he would be hypertensive, on medication. I would be making him whole wheat toast in the morning and he would complain that the butter substitute tasted like something a hog would turn up its nose at and speaking of hogs what he wouldn't give for just *one* slice of bacon . . .

I smiled so brightly then that Faith Jackson caught my eye and nodded ecstatically at me. I was rediscovering the Lord, I was coming back into the fold. I smiled back at Faith, thinking, I am imagining the feel of my husband's lips and tongue between my legs as he searches for a substitute for high-cholesterol foods. So there.

And then my smile faded abruptly. I thought, What the hell am I doing? Wallace—my husband? My cipher was more like it, my black man, or blackmon, or blakmon, however those Nation of Islam types wrote it, my knight in a shiny Coupe De Ville with rust damage on the running boards. I realized suddenly that I was angry at him, angry because he and not I had had the courage to play out the old story, to take a risk, to risk himself for me. I had just sat around, waiting. I had played at being a detective when all I really succeeded in being was Rosemary Krebs' maid, and in the end, it seemed, it had taken my father to bring us together.

7.05

Cora

IT WAS ROSA FIRST SAID SOMETHING WAS UP.

I don't suppose what she said surprised no one, but she was the first person to say it out loud.

She come with me to hear the Mayor's speech.

"Rosa," I told her, "you don't have to come if you don't wanna." But she said, "I'd rather not stay home alone."

"Sawyer—"

"Nuh-uh," Sawyer said. "I'm gonna go get *drunk*."

"You hush your mouth," I said, but Sawyer was already running out the door, his inhaler flying around his neck on its string.

"Rosa," I said when he was gone, "you don't feel well, you don't feel like people, you should just stay home, stay in bed with the A.C. on. Drink some mint tea, that'll settle you."

"Aw, Cora," Rosa said, and she sounded so far away. She was sitting at a table and I was behind the counter, finishing up my summer stew. "Cora," Rosa said, and the distance was all in her voice, "you so patient with me. I make you put up with so much craziness but you always treat me gentle and kind. I don't deserve you."

I stirred so hard I slopped a little stew onto the stove top, and it sizzled in the burner. "You stop that, stop with that kind of talk."

"Cora," Rosa said, "Cora, it's just something's wrong. Can't you feel it, in the air, all around you? It's like smoke, Cora, the air smells like smoke."

"Girl, that's just the pits you smelling."

"Cora!"

"The *barbecue* pits. Good Lord, woman, you jumpy as a mother hen."

"And you," she said, "you strong as one."

She'd snuck up on me somehow, and she placed her flat palm on the smalla my back. I put my left arm around her, and we rocked slightly as I used our combined weight to move the spoon through the big pot of stew.

"You just stick right here," I said, "and I'll watch out for you."

"I will," she said. "I'm sticking right here."

But I didn't believe her, and I had to repeat myself. "You stick right here," I said. "Don't ever leave Cora, Rosa, and Cora won't never leave you."

7.06

Divine

HE'S PROBABLY IN THE STUDIO," I SAID. "I MEAN, IF you want to say hi-lo."

"I guess," Colin said. "I mean, since I'm over here."

We made our way back there, using the worn trail Wade used. Inside, the studio was quiet as a church.

"Wade?"

I bounced up the stairs.

"Wade?"

I saw him then, coming outta my room—outta the room he'd filled up with drawings of me. As I went over to him he pulled the door to and locked it.

"Hey," I said.

Wade jingled the keys nervously before putting them in his pocket. "Hello," he said, "Divine."

Right then I knew something was up.

"Long time since I been in there."

"Indeed."

"I suppose maybe we should do a session soon."

"Indeed," he said again, and then we didn't say nothing for a bit.

"Colin's downstairs," I said finally. "My car wouldn't start."

Wade's eyes brightened. "Your car," he said, and he started off down the stairs.

"What about my car?"

"Is this," he said, sort of waving at Colin as we passed him, "yours?"

He turned round. He was holding something small and silver and shiny in his hands. It took me a moment to recognize it as my sideview mirror, and then, I don't know why, but for two seconds I was about five years old.

"Oh my golly," I said.

"Is that your sideview mirror?" Colin said.

"I-I-I think so."

"Let me guess," Colin said to Wade. "You found it in your mailbox."

"It's Sunday," Wade said. "There's no mail on Sunday."

"You found it today?"

"As a matter of fact," Wade said, "I found it half an hour ago." He walked over to me and put the mirror in my hands. "I found it on the porch railing."

The mirror was cracked down the middle and there was a little rust along the jagged edge of its broken arm. It was stiff and cold in my hands but it weighed almost nothing, like a dead kitten.

"Divine?" Wade said. He put a hand on my shoulder. "Are you okay? Divine?"

I shrugged his hand off. "I need a drink," and I pushed past him, pushed past Colin, who also tried to put a hand on my shoulder, pushed out of the thick smelly air of Wade's studio and into the thick dusty air outside, and I pushed through that as I made my way to the house. Wade and Colin followed along behind me. I could hear them talking but I couldn't make out what they were saying. Once or twice I heard them laugh.

They both laughed, but never at the same time.

Inside, I burned my throat with two thick fingers of Jack. When Colin and Wade came in the room behind me, they didn't say nothing, just kinda took up sides at opposite ends of the room.

"Divine," Colin said as I poured myself a second drink, "it's not even eleven. What's the matter?"

"What? You don't get it?"

"Divine," Wade said, and as I jerked my head toward him I felt the whiskey already working its magic. "Obviously he doesn't 'get it,' or he wouldn't be asking."

I hated the way he said *get it*, as if I was talking in a foreign language or using some outrageous piece-a slang. But I just looked down at my whiskey and I said, "He's after *me* now." It sounded silly, out loud, and I gulped some more whiskey.

"What?" Wade said. "Who—" but Colin cut him off.

"Don't be ridiculous. What even makes you say such a thing?"

My head spun over to him. "Who else does shit like that? Leaving around tokens, pieces, whatever, pieces-a your, I don't know, your *past* or something."

"Divine, you're not making any sense."

My head spun around to Wade. "I'm making perfect sense! Lucy's dress, Lucy's hair, Lucy's screams, Lucy's finger—"

I'd been ticking the list off on my fingers, but when I got to the last item I stopped, and my hand balled itself up into a fist all by itself.

After a minute or so I was able to go on again. "Colin's shopping bag," I said. "Colin's tape recorder. Colin's boxes. And now that mirror. *My* mirror."

"Divine," Colin said.

Spin.

"Divine," Wade said.

Spin again.

"Divine, do you really think Lucy's abductor left your mirror on the porch?"

I looked down at the mirror, which was still in my hand—further proof that it wouldn't go nowhere unless someone moved it. "Who else would even know it was *my* mirror?"

"Divine," Colin said, and I spun around. "Why should he know it was your mirror?"

"Cause he just does, doesn't he? I mean, he seems to just know these things."

"Divine," Wade said.

Spin.

"Divine," Colin said, and I spun around yet again. This time the big white plain of Colin's chest filled up my vision, which had gone a little tunnely from the whiskey and the spinning. I felt his arms closing around my body, which I suppose was meant to be comforting but was really kinda eerie, because I couldn't see them. His arms, I mean. I just felt them circling me, bearing down, getting tighter and tighter. "Divine," Colin said, "whoever he is, he's a *man*. It's a man we're talking about, not some omniscient being."

"I don't know what *omniscient* means."

Colin sighed. "It's not God," he said.

"Or Santa Claus for that matter," Wade said behind me.

Colin's hands ran up and down my back. "He can't know things he can't know."

For just a moment I relaxed in Colin's grip, but when I did the mirror slipped out of my hand and landed on the floor with a thunk, and the way we jumped, all three of us, was enough to make me tense up again, and I pushed away from Colin.

"What difference does it make anyway? It was lost, and he found it. He found it, and he returned it, to let me know that now he's got a eye on *me*."

"Actually," Wade said, "whoever it was, he returned it to me."

I looked over at Wade then, but he was looking at Colin. I turned to Colin, who was meeting Wade's stare with a stare of his own, and then Wade went to the bar, and poured out two drinks.

"I would like," Colin said, "like Wade, to accuse you of incoherence. But it all makes too much sense."

And then I was telling them how I lost the mirror out to the Big M last fall, about how it snapped off as I tore away from that old barn where

I found Eddie Comedy. I was telling them about that gypsy-type guy I let do me that night, Vlad the Impaler I called him, Vlad the Impaler who smelled like salt-and-vinegar potato chips but who couldn't tell me nothing about Ratboy, and then I was telling them about Ratboy, about all those nights we spent up toppa the grain elevator. I told them about the wheat stubble cracking under my footsteps and the satin bedspread crinkling under Ratboy's body, I even told them about how I'd dropped myself into the swimming hole and how the swimming hole had thrown me back out again, and then, I don't know, maybe it was the whiskey—it took a few drinks to tell the whole story—but all of it began to blend together in the telling, the night at the swimming hole and the night at the Big M and all those nights on toppa the grain elevator, but the one thing I didn't tell them about was what happened out to Noah's ark. Maybe it woulda been the perfect time to tell them, to tell someone, finally, but I just kept looking at Colin's forehead and seeing the words *Superior Bond* written there, and so I didn't say nothing about it.

When I finished, Colin was staring at me so hard that I had to look down. "Hear that," I heard him say, to Wade I guess, and I could tell from his voice that he musta been as drunk as me. "Not one *goddamn*, not one *shit*, not one—"

"*Fuck*," Wade said. "Not a single *fuck*." Something about the way Wade said that made me look up, and I was just in time to see him say to Colin, "Divine seems to have finally decided to be the little boy he never was," and drain his glass, which after a moment he refilled.

It musta been high noon by that time. There wasn't no shadows in the room and the whiskey in all our glasses had started to glow, it seemed, an amber fish tank kinda light, and just as I was thinking I was really and I do mean *really* wasted Colin said something like, I haven't been this drunk since the last time I saw Yonah Schimmel.

And Wade said, I haven't been this drunk since the last time Yonah Schimmel fucked me.

And Colin made a sort of choking noise then, and Wade was sort of mumbling to himself, Yonah, he mumbled, and Jonah, and John.

And Colin was whispering, Justin.

And Wade was whispering back, Justin.

And right then I knew why Wade hadn't let me in my room in the studio.

And I was thinking, *Justin?* Who was it who was lying in between them? Me, that's who. But who was they thinking about? That goddamned Justin.

Wade kind of rolled himself onto his feet then, rolled over and walked over to the wall of his living room and on the way he had to step over my sideview mirror which lay where it had fallen, and when he got to the wall he pulled a lump of something black from his pants pocket, charcoal it was, I guess, I mean, it was the same stuff he used to use when he used to draw me, and with the whiskey glass in one hand and the charcoal in the other he made these like one two three four black lines on the white wall, straight up and down and all the same length, and then with a slow and easy kinda gesture that seemed to go on for years and miles, he made a diagonal tally mark that connected them all together, and he turned back to me and Colin, and to Justin, who was in the room more than any of us were, and he said, "That's us," and it was, I swear to God it was, it was us and that's all there was of us, and I tell you *what*.

I'd rolled over on my side to watch Wade, and then, behind me, I heard Colin set his drink down on the floor, and I heard him say, "Divine," and then he said, "C'mere." Wade had turned around. He wasn't looking at me but past me, at Colin I guess, and then, real slow, he put the charcoal back in his pants pocket, and he left his hand in there with it.

7.07

Webbie

I FOUND HIM AFTER THE SERVICE IN THE PARKING LOT. I nodded unconsciously at twenty heads, twenty faces, twenty mouths which all said neither *Good morning* nor *Good afternoon*—there were no clocks in the church, but my father invariably finished either just before or just after noon—but *Welcome back the fold, Miss Webbie,* and I was thinking, I am not a *sheep* you imbeciles, as I made my way to the one car in the parking lot that didn't belong there, and then I waited. I watched him approach, his eyes scanning the lot, the street, the park, looking for me. When he was ten feet away I spoke.

"Hey there."

He held in both his hands a single sheet of pink paper, the coming week's events. His whole body shook at my voice and the paper split in his hands. It didn't rip, it *broke*, and he looked at it for a moment and then laughed once, and then he looked up at me.

"Miss Webbie," he said. "Fancy meeting you here."

"Fancy meeting you," I said, "here. Mr. Wallace."

He shrugged his shoulders. "Well, I guess there's no use pretending I just happened to be in the neighborhood. Although to tell the truth we *have* heard tell down to Wichita how Galatia's Reverend Abraham Greeving is a powerful witness to the Lord."

"Was that before or after you met me?"

"You mean, did I ask around, is what you mean?"

I shrugged. "Is what I mean," I said, and Wallace laughed.

"I asked around."

Ast. In New York he would have said *axed*.

We stared at each other for just a moment, and simultaneously burst into laughter, and even as I noticed his hands making funny, almost stunted movements, I noticed my own hands making the same movements, and I realized that we were both remembering, in our hands at least, the shape of the other's body beneath them, and when we had settled down, our feet, which also remembered our intimacy, had moved us a couple of steps closer to each other.

I said, "He's my father."

He nodded. "Greeving's not such a common name." He laughed a little then. "Back home, when I was growing up, boys used to tell stories about Pastor Littlejohn's daughter. Said she was *wild*. Said that's the way it was with preacher's kids. P.K.s I think is what we called them. Called you."

"P.K.s."

". . ."

"Was I—am I wild, Wallace?"

He looked down at the two pieces of paper in his hands. He crumpled them slowly, put one in each of his front pockets. Their rough outline was faintly visible through the gray polyester.

"Those are terrible pants," I said.

"Momma always said some men you judge by they Sunday best, others by what they wear on Saturday night."

"Six more days till Saturday."

"Just one, if you go backwards. Less than one."

"Six more days."

"Well, that was time enough for the Lord to make the world."

"Do you believe," I said, waving my hand at the church, the scattering congregation, my father. "Do you believe in all that?"

"Way I see it, a little faith never hurt nobody."

"And Hope," I said. "And Charity."

He smiled, blandly or benignly. "And hope," he said. "And charity."

I turned then, looked at his car, one hundred fifty miles of dust, and, underneath that, the shine of a fresh wash-and-wax job, and I knew that he had washed and waxed his car for me.

I spoke to the car. "I won't make you happy. I won't make you bacon in the morning and I'll make you buy new pants for church even though I won't go with you, and I'll complain that all you ever read is the newspaper."

"*The Eagle and Beacon*'s not a bad paper. And I can make my own breakfast."

I continued to stare at his car. The underside was indeed flecked with rust.

"A Cadillac," I said finally.

"My Daddy always said a good car had a back seat big enough for making babies, and then for taking them around after they born."

"Did your parents always speak in aphorisms?"

"Does your Daddy always quote the Bible?"

"Yes!" I nearly yelled.

He answered quietly. "Yes." He shrugged. "Usually." He smiled. "My grandma always said that a well-spoke word is like a gift."

"Did your grandma also read the Apocrypha?"

"Only if it was in the Bible."

"Did you really," I said, "did you think you could just *drive* all the way here and find me and carry me away in your *back seat*?"

He looked down at his hands again, but there wasn't any paper there, and he shoved them into his pockets. "Took me a few trips," he said, "but I did it. Found you anyway."

"A few trips?"

He looked up. "Seven."

"You drove up here *seven* times?"

"Nice drive." He nodded at his car. "Best suspension Detroit ever made. Like riding in a rowboat."

De-troit.

"Seven times?"

"You'd be surprised. It gets easier, not harder. Some things do."

"Some things?"

"Get easier, not harder."

"Momma? Or Daddy?"

"Neither," he said. "Wallace."

"Seven times," I said yet again, quietly, almost whispering, and then I finished. "For me."

"One thousand miles," he said, "each way. For you." He kind of gulped, and then he too finished. "That's all I got," he said. "That's what I'm offering."

7.08

Cora

SHE WAS FINE FOR A WHILE, AT THE PICNIC, SHE stood behind the table and she served up folks with a smile and a hi-lo and she spooned out extra meat to them that asked for it. But after a hour or so she began to get distracted, she wouldn't notice somebody speaking to her and she give them cornbread when they said they didn't want none, and then, like, she began missing the bowl with the ladle, and the second time she sent a big dollop of stew splashing all over the place I took her ladle from her and I steered her over to a chair and I said, "Sit," and she sat, and I said, "Stay," and she stayed. Later on I brought her some lemonade and she nearly jumped outta her skin when I touched her shoulder, and she had to use both hands to hold on to the cup. "Rosa," I said, "will you just *tell* me what's wrong?" She just looked up at me and smiled in a sad way. "How can I tell you?" she said. "How *can* I tell you?" "I'ma send you right on home if you keep talking nonsense," I said, but even before I was finished Rosa sort of giggled and she said, "Cora," and she set her lemonade down without seeming to notice that she spilled it all over the place, and she pointed at the big cottonwood trunk the Mayor'd set up at one enda Vera's parking lot. "Cora," she said, "there's a *man* inside that stump."

7.09

T. V. Daniels

AFTERWARDS FOLKS WOULD SAY, WELL HE PROBABLY couldn'ta done it any other way, but still—and I mean but *still.*

7.10

Lawman Brown

MYRA ROBINSON WASN'T AROUND, BUT SHE HAD A pretty good excuse. Rosemary Krebs wasn't there either, but she could come and go as she pleased, and she'd said earlier she'd try to stop by around four, for the speech. Darrell Jenkens and Dave Helman had been in and out all day since setting up the stump, loading up on food and beer. Dave said Darrell was helping him fix up that old '68 Mustang that'd been sitting on blocks in his back yard for going on three years now, though God save the first man who got behind the wheel of a car that'd been worked on by those two. It sickened him, he just had to say it, drinking in general struck him as a degenerate activity, and Founders' Day or no Founders' Day it was still the Sabbath. Well, he just hoped that none-a these folks thought they was *driving* home, that was all he had to say. He couldn't hardly blame Pastor Little and Reverend Greeving for not showing up: they'd preached to near-empty churches this morning, that was for sure. Lawman Brown had to admit he hadn't quite realized this is what three hundred plus people looked like when they was all gathered together. Shelly Stadler—now there was a finely developing girl although her cheeks seemed a little shinier than even this weather merited, and two times she had to cover her mouth with her hand when she burped—Shelly Stadler told him she'd sold three hundred and seventeen raffle tickets for the Booster Club, and they was limited one per, so assuming people was being honest then that meant just about everyone that was left in Galatea was at the picnic. Colin Nieman wasn't there, and his little friend Justin wasn't there either, and Wade Painter hadn't come, though that wasn't no surprise, and Lawman Brown was just as glad that Reggie Packman wasn't sashaying his little faggotty behind around. Webbie Greeving wasn't around either—well, it looked like that whole little set was boycotting the day, and that was just fine by him. It made his job that much easier. And of course a lotta people asked him where the Mayor was, and Lawman Brown just smiled and said he thought the Mayor'd be popping up any time now, any time. T. V. Daniels, he noticed then, T.V. wasn't nowhere around, and though T.V. wasn't exactly the biggest social butterfly around—Lawman Brown chuckled to himself at the thought of T. V. Daniels as a butterfly—nobody'd ever heard of him skipping a meal, let alone a free one. Lawman Brown supposed he'd be along soon enough.

7.11

Divine

AFTERWARDS THERE WAS JUST PIECES AND PARTS, AND trust me when I tell you I'm not using my own words to tell you this: but the pieces was like leftover from a jigsaw puzzle that'd been lost a long time ago, and though maybe you could tell that the puzzle had been pretty goddamn enormous, still, what pieces was left told you all you needed to know about the big picture.

There was Wade and Colin, first of all, each passed out on separate couches, and there was me in between them, cold tiles pressing against my chin, my chest, my belly and knees and the tops of my feet, and there was a breeze playing cold over my ass and my mouth.

There was my sideview mirror, and the little egg of sunlight it cast on one wall, and those five lines Wade'd made on another.

There was a glass on its side, and four long thin wet fingers of whiskey reaching across the floor toward me, and there was the painting Wade was going to make one day, of those fingers, and the story Colin was going to write, but I already knew there wasn't going to be no Divine in that painting, that story.

The whiskey had meaning, and the fingers and the floor and the shadow they was going to leave behind, but I didn't mean nothing.

I suppose there was nobody to blame but me. *I* taught *them*, really, I told them that this was the only thing I wanted, that it was the only thing that could comfort me. Who knew they would believe me?

I was the boy who cried wolf, calling the beast up outta the darkness.

Pieces and parts: a pile of clothes, which I sorted through for mine, and a headache that split my skull and blurred my vision, and above all the need to run run *run* the fuck away from there.

But I'd tried running once before, and it hadn't worked, so this time I just walked, and I walked real slow on a gravel road baked hard and hot that burned the bottoms of my feet right through my shoes. I walked right into town.

7.12

T. V. Daniels

IN ALL HONESTY DARRELL JENKENS WAS JUST ABOUT the last person T. V. Daniels woulda wanted to drive him anywhere, under any conditions, and certain things Darrell'd done that day had just about given literal meaning to the words *shit-faced drunk*, but the bottom line was that not only did Darrell know how to drive a forklift but he was willing to too, so there you go.

T.V. himself didn't drink that day, alcohol that is, except for his customary swig of Listerine in the early morning hours, but Darrell and Dave Helman had taken turns bringing him back plates of food, little baby plates if he said so himself, and Darrell and Dave didn't bring them nearly fast enough to suit his taste, but there you go again. Sacrifices had to be made sometimes, in the name of a higher cause.

Early in the morning, before Darrell and Dave had left to set up the Mayor's stump, T.V.'d examined the stack of pallets in Dave's shed. The examination consisted of him stepping on them, and when after six tries he came to one that didn't crack under his foot he had Darrell Jenkens drag it away from the rest.

Darrell had brought over the wingbacked loveseat from T.V.'s living room, and it rocked a little as he and Dave set it on the warped pallet, but Dave produced nails as thick as number two pencils and nearly as long, and, even drunk, he laid swift sure blows of a hammer on the heads of the nails, and he fastened the chair to the pallet, and he even bent the protruding ends of the nails over, for added security.

Every once in a while he giggled, Dave Helman did, and during the course of the day his giggles gave way to hiccups, and then to snores, and now he lay on his stomach in one corner of his garage, face turned to one side and his beer-softened and girlish bottom poking up in the air in a way that Darrell Jenkens said made him wish he had a cattle prod and a camera. Next to Dave's snoring body were the empty cups and bottles and cans of beer he had drunk, which over the course of the day Dave had used to spell out the letters of his name.

DAVE H was as far as he got.

T.V. looked at Dave from his position in the chair, and he frowned, and he pulled idly at the shoulder strap of his U.S.P.S. mailbag, and he smiled, and then Darrell Jenkens came back into the shed with a final plate of food for T.V., who ate it while Darrell Jenkens just sat there and stared at him, smoking a long slow cigarette and occasionally pulling on a bottle of beer. When T.V. finished Darrell continued to look at him fixedly, until T.V. said, "Can I help you?" and then Darrell kinda looked down, although not quickly enough to hide his grin, and T.V. thought maybe he heard Darrell mumbling, "What the fuck," under his breath. "You said four, right?" T.V. asked Darrell, and Darrell said, "I'm telling you, he set the alarm right in fronta me and Dave," and T.V. said, "Well, okay then."

T.V. checked his mailbag again, as if what was inside mighta gone somewhere, and then he and Darrell just kinda sat there for a few minutes, and then Darrell sighed and stood up and began gathering up all of T.V.'s scattered plates. He put them in a pile and then, without once looking at T.V., or, for that matter, at Dave Helman, he used the plates to spell out the letters of T.V.'s name on the floor of the shed.

TERRENCE VINCENT DANIELS, he wrote, and with the extra plates he wrote WAS HERE, and T.V. didn't mention that his first name only had one *r* in it.

7.13

Divine

IN TOWN I PUSHED MY WAY THROUGH A CROWD which'd gathered under the tent in the I.G.A. parking lot. Some folks was drifting toward the stump down at the north end, but I thought they looked a bit like army ants getting ready to carry off a stick, and me, I went for the food. Well, for the drinks really, but the food was right there too.

"Hey, Percy Schuyler," I said to Percy Schuyler.

Percy Schuyler's daddy has a fifty foot silo with a ladder up the side and a door on top, and one time when I was about fourteen or so Percy took me up there and opened the door and lo! the silo was full to about six feet from the top, and Percy and me dropped in and he gave new meaning to the term *planted his seed.* Afterwards, I shit wheat for two days.

"Well, if it isn't Quincy Cross, and his pretty little wife Cheryl."

Out to Sloppy Joe's Cheryl's nickname was cross-country cause she'd had affairs with just about everybody in Cadavera County I hadn't—plus, I suppose, plus about halfa the ones I had. Quincy took one look at me and grabbed his wife and steered as far cleara me as he could—in the process giving me a nice view of his big beautiful black man's butt, which Cheryl's cooking, I could see, was having an expansive effect on.

At the kegger I bumped into Richie Riose, and can I just tell you three things: one, his real name is *Ricardo,* and two, just like Dionne Warwicke, he added that *e* to his last name, and three, he's uncut, like just about every other wetback I ever had. Richie was kind enough to fill my cup for me, but he didn't actually say nothing to me and I didn't actually say nothing to him, I just kind of smiled and turned around.

And found myself face to chest with Sam Hall, who everybody still calls by the nickname *I* gave him, which was Sam the Butcher, and can I just add that I was born after *The Brady Bunch* went off the air. Now, Sam, let me tell you, Sam does what he can with what he's got—I think the term is *compensation*—but the bottom line is that he came outta his momma before he was quite finished. "Excuse me," I said to Sam, "I was just looking for the *meat,*" and I pushed my way past him.

At the meat table I found myself sandwiched between Titus and Ulysses Foster, and, well, I been *there* before, and it took me about two months to recover, so I forgot about any hot dog and squeezed out from between them as soon as I could. Some people wonder why two such fine strong men ain't married, but the answer Titus and Ulysses always give is that they waiting to meet a pair of twins just like them, and all I gotta say is that they better be Siamese twins cause Titus and Ulysses was still sleeping in the same bed last time I checked.

In a hot little corner of the tent I could see Rosa Stone sitting on a chair all by herself. She was rocking in a little circle like she was trying to screw herself right down into the ground, and while I watched Victor Bradfield come up to her and said something, but she didn't even look up.

"*Hey*, Victor," I called out, and he looked around to see who was calling his name, and saw me, and he took off without waiting to see what was up with Rosa. Victor Bradfield was my last conquest in town before Wade—

Right then someone shouted something, and then someone else shouted back, and before I knew it everybody was shouting and running toward the stump, which I thought was a helluva lot of excitement to show for the Mayor. In the crowd I saw Xavier Leroi. Who knows why his parents gave him that name, but there he was, looking a little sickly if you ask me, and kind of holding his side as he ran.

I kinda stood there for a minute or two and watched them all running towards whatever, and then, you know, then I heard the humming. I turned around and there was Lawman Brown, humming that goddamn song like he didn't know no other.

When he saw me looking at him I smiled as big and bright as I could, and I sauntered on over to him. Lawman Brown kept on humming, but his humming took on a kinda rattle to it, and I knew he was humming through closed teeth.

When I was right up next to him I just stood there until finally he stopped it with that bullshit noise.

"You got something you wanna say, Reggie?"

"Yeah," I said. I said, "First off, my name is Divine. And second." I stopped. I smiled. I almost put my hand on his dick to see if it was hard, but I didn't. "And second," I said, "Leroy Brown was a *nigger*."

And then I turned around and went to see what everybody was so excited about.

7.14

Rosemary Krebs

FOUNDERS' DAY.

My husband's invention, in case you're wondering, not mine. It seemed to me premature to consider anything founded yet—premature, or far too long after the fact.

Navy linen is the ideal attire for such a picnic: the linen minimizes the threat of perspiration, and the navy hides any evidence if you do, in fact, perspire. Some women complain that linen dresses always wrinkle in the seat, but, as my mother said, some women don't know how to *stand down*.

I had managed to accept and discard six different beverages without drinking any of them. Now I sat with a cup of lemonade on a chair at the front of the tent.

It was almost four, and Phyneas had said he would come on at four. Or come out, I should say.

"Afternoon, Mrs. Krebs," Portland Oregon Smith said. "Betty just asked me to ask you when we might be seeing the Mayor. Folks is wondering, is all."

"Good afternoon, Porter. A lovely day for a picnic, isn't it?"

"Yes, ma'am."

"How is Betty?"

"She's fine, ma'am."

"And Porter Junior?"

"We're all fine, ma'am."

"Well then. That's good." I looked down at my watch. "I expect the Mayor will be here any time now."

"Well," Porter said, or, rather, *welp*, "I'll pass the word on to—holy crow!"

"To whom?"

"Pardon me, Mrs. Krebs, but will you lookit *that*."

Porter let his voice trail off, and I stood up slowly.

I looked down at my cup then, to see if perhaps it had been switched with another beverage, something foaming and hallucinogenic, because, though I have seen smoke fill up my study window from a fire over a dozen miles away, for the first time in my life I did not believe my eyes.

The cup in my hand was plastic, and it appeared to hold only lemonade.

I looked up again.

T. V. Daniels was approaching the picnic.

He wore his United States Postal Service uniform. His mailbag hung off one shoulder.

His . . . hips spilled over the sides of the chair he sat in, which, I do believe, was actually a loveseat.

The loveseat he sat in rode ten feet up in the air, suspended by the tines of a forklift. Darrell Jenkens sat at the wheel of the forklift, which moved forward in fits and starts under the burden of T. V. Daniels' weight. A smile split Darrell Jenkens' face like a wedge cut from a wheel of sallow cheese, but T. V. Daniels' face was composed, almost dignified, although a patina of barbecue sauce dotted his chin and cheeks, and the forklift's vibrations caused his face to quiver like a pudding.

"Ho-ly cow," Portland Oregon Smith whispered, and I was distracted then, as I tried to remember if, when last he'd spoken, he had sanctified cows or crows.

Someone shouted then, and someone else shouted back, and the crowd began to surge in the direction of the stump and the forklift.

The forklift shuddered on.

I looked down at my lemonade again. It was not there. I thought that perhaps I *was* hallucinating, but then I looked farther down and saw my dropped cup and wet shoes.

The shoes I was wearing were red and made of suede, and if I left the picnic immediately I could probably wash the water stains out of them and brush up the nap.

I looked up at T.V. again. I will say this: his timing was perfect.

The bromide *waste not, want not* seemed particularly apropos in the face of his looming form, and I went home to save my shoes.

7.15

Divine

T. V. DANIELS TOOK THE STAGE LIKE SOMETHING WALKing outta your worst nightmare.

Took the stump, I guess you'd have to say.

Later on folks who was close by to the stump said they heard a ringing inside, like from a old-time alarm clock, and right on the stroke of four a trapdoor set in the top of the stump popped open, and a second later the Mayor's head popped out. I guess when you stop and think it was the obvious thing to happen, but even so there was a general gasp, although how much of that had to do with the Mayor and how much of it had to do with T.V. wasn't real clear. The Mayor's face when it come out of the stump was beet red and his hair and the collar of his shirt was glued to his skin with sweat, but his aw-shucks smile was stuck on his face like it'd been taped there, and he'd just managed to get one arm through to either like *wave* at his fans or maybe just to reach for the microphone that'd been baking on the top of the stump all day long, when the pallet the forklift was carrying, the pallet that was carrying all seven hundred and sixty-two plus pounds of T. V. Daniels, banged against the backa the trapdoor, which slammed against the backa the Mayor's head, and I tell you what: the Mayor even passed out goofy. His eyes rolled up to the sky and his head kind of wobbled back and forth like a balloon on a string on a windy day, and then he just kinda like sank back into the stump, his arm slithering in behind him like a rat's tail, and then the door slammed to.

Someone close to me laughed, just once, and then there was the sound of a mother's voice saying, Hush.

The forklift complained like a mule forced to work on a hot summer's day as it carried T.V. the last couple-a feet, and then I'm not sure if Darrell Jenkens actually shut the thing off or if it just like kinda *died* from the effort, but the motor cut off and when it did everybody's voices seemed like really loud in the air, and then people just sort of all shut up, cause what was there to say?

T.V. didn't stand up.

Leaned over doesn't quite describe how he picked up the microphone. I had this like X-ray picture in my head of T.V.'s skeleton buried somewhere inside all that fat, and even as his like skeleton bent just like anyone else's the rest of the like *mass* of him just sort of shifted, or maybe *melted* is a better word, and I distinctly heard Blaine Getterling saying, It's gonna break, it's gonna break, it's *got*ta break, and I wasn't sure if he meant the loveseat T.V. sat on, or the stump itself.

Then T.V. was sitting up again, panting from the effort of picking up the microphone, and when he switched it on the first thing you heard was a feedback squeal, and then the sound of T.V.'s heavy breathing amplified a hundred times.

I'd say that T.V. was waiting for everyone to shut up, but no one was talking. Everyone was in fact truly speechless.

T.V. was just waiting.

Then, finally, he spoke up.

"I have in my possession," he said, and he patted something that on him looked like a coin purse on a string, "I have in my possession several letters," he said, and I realized what he was patting was his mailbag, "documents, if you will, documents," he said, and he paused, and he smiled nervously, and then he went on, "documents which I think are of interest to more than a few men who live in this town," he said, and then, suddenly, for no reason I could think of, his eyes dropped to mine, and he finished, "men who are present in this gathering today."

It was only then that my blood ran cold, and I thought of running, but something held me there, the way a bird's held by snake eyes.

"These documents," T.V. said, "these *letters*, are addressed to one 'Ratboy,' a.k.a. Lamoine Wiebe, at various addresses in various parts of the country, and bear as their return address a local post office number which I happen to know is registered in the name of our very own Reginald Packman."

Well, that was a lie right there, cause I'd put that P.O. box in my name. *Divine*.

There was a general murmur in the crowd then, a creepier than normal sorta crowd murmur cause whenever I looked at someone's face it seem like *they* wasn't making any sound.

"You bastard!" I shouted then. "You stole my letters! You *fat* fucking thief!"

As soon as I opened my mouth the people around me backed away some, which had like two immediate effects, one-a which was to give me a little breathing room, and the othera which was to create a tight circle of bodies around me, and I knew then that running, which'd never really been an option, wasn't even a consideration no more.

I suppose I coulda denied that the letters was mine, but even if that thought had occurred to me, I wouldn'ta known how to do it. One thing I'd never done is I'd never *denied* nothing.

T.V. wasn't saying shit now. When I looked back up at him he was digging into the mailbag, and he pulled out a wad of letters, which he spilled onto his lap. He put his hand into the bag three more times, until his lap was filled with crumpled-up envelopes.

There was a sorta buzz as the pile of letters grew and grew and grew, and I tell you what: even I was kind of impressed. I didn't realize I'd been quite so *busy* in the past couple-a years.

"Each one-a these documents," T.V. was saying, "*each* and *every* one is marked 'Return to Sender.' " Only then did he look at me. "*I* did my job," he said. "I did my *job*."

It seemed necessary to answer him, and so I yelled, "And so did *I*, you great big *blob*."

T.V. ignored me. He just reached into his lap and picked up one of the letters.

"Evil," he said, and when he spoke his voice went faraway, and I had the distinct sense that he'd rehearsed this part of his speech, "evil is inside this envelope. Evil," he said, "is inside each of us. Evil," he said, "*is in our midst*. But evil," he said, and he ripped open one end of the envelope, "can be got at, and cut out, and removed—"

"Here now," someone yelled out, "there's no call to go opening up somebody else's mail. It's not right. It's not . . . legal."

I realized with a odd, a downright weird feeling that I didn't know who'd spoken. I mean I didn't recognize the voice.

T.V. seemed a bit taken aback. "Evil," he said, trying but not quite achieving the tone he'd set before, "evil must be *named*."

"Naw, naw, naw," someone else called out. " 'S'nobody's business but Lamoine Wiebe's and Reggie Packman's."

T.V. swallowed. His Adam's apple was in fact the size of a apple, and it was a sight to see. "The truth," he said in a voice that'd lost all its power, and he waved the envelope in his hand. "The truth will set you free?"

There was a general guffaw then, and for just a moment I thought maybe people was gonna take my side. Then someone else spoke.

"The thing to do is, the *right* thing to do is to give them back to their owner. To Reggie Packman."

It was like some strange thing'd happened. There was me, and there was T.V., and there was Everyone Else, and Everyone Else was like, I don't know, one person, but not even a person, one thing. One voice, one desire.

A mob, I thought then. A mob.

"Give em back!" the mob called out. "Let him have it!"

The mob was surging forward then, swirling around the stump, carrying me forward with it. A little circle of space was maintained around me, and high up on the stump T.V. was looking down with a kinda worried look on his face. Hands poked outta the crowd, pushed against the stump, which rocked back and forth, and then T.V.'s mouth was saying, Okay, okay, and he began throwing letters into the air. The letters caught the sunlight and flashed like sparks, and the saggy flesh of T.V.'s arms wiggled inside his shirtsleeves with the effort of his throws, and the mob's hundred hands reached out and snatched the letters outta the air, and it was still yelling *Give em back!* and *Let him have it!* and but underneath its shouts I heard another voice, a thin voice calling out *Help!* and *Let me out!* and at first I thought maybe this was my own voice but then I realized it was like the Mayor, calling from inside the stump.

Then a letter, wadded into a ball, hit me in the face.

It seemed like it weighed ten *pounds*, that letter, and it like to knock me out cold.

Another letter hit me in the chest, and I stumbled backward, my breath suddenly gone.

A letter slammed against my back, and I was pretty sure there was still a hand attached to that one, and I pitched forward into a onslaught of other letters and other hands which was waiting for me, and this time the hands made no bones about punching me straight out. Paper was curled into fists that caught me in the face and stomach, and as I bounced back and forth from fist to fist I had this like one *idea* which was that I had to stay on my feet. As long as I stayed on my feet I would be okay.

I had this idea too that if I said something people would snap out of it. People would remember who I was: a person, one-a them, a Galatian born and bred. But I couldn't say nothing, and even if I could all I could think to say was *My name is Divine*, and people was demonstrating pretty conclusively that that wasn't true.

Then an ankle snagged mine, and I fell.

What's funny is that I never passed out. I had a image in my head, of the Mayor's eyes rolling and his head wobbling back and forth, and I thought that that's what was gonna happen to me, but it didn't. As soon as I fell the mob closed over me like water, I had the distinctest sense that I was drowning, and that I was being tossed about by waves that were really kicks and punches, but my eyes never once closed, and there was sound too, a lot of sound, but it all had a underwater feeling to it too, one sound was more or less like another, voices, punches, the thumps and rips of the tent as it came down somewhere behind me, the crackle that was the beginning of the fire, and then I *was* under water, I was choking anyway, the air I pulled in was hot and thick and seemed to weigh me down and then, like a drowning man, I gave up and I relaxed and waited for it to happen.

And then the mob was gone.

I blinked my eyes.

Gone.

I blinked again. I turned and looked all around.

One end of the tent had collapsed or been pulled down, the end closest to the open barbecue pits, and that was where the smoke was coming from. There wasn't that much smoke really, and hardly any flames at all, but what smoke there was came from the burning of the nylon tent, and nothing stinks like burning nylon. As the tent burned it melted into little drops of oily fire that dropped on picnic tables, on paper plates and paper napkins and paper tablecloths, and these caught fire too, but not as quickly as you might think, it's like the fire was giving someone, anyone, a chance to put it out, and you could see just what was gonna happen if no one did.

I heard a voice then.

"Hey?" I heard. "Hey, is somebody there? Reggie? Reggie, you still there?"

It was T.V. I stood up slowly. I didn't feel no pain—I hadn't felt nothing since those first letters hit me—and I saw T.V. on toppa the stump, still sitting in his loveseat, looking at the fire.

"Reggie?"

No sound came from inside the stump.

I took a experimental step, to see if everything was working right. My body still felt like it was underwater. My arms and legs moved at a tenth their normal speed, as though they was pushing against something. I took a step, and another step, and then another step. Still, nothing hurt.

Then T.V. saw me.

"Reggie," he called. "Reggie, you gotta help me. Reggie, Darrell's done gone, can you run the forklift?"

I didn't answer him. It didn't even occur to me to answer him. I didn't hate him or nothing. I didn't feel nothing—for him, or myself for that matter, or the missing mob. I was taking steps, one after another, and waiting, to sink back down, or to break into pieces, or to disappear.

"Reggie? Reg—Divine? Divine, please. I didn't mean for nothing to happen."

And you know, I believed him when he said that. When he said that he didn't mean for nothing to happen. Nobody ever does, in Galatia. But all the same I didn't stop. I was walking. One step, and then another. I was walking away. I saw flames in the dry grass in Vera Gatlinger's back yard, which was next to her I.G.A. I saw the trail the mob had left as it'd moved away from me, and I turned, it was the only time I turned all day, and I walked in the opposite direction.

"Divine?"

I walked in a straight line. Step, and step, and step.

I noticed that the sun was going. Down, I remembered, the sun don't just go, it goes down.

Step, and step, and step.

Galatea was a small town, and I was outta it pretty soon. I was in Galatia, and then I was outta that too.

I was walking east.

Step by step by step.

My name is not Reginald Packman. I did not know people hated me so much. In fact, I don't think they do.

My name is not Divine, and people do not hate me either.

My name could be Eric Johnson. Everyone hated Eric Johnson.

Maybe I do not have a name. Maybe that's what people hate.

I have many names, and I hate them all.

Step, and step, and step.

7.16

Eric Johnson

JUNE 26, 1984

My name is Eric Johnson and I live in a land of make-believe.

My Momma says she ain't cleaned house since long before I entered her life and for once it's not too hard to believe her. The air in here's so thick with dust motes they seem drawn in—as in, drawn with a pencil, or a crayon—and they float cattywampus from room to room, millions and millions of silver flecks the size of nickels and dimes and quarters all bouncing off each other and flashing in the morning light, and I tell you what: they make morning a special time around here, a magic time my

Momma would say, and even though I don't believe in magic I believe in my Momma, or I understand her, which is tantamount to the same thing. My Momma calls it fairy dust, says that's why she won't sweep it up. I tried to explain to her that ninety-five percent of household dust is actually human skin but she said that don't make no nevermind. Sometimes I wonder if she was trying to say we was, I mean we *were* fairies, but I figure I'm better off not asking that question, or leastaways not asking her. At any rate, the dust *does* change things. It affects sight and sound and touch. My hand at the end of my arm seems a mile away, the lines of the book I'm reading waver like the surface of Webster Reservoir on a windy day. Dust settles on everything, countertops, bedclothes, food, even doorknobs if they ain't turned every five minutes, and when it lands on my skin its touch is barely felt but still there, a thousand times lighter than the footsteps of a fly—I was going to say a fairy but I'll stick with the real world cause for once the real world's good enough—and as I read and sweat pools on my arms and legs and belly it rolls off me in thin brown streams and zebra stripes my entire body. Walking to the bathroom or kitchen is like floating. Somewhere, down there, is the floor: little mushroom clouds spring up with every step I take, swallowing my feet and damping out the noise they'd make otherwise, and if I whip my head around I can see the dust rushing into the empty space I've just walked through. My Momma says that anybody with open eyes and a open heart can see magic, and if that's true then it *is* magic, what goes on in our house on a Saturday morning. On the floor in front of every window there's a square of light colored red or blue or yellow from where it pushes through the used-up bath towels my Momma nailed over the windows in place of curtains. Words have been known to show up in the dust on top of a bureau or countertop, words like A *fool hath no delight in understanding, but that his heart may discover itself*, and so on and like that, and let me just lay your suspicions to rest by telling you that my Momma can sign a check but only after Vera Gatlinger at the I.G.A. or Yankee Carting at the TruValue makes it out for her. Sometimes the TV works fine and sometimes it don't work at all. Sometimes I hear tinkling piano music coming from the attic, which is nice, but sometimes I hear the clankety-clank of drums in the cellar, which ain't. Isn't. Is *not*. My Momma never buys nothing except liquor but even so the icebox is always fulla food. Around here a turn of the faucet is less likely to yield water than a shot of dry air or golden rust. My Momma told me one time she turned it on and out come a little red-gold-green garden snake—but she also told me that she bit into a apple once and sank her teeth into the gold coin she wears around her neck now, and, too, she told me I didn't have a daddy, she says she made me by mixing the dust of a bone chip she found inside her very own bellystone with a quart of Puerto Rican rum and drinking it at midnight by the light of a full moon. My Momma swears that the bone chip came from a great pale whale that lived and died a million years ago and that's why I turned out the way I am.

That's why I turned out white.

7.17

Colin

IN A STORY, THE ONLY REASON SOMEONE FALLS ASLEEP after sex is so the other person can slip away. Lovers don't fall asleep after sex—old married couples maybe, but not lovers—and I had never allowed myself to use the device because it seemed to me nothing more than a clunky piece of plot machinery. Yet after I had shared Divine with Wade—or perhaps I should say, after we had split Divine between us—Wade and I both fell asleep, and when I woke up I realized that there was a legitimate motivation for zoning out, besides everything we'd had to drink. Going to sleep so soon had made the sex seem like a dream, a nightmare perhaps, but at any rate something unreal and therefore requiring not explanation but interpretation. Because I couldn't have told you *why* I'd done what I had, but I could see immediately what it *meant*.

Divine was gone. Though there was nothing to indicate he had done anything more than absent himself from the house, I felt a certain emptiness there, a hollowness, as if when he'd left he'd taken with him not just his body but some essence of himself he would normally leave behind, and return to. So I left too. I wanted to find him, not to stop him really, because I think he was right to flee us, but to make him safer on his journey. I tried to slip quietly from the room but Wade's voice caught me.

"Colin Nieman," he said.

I stopped, turned around. Wade lay propped on one elbow, his gray shirt hung open on his skinny torso like parted curtains. Fucking Divine seemed to have cleared the air between us, and we proceeded straight to the point.

"I would like, if I could, to ask my own question about your novel."

I looked at him; I neither allowed nor denied his request. "I would like to know," he said, "where you got the names Martin and John."

"Martin and John?" I said. I looked at Wade for a long time, wondering if there was something Justin had told him that he'd not told me, and finally I shrugged. Did it matter? "They're names from a dream," I said. "Justin's dream. They're names he called out in his sleep."

Wade nodded his head; he smiled slightly, as if I had confirmed something he'd already guessed. "I sometimes wonder if we might all be Justin's dream."

Something in his comment infuriated me—not his words exactly, but the complete lack of emotion with which he spoke them, and I suddenly started shouting. "You think you *understand* Justin, don't you?"

Wade didn't look at me. "I think I understand myself," he said, "which is more than you can say about yourself."

"You still blame me, don't you. You, you're like Cora, or Webbie. You think I upset some delicate balance by coming here, and that all of Galatia has to pay for my crimes."

Wade didn't answer me, but, very slowly, deliberately, his eyes closed.

"And Justin," I said. "Justin especially has to pay. That's what you think, isn't it."

Wade's voice came from behind his closed eyes, as if he were concentrating, working hard to remember a speech he'd learned long ago. "I wouldn't say he's had an easy time of it," he said, and I wondered if it was Justin he referred to, or if he really meant himself.

My own words, when they came, seemed as distant from me as Wade's had seemed from him, as rehearsed, recited, I should say, and I felt as I had felt so often recently, that we were all following someone else's script. "That's your Justin," I said. "Not mute but muted, not silent but silenced. Well, listen to me, Wade. He painted himself into the corner he's in, and it's *you* who keep the paint wet for him by indulging him in his little melodrama. You feel sorry for him, you call him a victim. But it's you, Wade, and me, and Lucy Robinson, who are Justin's victims."

At Lucy's name Wade blinked his closed eyes, but he didn't speak.

"An eye for an eye, Justin once said to me, a tooth for a tooth, a book for a book. Yes, a book for a book. I stole *The Beast* from him, he said, I published it, I made it real. But don't think he let me get away with it. *The Beast* and *The Land of Make-believe*. I had taken his, so he had taken mine. But you still have *The Beast*, I said, it's right there on the shelf. And you, he said, you still have *The Land of Make-believe*, and he upended a sack he was holding, a sack which wasn't important until he emptied it. And what came out, you ask me. What fell to the floor? Why, my book, of course. Every word of my book, every single word. Yes, every *single* word. Justin had taken a scissors to my manuscript, to fifteen years of labor, and, word by word, page by page, year by year, he dismembered it completely. It's all here, Justin said, it's all yours. Every single word."

Wade's eyes suddenly opened, and in them I could see a vision of his own paintings, shredded at Justin's hands and blowing away across his beloved plains. Very quietly, almost whispering, he said, "What did you do?"

"What did I do? I laughed in his face. I said, You think you can destroy a story just by cutting it up in little pieces? I grabbed a handful of words. I said, Once this was just one story; now there are *this* many. I flung my words at him, I had the satisfaction of watching my story fall like dirty city snow all over the apartment, so insubstantial that the slightest breeze whirled it away in eddies and falls, yet so widespread that, like a net made up of a hundred times more open space than solid materials, its few threads were enough to trap everything it fell on. And you think he's *helpless*. He is *eating* you, and you don't even know it."

Wade didn't say anything for a long time, and then, finally, he pulled his shirt closed on his torso. I thought of curtains again, closing this time, like curtains drawn shut on a stage.

"Tell me," he said then. "When the two of us remember this day, who do you think will claim the final responsibility? You for initiating it, or me, for joining in?"

"That prize," I said, "I suspect, is one we shall fight over to the bitter end."

Wade closed his eyes then, draped one arm over them. "It already *is* bitter," he said. "I only wish it were the end."

7.18

T.V. Daniels

THE TENT BURNED SLOW. EARLIER IN THE DAY DARRELL Jenkens had told T.V. that Yankee Carting always gave it a good hosing before the picnic, to clean it and to cool it down and to guard against fire. Well, it did burn slow, but it was definitely burning.

Smoke grew outta the fire in tufts as thick as black whipped cream. It had the peculiar stink of dog hair on fire, and when an occasional plume of it engulfed the stump, T.V.'s eyes watered and he choked and covered his nose with his empty mailbag.

Divine had gone, and the crowd had gone, and Darrell Jenkens was gone too, and the Mayor had stopped making any noise a long time ago.

T.V. still had not stood up, because he was afraid one of the pallet's boards would crack underfoot and he would fall off what to him seemed like the narrow surface of the stump. So he sat there, and tried not to look at the fire.

At some point he noticed the microphone, squashed between his hip and the side of the loveseat, and he picked it up and tapped it experimentally.

A hollow boom rattled out of the speakers.

"Hello?" he said. "Hello? Is anybody out there?"

He waited for a moment and then, hearing nothing, he set the microphone down.

He gagged as a fresh wave of smoke washed over the stump.

He still didn't stand up. Instead, he rolled forward, slowly, slowly, as slowly as he could he leaned forward until suddenly the front legs of the loveseat snapped under the strain and T.V. pitched onto his chest and stomach, and then with a crash he heard more than he felt he fell to the ground twelve feet below. He bounced once, twice, three times, and then he was still.

7.19

Colin

IN FACT, I SAW THE SMOKE, AND I DIDN'T THINK ANYthing of it. Everyone in town had been talking about the barbecue for the past week, and I had seen the size of the pits: they seemed easily deep and wide enough to produce a column of smoke as large as the one I saw, or, I should say, as small, because the thin black ribbon that spired from the center of town seemed tiny and harmless, a dust devil as opposed to a tornado.

But as soon as I got into town I knew something was wrong. The feeling wasn't intuitive: a wide swath of destruction cut a path across Monroe, broken fences and mailboxes, trampled hedges, the smashed window of a parked car. As I crept along in my car I could see what looked like the footpath of a large herd where it had crossed the street, a beaten-down powdery trail like the track of a giant snake, and then I saw the I.G.A. parking lot, and the stump, and the forklift, and the half-collapsed and burning tent. I turned the corner and gunned it then, but the sound of spitting gravel brought a blush to my cheeks, and I slowed down immediately. I was not a hero; I was not going to rescue anyone. I was just going to see what had happened.

The stump canted slightly. Something, probably not the forklift since the stump angled to one side of the forklift's path, had tried to knock it over. On top of the stump the remains of something—a chair?—lay in splinters, as though an anvil had been dropped on it as in a Saturday morning cartoon. Beer cans and bottles and plastic cups littered the parking lot, and a gust of wind scattered a stack of printed paper napkins like large gingham snowflakes. The tent itself burned slowly and noxiously. The smell of roasting flesh mingled with the smell of burning petroleum, and when my eyes and mouth watered I wasn't sure if it was because of the bad smell, or the good smell, or the combination of the two. I stared at the fire, at the several little fires, for a long time. I thought about getting a hose from a house next door, or calling 911. Did one call 911 in Galatia? Is that how one responded to an emergency here? I wasn't sure, and, at any rate, the point was moot, because I didn't do anything in response to the fire except sit in my car and watch it burn. If I had any thought about the fire at all, it was just a dim wish that it would burn out of control, that it would take the whole town down, because I was going to leave it now, and if the town burned down then I would feel less like I was running away from something than that something had been taken away from me.

Something caught my eye. A gray-haired head poked out from behind one of the half-dead elm trees that lined Jefferson, a gray-faced figure that withdrew as soon as it had seen me. The urge to flee left me as quickly as it had come, and I jumped out of the car and raced toward the tree. My footsteps crunched loudly on the prairie's debris, and at the sound of them the figure dashed from behind the tree and began to run from me.

"Rosa!" I called. "Rosa, wait! It's Colin, Colin Nieman!"

It occurred to me that there was no reason why my name should make her stop, and she didn't stop; she kept running, and a red bag that hung from a strap over her shoulder banged and bounced off her hip. It occurred to me that no one had ever run from me before, like this, in fear. Justin had never run from me in fear—from disgust maybe, but never in fear—and it gave me pause, the idea that I could strike a fleeing terror in someone's heart. I slowed some, but still, even a halfhearted effort on my part was more than Rosa could manage, and I caught up with her easily. I had only to lay a hand on her shoulder and she stopped, which made me glad, because I didn't think I could have knocked her to the ground. I would have run beside her for miles before doing that.

I'm not sure if Rosa had been talking before we stopped running, or if she started immediately upon my touch.

"You gotta go!" she gasped. "Gotta go, go go go. Get on, you, me, everybody. Got to *go*!"

"Rosa, calm down. Calm down now, catch your breath."

Rosa's eyes rolled wildly, looking everywhere but at me.

"No time, there ain't no time. No time atall. Got to just get on go and get *out* of here, before it's too late."

I put both of my hands on Rosa's shoulders then, and turned her toward me. I hated to use my strength like that, but I could think of nothing else to do. I stared at her until her eyes finally caught mine, and I held her eyes then, until she calmed a little.

"I'm not going anywhere," I said then, "and neither are you. Not just yet. Now take a deep breath and get hold of yourself, and tell me what's wrong. What happened here?"

Rosa's eyes stared into mine as if she had been bewitched, but after a moment I realized that I was just as powerless to turn away as she seemed to be. She stood tensely between my hands for a moment, and then, with a deflating wheeze, she sank to the ground.

"Oh it's no use," she said, whispered really, or sighed. "No use, no use, no use."

I dropped to my knees beside her. "What, Rosa? What's no use?"

Rosa looked up at me. A tear had fallen from each of her eyes, and they made muddy lines in the dust of her face. They looked fake, made up, like the tears a clown paints on his face, or the vertical slits that slice down the cheeks of marionettes. She put a wet hand on my cheek.

"I like you, Mr. Nieman, I always have. Everyone else knows you for a arrogant and maybe even a ruthless bastard, but me and my Cora always knew you weren't a bad man. Just outta place."

"Rosa—"

"Just troubled is all. Plagued." Her hand gripped the skin of my cheek so tightly I thought she would cut me. She said, "I *know* about plagued."

"Please," I said, "Rosa—"

Her hand dropped from my cheek to her lap, and she looked from my face to the ground.

"You think it was you, Mr. Nieman, but it wasn't."

"It wasn't me, Rosa? What wasn't me?"

"You think it was you who upset the balance, like Cora said. Here in Galatia. But it wasn't. It was me."

"Rosa, I'm afraid I don't understand."

"The balance, Mr. Nieman. Every place has its balance. Good and evil, life and death, God and Satan, Mr. Nieman, swinging on either side-a the scales. You think it was you who upset the balance, but it was me."

"Rosa," I said. "Rosa, Rosa. Why does it have to be anyone's fault. I mean, besides the person who's done this thing."

Rosa looked at me as though I were a child. "Eleven years, Mr. Nieman. He's had eleven years to do something if he wanted to."

"Eleven years?"

"Five years ago I showed up. You ask anybody, things started happening then. Things went missing. Bedside lamps, toothpaste, the batteries outta people's cars. Odds and ends, not the kindsa things a thief takes. It was like *shopping*."

Suddenly I understood her. "You're talking about Eric Johnson."

"Oh, he started slow, Mr. Nieman, started small. Like a snowball on toppa mountaintop. But it's been growing and gathering speed, ever since I come here. You"—she laughed a little—"you just showed up for the end."

"Now *listen* to me, Rosa. Eric Johnson is *dead*. Eric Johnson was killed by a lynch mob. They killed him, Rosa, do you understand?"

Rosa looked confused. "Killed him?"

"Yes, Rosa. Killed him."

All at once she smiled, sweetly, innocently. "He ain't the sorta person who just . . . dies."

"Yes, Rosa, he is. He did. He *died*."

She was whispering now, her voice so quiet that I had to put my ear close to her mouth. "Then where is he?"

"Dead, Rosa. He's *dead*."

And then she was shouting. "Then where's his *body*? You don't just die except you leave a body behind! You don't just die! You got to have something to show for it."

She jumped up then, and would have run away if I hadn't held her. She fell against me, and again she started to mumble, "It's all my fault. Mine, all mine. The fault is all mine."

"Rosa," I said, "please, believe me, you didn't do anything." I had an odd sensation as soon as I spoke. I had believed my words before I voiced them, but as soon as they were out of my mouth I felt them to be false. I didn't know—I didn't have any idea, even, what Rosa was talking about—but nonetheless I knew that I had not spoken the truth.

"I came here, I brought the world with me. I brought the world to Galatia."

"By that reasoning I'm just as guilty as you. Didn't I come here, with my money, and my culture, and my Justin? I brought things too, I brought more than you."

I felt Rosa shake in my arms, and it took me a moment to realize she was laughing. "Oh, Mr. Nieman, oh, you silly boy." She sat up, looked at me. "You always trying to own everything," she said, "always trying to make it yours. Yes," she said, and she paused for a long time. "You brought things. You brought everything maybe. But I," she said, "I brought *you*."

"Rosa?"

The tears in her eyes almost had a glow to them now, and I had time to think, She's more than a little crazy, before she spoke again, in a voice that was racked by regret and sorrow.

"First the mother comes, and then the son."

Something in her words shocked me, and I had to fight the urge to recoil.

Rosa shifted the red sack that hung from her shoulder to her lap.

"When I come here," she said, "I walked here. I walked away from everything just to get here, every man and every woman that was ever a part of my life I walked away from. My body has loved men and women and given birth to boys and girls and I watched em all each and every one of em grow up and grow old and die, a hundred times that's happened to me, a thousand, oh, Mr. Nieman, you don't know the history I walked away from, just to get here. But I did. I walked away from it. I left it all behind. Everything. A thousand miles I walked here, naked as the Lord Almighty made me, and I didn't even know this was where He was sending me till I got the sign."

She unzipped her bag then, folded it open. A bellystone sat in there, a whole one, the size and shape of a cantaloupe. Instinctively I reached to touch it, but she folded the bag closed.

"*Mine*," she said, and she sounded like a mother scolding a young child. "This was *my* sign. It was left for me in the middle-a the road. There was carnage all around it but this sat untouched and pristine, unopened, a whole world all its own and glowing with the Lord's glorious sunrise, and even as I saw it I saw another glow in the distance, the same glow, and then I knew just where I was supposed to go."

She was looking behind me then, over my shoulder, and I turned to stare with her and saw the crest of the bald bluff, almost blindingly white now with the late afternoon sun.

I turned back to Rosa. "Carnage," I said. "You said carnage. What carnage, where?"

Rosa blinked her eyes slowly. "Where?"

"Where was the carnage, Rosa? Where was the bellystone?"

Rosa clutched the sack in her lap. "It's mine," she said, and now she sounded like the child. "It was *my sign*."

"I know it's yours, Rosa. I don't want to take it from you. I want to know where you found it."

"Where?" Rosa looked confused. "Why, it was where I come from. Where I was born." She looked up at me. "Where Galatia was born. And you too, you was born there too."

Despite myself, I shook her. "*Where*, Rosa? Where was I born?"

Rosa shivered a little, and shrank around her bag. I had a vision then, of her disappearing into the bellystone like a genie into its lamp. But then she looked up at me and a bright smile split her face and a crazy light filled her eyes.

"Why, Kenosha, of course."

"Kenosha?"

"Of course," she said. "Where else?"

7.20

Eric Johnson

TODAY IS MY THIRTEENTH BIRTHDAY, BUT PAY NO ATtention to that. By the time I could crawl I knew—or I felt anyway, and sometimes feeling is the same as knowing—I understood that time had little relevance for me: there would be a time when I was alive and there would be a time when I was not but either way I was going to be alone or I was going to be miserable, and that wasn't going to change whether I shit into a diaper my Momma changed or a toilet that emptied into a septic tank I had to call Stan Robinson up to pump for me. Of course I didn't have the words for that when I learned to crawl. As far as that goes, I didn't have them when I was thirteen years old neither—I'm just telling you. I'm telling you there ain't no peace in this town of Galatia, oh, excuse me, Gala*tea* now, there isn't any peace for someone who looks like me, no matter how old or young he is, no matter what his name is, or the name of the town he lives in. I'm not black and I sure as hell ain't white: what I am is ugly, and you might think I could just leave Galatia but I'm pretty sure I'd still be ugly no matter where I went. Another thing my Momma says is that some magic comes from outside and some from inside, and if I *do* have any magic it's my ability to make anyone who sees me recoil in horror.

Uncle Sawyer and Aunt Cora come over round noon for my party. It's just them and me and Momma, who's still asleep when they knock on the door. True, they been promising all week they'll come over, but I have to admit I didn't really believe them until I heard their car on the driveway dirt and so now I have to hurry-rush and slip out of the bed and get dressed without waking Momma. When I finally pull the door open a rush of my Momma's fairy dust is sucked out the doorway and Uncle Sawyer and Aunt Cora cough and wave their hands in front of their faces and make a general carrying-on, but even so I can see that Uncle Sawyer has a shiny silver-wrapped box in one-a his hands that he's taking care to not jiggle around, and Aunt Cora has a cake plate all wrapped up in tinfoil in one-a her hands, and it's all I can do not to grab the present and the plate and run for it, but I don't, I hold on to the door and I hold still and the dust settles down and then Uncle Sawyer and Aunt Cora stand up straight and smile down at me, and almost at the same time they sing out "Happy birthday" to me, but neither of them says my name. I guess

I should tell you that my Momma named me Eric after her daddy, which everyone thought was more than a little disrespectful seeing as how my Momma gave birth to me outside-a the sacred bond of wedlock and all that, but my Momma said she had her reasons, and so anyway most people don't call me anything except for Uncle Sawyer, who just calls me Bro.

Now, Uncle Sawyer and Aunt Cora are just about the prettiest people I ever laid eyes on, and they are so in love. Now that it's summer they're both dark as the old oiled walnut bed in their bedroom, and Aunt Cora has that funny red tint going on too, her Cherokee heritage she says it is, you can also see it round her eyes and cheekbones and lips, and even as the two of them say happy birthday to me I can see their attention is really on each other, which doesn't bother me all that much because that's just how it is with them. Uncle Sawyer wobbles a little bit, even I can see he's faking being drunk just so's he can rub his arm up against Aunt Cora's arm. He's wearing a clean pair of faded overalls and she has on a sleeveless summer dress made out of a pale blue fabric with tiny white flowers all over it, and when Uncle Sawyer rubs against her Aunt Cora giggles and slaps his arm and says, "Stand up straight you fool man, anybody looking at you'd think you was drunk at noon on a Saturday," and then, just for good measure, she jabs her elbow in his ribs. "Marsha still sleeping," I say then. "She was out to Sloppy Joe's till all hours and plus too she come home with a bottle in a bag, she tried telling me it was Co-Cola but I told her she shoulda said it was 7-Up cause at least that's the right color for whatever it was, gin I think. And anyway pop fizzes and gin don't." Uncle Sawyer and Aunt Cora manage to hold on to their smiles and so I say, "She drunk up the whole bottle," and then Uncle Sawyer clears his throat and says, "Well, yes," and he says, "Cora honey," and he says, "Whyn't you get the birthday boy ready for the picnic while I go see if I can wake up my sister." He makes a big show of handing over my present to Aunt Cora and he wags a finger at me and says, "Now, don't you be shaking the box cause then there won't be nothing lefta what's inside," and then he goes off to the bedroom. Aunt Cora takes the cake and the box to the kitchen table and when she sets them down a cloud of dust rises up and sets her to coughing again. "Good Lord, child, how *do* you breathe?" she says, and then, while I watch in wonder, she goes from window to window and without a care in the world she pulls the bottoms of all the towels off their nails and folds them up over their tops and then she opens every sticky protesting window wide. "Got to get some fresh *air* in here," she says, and every time she bends over to open a window her butt is outlined inside the thin cotton of her dress, and when she pushes the window up high her titties stick out from her chest like they separate things that only her bra holds on to her body. "Never seen so much *dust* in all my life," she says. "It's like living in a dream."

When Uncle Sawyer comes outta the bedroom with my Momma, me and Aunt Cora are sitting in the living room. Aunt Cora is staring at a TV program that sometimes is ladies' golf and sometimes men's bowling, and I am pretending to read my Tarzan book but really I am watching the Kansas wind that blows through our house. I am watching it for the simple reason that I *can*, because something that is usually invisible is for once easy to see: outside the window there's just a clean clear hot day, a day like any other day, but in here the dust makes the air currents as visible as water flowing down the Solomon River. It's as though a flood is moving through our house, it's as though we're fish, and because most all the fish I have ever seen have been in fish tanks I have the eerie sensation that someone is watching me—although that's a sensation I have all the time, and might just be because the windows are, for the first time in my memory, uncovered, and so if someone wanted to they could, in fact, look in.

"Miss my baby boy's *birth*day," my Momma is saying as Uncle Sawyer leads her out the bedroom. He got her to pull a dress on over her nakedness but underneath her body's moving about every which way. "What kinda foolishness you talking to me, Sawyer Johnson? As if I would miss my one and only child's birthday. As *if*. Eric," she yells then, "Eric," she says, a little more quietly, "baby boy," she says, "you run and fetch your Momma some-a that aspirin out the medicine cabinet. Your Momma's got a headache the size-a this town and she could sure use some aspirin." I get the aspirin and I bring them to my Momma, along with a cup of whatever it is she keeps in the flask in the medicine cabinet, which is what she really wants, and my Momma takes the cup from me with a smile and a wink that pulls at one side of her face like a seizure. "And you brought me water too," she says. "What a good little boy you are." Her hand on my hair is rough and clumsy and pulls away as soon it's able, but the hand that raises the glass to her mouth is gentle and steady and slow, and my Momma drinks something that I think is vodka—really cheap, really bad, really *warm* vodka—in slow steady gulps, in order to pretend it's water. When she's finished she makes a gasping noise she tries to mask with a lip-smacking sigh of satisfaction, but Uncle Sawyer has a frown on his face so severe that it pulls lines down his cheeks from the bottoms of his eyes all the way to the long point of his cleft chin. "What?" my Momma says, feigning innocence, and Uncle Sawyer don't say nothing, *doesn't* say anything, I mean, he does not speak, but he does take her glass away from her and he hands it to me and says, "Well, Bro, looks like you better get your Momma some more water. She done drunk up her first glass and forgot to take her aspirin." My Momma looks at the two little pills in her hand and tries to smile; over on the couch Aunt Cora is watching TV intently, and when our silence continues she jerks her head in our direction, then back at the TV, and after a moment she says, "Strike? What you mean, strike? He knocked em all down." Uncle Sawyer catches hold of my shoulder when I head toward the bathroom, steers me in the direction of the kitchen. "I wanna hear the sink running," he says to my back, and then after a pause in which I know he's thinking what I'm thinking—that it's easy to fill a glass with liquor under cover of the sound of running water—he says, "But not *too* long."

7.21

Cora

SOMEWHERE IN ALL THE CONFUSION I LOST TRACK OF Rosa.

I wanna say that I don't know what come over people besides maybe too much beer and too much sun, but that would be a lie.

That man up on that stump, T. V. Daniels. Well, he'd set at my table more than once. We'd all fed him, and now we was looking at what we'd grown.

And then too ain't no one didn't know what those letters was about. Oh, Reggie. I told him once that he was fool crazy to think a couple-a letters could save him. Nowadays it takes a video to get people excited, or at least some good color pictures, but if he was gonna do it I said at least take the trouble to do it right. Think of them *like* pictures, I said, make copies but keep the negatives safe. But Reggie. He just said, *I'm* the negative, and left it at that.

Well. As soon as T.V. showed up I grabbed ahold tight of Sawyer's arm, and when it came pretty clear to me things was gonna get outta hand I looked around and around for Rosa too, and when I couldn't find her I figured she musta gone on home, and I took me and Sawyer there as fast as his wheezy lungs would let us go.

I knew something was wrong even before I climbed up the front steps. The screen door was flapping in the breeze, and the inside door was wide open too.

It was Rosa who'd closed it when we left. Closed it, and locked it. Just in case, she said, she always said. Just in case.

The door was open but the blinds was closed, which the blinds'd been open when we left.

Inside I didn't even call her name. I just sat poor confused Sawyer down in a chair and run up to the bedroom.

The bellystone was gone.

Five years she hid it from me and I pretended not to know about it, and now it was gone.

I was surprised I wasn't surprised. But I wasn't.

And I was sad I wasn't sad. But I wasn't that either.

Both them things would come later, I knew, but right then I felt just like that little corner in the backa Rosa's bureau looked: empty except for a few dusty crumbs that coulda come from a stale loaf of bread.

I went back downstairs to the café, and Sawyer.

"Momma," Sawyer said.

"What you want, honey? You feeling okay?"

"Momma," Sawyer said. "Look."

I looked at Sawyer first, but he was pointing away from himself, pointing up, I knew just where he was pointing without looking but I turned and looked up anyway.

The picture of me was gone.

The Sawyers was there, botha them, but I was gone. The kitchen stool was behind the counter, right under the pictures, and there was the outlines of two footprints in the cushion on top, and there was a third outline on the wall where my picture shoulda been.

Then I was *surprised*, and I was sad too, and I sank down into a chair and laid my head on a table and bawled out loud, cause she'd left me but she'd loved me, she'd took the bellystone to tell me she wasn't never coming back but she'd taken my picture to show me it wasn't *me* she was leaving, it was Galatia and whatever it was in herself that she was running from, that'd driven her here and now had driven her away, and I cried and cried and cried then, because Rosa was my second chance and ain't no one gets a third. Sawyer come over and put a hand on my back and he whispered *Momma?* but still I cried and it was all I could do not to shake his hand off me. Aw, Sawyer, if I could blame you I would, and if I could free you I would do that too, of me, of me and Rosa and your daddy and Galatia, but we *all* gone now and if you see anything at all it's just ghosts of who we used to be, and Sawyer like the rest of us you're stuck, and like the rest of us you'll build a city one day, and maybe, just maybe, if we lucky and you lucky, the city you build will be a beautiful city, and we can all come home at last.

7.22

Colin

I DROVE HOME FIRST.

I asked Rosa if there was anything I could do for her, if there was anyplace I could take her, but she said no, no there wasn't nothing she needed, and when I put a hand on her shoulder and tried to steer her toward the Range Rover she writhed beneath me like a mouse beneath a cat, and when I took my hand off her she ran in the opposite direction, from the car, and me, and Galatia, and this time I just let her go.

On the way home I passed Myra's house. I passed the place where, last winter, Lucy had been abducted, but I tried not to think about that. I did glance at the mulberry tree there, and I noticed for the first time a thin yellow ribbon that someone, Myra probably, had tied to it; the ribbon was frayed and faded now, and virtually invisible through a thick growth of leaves and dark red and purple berries and the shiny green of an itch-ivy vine, but all I could do was marvel that I had never noticed it before. It amazed me how much Lucy Robinson's disappearance had changed our lives, and yet how little we actually thought of her. Myra's house was less than a hundred yards from the tree, I realized then—so close, Lucy had been so close to home—and on her front porch Myra was standing with both hands wrapped around one of the posts that supported the porch roof. She stared fixedly at Galatia, and I glanced in my sideview mirror and saw that the smoke was still a single thin column spiraling up from the center of town, and I glanced at Myra and saw that she was swaying slightly on her dead feet, swaying like the column of smoke behind me, swaying like a dancing cobra or a dust devil or a single strand of prairie grass, Myra, swaying like an animal or something inanimate, and I resisted the urge to stop and wave, or stop and shoot her like I had shot Charlene.

At the house, black flakes of obsidian sprayed against yellow limestone as I skidded to a stop. Inside, I went straight for Justin's cupola. I called his name as I ran, not because I thought he might answer me, or even come to me, but because I didn't want to burst in on him and scare him. I wanted him to know it was me.

He stood in the center of the cupola when I reached the top of the circular stone stairway. He had opened the door for me, and for a moment I paused on the landing, unwilling to violate a space he had made sacred to himself, and to unknowing.

"Justin," I said, and I stopped. I so wanted to know his real name, to use it just once.

Justin's feet were pressed together, and he rocked slightly on his heels. Behind him a window gave onto Kenosha. It wasn't visible but still, I knew it was there.

And then I made a choice.

"John," I said, and took a step toward the room. "Lucy," I said, and stopped again. "I think Lucy is in Kenosha."

I couldn't swear to it but I thought Justin shivered a little, when I said the name Lucy, or when I said the name John. The light came from behind him and shone in my eyes, and his form already shimmered slightly.

"I'm going there," I said. "I just wanted to tell you."

This time I was sure he didn't move.

"Listen," I said, "whether she's there or not, when I come back we're leaving. It's over, do you understand. It's all over, and we're going home."

He stood and stared.

I noticed that his hands were balled into fists. I wondered if he had willed them, or if he was even aware of them.

"You should pack," I said quickly, "because we're leaving the second I get back. You should—aw shit," I said. "I'm sorry it came to this. I—Goodbye, Justin. I'll be back as soon as I can."

7.23

Nettie Ferguson

SHUT THAT DAMN DOOR,'' LAWMAN BROWN SAID TO Nettie Ferguson, "and for God's sake don't tie up the phone line. Just sit down and for once in your life shut up."

Nettie Ferguson looked blankly at Lawman Brown for a moment, and then she did as she was told.

After a moment Lawman Brown said, "Are they gone?"

Nettie Ferguson didn't say anything.

"Are they gone?" Lawman Brown said again.

Nettie Ferguson still didn't say anything.

"Command Central to Nettie. Nettie, I'm talking to you. Are they gone?"

Nettie Ferguson sniffed. "You told me to shut up."

"And now I'm telling you to talk."

"Well, what I was gonna say is that this day reminds me of that time way back in Kenosha, good golly, it seems like so much more than twenty years—"

"Nettie! Are they gone?"

"They're gone," Nettie said. She sat silently for a moment, and then she ventured, "North?"

"Toward Rosemary Krebs'."

"North."

Lawman Brown paused for a moment and then he picked up the telephone and set the unit in his lap. "I suppose maybe I should call Mrs. Krebs."

Nettie Ferguson raised her voice slightly. "She said not to disturb her under any circumstances."

"Well, I don't suppose she was expecting a visiting party."

"I do believe she said that the sun had given her a headache and nothing short of the Second Coming merited a break-in on her peace and quiet."

"Well," Lawman Brown said, "I guess she did say that."

". . ."

"You said they was heading north?"

Nettie Ferguson waved an arm. "North."

"Heck, they could be going anywhere."

Lawman Brown took the phone from his lap and set it back on the desk. When he set it down it made a short sharp ringing noise which vibrated through the room's silent air.

Nettie Ferguson sniffed loudly. When Lawman Brown didn't react she said, "Allergies?"

Lawman Brown tapped his fingers *tum-tum-tum* on his desk and stared into space.

Nettie Ferguson sniffed again, then wiped her nose with one swollen knuckle. "Pollen count's been through the roof all week."

Tum-tum-tum.

"Me, I like that Clor-Trimeton myself, but they was out of it over to Vera's I.G.A., so I had to get me some-a that Sudafed Hay Fever Plus, which just don't work as well. For me anyway." She sniffed again, loudly, and when Lawman Brown still didn't react she said, "I never thought I'd see the day?"

Tum-tum-tum.

"Well, look," Nettie Ferguson said, "and it was right about the same time of the year too, wasn't it? Well, of course it was. I mean Founders' Day here is just a month or two after burning day there, I mean, you'd think I'd remember the exact date but I'm not even sure if it was May or June. But I do remember that it was hot as a *oven*. Hot as a oven, I tell you, there was times I thought my hair was going to catch fire and you know it was a miracle more people wasn't caught. Now, you wasn't there if I recall, I seem to recall that Rosemary Krebs had you running an errand for her down to Bigger Hill that day, and what was I saying, oh yes, I said that to her, to Rosemary Krebs, she and me ended up right next to each other on the edge of town and I leaned over to her and, well, I mean, of course I leaned over, I guess that goes without saying, I leaned over to her and I said, It's a miracle more people wasn't caught, because by then you could tell that most everybody in town'd made it out okay, praise the Lord, and do you know what she said to me? Do you know? Well, of course you don't, you wasn't there and even if you had been there you'da been with the men fighting the fire and so I'll tell you. I have observed, she said, Ah hayahve ahb-zayaved, she said, just as Georgia as the day she was born and her married to Phyneas Krebs twenty years if it was a day, Ah hayahve ahb-zayaved, she said, that the denizens of this part of the world are habitually laconic, I swear to you that was just the words she used, the *denizens* of this *part of the world* are *habitually laconic*, she said, but she said that when someone lights a fire under their, excuse me, but she said it first, under their *ass*, she said, they really get a move on. Well, did you ever? I mean, in your life? How is it that when certain people use filthy language it's *you* they make feel dirty? But still and all, it did make me think. I mean it made me wonder. I wonder, *are* we quiet folks? Or are we really a bunch of busybodies who just don't like to admit it? I mean, something like today, or that day. It does make a body wonder."

Nettie Ferguson paused for breath.

Tum-tum-tum.

"Eustace?"

Tum-tum-tum.

"Eustace?"

Lawman Brown continued to stare into space, and when his mouth did finally open Nettie Ferguson like to jump out of her skin.

"Did you say something, Nettie?"

7.24

Eric Johnson

NOW WE'RE IN A FIELD OF YELLOW STONE.

The field is outside of town.

Way outside.

Another thing Uncle Sawyer and Aunt Rosa promised me was we could have my birthday picnic in the park at the center of town with the willows and the windmill and the goldfish tank and that soil that is always wet and springy with thick green grass, but as Uncle Sawyer heads us all to his car he tells me, "Gonna be crowded there today. Cora told me Reverend Abraham's having a outside meeting with the Church Ladies and some-a the other elders." When I point out that the park is completely empty Uncle Sawyer just shakes his head. "Starts at one," he says. "Cora told me." By then it was quarter past but I didn't mention that, and for her part Aunt Cora held the cake on her lap and stared out the window so hard as we passed through the new part of town you'd think she'd never seen white people before. I don't think I'd be as disappointed as I am if Uncle Sawyer and Aunt Cora had gone ahead and broke their very first promise to me, the promise of the picnic itself, but there you go: hand someone even the tiniest part of your trust and you leave yourself wide open for their betrayal.

I sat back in the back seat then and watched my Momma poke through the picnic hamper that filled the space between us. "What you got in this big old basket here," my Momma said, pushing aside wrapped sandwiches and Tupperware containers until at last she found what she was looking for: a little brown bag enclosing the slightly convex shape of a wide liquor bottle. My Momma looked at me and winked and patted the bottle and put it back in the basket, sated for the time being by the glass I'd brought her earlier and by the promise of what was to come. She closed the hamper and sat back in her seat and said, "Looks real good, Coretta, I have to say. Looks like you made us a real good lunch."

Uncle Sawyer calls where we are now the hinterlands. This field I mean, not Kansas, not Galatia. Technically this field we're in is a part of the Deacon spread, which I guess I should say that it belongs to Old Lady Bea now, but it's way far out in the middle of nowhere. The Cave of the Bellystones is miles closer to town, even Noah's ark is closer in; if it comes right down to it, we're in Kenosha territory now, or what used to be Kenosha. The land here isn't really arable. It's uneven and studded with the limestone deposits that were quarried to build the limestone house. The usable stone was mined long ago; now the area is just a mess of limestone shards that'll cut up your ankles if you ain't careful, if you're not, I mean, if you are not careful then the shards will lacerate your ankles, and there are these deep squared-off pits boring into the earth, some of them have what look like bottomless pools of water in them and some of them are bone dry and don't ask me why that is cause I don't know, and anyway pretty much nothing larger than a kangaroo rat or a rattlesnake ever comes here, and my Uncle Sawyer, who's always kind of liked the place. Something I once heard Aunt Cora's friend Webbie Greeving use, Reverend Abraham's daughter Webbie, the one that's off to college now, something I heard her say is "harsh beauty," which phrase she was saying to characterize whatever attraction the Great Plains might have had to the people who chose to settle here. I always kind of liked Miss Webbie. I guess if you believe in such a thing—*harsh beauty*, I mean, not *choice* or even *settling*—then the abandoned limestone quarry is exactly what she was talking about: to me it looks a hell of a lot like the surface of the moon except it's a damn sight hotter, and the sight of that long line of smoke and ashes just over the horizon gives me the heebie-jeebies. I'd just as soon sit down under a shade tree and wash down Aunt Cora's roasted chicken sandwiches with a cool drink of water from the well in the park. But I guess Uncle Sawyer didn't want to be disturbed. I guess he thinks it's easier that way, for me, or maybe he just thinks it's easier for him.

There's potato salad to go with the chicken sandwiches, and thin seedless moon slices of cantaloupe for after, and it seems like forever before we get to the cake. Before we can eat it Aunt Cora pulls out a little box of candles which strikes me as odd, given the wind, but she sticks thirteen of them in the cake plus one to grow on and she lights them all with a lighter she produces with a flourish from another pocket and all the candles catch right off and burn in the wind, tiny contained light balls under the big bright sun. I find out why they burn so easily as soon as I try to blow them out: they're those trick candles, the kind that don't go out and if they do go out then come right back on again. I blow once, hard, and they all go out, some-a the candles even bend over in the sun-softened frosting, but in a moment they pop back alight with a little ticking sound, and they flutter in the wind and drip little balls of pink and pale blue and yellow wax on the deep dark frosting of my cake. I look at Aunt Cora, Uncle Sawyer. They both have big mischievous smiles and a little shine on their foreheads from the bottle of schnapps they been helping my Momma polish off. I look at my Momma. She's cradling a cup in both hands, holding it just above her gold pendant and just below her nose. Her eyes are closed and her nostrils flared, and her chest is rising up and down as she breathes. I look back at Uncle Sawyer and Aunt Cora again, and then, one by one, I pull the burning candles out of the cake and throw them on the rocks, and then I stick both of my hands into the cake and rip away about half of it, and as I get up and walk away from the grown-ups I am already shoving my face into my hands and stuffing as much of the cake into my mouth as possible. The cake is chocolate. Aunt Cora wanted to make me angel food, but my Momma laughed and said I wasn't no angel and told her to make devil's food, my Momma didn't know I was in the other room or maybe she did, but she said make that boy something as black as possible cause whatever color he be on the outside, on the inside he as black as the devil himself.

7.25

Colin

I WALKED.

There were reasons. I wanted to leave the car at the house for one thing. For Justin. Just in case.

And I had seen the pieces of Lucy her abductor had sent us, her dress, her hair, the pictures of her broken body, her fingertips. I was in no hurry to see what was left of her.

And it was a beautiful day.

The sun was a hot orange diffusion in a cloudless sky, the stubbled ground its man-made mirror.

I ran actually. Okay, I jogged. Maybe *loped* is the right word. I debated with myself as I went. I filled my mind with thoughts of just how I was moving over the ground so that I would not have to think of anything or anyone else. I didn't fly, nor did I crawl, or slither, or swim. I thought, There are only so many ways a man can move himself along his path.

At one point I stopped. It was on the hill from which Rosemary Krebs had told me that one could, at one time, see both the steeple of Abraham Greeving's church and the cresting wave of Kenosha's grain elevator, and I stopped when I reached that hill's summit, because, far in the distance, I saw the gray cloud that marked Kenosha and its distant fire. A few hundred feet away, I knew, the little pointed fortress that enclosed the cave poked from the ground like the sharpened end of a pencil; a mile farther on lay the ashes of Noah Deacon's ark, and perhaps four miles beyond that lay Kenosha. A mile and a half behind me—I didn't turn, lest it should be gone—stood the limestone house, and behind that lay Galatia, and at the foot of everything towered the bald bluff, and I didn't turn to see if the flames had been extinguished or had grown out of control, if the pale crest of the bluff was fringed with hoary gray stubble and spat forth children in tongues of flame.

I started walking again, loping, jogging, running, and eventually I was there.

A wobbly ring marked the fire's ancient border like a tideline, and the grass on the inside of the line was thicker and greener than the grass on the outside, but everything else was a ruin. Asphalt that had once run in a clean grid had melted and hardened into random swirls and puddles, and the brick and cinderblock and stone foundations of houses poked from these pools like the tips of skeletons from ancient tarpits. The scene was somehow post-apocalyptic and prehistoric at the same time, and I had to remind myself that Kenosha had burned less than a quarter century ago, and that nature had only just begun to erase Kenosha. Already drifts of dust and tumbleweed piled against the west side of anything that stuck out of the ground more than a foot, which wasn't much, and it was easy to see how one day the land would swallow Kenosha entire, in the same way it had swallowed so many cities in history.

It wasn't a difficult search. There was only one place to look really, and that was among the cluster of brown brick walls that marked the site of downtown Kenosha. A bank, Myra had told me, a supermarket, the school building. As I approached them I saw that the walls were nothing more than hulls: the debris of the structures they had once enclosed had been bulldozed into a single mound at one end of what I guessed had been the school. Dirt had collected on the mound, and grass grew there, and thin green itch ivy, and twisted stunted trees, but the whole pile looked both so fragile and so impregnable that it was hard to tell if the roots of the plants held it together, or if the piled trash had trapped the plants among its folds. The pile drew me, and as I walked closer it seemed to grow from the ground like a hibernating locust, awakening. But that wasn't really what it looked like.

What did it look like?

It looked like a bellystone. Either a halved bellystone, flat end down, or a whole bellystone half buried in the ground, and if I hadn't known I was at the right place then I knew it as soon as I thought that, and I also knew why I had been wrong to assume Lucy was in the Cave of the Bellystones. Lucy was not in the Cave of the Bellystones. Lucy was *in* a bellystone.

When I got to the mound I walked around it slowly. At first it appeared solid, but soon enough I noticed half a dozen partially camouflaged holes. The shadow cast by the charred backboard of a basketball hoop was actually the empty space of a tunnel; a car's door opened onto an empty shell, and the other side of the car opened onto a black emptiness; a huge drape of colorless cloth hung over another hole, and so on. At each entrance the grass was crushed but not completely worn away, and in a bare patch of dirt in front of the stubbed-out end of a galvanized-steel culvert I saw several footprints, and I recognized these feet, their size and the deep stamp they had made in the land, from the stairwell that led to the cupola.

The culvert was big, nearly three feet around, and I got down on all fours and crawled into the hot tunnel. For a few seconds the light behind me cast my shadow before me, but soon enough it was gone, and I hit my head on the uneven side of the culvert several times, and nearly fell over when it dipped sharply. Eventually I was out of it, and the air cooled and I could feel the space open up around me. The hairs on my arms and legs and chest tingled from a slight movement of the air. I stood up then, slowly, one hand raised to protect my head from an obstruction that never came. The breeze played over my sticky skin. I started forward, my hands stretched out in front of me now, and as I walked I noticed here and there a distant glimmer of light. So the fortress wasn't so impregnable after all, I thought. It wasn't a fortress at all, or even a bellystone, it was just a pile of old shit. My sight came back slowly; the black resolved itself into lighter and darker patches, into shapes and shadows, and I stumbled along slowly. Things cracked and rustled underfoot, and I knew that it was pointless to attempt stealth. I thought of shouting out even, but something held my tongue. The sound of my approach said enough.

It was impossible to tell how long I walked, or how far. It seemed I went on for hours and miles. I was sure that I was caught on some loop that led around and around the mound, but I couldn't tell if I was spiraling deeper into it or merely circling its perimeter. More times than I could count the path split and I veered to the left the first time because that seemed to be the way deeper in, and at each successive fork I veered left again. The air seemed to be getting hotter, but that could have just been my exertion. At some point, though, I realized there was no turning back because I had no idea which way was back, and so I continued to walk, one foot in front of the other, step and step and step.

And then I knew I was there.

The piecemeal walls of the tunnel seemed to disappear from beneath my trailing fingertips, and I felt again the expansion of space around me. I didn't realize my breath had been echoing in my ears until the echo disappeared, and I hadn't noticed that the faint differentiation of shape and shadow had also disappeared some time ago, and that I could truly see nothing. I took one more step forward and felt something light and hard bounce off my foot, followed a moment later by a hollow metallic clank. For some reason I knew that the sound I had heard was one empty tin can striking another.

I stopped walking.

I turned around slowly, looking for even a single glimmer of light, but I saw none.

A stink hit me then. I realized I had been smelling it for a long time, but all at once it assaulted my nose and the gorge rose in my throat. What I smelled was shit and piss and rot and flesh that was not merely unwashed but festering, a smell I have only ever encountered in the slums of certain Indian cities and the cardboard shanties that used to fill Tompkins Square Park, but in the enclosed space of the mound it was not merely disgusting or nauseating but truly horrific, and more than I wanted to vomit I wanted to run away. But I was lost in the darkness, and the idea of forward and backward or left and right seemed not just useless but meaningless now, and so I stood stock-still, retching slightly, and before I could decide what to do an electric light snapped on. I had time to see the pulsing walls of a cave, an uneven floor covered with something that I recognized instinctively as the black foamy underside of wall-to-wall carpeting, a ragged chair, a stack of charred pillows and bedding, and a pile of something else that I did not immediately recognize as Lucy, I saw myself poised as though on a tightrope, one foot directly in front of the other and my hands stretched out on either side of me, but I did not see the light nor who had turned it on, and then something struck my head, and what I thought of then was Jewel, Jewel and the one I had named John, and then the room disappeared again, and so did I.

7.26

Wade

AFTER COLIN LEFT I CLAIMED SLEEP'S ESCAPE AGAIN. I could say that sleep's escape claimed me, or I could say that sleep and I escaped together. I could dress it up in as many different and colorful phrases as you like, or even as you don't like, but the simple truth is that after Colin and I had said the few words we had to say to each other I closed my eyes again, and I kept them closed until I was sure he was gone. When I was sure, I opened them again, and then there I was: Wade Painter, the biggest fool who ever lived, in a town of very big fools indeed. Colin was gone, of course, and so was Divine, but it took me a moment to realize that Divine's sideview mirror was also missing, and I searched my drink-muddied brain for any memory of it from the first time I had opened my eyes but I could find none, and this seemed the day's biggest loss. The little innocuous thing which I had wanted to blame for the day's mess had vanished, and now I was left with just the mess itself, unadorned and unmitigated, and I could no longer pretend that anyone was to blame but myself. You could say that Colin had a hand in it, or even Divine, but in the end—or, I should say, in the beginning—only one person had introduced Colin to the limestone house, and that was me. The truth is that I had wanted Colin to move here because I had disliked him immediately upon meeting him, and I believed that if anything could beat his personality it was this town's, and I was right, but I had not quite foreseen the battle royal that would precede Colin's fall. And I had wanted him to move here, and bring Justin with him.

I got up. Off the couch, I mean. I got up and I left. I left our mess untended, the stains of whiskey and other things. Oh, why be coy: I left the stains of whiskey and cum and shit smeared on the floor, and I looked for but could not find my shoes, and I walked out of the room and closed the door behind me. It seemed to me then and it seems to me now that had I attempted even a cosmetic cleansing I would never have stopped scrubbing, and so I closed the door behind me, as I said, and I walked to my studio in my bare feet.

Where else was I to go? I wasn't hungry, and I wasn't tired, and the light was still good.

On the floor of the hall leading to the back door I found Divine's cigarettes, a book of matches tucked into the cellophane, and I retrieved them and dropped them in a pocket of my pants.

In the studio I wandered from door to door, room to room, floor to floor, but my eyes didn't see my unfinished paintings waiting to be completed; instead I saw the ghosts of tables and chairs and beds and bath towels and pots and pans and plates and area rugs, and I laughed a little to think I could have ever taken this house away from my parents, away from my family and my past.

Eventually, inevitably, I found myself in front of the door to Justin's room. Divine's cigarette pack was slick and cool against my hand as I reached in my pocket for the room's key, and then I was inside, I was in my childhood bedroom and I dumped the key and the cigarettes and two dimes and a nickel to the floor, and I looked at this new mess I'd made for a long time until the room gradually asserted its presence and all those other things, those other thoughts really, were pushed from my mind.

Only one picture of Divine was still visible. Only one shot, a sketch of his smirking face and wide eyes. The rest of him was covered by pieces of Justin.

A sketch pad and a piece of charcoal seemed to wait for me on the floor.

I looked around for something to draw. I looked around for Justin, I suppose, or Divine, or myself, but none of us was forthcoming. None of us was visible; none of us was in the room anymore, and all my eyes saw were black lines on white paper and the things that had fallen from my pocket, a single key and a pack of cigarettes and two dimes and one nickel, and a voice that should have been Yonah's—or perhaps Justin's—whispered, *Gone away. Not for you.*

I held the pad in one hand, the charcoal in the other, and I sat down in the center of the floor, and, like Justin, I closed my eyes.

One of the things you learn in life drawing is that the picture doesn't come out of your hand, it comes out of your eye, and so your hand should follow your eye and not the other way around; and one of the first lessons in any good life drawing class consists of drawing an object, often your own hand, without even looking at the drawing. The result, inevitably, is a mess, a map of unfollowable lines, but in a way I never quite understood the lesson was the lie that proved the truth of the eye's superiority, and I never forgot it, and over the years I repeated it often, and in a drawer downstairs I had the shredded remainder of dozens of these squiggled pages, and the only thing I can say about them is that *they all looked the same.*

Yonah once got an offer of several thousand dollars for those sketches.

He had the check actually, and he was packing the sketches up when I caught him, and I wasn't sure if I should rip up the check or the drawings, so eventually I did both.

My eyes were closed.

In this room it wasn't myself I drew, but Justin, and Justin wasn't there, so I closed my eyes.

My first impulse was just to fill the sheet completely with blackness, because that's all I saw, all I saw when I tried to conjure an image of Justin, and then I thought I should leave the page blank, because blankness had replaced the blackness, blankness felt much closer to Justin than blackness, but eventually the memory of what I thought his face looked like returned to me, and I began to draw.

I don't know how long I drew, but when I opened my eyes the room was dark. A faint glimmer of light came off the key and the pack of cigarettes and the two dimes and one nickel I had dropped on the floor, but the shape of what I'd drawn on the pad was invisible to me.

The light came from the distance, from Galatea, which was on fire, and I needed more of it.

I mean that I needed more light.

I said it out loud. *I need more light*, I said, and the voice which said these words was the same voice that had said, *Gone away. Not for you.*

I reached for the cigarettes, and the matches tucked into the pack's wrapper.

I lit a match.

I looked at what I had drawn for a long time, and all I can, all I *will* say is this:

It looked like my hand.

And then I dropped the match on the pad.

The match sputtered and then it went out, and, after a long moment and another glance at the flames on the horizon, I lit another match and this time I applied it to the edge of the paper and I held it there until the flame took and began licking up the page like a dog's tongue licks a spill of milk from the floor, and then I set the burning pad on the floor atop the one remaining picture of Divine, and I left the room, and I left the house.

My parents' house.

The wind was blowing from west to east, and barefoot still, I set out west across the stubbled field, and I did not look back to see if I had succeeded or failed, because I no longer knew what the terms of success or failure were. The air smelled like dust, and dust, I should tell you, does not smell like smoke, but it smelled like smoke to me.

7.27

Lawman Brown

THE PHONE RANG.

Nettie Ferguson reached for the extension on her desk, but Lawman Brown sliced a finger across his throat.

He let it ring seven times before he answered it. By the third ring Nettie Ferguson had to sit on her hands to keep from grabbing the phone, and by the seventh she was positively quivering in her chair.

On the seventh ring Lawman Brown picked up the receiver.

"This is Sheriff Brown."

The voice on the other end of the line was slightly hoarse. Lawman Brown immediately thought the person was trying to disguise his voice although the truth was it sounded like maybe the person had just woke up.

"Lucy Robinson is in Kenosha" is all the voice said, and then the line went dead.

7.28

Eric Johnson

BUT LIKE I TOLD YOU: YOU CAN'T NEVER GET AWAY. I find me a little quarry, maybe ten feet deep, one with a thin triangular pool of water filling the low corner of its sloped base and a cloud of mosquitoes hovering just above the water's scummy surface, and I climb down, using the niches left behind by drills and chisels. But I don't get away. Down there there's a shadow. Down there the temperature drops ten degrees, and the mosquitoes move away from the water and begin to circle my arms and legs like a thousand tiny moons, and on a little ledge no wider than my thumb enough soil has collected for a stunted stalk of wheat to take root, and down there, too, there are the voices of my Momma and Uncle Sawyer and Aunt Cora. Some little trick of acoustics carries their voices straight to me, as if I'd picked up a telephone extension they was already talking on. "Marsha," Aunt Cora is saying, "you not gonna let him stay down there, are you? He could hurt hisself." "Boy's big and fat but he ain't clumsy," my Momma says, "big and fat and white," she says, "but he can climb trees like a monkey," and Aunt Cora says, "How can you talk about your own son—" "Aw hush," my Momma cuts her off. "He is my own, and they ain't no use in holding illusions about what he is." "What he *looks* like," Aunt Cora says, "not what he *is*." "Same difference," my Momma says, "round here anyway." There is a little silence then, and then Uncle Sawyer says, "So how's things down to the factory?" and my Momma says, "Shit, where you been at, boy? I ain't worked there in two, three weeks now. Laid off," she adds after a little pause, "cutbacks." That's a crock of shit, of course, and it's not like nobody don't know it—the plain truth is Momma went in drunk one too many times—but all Uncle Sawyer and Aunt Cora say is "That's too bad" and "I'm sure they'll take you back on soon." "Well," Momma says, and I can even hear her sniff, "gimme some more-a that stuff, will you? What you call it?" "Peppermint schnapps," Uncle Sawyer says, and my Momma says something that sounds like "schnot," and then she laughs and says, "Gimme some more-a that peppermint snot."

There's something funny about hearing my Momma and Uncle Sawyer talk without seeing them. Some more family history: Uncle Sawyer's real name is Marshal to my Momma's Marsha, and according to legend he's my Momma's twin. I say according to legend because looking at them you'd never even suspect they was, I mean they *were* related. Uncle Sawyer, well, there's an economy about his body, it's not that he's short, just that his body doesn't take up any more space than it needs too, and his skin is just *so tight* that not only is Uncle Sawyer lean but it's impossible to ever imagine him becoming fat. One time after he'd done some night planting for Kendall Hendricks—old Kendall's real superstitious about when he'll put seeds in the ground—I happened to be over early the next morning and Uncle Sawyer was sleeping the sleep of the dead, it was April, I think, or May, but it was a hot morning and Uncle Sawyer was sleeping on top of the sheets. Aunt Cora was out to the I.G.A. getting some real maple syrup for the pancakes she'd made me, and Uncle Sawyer was asleep in just a pair of boxer shorts. One thing about Uncle Sawyer that does look like my Momma is the color of his skin, which like I said in the summer is the same color as the dark walnut wood of the bed he shares with Aunt Cora, and, well, I was only four or five then, and for some reason I just had to *touch* that beautiful brown skin that Uncle Sawyer and my Momma and my Granddaddy who was still alive and living with us then all had. I had this overwhelming urge to prove to myself it was real, that it wasn't, like, painted on, that it wasn't a hoax they were perpetuating on me, who didn't have it, and so I tippytoed over to the bed and I put one hand flat on Uncle Sawyer's back. It was hot and there was a film of sweat on it and *aha!* I thought, *it is paint*, but when I took my hand off it wasn't no different, my hand, I mean, it was still white, and Uncle Sawyer's back was the same too, as dark and deep as chocolate sauce, it was just sweat I'd felt on his skin, but then I noticed that where my hand had touched him the sweat was gone and in its place was an even darker patch of skin in the shape of my hand and all the sudden I put my hand in the exact same spot on his back and then I put both of them on him. I put my hands on the hot slick skin of his back and at first I just left them there until, very slowly, I began to rub, I pushed my hands back and forth over Uncle Sawyer's back and like I said before his skin was so tight it was like my hands was pushing over the vinyl upholstery of their new living room couch, back and forth I pushed my hands and as they went the sweat was pushed away and Uncle Sawyer's skin seemed to get deeper and darker, blacker and shinier, until what I was reminded of wasn't walnut wood or chocolate sauce but the tar pits I'd read about once, and as I pushed and pushed I imagined my hands slipping into the tar of Uncle Sawyer's skin, slipping inside his body, pulling me in after them, I was gonna dip myself in his deep well and come out as dark as he was, as *real*, a real live black man. But what happened instead was that after a minute Uncle Sawyer—his face was turned away from mine on the pillow—Uncle Sawyer made a little sighing sound which confused me and I didn't know whether or not I should stop and then Uncle Sawyer made another sound, a sound like you make when you take your first bite of sweet potato pie and it turns out to be still warm and fresh and full of the flavors of cream and brown sugar and coconut, and then Uncle Sawyer's back arched up under my hands which kind of brought them into contact with the waistband of his underwear, they even slid a little under it a little, and that if anything should have impressed upon me his solidity, demonstrated to me the futility of my task, but still I kept rubbing and praying that somehow he would let me in on his secret until finally, at last, the front door opened and closed in the other room and a moment later Aunt Cora's voice called out, "Eric? I got you syrup for your pancakes," and Uncle Sawyer and I both froze, he lay there with his face turned away from me and he didn't breathe, and I stood there with my hands splayed about the small of his back and then, quickly but silently, I backed away from him, I never turned around, it was as if I wanted to reverse whatever it was I'd just done so that it wouldn't ever have happened, and I slipped backwards out of the bedroom and backed down the hallway and I even pushed the bathroom door open with my butt and after a minute I flushed the toilet and then I came out and Aunt Cora was pulling the pancakes out of the oven where they'd been keeping warm while she was at the store and then we sat down and ate breakfast and Uncle Sawyer didn't get up until well after noon, by which time I was already back at my house.

But I was talking about Uncle Sawyer's voice. I was wanting to say how it sounded just like my Momma's. Which was my point, a long time ago: that Uncle Sawyer—by birth Marshal, he got his nickname, Momma told me once, "on account of he was always playing with wood," which she seemed to think was very funny—Uncle Sawyer has a voice that sounds exactly like my Momma's, lending credence to the idea that they really are twins, and yet my Momma's such a flop and Uncle Sawyer's so fine. It gives me, I'm not sure what to call it, but *hope* is what I want to say, hope that if he could turn out to be such a different person than his twin sister—and their daddy too, I remember, he was a real mess of a man, their momma being dead since a long time before I was born—then maybe I can change too, maybe one day things will all come together in me like they did for the ugly duckling who became the beautiful swan, I won't have to be tarred and feathered or painted with my Momma's fairy dust, the change'll come from inside of me.

I'm finished with all my cake and the mosquitoes are biting hell out of my arms and legs. I climb up out of the hole then, rub my eyes and rub my stomach and say, "I don't feel so good." I say, "I wanna go home," and Uncle Sawyer says, "Sound like somebody had too much cake," and Aunt Cora says, "Boy, come on over here and let me wash your face. Looks like somebody done dropped you in the mud," and then she giggles once, a drunken giggle, and then she claps her hand over her mouth and doesn't say nothing else, and in the silence my Momma lets out a slow loud belch. "Well, ain't you even gonna open your present?" she says. I'd forgotten all about it, and now, looking at everybody's bright expectant faces, I am forced to sneer at them and rub my hands over the smeared frosting on my face. I look at Aunt Cora and pull out the most derisive, dismissive voice I can manage and say, "It was your cake made me sick. It was *bad*," I say, and I turn to Uncle Sawyer and I fix his eyes with my own and all I say is "You can keep your shit. I don't *want* it."

I never did find out what was in that box.

What's waiting for us in the dust on top of the TV after Uncle Sawyer drops us off is this: *How doth the city sit solitary, that was full of people.*

My Momma spends the rest of the day nailing the towels back up over the windows. By the time she's finished it's dark out, and she goes to bed.

Later on the piano starts playing upstairs, and the drums answer it from the basement. I shut off the TV that I was watching, but before I go to bed I read again: *How doth the city sit solitary, that was full of people.*

There isn't anything too miraculous about bad plumbing or clanking pipes in the cellar or mice running along the keys of the old piano up on the abandoned second floor of our house, although don't ask me how it got up there. As for the words written in dust on the top of the TV, well, I'm forced to admit that they come from no man that I know of.

In the bedroom with the towels tacked up over the closed windows and with the door shut tight it's as dusty and dark as it ever was, and in the bed next to me is my Momma's body, it seems like that when she's passed out and naked, something that belongs to her but isn't really her. She's sweating and snoring and spread wide over her side-a the bed, and there are funny smells coming out her mouth and her pussy, and then, like I did a long time ago with Uncle Sawyer, I start rubbing on my Momma, I rub that black skin which in this light or lack thereof doesn't show no change but I keep rubbing anyway, hoping to find what it is that all that blackness hides, what it is that it *means*, and then I start rubbing on myself too, my hands making smaller and smaller circles as my arms get tireder and tireder until finally they've just spiraled down to the center of our bodies and there I keep rubbing, keep pushing, keep praying that somewhere under my skin I'll find my Momma's, and if not that then maybe somewhere inside my Momma I'll find me.

Tomorrow Lucy Robinson will point her finger at me and scream.

Tomorrow the pointed flames of lit torches will stab at my feet as I hang by my thumbs, but I will concentrate on the gurgle of the water in the Solomon River beneath me, and not feel the flame, not feel the jerking pain in my thumbs as I try to kick away the torches that stab at my feet. I concentrate on the river's sound, and on its smell too, the cool cool smell of water, and eventually, after first my right thumb goes, and then my left, I will feel it all around me when I fall into it, and I will feel it inside me too, as it rushes into those two new holes in my body.

7.29

Colin

A DROPLIGHT DANGLED FROM THE ROOF ON A GREASY yellow cord, and this is where the light had come from. The protective housing that normally shielded the bulb had been ripped away, and the naked bulb showed so brightly that it was invisible unless I looked at it from the corner of my eye. The space the light illuminated was neither room nor cave; it struck me as nothing more than chance emptiness where solidness could have been, and it was impossible to tell if the hollow had formed when this pile had first been bulldozed into place, or if it had been excavated later. Everything that made up the floor and walls and roof of the room—you see, already a lack of vocabulary has forced me to familiarize the place—everything was burned and broken and piled together so thickly that almost nothing was recognizable. The melted steel spokes of what might have been a bar stool stuck through one part of one wall; a line of jagged studs poked from the ceiling like the broken teeth of some giant's comb; the limbs of half a dozen human beings were, I was pretty sure, the charred remains of display mannequins, but that was all I could make out. Everything else was inky black and indistinguishable, except for me, and Lucy Robinson, and the man who held us here.

I cannot bring myself to describe Lucy Robinson. I will only say this: she was not yet dead, although the only people I have ever seen who looked anything like she looked lay in the AIDS wards of New York City hospitals, which, I suppose, is another way of saying that Lucy Robinson looked as if she would not be alive for very much longer.

And I cannot bring myself to call the man who held us Eric Johnson. Oh, I knew it was him—who else could have possessed that skin, and those hands, who else had so much reason to hate—still, the figure who caromed about the room seemed somehow more and less than human. I know I am giving in to so many of the old prejudices when I say that, but what else can I say?

He had tied my hands behind some kind of post that stuck from the floor, and it seemed he had been waiting for me to open my eyes because as soon as I did he grabbed one of Lucy's ankles in both his four-fingered hands and dragged her naked body into my line of vision. He only left her uncovered for a moment; then, when my eyes would not leave her form for his, he pulled what looked like an ancient vinyl tablecloth from a recess in the wall and spread it over her body. One of her hands—one of what remained of her hands—poked from beneath the covering, and he kicked it from view. Then there was just the mound of her, falsely blooming under flowers that had melted like Dali's timepieces, and the slight wheeze of air escaping from her lungs didn't sound like breathing as much as it sounded like something broken and winding down. Throughout the operation she made no other sound, and our captor made no sound at all.

After that he just stared at me. He squatted down on his haunches, and sometimes he used one of his mangled hands to poke at my head. When he brought them close to my eyes I noticed for the first time the long mottled scars from missing strips of flesh that ran up both his forearms to his elbows, and the little splinter of naked bone that poked from his left hand where his thumb should have been; on his right hand there was just a hollow red-lipped pucker carved into the side of his palm like a second mouth or anus. The splinter wiggled agitatedly, and it held my eyes like a hypnotist's pendulum. As I looked at it I could hear bone snapping, but I wondered what, exactly, flesh sounded like as it tore like wet cloth.

He poked at my face with those hands, those arms, that body, he slapped me sometimes, once or twice he pulled back as if to punch me but always he turned and directed his blows against the covered body of Lucy Robinson, who seemed to absorb the impact in the same way a partially stuffed feather pillow does.

He avoided her stomach though, I noticed. He kicked her in the legs, and the arms, and the head, and when sometimes he kicked part of her out from under the tablecloth he kicked it back in.

After a while he began to cry. Some color came to his pallid cheeks, a veiny swelling blush that seemed to rise from his skin like hillocks from a flood basin, and then the tears began to fall thickly. Soon he was sobbing, and thick cries began to push out of his throat with gobs of spit. They were the first human sounds he had made before me, and they seemed to spur him to even greater histrionics: he sobbed, his body shuddered, he fell forward onto his hands and knees and his head hung low to the floor, his mouth open, spit drooling from it, and then flecks of blood, and then the muscles of his abdomen began to convulse until finally a thin stream of bloody vomit pushed out of him. He caught some of this liquid in his hands, and he looked into it for a moment, and he turned and looked at me, and then I was scrambling and trying to get away but I couldn't and I caught the splash of it full in the face. The smell and the taste of it caused my own stomach to heave, but nothing came out, and after several shuddering moments the attack passed, and then I was left with the hot foul liquid cooling on my cheeks and chest, and when I thought of that I was surprised, surprised that it was warm I mean, almost welcomingly warm, and I was reminded that the creature before me was a man, hardly more than a boy, barely older than Justin or Divine, and then, without conscious effort, I spoke. I had meant to spit his vomit out of my mouth, but instead I spat out his name, and my own.

"Eric Johnson?" I whispered. "My name is Colin Nieman."

Breeding always shows itself in good manners, my mother used to say, and despite myself I laughed a little.

He was up in a fury then, and his fists and feet struck me a dozen times until suddenly he fell back and screamed at me. The sound was unintelligible; I wasn't sure if he'd attempted words or not, but after a moment he seemed to calm, and this time when he spoke I did understand him.

"Eric Johnson is no more," he said. "My name is Noman Never. Whatever I was is so long buried that it no longer exists, and so I take my revenge in secret and without fear of retribution, and I leave it for others' backs to take the whipping meant for mine, and for whoever it was they thought I might once have been."

I stared at him for a long moment, and then I said, "Your name is Eric Johnson. You were born in the town of Galatia twenty-four years ago to a woman named Marsha P. Johnson by an unknown father, and despite whatever mutilations and injustices have been heaped on you, you remain Eric Johnson."

"My *name* is Noman Never!"

"Your name is Eric Johnson, and eleven years ago you were hung by your thumbs for molesting the girl Lucy Robinson who now lies between us."

"My *name* is Noman Never, and *I* never touched her, never!"

"No," I said. "*You* never did. Her father did. Lucy's father did. Stan Robinson, who delivered the punishment meant for him to you."

He stared at me, eyes wide and mouth agape, and then he spun around in a circle and kicked Lucy in the head, and he screamed, "*It* has no name, and therefore no father!"

"Let me go," I said. "Let Lucy go. There's no point in keeping this up any longer. Let us go." I sighed. I didn't believe what I was saying but words spewed from me with the urgency of salmon swimming upriver to spawn, and die. "Let yourself go, Eric."

He lunged at me then, leaping over Lucy's covered body and grabbing me by the throat and knocking my head back and forth against the post I was tied to. "I am doing the telling," he screamed at me. "This is my story now, not yours, not you, Nieman."

He continued to shake me until my neck slipped from his awkward grasp, and when I could breathe again I said, "You don't really believe that."

"*I* am telling the story!"

"The story," I said, "is telling you."

But he went on as if I hadn't spoken. "I didn't do anything, do you understand. I was punished for something I didn't do, punished but left alive so that my mutilated body would serve as a warning lest anyone else transgress. So I tell you: I too punish the innocent, and I too leave them living. I too shall make truth out of lies, and so: Lucy. For she is Lucy, and always shall be Lucy, forever and ever Lucy," and with that he leaped backwards and he pulled the cloth from her body.

I closed my eyes before I saw anything, because I wanted to say something and I didn't know if I would be able to speak after I looked at Lucy.

"They didn't leave you alive," I said to the blankness of my closed eyes. "They came back to kill you."

"They let me fall like spoiled fruit. They left me to fester and rot."

"They didn't leave you. You left them, before they could kill you. You escaped," I said, and then I opened my eyes, "and you didn't even know it."

I saw Lucy then, and my mouth remained open, but the only thing that emerged from it was my breath, as ragged as her body.

My silence seemed to give him back some of his poise, and more pilfered words spilled from his lips. "Behold your wife," he said. "Behold the woman who dared to look back, and so was transformed into a pillar of salt. But I have made her flesh again, for you, Nieman, I have prepared this marriage chamber for you. In the morning the mother shall see the blood upon the sheets hung out the window, and know that her daughter fell, heretofore pure, before your attack, and forever after you shall be known as man, and wife, and child."

"Eric," I said. "Eric, Eric, Eric."

It wasn't my intention to infuriate him further. It wasn't even my intention to speak. But still the word was there, over and over again, and it caused him to hop about with rage, and at the last he kicked Lucy in the head yet again, and it snapped over, and her swollen stomach continued to rise and fall, but other than that she didn't move.

"Eric," I said, "you did nothing wrong."

"But there you are wrong, Nieman, who was born forty-four years ago to Ellen Powys and Charles, and who once had a wife named Susan and now has a lover named John and a net worth of seventeen million dollars."

"Justin," I said. "His name is Justin."

"The name Nieman appears on two books, only one of which Nieman wrote, and Eric Johnson's is the same sin, a sin more original than miscegenation. For Eric Johnson's is the sin of being born, or, in his case, of not being born. Of not being born black, and not being born you."

"I don't understand."

"Then you shall never understand, for my part in this story is over. I leave now. Soon all of Galatia will be here, and then your part will be over too."

"All of Galatia?"

"A mystery, Nieman. One more mystery. At the end everything is vagueness instead of clarity, more questions are reaped than answers sowed."

"But one thing is clear. Your name is Eric Johnson."

"My name is Noman Never."

"Your name is Eric Johnson."

"My name is Colin Nieman."

"*My* name is Colin Nieman."

"Your name is Eric Johnson."

And with that, he was gone.

7.30

Cora

THERE WAS FIRE BEHIND ME AND FIRE IN FRONT TOO: the fire of the sun setting the western horizon alight. A thousand times Sawyer asked me *Momma where we going? Where we going Momma?* but it took me a thousand and one before I knew the answer. *We going away,* I said. *We going far, far away. We gonna be free of this land. Finally,* I said, *we gonna be free.*

7.31

Rosemary Krebs

THE NIGHT WAS HOT AND I HAD BROUGHT A GLASS OF iced tea out onto the porch with me. By chance it was the first pitcher of iced tea I had made myself since Webbie Greeving left my service, and I was thinking that in some ways it was a relief to be rid of her, because she made a vile pitcher of iced tea. I suppose she did it on purpose—that is often the case with servants—but it is just as likely that she simply lacked any talent in the kitchen. At any rate, a muddy brown pitcher of what my momma always called nigger water had seemed a small price to pay to no longer have to clean my own house, and I was wondering if there was any way I could use tonight's ruckus to procure a new maid, preferably one who knew her way around the kitchen as well as the broom closet.

In fact, I half hoped that Coretta Johnson might be among the crowd now making its way through the gaps in my lilac bower, although I doubted it. Coretta Johnson had always seemed rather well behaved. Still, a town the size of Galatea doesn't need two restaurants, especially not two restaurants that serve the same cuisine, and a single mother only has so many options.

There was fire on the horizon, but after Kenosha, what is such a thing as that? And besides, *I* had not lit it.

I sipped my iced tea and waited.

The crowd poured into my yard like water into a bottle, spreading out within the bower's boundaries and slowly surrounding the house. Their voices were at once clear and indistinct: what they were trying to tell me was that they had come here to take umbrage with me, but, whether they knew it or not, what they meant was that they had come here to take orders. I could tell just from the way they avoided trampling my lilacs.

There was a collective stench of liquor-laced breath, and I was grateful that I hadn't indulged myself in sugar in my tea, just this once, but had stuck firm with fresh fragrant lemon juice. I held the glass under my chin and inhaled the sweet clean scent, and I waited for the stragglers to file into place.

At length I judged that the only movement in the crowd was a general milling about and not the arrival of new bodies. The entirety of Galatea was displayed before me, around me, behind me; it just fitted within the confines of my lilac bower—one more body would have tipped the balance against me—and as I waited for the poor soul who would be the first to dare to speak, I allowed myself a proud smile behind the cover of my glass of iced tea. This—this crowd—was a real accomplishment, worth so much more than a fortune, or a painting, or a child. There were three hundred children before me, three hundred paintings, three hundred fortunes. I am speaking of human potentiality here, and not necessarily actual conditions. I am speaking of the particular alchemy of a mass of human bodies all brought together in accord with a plan larger than any of them, and the sight of these faces, not just the dark ones, but the fair ones and those that were neither as light nor as dark as they should have been, the sight of all these faces made me ever so briefly envious of the simplicity of my ancestors' plantations. Well. They had had the law on their side then, and the church, and three hundred fifty years of history and common sense, and if it could be argued that my methods were not always genteel, then I would be forced to offer an admittedly weak response: context is everything.

Times had changed.

Once upon a time in America you punished the strongest and weakest members of your opposition, and the masses fell into line. Now one had to tolerate the strongest and coddle the weakest, and punish all the rest. It seemed to me that the old methods were easier on everyone concerned, but there's no point in being sentimental.

A voice called out from the middle of the crowd.

"Rosemary Krebs!"

I could not immediately place the voice, and I put my glass of iced tea on the porch railing. I could tell that the speaker was male, but that was all.

"Good evening," I said.

"We don't want none of your double talk, Mrs. Krebs."

The speaker was white as well.

"By no means," I said. "By all means."

"We want justice."

Sheldon Stadler.

"We want our town back."

Sheldon Stadler owed three back payments on his mortgage on his house in town. He was two months behind on the lien he had taken out against Wilma's farm, and I knew too that Wilma Stadler, who baked the cakes and pies sold at Elaine Sumner's Sumnertime Café and at Art Penny's café in Bigger Hill, was pulling in more money each week than Sheldon was.

Elaine Sumner hadn't made her mortgage payment last month. It was the third payment she had missed in two years.

"If you don't give it," Sheldon Stadler was saying, "we're gonna take—"

"Sheldon Stadler," I said, and right away he shut up.

"Lucy Robinson," I said, and then everyone in the crowd started to speak. I didn't raise my voice. I knew the people closest to me could hear me, and they would spread the word. "Lucy Robinson is in Kenosha," I said. "And so is Colin Nieman."

Then I picked up my glass of iced tea.

My words worked their way from me like ripples spreading out from a pebble dropped in a pond. At length everyone was silent and stood facing me again. Torchlight sent flickering shadows over their faces, and the fire in the distance seemed like nothing more than an orange crayon line drawn between the black plane of the land and the deep blue plane of the sky.

I put my glass of iced tea down without drinking from it.

I said, "I too would like to see justice done."

The crowd pushed their way out of the bower somewhat less orderly than it had entered.

Alma Kiehler, I noticed, broke off several branches that snagged in her hair.

Alma Kiehler had helped out at Coretta Johnson's café for a while, before Rosa Stone had shown up in town.

It was hard to tell in the dark, but it seemed to me that Alma Kiehler was just about the same size as Webbie Greeving.

7.32

Colin

WHEN I OPENED MY EYES HE WAS GONE.

There was a fresh ache in my head. I guess he had hit me. I put a hand to my head, and realized that he had untied me.

I thought of leaving too. He had left the light burning, and I could see the mouths of perhaps half a dozen tunnels, but I could see less than a foot into any of them, and I had no faith that any of them actually led anywhere, unless one knew which turns to take in the dark, and while I had found my way here without any difficulty I was pretty sure it wouldn't be that easy to get away.

And then there was Lucy.

Lucy Robinson.

Lucy looked like something that had been built and then torn down again. She looked like a stage set after it has been struck. What she had been was visible in the pieces left behind, but she was no longer what she had been, nor would she be, ever again.

Oh, I'm equivocating, I know, hiding behind metaphor, but when I try to approach her body I find I can only do so piecemeal, just like Noman Never.

The things which had been Lucy's hands were just blackened lumps now. They had been dipped in something which probably had been hot tar, and I suspected that he had done this not merely to hurt her but to cauterize her wounds, to reduce blood loss and the risk of infection, to keep her alive.

Something had been burned into the skin of her abdomen, and while I suspected, given Noman's nature, that it was a word, a name probably, or possibly just a line drawing, whatever it had been, the swelling of Lucy's womb had rendered it unrecognizable.

A brown crust ringed her mouth. I willed myself to make the less nauseating connection with the empty cans of dog food that littered the floor.

There were books too, I noticed then, hundreds of swollen water-damaged filthy books piled as though for burning and not for reading, but I knew, from the way he had spoken, from the way he had put on and put off pose after pose, that he had read them, and for some reason the thought of him handling those books with the hands he had used on Lucy Robinson made me more ill than what he had done to Lucy herself.

And there was a television. I hadn't seen it before; I don't know if it hadn't been there, or if it had been covered up, or if I'd just missed it; I didn't remember seeing the books either. It was an old console television, and a power cord trailed around its legs before disappearing into the shadows in the wall, and an antenna wire ran up to the ceiling. Still, just to be sure, I crawled over to it slowly, giving Lucy's body a wide berth, and I turned it on. The screen hummed and glowed into life, and then a black-

and-white image of a computer-generated weather map appeared on the screen. There was no sound, and I watched a smiling young weatherman point out tomorrow's forecast.

Sunny skies.

Hi: 113.

Lo: 87.

Winds: E/SE at 10–25 mph.

Chance of precipitation: 0.

7.33

Justin

HE LEFT ME THE CAR. HE LEFT ME SO MANY THINGS, his money, especially, and the last charred remnants of his love, and the particular smell that always followed him around after sex, but above all this he left me alone and he left me the car.

Once, when I was a child, not so young that I had to be accompanied by my parents but young enough that I still held on to one of the most basic of childhood dreams—I wanted more than anything else to fly—I went to a carnival that had come to our town, and with the money my parents had given me to ride the Ferris wheel and the roller coaster and navigate my way through the fun house I bought up every helium balloon I could find in the place, and I took them, in ones and two and little bunches, to a little alcove I had found between two tents, and I tied them to two cinderblocks and left them there. It didn't occur to me until years later that two cinderblocks weighed less than I did or I would have abandoned my quest immediately; but at any rate, after two hours of scouring the carnival from one end to another I had collected what seemed like hundreds of balloons—and run out of money—and then I secreted myself in the alcove and began to braid the balloons together with a ball of kite string I had brought with me. The day was windy, I remember, an irregularly gusting wind that whipped down the narrow alcove and knocked the balloons against my face and tangled their strings together, but I persevered, and at last I succeeded in braiding all the balloons into an oblong shape that at the time I thought looked like a bunch of multicolored grapes but which now reminds me of a microscopic photograph of the alveoli of a lung; and then, very carefully, I untied the balloons' anchors from the cinderblocks and wrapped them one bunch at a time around my wrists and ankles. The balloons seemed to tug mightily against my limbs, and my heart was pounding with excitement and in my mind I was picturing the pointed tops of tents seen from above, the stunned faces of Ferris wheel riders as I waved at them, the deep blue of a sea that was farther away than even I realized, and when I had fastened the last of the anchor lines to my body I released my hold on a tent wire I had been grasping for dear life, and as I felt the balloons lunge for the sky I jumped with them, jumped into the air . . .

. . . and almost immediately fell back down again. I say almost. There was something, a moment, a lift, a feeling—maybe it was only a feeling—and then I was on my face in the dirt, and a moment later a gust of wind ripped one of the balloon bunches from my wrist. The strings sliced my skin open as they pulled free, and when I shifted my eyes from my bleeding hand and back to the sky the balloons were already gone, blown over the edge of one tent or another.

Colin left me like that, like a lie I no longer believed in. He left me with a sense of the limitations as well as the reaches of my humanity, but because I still needed some fiction to cling to, I went searching for another. Before I could get away the door knocker sounded through the house.

It was Myra Robinson.

She didn't give me time to greet her. She merely grabbed my hand. I thought she was shaking it at first, but then I felt something small and hard pressing against my palm. When Myra withdrew her hand, I saw a small black pebble in my hand. I wasn't sure, but I thought it was a piece of obsidian from the stone moat which ringed the limestone house.

"This is every word Lucy ever spoke," Myra said to me. "Maybe one day it'll help you to talk again." She kissed me then, on the forehead, and then, wobbling wildly on her numb feet, she made her way back to her car, climbed in, and drove away.

So I took his money, and I took the car, and I took also a little piece of the mural Wade had painted in the cupola, the varicolored bird who flew heavenward in search of the lost husband of a woman named Beatrice, and I took also the stone that Myra had given me, but I left behind the bellystone, just as Beatrice had, and for all I know it waits there still, for whoever comes next.

7.34

Webbie

WHEN WE WERE TWO HOURS OUTSIDE OF GALATIA THE sun finally hit the horizon's edge, and its glow seemed to spread like wildfire across the prairie. The sky was streaked purple and orange and black and pink and a deep cerulean blue, and as my mind catalogued these colors I suddenly thought that I would miss Wade more than I would miss anyone, Cora, Divine, even Justin, even my father. I would miss the smell of him and the way his eyes seemed to hold the imprint of the last painting he had worked on, and I would miss, too, the chill of his hands, the one time I had let him put them on my breasts and he had tried to pull my nipple into his mouth. I would miss that too. I looked over at Wallace then, and I wondered if I would ever see anything less solid than a steering wheel in his hands, a drill bit, a fork, and Wallace looked over at me and the sunset's light brought out the freckles on his cheeks and made them glow. He had a wry expression on his face, as if the melodrama of running away together embarrassed him, just a little, and the smile he gave me was, I think, meant to reassure me more than anything else. He took one hand off the steering wheel and placed it briefly on my thigh, and then he returned both his eyes and his hand to the task of driving, but in the fresh curve of his palm I saw a memory, an echo of a shape that I had never seen in Wade's hands, or anyone else's, and that was the shape of my leg, the shape of me.

7.35

Colin

THE STUMBLING CRASHING APPROACH I HEARD WAS not, I knew, the return of Noman Never. He knew these paths, knew, too, how to place his feet so they made no sound.

I turned the television off, and I waited. I thought of turning off the light but I didn't know how.

A hand appeared first, clutching a pistol, and then a brown-sleeved arm and a badged chest and the wide white dirty hat of Lawman Brown.

He saw me, and then he saw Lucy Robinson, and he looked at Lucy Robinson for a long time with a bewitched expression on his face, mouth slightly open, eyes steadily glazing over, and all at once he pointed his gun at her, and before it even occurred to me to stop him he pulled the trigger. Her sheared scarred head snapped about, and even as my ears rang with the gun's report I heard Lucy's rattling breath for the last time, and after the echoes of the gunshot had faded there was only silence.

Then Lawman Brown turned the gun on me. He aimed the gun at my head but kept his slightly unfocused eyes pointed elsewhere, as though, if he met my gaze, I might snap him from his own spell and capture him in mine.

"I'll tell you the God's honest truth," he said.

I didn't say anything.

"The truth is I don't believe you had anything to do with this here. With her."

He waved a hand now, his free hand, but he didn't look at Lucy.

"But that don't matter," he said, and he stopped short, and then he took a deep breath. I could see the words taking shape in his head, words borrowed from some other story, words that he would later parrot to anyone who asked. "I'm gonna shoot you," he said. "Yes I am. Shoot you dead. And just for good measure I think I'll shoot myself too, in the arm maybe, or the leg. And then I'm gonna tell everyone that you did it, shot her and shot me and shot yourself too."

He stopped again, but I still didn't speak.

"Well," he said, "I don't really expect anyone to believe me. No I don't. But that don't matter neither. Cause I learned something today, and what I learned is this. People, people around here anyway, and I'd wager that Galateans ain't all that different from the rest of you, people don't want to know the truth. They just want a explanation, and a end to things."

He seemed done then. He looked at me, and he looked at the gun in his hand, and then he lifted a second hand to the gun in an effort to steady his trembling hand, and then he looked back at me.

I stared at Lawman Brown, and at the dark gun that was pointing at me, its barrel bright with reflected light, and I tried, I tried very hard to understand everything he had just said, but I was distracted by Lucy, by Lucy's finally stilled body, and that sight wiped away all the words he had spoken. I was wondering if he hadn't actually done the right thing.

When the shot rang out I didn't flinch, but when Lawman Brown dropped his gun and pitched face forward onto the floor I have to admit I was surprised, and I gasped and checked myself for wounds and then I looked all around the cave and it seemed a fitting end to things that the face that finally emerged from the darkness of a tunnel belonged to Abraham Greeving, followed shortly by the straining faces of two of his Church Ladies, Faith and Hope, or Hope and Charity, or Faith and Charity, and, tottering slightly, the three of them made their way into the room.

Abraham Greeving had been leaning on the women, but as soon as they were on level ground they released him and he handed his gun to one of the women and retrieved his cane from a crooked elbow and leaned on it heavily.

"I won't ask how you got here."

"With much difficulty," Abraham Greeving said, "and with the assistance of the Lord."

The woman who had the gun dropped it like a soiled hankie into her purse, and the other pulled the tablecloth over Lucy's body.

"I won't ask how you knew to come here."

"Someone called Nettie Ferguson," he said. He pulled a handkerchief from his pocket and dabbed at his brow. "Someone called the police station," he said, "and Nettie waited until Eustace had left and then she did what she always does." He pushed the handkerchief back in his pocket. "I expect the word's out by now. I expect the whole of town's on their way here."

"And I won't ask why you shot him."

"I shot him," the Reverend said, "because it was my *turn*."

"I won't even ask why you don't shoot me."

Now the Reverend shook his head, and he smiled, and he said, "So like a sinner, to wonder why he hasn't been punished for his sins."

The Church Ladies nodded assent, but, thankfully, didn't speak.

The Reverend looked at me.

"I didn't shoot you," he said, "because you never done nothing to *me*."

"I don't mean to seem naive," I said, "but I don't understand."

"Eustace Brown," Abraham Greeving said. "Howard Goertzen. Eddie Comedy. Odell Painter. Stanley Robinson." He ticked the names off on his fingers, and the gesture seemed in some ways the most macabre event of the entire day, given the proximity of Lucy Robinson's hands, and Eric Johnson's hands, and the withered fingers the Reverend was ticking.

"These are the five men who killed Eric Johnson, and it has been my task to revisit on them their own actions."

"But Eric Johnson isn't dead."

"That's where you're wrong," Abraham Greeving said. "Eric Johnson is as dead as dead can be. More dead than Eustace here, or Lucy Robinson, or you, or me."

I shook my head. "I still don't understand."

The Reverend smiled wryly. "It's a God thing," he said. "You wouldn't understand."

I started to speak again, but he held up his withered hand.

"The town is on its way, and it will take me some time to negotiate my way through these tunnels." He looked at me. "I will leave you here," he said, "because, as I said, you never done nothing to me."

"And the townspeople?"

The Reverend paused, and then he said, "I expect, Mr. Nieman, that you will tell them a story, and if that story is good enough then you don't have nothing to worry about. At any rate," he said, "it's never too late to ask the Lord for His aid."

He began to turn to leave then—it was an arduous process for him, turning—and I said, "Please. I *would* like to ask one question."

The Reverend paused.

"I would like to know," I said, "if you waited."

"Waited?"

"Until he shot Lucy."

The Reverend's face clouded momentarily. He frowned deeply, but then his face cleared and he blessed me with his last and warmest smile. "So it's true," he said. "You *are* a man of words."

7.36

MY NAME IS ANGELA.

One day my mother was playing with her fairy cousins by the stream that ran through the fields where they lived. They made boats by folding heart-shaped leaves around pebbles that served as ballast, and then they raced their vessels down the stream. The fairy whose boat won the race, my mother told me, would be the one first taken in marriage, and that day my mother's boat was fastest by far. She ran along with it, laughing so gaily at its merry progress that she never grew tired and never realized that she had long ago left her companions and their boats far behind. She stopped only when her leaf grounded against a tree root that grew into the water, and then, slipping off her shoes and holding her skirts high with one hand, she waded into the cold water and retrieved her boat with the other. Suddenly she heard a voice from high above. "Who are you, and what are you doing here?" My mother looked up, and for the first time she realized that she had run into the forest that bordered the fields where she lived. She looked all around but saw no one, just the tall trunks of trees and a distant kaleidoscope of leaves and sky. "Who are you?" another voice demanded. "What are you doing here?" said a third, and this time, as the words were spoken, my mother noticed that the branches and leaves of one tree, of the tree connected to the root which had stopped her boat, were shaking slightly, and even as she stared at it the tree bent itself over at the trunk and what my mother had thought was merely a collection of knotholes was revealed to be mouths and eyes—many mouths, and many, many eyes. "Tell me your name!" one mouth barked, and my mother was so startled that she dropped her skirts into the water, but other than that she remained absolutely still, and she stared into each of the tree's blinking eyes. "My name is Angela," she said at last, for my mother and I have the same name, just as her mother was named Angela, and my daughter, too, shall be named Angela. "Why have you left the fields and entered my forest?" another mouth demanded, to which my mother replied, "I'm very sorry, but I didn't notice. I was only following my boat." "What *boat*?" a mouth said, and another said, "I don't see any *boat*," and it blinked, and then my mother realized that on this tree eyes and mouth were the same thing. "This boat," my mother said, and held up the hand containing the leaf-covered pebble. The tree bent closer; eyes squinted, mouths frowned; eyes frowned and mouths squinted and then one of these holes hissed a "Bah!" and another said, "I see only a *leaf*," and then the tree's limbs rustled and a shower of its own five-fingered leaves fell on my mother and clutched at her hair and clothes. "What use have I for *leaves*?" "Not just a leaf," my mother said, "but a leaf with a stone folded into it," and she unfolded the leaf to reveal it. "*Stone?*" a mouth said. "What is this *stone?*" "A rock," my mother said. "Small and solid and too hard to break." "*Stone,*" another eye blinked. "I never heard of such a thing. I know dirt and water and sun and air, and trunk and branches and twigs and leaves." "And birds," another mouth said. "Yes, birds, who come and stay and then fly away. But . . . *stone?*" And then my mother knew what to do. She brought the pebble to her lips and kissed it. "Mmmm," she sighed, "delicious." "What, the *stone?*" My mother kissed the pebble again. "It tastes so good," she said. "Good?" "Good?" "Good?" the holes all panted, and my mother couldn't tell if the liquid that leaked from them was spittle or tears. "Here here, give us this good. Give it to us *now.*" My mother smiled then, and kissed the pebble a third time to complete the spell, and then she tossed it into the nearest opening. The tree was so greedy it didn't even try to chew, it just swallowed the pebble whole, and almost immediately an awful rumbling commenced deep within it. "Good?" "Good?" "Good?" the other mouths asked, while the mouth which had swallowed the pebble gagged and choked and coughed. It turned into an eye but could only leak tears. Then it was a mouth again, and it spat, but instead of the pebble the pale green shoot of a vine emerged, a single thin spiraling line that seemed to curl out endlessly. It grew longer and thicker and sprouted heart-shaped leaves and fresh tendrils which also grew fast and thick, winding themselves around the tree's trunk and branches and twigs, blinding all its eyes and binding all its mouths and growing and growing and growing until the entire tree was just a shiver lost inside the vine's coiled layers. And then, at the last, a few stray lines of vine detached themselves from their prisoner. They snaked down to my mother bearing a tiny parcel all wrapped up in their leaves, and they deposited it gently in her arms. She picked the leaves away, and there I was. I remember that she stared at me in wonder for a long moment while I stared back, and then she kissed me on the forehead. One, two, three, four, five, she counted the fingers on my left hand. One, two, three, four, five, she counted my right, and there, clutched in my palm, was the pebble she had thrown in my father's mouth, smooth now, and shiny, and dark and wet as my new eyes. "Angela," my mother said when she saw the stone. "Your name is Angela." She said, "We are some of us born different and we are some of us born the same." She said, "Angela." She said, "You did not come out of me but instead came into me," and she took the pebble that was in my hand and put it in her mouth. "*In me*," she said, swallowing. "Spelling is the easiest magic of all," she said, "and now you are *mine*." All around her swirling skirts the water ran red and thick and warm, and then, slowly, slowly, slowly, it lost its color and revealed a bed of a thousand thousand thousand pebbles, each of them waiting to be swallowed, each of them desperate to be born.